MW01170173

DESTINY SECRETS

WEALTH TRANSFERS
VOLUME ONE

CAROLE STOVALL HAMILTON

WESTBOW
PRESS®
A DIVISION OF THOMAS NELSON
& ZONDERVAN

WestBow Press books may be ordered through booksellers or by contacting:

WestBow Press
A Division of Thomas Nelson & Zondervan
1663 Liberty Drive
Bloomington, IN 47403
www.westbowpress.com
844-714-3454

Because of the dynamic nature of the Internet, any web addresses or
links contained in this book may have changed since publication and
may no longer be valid. The views expressed in this work are solely those
of the author and do not necessarily reflect the views of the publisher,
and the publisher hereby disclaims any responsibility for them.

Any people depicted in stock imagery provided by Getty Images are
models, and such images are being used for illustrative purposes only.
Certain stock imagery © Getty Images.

Scripture quotations are taken from the Holy Bible, King James Version.

ISBN: 978-1-6642-9810-1 (sc)
ISBN: 978-1-6642-9811-8 (hc)
ISBN: 978-1-6642-9812-5 (e)

Library of Congress Control Number: 2023907386

Print information available on the last page.

WestBow Press rev. date: 9/27/2023

I dedicate this book to the souls
who loved freedom of religion.
First to Jesus Christ
who overthrew the moneychanger's tables,
making room for true worshippers
to have a sacred place to pray.
Second to the Protestants far and wide
who held the line until God provided
a nation for religious freedom.
God bless America!

FOREWORD

I had a World History teacher who taught like he was writing for the National Enquirer. No one fell asleep in that class.

But it was my dad that lit a fire under me the month before I began homeschooling my kids.

He and Mom took the three of us on a ten day road trip. From Athens, Georgia to Savannah, up the coast to Cape Hatteras and old Williamsburg, across to Bird-in-Hand and Gettysburg, finally going home through the coal country of West Virginia.

At Kitty Hawk I became captivated. The Forest Ranger who managed the lighthouse lectured about what Sir Walter Raleigh and his crew found when they landed there, a Paradise comparable with the Garden of Eden. The doctor who had recorded the abundance, the beauty and pristine wilderness captured my imagination with the same adventure fever it must have had as it was told long ago. Those giant hardwood forests built the ships "where the sun never set on the British Empire."

It reduced the Garden to shifting sand, never to recover.

America with its diverse culture and independent thinking cannot teach its history by limiting it to the viewpoint of English Puritans and Jamestown, skimming over the rocky places of things that didn't work out. Like the fall of New Amsterdam, the curse that fell on the entire Dutch fleet, and how William Penn died penniless.

We are so much more than that. In the hearts of all true Americans, may we recover the original blessings of God. And for all who want nothing more than to honor Him and build the kingdom, may you receive His destiny secrets to your life and His wealth transfer to accomplish His dreams.

Carole Stovall Hamilton

Chapter 1

"FOR WE KNOW IN PART, AND WE PROPHESY IN PART."

1 CORINTHIANS 13:9

IN THE YEAR OF OUR LORD, 1638

I don't know how my mother knows danger is near.

"You want some chicken, son?" she asks this morning, rising from her prayers, "Get your boots on."

She is solemn, not her usual self. She senses something moving cautiously through the yard, looking over her broad shoulder, brushing back her auburn hair.

Near the woods, she holds our chicken down and takes its head tightly in her right hand.

"Get behind me," she says, and I do.

The chicken squawks, struggling. I sneak a look as she whirls the hen around, wringing the neck. It cracks.

The feathered carcass flops wildly on the ground while Mum's chestnut eyes scan the hills, her lip tight.

I want to ask what's troubling her, but I don't.

Resolutely she lays the head on a stone to chop it off, blood spurting across the grass.

Back inside, she scalds the carcass in boiling water, and I help pull the feathers out.

She doesn't smile. There is no song in our house today. She busies herself without looking at me.

Something's wrong.

Dried onion with an aroma of poultry steams in the kettle. Mum forks the whole chicken onto a platter on the table.

I almost sit down, but her head jerks toward the noise close to the house.

"Hide!" Mum whispers harshly.

I scramble up in the loft while she whisks away my plate.

I watch her calm herself, eyes locked fearfully as the sinister clomping rises on the steps outside our door.

Silently she hammers the table with a clenched fist and *seals that memory in my mind forever.*

I settle deep in the hay with a view of the room.

He opens the door, clamoring metal against metal of armor, and wrenches his throat above the metal breastplate rim.

I can see him clearly, a vein near his temple throbbing, his earthy odor overtaking the room. He pants.

He takes one step and raises a brow. Slowly he saws a slab of juicy chicken breast with a field knife and slides it between his teeth.

Her eyes dart. The only noise is his chewing.

He steps toward her and blocks my view.

I hear her gasp, then moan.

Mum! Tears cloud my eyes.

He shoves her down on the bed and she faints away.

He grabs the whole chicken and clamors out.

Trembling, I peer through the crack. Soldiers clank loudly, rushing on horses toward those in the square, swinging spiked metal balls.

I cannot stand to look outside.

While the sun shines and the trouble continues, I crouch afraid under the musty straw.

At dusk, it's quiet. I creep down and peek through the crack watching the ragman remove clothes, roll people over who are swarming with flies, and throw rocks at vultures. He high steps over piles, carefully choosing garments.

I kneel at Mum's side and see dried blood. She moans while

I stare at droplets of sweat on her face. A single tear slides into her hair. *She knows I'm here.*

Her icy fingers search for my warm hand, while she whispers a desperate prayer, "Lord, take care of my boy."

Her grip goes limp, her chest now still. The eyes glaze.

Is that all? I swallow, not daring to make noise.

Slowly, I return her hand and wipe my tears.

I lean close *hoping to see her chest rise and fall, hoping her eyes will look at me.* No, she doesn't.

It seems my heart stops. I cannot cry. So afraid.

Panic. Now what? Should I run away?

I put my boots on and crack the door. *Go where?*

The cold breeze blows in, and I shudder. I have outgrown my coat. I reach to the peg and wrap myself in Mum's clan shawl. Her smell is on it.

I think *of her snuggling me in her arms.* I think of *her smiling at me.* I have a sour taste in my mouth. I can't look at her. I won't!

Now the smell of smoke is in the air. I see it making a dark cloud over the hill. The king's men are burning barns.

I'm caged. It's getting dark outside.

I watch soldiers like hornets, landing here and there, robbing the households. They are drunken, unruly.

They will come here! My heart quickens.

Is this when I should run? Where?

I hold the door ajar and see a hulking figure looming through the knee-high grass. He lumbers across the meadow, coming close.

I close the door crouching back in fear.

Near the opening, out of sight, I watch the man.

He's bearded, tall, near our house. *Oh no.*

Heavy boots tromp up the steps. I hold my breath, every muscle tight with dread.

I don't want to die.

The stranger shoves the heavy door open. I stay behind it, peeking a stare at him.

He goes to Mum softly, a whimper in his throat.

He hears me breathing and turns.

"Gerrit?"

He sobs, lifting my skinny frame in his arms.

"Don't ye know ye own Father?" he whispers.

I didn't.

I'm stiff from fear, but I put my arm around his neck, as he sees the light in my pupils from the fire blazing in our village.

Quickly, he hoists me up.

The ragman shouts. "Halt! You there! Halt in the name of the king! I'll report you!"

My father turns an angry glare.

The beggar backsteps.

Near the gates, soldiers leave houses with food, tossing hay in the doors. Another regiment on horseback rattles over the bridge torching hay scattered through the village.

In the twilight, my father flops me over his shoulder like a sack of potatoes and runs into the dark, scaling the rock wall and hedges among the cornstalks. Cows are agitated and moo in the pale moonlight, until I no longer hear any soldiers.

He crosses through the woods, and sets me down in the grasses, glancing at the orange glow of fire in the night sky.

He puts a hand on my shoulder, eyes twinkling with tears.

"Don't worry. You're with me," he whispers.

From under his shirt, he pulls a crusty bread heel and raises his brows as he offers it to me.

I rip it with my teeth and clutch it like a treasure.

He looks me up and down, asking, "How old are you?"

"Nine years," I answer, *aware my dark hair is like his.*

Then we scramble down the rocks to the riverbank. His hands come tenderly together to dip for me to drink.

I wipe my mouth on the back of my sleeve.

His lip tightens, and he hugs me to his side, pointing to a massive ship far out on the water, a magnificent vessel with proud flags and broad sails.

Silently I hurry beside his long strides, crossing the fields till we reach a dinghy where the water laps the reeds.

Frogs grunt frolicking in the mud.

I might have caught one when I was younger. Not anymore.

As he rows across the harbor, *I know I will never be a silly boy again.*

Moonlight rests on his loving smile.

He understands my broken heart.

I tell him everything, how I hid like Mum said, how she knew something bad was going to happen and tried to cook the chicken for me. I told him her last prayer.

He stops, wipes his eyes with his hand and whispers, "A fine pirate you'll make."

I'm comforted that he says it that way.

He rows quietly on. Slap, slap. No more words.

The night clouds part for me *to discover in absolute wonder, the tall ship like a castle towering behind him in the moonlight.* I hear it creak, shifting in the deep saltwater.

I gaze high at the giant lantern burning from the bow, and two iron cannons poking out from the belly, while we climb a rope ladder hanging over the sea, my father behind.

So elegant the golden letters *Zeehaen* look to me, as my hands touch the delicately carved wooden rails shaping the bow. It is colorfully painted and tiled. How powerful is my first impression of the massive wooden fluyt with its trunk-like masts and heavy knotted rope lines, rolled up waiting to direct the force of the wind in full sails.

I think, *"Here is a safe place."*

"Ho!" calls a soldaat, "Who goes there?"

"Brinkendorf and son," says my father.

My father proudly stands with his hand on my head.

"Where's it's mother?" the soldaat spits.

In two quick paces, my father confronts him, nose to nose, and defiantly sticks his chin out.

The soldaat's eyes bulge, returning a smug stare back.

My father's hand covers half the soldaat's face and pushes him to the boards.

The contest ended, my father politely offers a hand-up.

By now, several men are roused and come to see.

No one speaks a word.

Two pull our rowboat up and place it in grooves on deck.

A call is given to "Man the sails."

I feel the ship lurch as the canvas grabs the night wind.

I'm given a cold bowl of beans and go to sleep in a hammock with Mum's plaid shawl up to my chin.

Alone, I force away the bad memories of today. I will not let myself cry like a baby. I decide I will make myself think like a man and I wonder, How will I like being a pirate?

Chapter 2

"... FORGETTING THOSE THINGS THAT ARE BEHIND,
AND REACHING FORTH UNTO THOSE THINGS WHICH
ARE BEFORE,"

PHILIPPIANS 3:13B

Come morning, I awake feeling sick and forget where I am, falling kerplunk from the hammock. The stench reeking from the wood overpowers me, and I heave till my belly is empty, leaving me weak and dizzy. I cling to the wall hoping to balance myself, leaning with the tilt of the ship, jabbing splinters in my soft palm.

I gain resolve and open my eyes. Rats scurry near the wall. Terrorized, I run quickly to find my father.

In the dark passageway, past the creaking cannon, I make my way to the sound of men's voices.

I round the corner and stand in the door, listening.

Over breakfast, my father tells what happened at home.

"The little peep didn't know me," he spouts.

The crew men are angry, ready to defend my mother.

I don't want to remember and mount the steps for some fresh air. To focus on the horizon helps me not be seasick. I wander higher away from the sail lines and lean on the colorfully painted slats of the beakhead. A surly frown from one of the men signals me I shouldn't be there.

I cross the main deck, looking things over.

What a beautiful vessel, commanding the wind and sea.

At once I fall in love with ships, and their speed as the wind tosses my hair and soothes my feverish brow. This will be my home now. I believe I am destined to be here.

Now the breeze picks up. The boatswain orders to hoist the topsail, and I am in the way.

I bend under the riggings and go back to hear my father.

Listening to his adventures, I can tell the weathered sailors observe his muscled forearms while he brags.

He pecks his stout forefinger on a knothole and forcefully states, "Our enemy proclaimed execution for all heretics declaring it was unlawful to pray in private, read the Bible, or refuse to bow to their images in the street."

He puffs out his chest and says, "Me own Father fought the Spanish fleet at Haarlem. Thirty thousand men strong they were. The cannon roared for three days and breached our city walls. Prayers went up. Ideas came down. Their greedy militia crossed the ditch and met a surge of men, women, and children fighting back with showers of homemade missiles, blocks of stone, boiling pitch, blazing hoop irons and live coals."

The men roar with laughter. My father pushes his plate away, their faces full of anticipation. He is solemn.

"When the troops left, it was a month before they tried that again. The enemy dug trenches by day, but at night, ha-ha!" my father says and raises his brows, "Our people sneaked in their camps, burning tents, and seizing cannons."[1]

I watch their respect surround my father. My mother had a Bible. Why is she dead? I'm afraid to ask.

"We pirate for the power to protect all Protestants," father says, "Imagine my terror as I see fires near my house."

The sailors around him tighten their jaws.

He grips the mug and his lip quivers. His eyes turn to me.

A look passes between us, *a bond all can see.*

I run to his side and bury myself in his embrace.

The men shoot looks at each other as they rise to leave, a binding of purpose.

It is my first glimpse of their unity, a rare and precious agreement of souls I will never forget.

Then I look for something to eat.

Near the back wall, the Commander speaks to my father alone, something about "hearing a word of knowledge from the Holy Spirit," and *it echoes in my mind.*

Another thing I will ask my father when the time is right.

I decide no complaints will come from me. I must become a man overnight.

With his arm around my shoulders my father tells me our people are at war, and we pirate the seas for the cause of the Netherlands.

On deck, I watch his burly arms pull the ropes taut to maneuver the wind. As skipper, he possesses a strong work ethic.

I do my best to please him and be by his side.

It's a fighting ship. Experienced men row lines in the hull while others climb high beams for massive sails to furl, their wiry silhouettes growing small against the clouds.

Now someone walks toward us.

"This is Gerrit," my father introduces me.

A broad-shouldered man with white hairy sideburns nods.

"Yah. Everyone calls me the Swede," he says smiling, "You like being on the ship?"

I make a squirrely face, and my father pokes me.

"He has my blood. Give him time," my father says.

I look out across the sea.

When the fluyt glides smoothly through the sparkling ocean, it's a lovely sight. Ahh, yes. And the fresh smell of salt spray in the wind thrills me.

Following him becomes my habit. By afternoon he sends me below.

He must get tired of having a boy by his knee.

Later I'm given a job as the cook's helper. I pluck weevils from the flour and feed the fire carefully without burning myself. I peel turnips and chop cabbages.

"Don' be a feeding the cat, boy!" the cook roars over the

splashing waves, "His job is feeding himself. The cat is not fat because he's lazy."

I see vermin scampering along the wall, with prominent whiskers. Their noses and feet are pink, their eyes beady.

Soon dinner is ready.

I clang the bell, and the cook says, "The water's calm. That means dagger match tonight."

He nods toward the galley as the men file in, talking.

My father works topside, so I eat alone knowing no one.

The cook and I wash the dishes in the barrel while the men draw straws of different lengths and line up.

Finished I perch myself on a barrel by the Swede and he whispers, "They bet on who can spear a rat."

Everyone is quiet.

In the shadows, away from the table, the sailors stand motionless poised to strike, daggers raised in full focus on the target.

Against the back wall of the galley, hunks of cheese wait, smelling its attraction for the hairy vermin. At first sight of a rodent, I hear the whir of the flying blade and thud. He missed.

The rat stops, squeaks, and hurries for the cheese. More rodents sneak in. No noise. Like a flock of startled geese, the daggers fly across the room, spearing two, missing seven with the thuds in the wood sounding like a distant drum. The cheese is gone. The rats disappear.

The men grin and retrieve their knives, poking one another.

It's magnificent! I want to try it.

When I ask, they scowl and say, "We can't play every night. They'll get wise."

I take that to mean, "Don't get in the way."

They're tired and bored. I understand.

I wander away.

When the sun sets, my eyes scan the shore.

"The Age of Opportunity beckons with wealth and adventure," my father winks, "Tomorrow, we'll be at Leiden. I will show you wonderful things my son."

10

Chapter 3

"...FEAR GOD AND KEEP HIS COMMANDMENTS, FOR
THIS IS THE WHOLE DUTY OF MAN."

ECCLESIASTES 12:12, 13

During the night, a strong breeze pulled us. We are at
Leiden by dawn.

My father pokes me, "Wash your face and hands. Tie your
hair back. Pull your sleeves down."

He hands me a chunk of lye soap, a brush, and a leather
cord.

At the wharf, sparrows chirp their early morning chatter
across the roof ridges and flit about the treetops.

Off the dock, I walk behind my father, awkwardly slow.

"Come along, Gerrit. Keep up," he urges.

I try to, but there is so much I find fascinating.

The streets are crowded with strange-sounding people.

The waterways are brick lined, the grass cut neat. I gawk
at women in aprons and white peaked hats, washing the street
with soap and a broom. Every curved gabled house is built of
yellow brick with flower gardens.

I don't know where to look next.

The buildings soar five houses tall above children playing
freely. Delicate artwork is painted around the windows and
corners. And the arms of the windmills match the sails of our
ships. They whirl around, pumping water through the rows of
canals.[2]

I could never dream such a lovely place existed. The carved wood on everything is in itself a wonder.

"They print our Bibles here," Father whispers as he goes inside the Dutch Reformed Church.

Emanuel de Witte (painter)
"The Interior of the Oude Kerk, Amsterdam"
c. 1660 - oil on canvas

Patrons' Permanent Fund
Courtesy National Gallery of Art, Washington

I stare at its whitewashed walls stretching high, held together by thick black beams, sun shining through colored glass pictures in the windows.

There is a large Bible with brass fittings and buckles resting on the front altar. My father kneels and kisses it. He swats me and motions I should kneel. I do quickly.

"Pray," he says.

My heart pounds but I do not do it.

He looks questioningly at me.

"I forget how," I say weakly, looking away.

It's not true. I don't know why I can't pray. God seems far from me.

My father puts his offering in the receptacle, and we leave.

There are taverns and music halls and people smoking tobacco. I stare at their strange clothing, embroidered vests, homespun shirts, and leather britches. Women have tight caps tied around their pink faces. Dark-skinned men wear turbans and long robes with wide sashes, and turned up shoes, puffing long curved pipes.

All of them trade in the streets, buying, selling their wares.

I can't keep up with so many new things at once.

"Many books are published here. Scientists and writers from other countries have innovative ideas. Cross the walk bridge Gerrit, over to the Rapenburg," Father keeps talking.

He means the University, a grand two-story building, handsome with leaded glass framed windows and an arch in brick. We sit under a tree and listen to the languages of young men who come and go at its entrance.[3]

My father pats my knee and smiles.

"Have you ever tasted a cinnamon bun?" he asks.

"What is that?" I say wondering.

Nearing the bakery, I get purely lost in the fragrant smell of fresh yeast baking and delightful spice.

Inside, my father knows the baker by name. They talk, *but I cannot pay attention for anticipation at the delights displayed under glass. I look closely at every one dusted in white powder or glazed in icing with a single berry on top.*

He chooses two and pays.

We go outside in the sun, and Father places the cinnamon bun on the bench beside me. I look shyly at him. He nods.

Oh! It is better than the smell. I devour it ravenously, which makes my father laugh. *And I feel special.*

Now we must get back and make sure the cargo is loaded evenly. He passes our mates and makes a friendly salute.

They drink and talk with women.

He tells me this stop is only for fresh food and water.

By afternoon, we sail again, and my father hugs my head.

"You will go to university someday, I promise," he says.

The Swede behind him nods at me, while his strong shoulders throw huge fishing nets over the side by himself.

Before we arrive at Amsterdam, cheese is again put on the lower decks to clear our ship of rats before we unload.

I watch the men stand behind crates anticipating targets.

Down the rail, Father lets me cut off fish heads and slice the small ones for bait. I chop in a rhythm Mum taught me.

Up the deck, our crew makes silent gestures.

The sails flap loudly in the breeze while the cheeses sit scattered in places. They must have seen a rat's head because the men crouch down and wait without a stir.

Several vermin race out of the galley. Daggers fly, and I turn my head quickly.

Then something brushes over my foot. I flip my knife on the ugliest rodent you ever saw.

Augh! I got one!

A loud cheer goes up for me.

I'm surprised.

Father picks it up with the shepherd's hook for all to see.

The Swede calls me "Tiger," and the others nod with a grin poking one another.

Suddenly I have earned respect among the men.

They say I must practice and be ready if we attack a ship.

My father doesn't smile. He will not look at me.

"Wash your hands and the knife," he says sternly.

By sunset, I view Amsterdam with its jagged silhouette skyline. We are landing. The men anchor among a forest of other grand ships bearing the Dutch East India Company "VOC" symbol, a few with the "WIC" emblem.

We have business at headquarters. The commander disembarks into the rowboat with us, carrying the ship's lading account and the log.

Down the Herengracht Canal, my father rows while I gaze up at more rows of steep buildings with the curve edged roofs of overlapping tile. Constructed entirely of yellow brick flat-faced, they have glazed windows and cheery flower boxes, hanging over perfectly clean cobblestone streets. The stones run all the way up to the foundations.[4]

Nowhere is any mud to step in. Every inch sparkles.

Each canal and bridge is arranged neatly parallel.

We see the Commander get off at Millinery Square on his way to report and leave the boat tied up for him.

"Keep your hands behind your back," my father says and takes me by the arm into a merchant's shop where folded clothing is stacked in sizes.

The store smells of leather and wool and candlewax.

In the rear, stacks of beaver pelts wait for the hatmaker.

Two large looms are weaving textiles, one colored blue.

"We expect a load of indigo any day, my good man," the merchant says to my father, "If you like a garment fitted to your taste? Or a beaver hat to keep the rain off ?"

"No. His size," my father motions toward me.

I get my own clothes and big boots. He says I will fill them out soon enough and hands me a pair of gray woolen stockings.

I am grateful to have leather gloves and slide my fingers inside with pride.

The shopkeeper rents us a small boat, and we walk down the pier.

Father climbs in, saying, "I'll show you our city raised from the sea," and he mans the oars while I gaze up.

The vessel glides smoothly past six-story narrow buildings, with their artistic embellishments and brass lanterns. Everywhere sailboats and rowboats are tied.

"Windmills churn the water, keeping the land dry," my father says, "I will tell you why, before you go to sleep."

We pass the Fish Market, full of traders and smelling of steamed crab. Women inspect the day's catch with fingers probing the scaly skin. Coins exchange hands beneath strings of salted, drying fish.

My father delights in my curiosity. *I am wiggly excited,* and he stops to buy us hot pretzels wrapped in muslin and a chunk of orange cheese. I watch him carve some off for me. I sniff the cheese and indulge myself.

My cheeks hurt from grinning so much.

"Every voyage we made took a year. Left in summer.

Returned in summer. Came back with loads of raw silk and barrels of spices. From Jakarta and Hirado," he says, resting to swat a fly, "Gerrit, the Bible says there are paths in the sea, currents that pull the ship or hinder it.[5] After my Commander Hyen brought in the Spanish ships, the Dutch East India company exploded with success. All the men of the country invested in it. At Middleburg, ship construction developed rapidly which began a race to set up monopolies in every corner of the world. In the years I've been a pirate, our country has become rich. Now we have the Portuguese market on cinnamon and are the only traders with the Shogun in Japan. Our ships return with silver. Nothing compares with our country's luxury and exotic opulence."[6]

As we ease through the crowd, my father nods at others, *and I copy him, playing the man.*

Johannes Lingelbach
"Dam Square with the new Town Hall under Construction" c. 1656

Wikimedia Commons / Public Domain

When we are out of earshot, Father says, "King Solomon was the richest man that ever lived, but he loved many strange women, and they turned his heart to worship idols[7] and ruined his country with sin. I saw this overseas in the East and my heart was pained."

He supposes I understand.

I study his face.

He looks away.

"That's why I chose to work for the West India Company.

We trade with colonies in the New World. And the day I made that decision, I met your mother, here."

"In this city?" I ask.

"Hmm," he grunts, his eyes looking down.

"She had fled Scotland with her neighbor's family. Just a thin little beggar of fourteen," he remarks.

I cherish every word with anticipation.

"There was a cottage prayer meeting in the countryside. I went out of curiosity. An old woman that lived by the windmill had taken the Scots in, bless her soul. The old woman told us her grandfather helped build the windmill, the most ancient in the Netherlands. God showed them how to drain the water off the fields with sails like a boat and a wheel in a wheel, while reading passages in the book of Ezekiel[8]," she divulged the secret, "We prayed for a way to escape the persecution. They had pushed us to the sea. Digging the dirt from the canals to build up the shore we used the windmills to pump the water back out and created more land. God showed a way where there seemed to be no way."

"Hearing the old woman tell Dutch secrets made me wish I could read. Then your mother read aloud bending over the heavy Bible on the table. She described what the prophet saw in visions of God, lightnings and whirlwinds and creatures with wings that sparkled like fire. They moved forward with the wheels moving within a wheel. And then she read about the thundering voice of God from within a glittering blue dome with a throne above and a figure towering with brightness everywhere, the way a rainbow springs out of the sky.[9] What she described was," he blinked, "Was the glory of God! Oh Gerrit, all of us got on our knees. The presence of the Lord was there. Some wept while most of us whispered prayers. After a while, a tune was being hummed and those that knew it began to sing. The old woman prophesied, her hands raised and her face shining gazing upward."

"This nation shall gather the riches across the sea. Your men shall build swifter boats and have favor on distant shores. Angels shall attend thee, and you will protect my Word, provide for the stranger and their people shall serve you for the shields of the earth belong to Me[10]," she cried.

"We all kept a holy hush. Never make fun of the Holy Ghost, Gerrit. It cannot be forgiven,"[11] he whispered.

And he looks deep into my eyes. His lips are firm.

He is finished.

Though I want to ask about my mother, I know better. We share the sorrow in a silent way.

We pass the Oude Kerk, the oldest building, once a Catholic church and face the Dutch East India House.

Father explains, "The company is made up of traders who the States-General gives privileges to, like the monopoly on trade east of the Cape of Good Hope. Their goal is finding spices, textiles, and metals produced in Persia, India, China, Malaysia, Indonesia, and Japan."[12]

He's proud to be Dutch.

While we row he says, "I don't see the fear of God like I used to. The love of money has corrupted our people. It troubles me there's no longer a holy standard."

Back on board, I ask if we are Protestants. Father wears a frown. He leans on the cabin wall and bites his lip.

"Yes," he closes his eyes, then opens them turning toward the sea, "We believe in the Creator, the God of your mother, the Cross of Calvary, and the Blood of Jesus Christ, from the Holy Bible, when you learn to read."

"Can you read, Father?" I ask *so boldly, it shocks me.*

He checks behind him.

"Get to work, Tiger! No slacking! A boy must pull his weight around a ship!" he grumbles and hoists a barrel.

I glance from the cook's door as my father wipes a tear.

I know he loved my mother. She was Scotch-Irish. To hear him tell, he was the envy of all the sailors on account of her gentleness and charm. A beauty she was not. All the same, a kind soul who mothered me and adored my father. He respects her religion and makes sure I can stay with him. We are harnessed

18

together by the love she gave us. He shows his love by taking care of me.

He can't read. I guess it.

And I learn a lot from what my father doesn't say.

Chapter 4

"AND ALL THIS ASSEMBLY SHALL KNOW THAT THE
LORD SAVETH NOT WITH SWORD AND SPEAR: FOR
THE BATTLE IS THE LORD'S..."

1 SAMUEL 17:47

When the men are below for the night, I stay up with my father to keep watch with him.

"Your mother read parts of the Bible to me, Gerrit. She told me about Jesus promising to baptize us in fire and give us gifts of supernatural power," he says, "Secrets of blessing because we please God."

"Like what?" I ask.

"Like how I knew to come and get you. Holy knowledge from God when we need it," he says.

I want to ask why he didn't come before she was killed, and my dark expression must have been noticed. He is caught in the middle of the lesson without answers to our unspoken questions.

He nods and proceeds, "Hmm. David was a shepherd, a boy true in worshipping God. He sat alone by the stream when a bear came out of the woods to attack his sheep. The Spirit of God came on him, and he wrestled the bear and killed it, with a dagger, like yours Gerrit. Another time a lion threatened his flock. David killed it too.[13]"

I gasp. Then swallow.

My father chuckles, curling the rope over his shoulder, directing the sails to the mounting breeze.

"Now, David practiced day and night with his slingshot. He became familiar with the weight of stones and the exact whirl to fling his aim with accuracy," he says.

"Like our knife throwing at the rats," I add.

He raises his brows.

"Yes, David's faith increased by his daily worship and prayer," my father says, "As the boy grew older, the day came when David saw a giant nine feet tall in full metal armor on the battlefield, cursing God Almighty and strutting defiantly before the soldiers of the king."

"He's going to fight the giant, isn't he? " I guess.

My father grins.

"Both armies watched as young David stepped out to meet Goliath with only his slingshot. It embarrassed the giant to anger. He cursed David's God. So, David declared 'Come to me and I will smite you because the battle is the Lord's and He will give you into my hands so that all the earth may know that there is a God in Israel[14].'"

"Oh no! He didn't," I say amazed.

My father smugly replies, "Heh-heh. David ran forward, twirling the sling. God guided the rock to hit the one place not covered, his forehead. Down the big brute fell."

I giggle in delight, beaming at my father, the storyteller.

He takes a deep breath and sticks out his chest.

"Bravely, David rushed to the body and pulled the massive sword from the giant's hand. Like your rat on the hook," he teases.[15]

"Because the Spirit of the Lord came upon him?" I ask.

My father considers me with a long look.

"What do you think?" he questions back.

"We can have the Spirit of God come on us, too," I say.

My father nods. His lips are firm.

There is silence between us now. The boat creaks slightly, pitching on the wave. The wind is winding down, and we float along under twinkling stars. Moonlight glistens shafts of white behind clouds creating a mosaic of blue hues.

"Where are we going, Father?" I ask.

"The trading post. New Amsterdam," he says, irritated.

His tone hurts me. I wish I was more of a man. Then he wouldn't have to bother with a boy.

I leave him and go below where men are snoring and I sway in my hammock, thinking of David's victories.

A storm must be brewing. The ship is heaving so strongly I fall out of the hammock.

Climbing the hatch, salt spray stings my face, and I hear the lightning crackle.

"Get below!" Father yells as he hurries to lower the sails.

The next day my father tells the cook I must be trained and decides to give me "a go at the ropes". My hands blister. My shoulders ache. I sunburn hot and pink.

At night he rubs my back and arms down with pig lard. I sleep hard and wake up late, while he keeps the training up. For ten weeks, we sail across the Oceanus Atlanticus, my apprenticeship fitting me as a crewman.

And sometimes he teaches me "father to son" things about my person.

He says, "Daniel and his three friends were taken prisoner by a pagan army, but Daniel determined he would not defile himself, so God gave him the gift of interpreting dreams and wisdom beyond the other boys[16]. I pray you will have spiritual gifts and please God. Will you do that, Gerrit? Try to please God?"

I lower my head and nod in awe of such a responsibility.

He says, "Whatsoever ye do, do it heartily, as unto the Lord"[17], meaning don't go about your work in a lazy way. Be dependable. This shows gratitude to God for giving you a good brain and a healthy body."

I watch him. He never wastes time. He is friendly and helpful, paying attention to all the jobs men do around him.

"Keep peace in your soul, and it will show on your face. If you war in your mind with others, it will spill over into a fight.

Don't pick up the surly brogue son," he warns as we take inventory of rations in the back room, "It's ungodly. Proud words cause trouble."

I'm quiet.

He realizes I don't understand.

"We must all give account to God for what we say and what we think[18], Gerrit," he says softly, pointing at my chest.

"But Father," I argue, *wondering how to be so good.*

"Tis not my law. God requires it," he says, "Keep your mind clean, as well as your body. Your hands touch many places. Rinse them in saltwater often. The rats roam everywhere, leaving their droppings, chewing through the burlap. Never walk on this ship without your boots. And scrub your teeth with cloth and oil."

When we eat in the galley, *I notice many of the men have sores on their arms or faces. Most have rotted teeth. Not my father. He watches out for me.*

My father shows me how to cross off the days on a calendar painted in the hull. I show him, I know numbers to one hundred and how to write the alphabet.

Sometimes I like hanging around the Swede and learning his language. We work in the galley kitchen, a welcome place where I go when my father has moods.

Today, my father sits me down.

"I have memorized some of the Bible. It has secret holy power to strengthen your soul," he says, searching my eyes, "I will teach this to you."

"What is memorize?" I ask.

He says, "I say the words first, and you say them back to me. We repeat them until you know them by yourself, until you learn them by heart. Now I say it, 'Your word have I hid in my heart, that I might not sin against thee.[19]'"

I look at him.

"Say it, Gerrit," he says.

And I do. He says eight words and waits. I tell them back. We practice a while. Then I get better and learn it all.

We work some more, and he comes back to where I am.

"Say it for me," he says.

I forget some of the words, so he reminds me.

When the cook blows the conch shell for dinner, Father passes me and asks again, "Do you know it?"

I say it for him. He smiles.

"See, we get it in your heart," he says and thumps my chest with a flick of his fingers.

For a few days, Father makes me meditate on the first one and plant it down deep, he says.

I memorize one verse at a time.

With repeated practice, I learn the twenty-third Psalm, "The Lord is my Shepherd. I shall not want. He maketh me lie down in green pastures. He leadeth me beside still waters. He restoreth my soul. He leadeth me in paths of righteousness for His namesake. Yea, though I walk through the valley of the shadow of death, I will fear no evil for Thou art with me. Thy rod and thy staff, they comfort me. Thou preparest a table before me in the presence of mine enemies. My cup runneth over. Surely goodness and mercy shall follow me all the days of my life and I will dwell in the house of the Lord forever,"[20] I say.

While I treasure these scriptures, *I listen most to how my father believes they guide our faith.*

"Your mother used to tell me Jesus is the Prince of Peace," he says, "He calmed the storm at sea.[21]"

That arrests my attention, but my father is melancholy.

If he talks about Mum, I keep quiet. She is a subject he feels with mixed emotions. I know better than to press him.

He seems happiest teaching me things.

"Sheep are easily frightened, unable to defend themselves. A babbling brook muffles the sound of a stalking animal. They don't like that. They drink where the water's still," he says.

While summer lasts, I think *of God as a loving presence like my mother.* I think of *her living in heaven and wonder what it's like. Like Amsterdam, maybe, with peaceful, tidy streets and happy people busy doing things?*

When we near land, birds fly about. The sailors are anxious to go ashore and get off the ship.

I hear them talk about the food they want to eat and their hopes of finding true love. They shave one another on deck, borrowing fresh clothing from one another.

My father smiles at me, *embarrassed possibly.* I return it innocently.

It's hot midday when we pull in among the shipping masters, laden with goods from the West Indies to trade.

Their cargo holds citrus fruit, sugar cane, coffee beans, bananas, grapes, rice, barley, and olives from plantations.

Slave ships anchor out from the beach, but our men scowl at them. I hear whispers and see their eyes narrow. What goes on behind the closed hatches, our men want no part of.

New Amsterdam is a rude disappointment to me.

It's a muddy trading post of thatched roofed cottages scattered with pigsties and rickety fences. There is no pier. No place to dock. Enormous quantities of goods are maneuvered onto smaller boats and rowed in, requiring constant manual labor. The stumps of trees dot the shore in front of the wooden fort and the manure along the crude paths *holds no candle to Amsterdam.*[22]

I ask my father why it was named New Amsterdam?

He looks at me and tightens his lips. I watch him roll the barrels onto the dingy, waiting while he heaves the wooden cases of dry goods for the colony store.

After we cross the inlet between the boat and the beach, he leads me in wet boots down a shady path, and we eat at a tavern, both of us watching people. The turnip greens taste good for a change and the buttermilk.

Without looking, he says, "See these people from many countries? They come because this is a place where dreams come true. Where I always wanted us to live. Far from what your mother went through. An ocean away from war."

In one corner an artist paints a peaceful scene of the port, *nothing like being here.*

My father is despondent, and I choose to be patient with him.

We spend the afternoon sitting under the shade trees watching other ships unload. He nurses a jug of brandy and I savor a luscious peach, *sadly reliving thoughts of my mother.*

At sunset, he rises quietly, and I follow him, back onboard the boat and he wanders away.

The Swede sees I'm lonely and pokes me in the shoulder.

"Gerrit, me boy, come see the furs we haul this trip," he says and jostles down the steps with me in tow.

"Maybe you want to learn more of my language," the Swede grins as we enter the ship's storeroom, and I gasp.

Almost touching the ceiling, are banded layers of beaver pelts, stacked along the length of the hull. The stench is suffocating. I gag, and cough and the Swede erupts in laughter, leading me back to fresh air.

"First words will be 'stinking ship'," he says, grinning.

My father did not bunk that night. He passed me on deck, acknowledging me with a squinted eye.

In the galley, the Swede pushes a plate of fried potatoes in front of me and a crock of tomato relish.

"He'll come 'round, just wait and see." he says, "Have some chow-chow. Is good together."

I pout and pick at the food while he makes silly songs and sits by me until I laugh at him and have some. Then he takes me up to the sterncastle, and we watch the shore grow small.

I learn a little Swedish.

Mostly he shows me how to cheer people up, especially yourself, even if he's being silly.

Chapter 5

"They that go down to the sea in ships, that do business in great waters; These see the works of the Lord, and his wonders in the deep. For He commandeth, and raiseth the stormy wind, which lifteth up the waves thereof. They mount up to the heaven, they go down again to the depths: their soul is melted because of trouble."

Psalm 107: 23-26

My father sleeps most of the next day coming round for dinner and eases in by me on the bench.

"Everything all right?" he asks.

I nod, my mouth full of corn pudding.

He grins sheepishly and glances at the Swede.

Father says, "Found yourself some ripe old company."

It's a joke between them, and I watch their interaction.

With his fork pointing at the Swede, my father says, "Now there's a man could've been skipper if he'd only been Dutch. Pity the shame. Such a fellow deserves respect."

The Swede politely rises and winks at me, leaving us alone. *It's hard to say if my father felt jealous or grateful, but he filled the evening with advice to me as if he had little time left to do so.*

"There was a man who loved a woman like I loved your mother, and the woman couldn't have children. In those days, men had more than one wife. This man, Jacob, had two wives, sisters that competed for their husband's love. The one he loves is named Rachel. She's pretty. Her sister isn't, so the father tricks Jacob into marrying the sister. In the dark, he doesn't know he's been given the wrong one," he says, "The next morning the father now traps Jacob into working seven more years for his chosen bride."

I'm wide-eyed, *but it's over my head.*

Still, Father continues as the tables empty, and we sit alone in the dining hall. Only the cook is noisy in the kitchen.

"Now the ugly sister begins having sons, one, two, three, four. Then Rachel offers her handmaid to Jacob, more babies. Now Leah does the same until Jacob has ten boys, but none are Rachel's. Jacob prays for her to conceive and finally, Joseph is born."

"From that day, the older brothers are jealous of Joseph."

Jacob makes his favorite son a coat of many colors and takes Joseph along trading, teaching him business and manners, trusting him with handling wealth," he says and *gives me that "once-over look", to make sure I'm listening.*

"It seems like Jacob intends to give him all he owns, and his brothers are burning with envy. They suspect he might become their master and grumble about it while working in the field."

"Over family dinner, Joseph tells them he had a dream about the stars of heaven bowing down to him, which incites anger their father can see. So, things are at a breaking point," he says forking a bit of meat, "When there's an opportunity, they capture him and sell him as a slave to a caravan going to Egypt."[23]

"Oh, Father, they didn't!" I exclaim.

He raises his finger peacefully.

"But God had his hand on Joseph," he tells me, "He found favor with his Egyptian master who promoted him to manager. Soon he is the keeper of the entire rich man's estate, gaining valuable experience. The master's wife, like the devil, tries to tempt Joseph to sin. He won't. His heart is true to God and his owner, so she lies and says he did something bad, which throws him into prison."

"But why didn't his father come and rescue him?" I ask.

He says, "Because the brothers smeared blood on his coat and told their father a wild beast must have killed him. Well, while Joseph is in prison, he has time to meditate on his dreams and ask God about them. He prays and serves with a pure heart, pleasing our heavenly Father. When two of Pharaoh's servants are thrown into prison, Joseph is their guard, and each of them has a dream. Joseph has the gift of interpreting dreams. When he interprets their dreams, it happens exactly the way he described."

"What happens to Joseph now?" I ask.

My father leans back, smiling and says, "God placed him at the right place at the right time. God gave Pharoah two dreams. Joseph is the only one that can interpret them, and it causes him to be appointed Prime Minister of Egypt. He oversees the granaries during a world famine and when he is about thirty, his brothers come to Egypt bowing, asking for food, like he dreamed. After so many years they didn't recognize him. But he knew them when he saw them."[24]

"He will punish them and say no, won't he?" I ask.

"No Gerrit. Joseph is tender-hearted, God's man. Whatever you do, whatever lies before you, keep your heart tender with all diligence. Out of it are the issues of life.[25] Nothing good can come from a hard heart. Joseph tests them to see if they're sorry for what they did. When they convince him, he welcomes them to Egypt, rescuing them."

I say, "You mean, God was behind the world events, the weather and the nations?"

"What do you think?" my father waits for me to weigh the story.

I nod.

He continues, "He planned for Joseph to become the leader. God planned to transfer the wealth of Egypt to His people when He took them to the Promised Land."

I speak up, "Mum told me about Moses. The Ten Commandments[26] are the rules of how He wants us to live."

"Tomorrow, I want you to memorize them," he says, reaching for another cracker.

I follow him up, and we stand in the night breeze looking out over the moonlit waves, the wind blowing across it in rippled diagonals.

"God rules the world. He puts down kings and replaces them. He transferred the wealth of our enemies to us, and I was there, a week of miracles," he said, looking at the stars.

We cross the Atlantic in nine weeks, the weather being mild, and the boatmen experienced.

I memorize the Commandments and the Beatitudes.[27]

Arriving at sundown, we have no time to go to Amsterdam. We must sail back to the New World for another load and return before icy conditions. My eyes strain to see the city from the poopdeck, with the cobbled thoroughfares pulsing by lantern light.

Hyacinths fill the night air with fragrance blown by the constant flow of the windmills scattered across dewy fields of tulips.

I smell cinnamon and ask for a bun to be fetched from the men who go ashore. They bring me two.

At midnight we leave speedily away with passengers and supplies.

All our return trips carry foreign people who hope to live peacefully in the New World. They speak broken Dutch and wear serious expressions. I look at their peculiar clothing and keep out of their way.

In the galley at mess time, the stories spin around pirates.

Each man tries to out talk the last, and even I know some of it to be pure lies.

Every one of the crew has a turn to entertain with storytelling and men's brags.

The Swede says a sailor will lose his soul if he operates a slave ship or kills without provocation.

The cook spits and shrugs, "Pirates don't have souls."

That was offensive to everyone. To mention a holy belief, in an unholy way, causes them to become solemn.

It alerts my father. He leans on the table and grins.

Jan Lievens
(Leiden 1607 – 1674 Amsterdam)
"Card Players" - c. 1625
oil on canvas

DeWitt, Lloyd and Arthur K. Wheelock Jr., "Card Players" (2017). In The Leiden Collection Catalogue, 3rd ed. Edited by Arthur K. Wheelock Jr. and Lara Yeager-Crasselt. New York, 2020–.

"Never a better Christian pirate breathed the salt air than hearty Commander Piet Heyn," he says in a challenge.

Brows raise. Only the slap of the sea dares make noise.

I sense secrecy and latch my ears not to miss the details.

My father draws in his chin and blinks hard.

"God in heaven plans payday for everyone," Father says, "In 1628, the year I took a wife, He rewarded the Dutch. Sixteen heavily loaded Spanish treasure ships we captured. Hedged them in the Bay of Matanzas on the Cuban coast!" he says, whirling hands in the air.

The men cheer and whistle, but he holds one hand up for attention. They lean close.

"At Salvador, we took over thirty Portuguese merchant ships," he says, "We chased ships from Venezuela and Mexico, and after musket volleys from our sloops, the crews of the galleons surrendered. Hyen captured twelve million guilders worth of gold, silver, and expensive goods. In a month, our country became the leading world power."

Nods around the room become smiles of awe.

Then he points a finger, "Without bloodshed."[28]

Mouths fall open, overwhelmed. Gasps are heard.

"We took no prisoners. He gave Spain's soldiers supplies for a march to Havana. Pien had been in prison at Cuba years before. He spoiled those who owed him justice stripping Spain. We kept the ships. We kept the gold."

My father says, "We're the most successful pirates on the high seas. Honorable men, taking spoils from our enemy."

There's pride on their faces as they go back to work.

After they go above, the lantern sways in the hull, and Father looks at me long, knotting his thoughts.

"To be a Dutch sailor is a worthy trade, Gerrit. We purposed as a nation to protect the Protestant faith, to live by the Bible, and use the weapons of warfare God gives, including supernatural strength, wisdom, discernment, miracles, things like that.[29] Jesus sent Peter to get a coin from a fish's mouth.[30] To have holy gifts is an asset to the company. I came home with rewards, son," he says.

I admire him so. Does he know?

With new courage, I climb the sails to keep watch as the sun sets.

When the North Star disappears, and bolts of lightning pierce the black sky, I'm relieved from duty and go below.

Later, I awake to a mighty gale, the ship tossing high and

laying over low. The crew scramble to climb above but none of us can make it up the hatch. In the darkness, the mildew of the hull smells heavy as the men cling to the railings. Soon, the sloshing of water fills our floor.

I panic and call "Father!" who doesn't hear me, above the booming thunder and crack of lightning.

But I hear him, shouting for all hands on deck and calling on God to help us.

Chapter 6

"A MAN'S GIFT MAKETH ROOM FOR HIM AND BRINGETH HIM BEFORE GREAT MEN."

PROVERBS 18:16

Morning light finds me on the shore, being drug by two men in sea-soaked clothes and forced to stand.

Aware I am not in good company and not understanding the language, I try to gather my wits.

At once, I'm clubbed. I bow and see I'm missing the new boots. *Eleven, and barefoot. I never.*

The *Zeehaen* is broken, shattered wood against the rocks, and four of us swept ashore. Parts of it float on the waves. Beams lie scattered across the sand, and the golden name gleams through the seaweed, tangled in rope.

My father is gone.

I stare into the deep, aching beyond words. Foreign men put us in a rowboat. Me, the first mate, the navigator, and the Swede, are taken prisoner.

I look down at my clenched fist and recall my mother's hand silently pounding the table on her last day.

Once on board, we are taken below and chained with the slaves in a row.

If only I understood their language. The navigator does. He explains in whispers.

The hours creep along with anxiety in our minds.

The wood reeks of foulness. Unable to eat their frothy soup and stale black bread, I force myself to drink water.

About sundown, we're loosed from our shackles and brought single file up to the deck.

Anticipation mounts.

As we near another vessel, I see Dutch national flags, and *I can only think of my drowned father.*

I want to cry.

Why didn't I die with him?

They are moving us now, by rowboat and hauled up like fishes in a net.

We're dropped aboard the Dutch ship, and *I count it the prayer of my mother that I was not sold into slavery.*

I decide then I will memorize any language I can.

I'm covered with sand as I stand barefoot and hungry.

In his quarters, the Commander gives credit of our release as a service of the Dutch West India Company and sends the men to work detail, leaving me last.

He eyes me critically.

"The Swede says your father served under Commander Piet Hyen. Hmm. My respects to his memory. I've traded for your passage. This is *The Arms of Amsterdam*," he says and looks at my big feet.

Someone hands me a hardtack biscuit and a cup of tea while he proposes a bargain.

"I have no use for a boy. But I am a compassionate man and wish you no harm," he says, "Has your father given you any 'trade secrets' or confided certain, uh, valuable information, I might find profitable?" he inquires.

I dare a glance at his face *while my mind tightens to respond as a man.* I stiffen straight and tall.

"Yes, your grace. I think so," I look him in the eye and say, "I'm proud of the Dutch legacy he vested in me, being his only child. He often talked to me about the Holy Spirit coming upon the heroes of the Bible. What's more, he and the commander discussed getting revelation words of knowledge that directs good men for prosperity and to be victorious over enemies. Secrets from God."

With this he's delighted. He looks at me as he gives the next orders.

"Feed him well, as much as any man, and dress him for the fine class he is. He will make himself worth it," he says to the quartermaster, leaning back and eying my response, "Until we reach New Amsterdam, you are my apprentice, so to speak. Eat at my table, sleep in the next room, and no manual labor. You'll learn navigation, and I'll learn the secrets your father divulged to his son, hmm?" he says.

I step forward reaching to shake his hand, but he pretends not to see it, so I follow the first mate up the hatch, gulping my tea and savoring the hardtack.

I am an orphan and have no one to love me anymore.

After dinner I find out the Commander of *The Arms of Amsterdam* is ravenously interested in the gift of spiritual knowledge.[31] He wants to know where it is in the Bible and makes me find it. I talk until I'm tired.

Laid on my cot, I'm given a respectable change of clothing. Not for work like the scallywags. Not fine as Amsterdam either. Only better than I've ever worn before. I wear smooth boots of calf leather, golden and not broken in. I have a white shirt that's long as a nightshirt and that's tucked in by a blackened belt with a buckle. And the mate left a faded grey jacket with pockets, folded with my under things. It's too large, so I cuff the sleeves.

Each day, I report for more questions. The Commander is anxious. He keeps the door closed while he questions me.

I tell him how my mother died. I tell him about her plaid shawl I lost when the ship went down.

I say, "Both my parents could sense danger."

He gives me rapt attention, his concentration centering on every mention of spiritual power. I watch him plow through the scriptures, sometimes reading it aloud.

He finds where John the Baptist says, "He (Jesus), will baptize you with fire and thoroughly purge His floor."[32]

"What does this mean, 'baptize you with fire'?" he inquires, *but I don't know.*

I shrug and he delves more buried into his investigation.

Presently I ask if I can be dismissed, and he nods.

I wander away, *hoping to catch a dagger-throwing match, or maybe the cook will give me a bite of something.*

That afternoon, *The Arms of Amsterdam* navigator takes me under his wing and explains how he uses the compass, the sextant, and our maps. Our navigator stands by to assist.

Winking, he remarks how anyone appreciates a polite young man and then points at me.

I won't forget this encouragement for my tired soul.

The next morning, I rise at dawn to bring them both a hot biscuit wrapped in muslin, before breakfast is called.

The sea gulls are hunting, squawking as we sail along.

"Where are we?" I ask as they make their notations.

"Four hundred miles northwest of Jamestown," the navigator says.

I ask, "Where did my father go down?"

Both men quietly look at me and then at each other.

Our navigator blinks solemnly and says, "Cape Hatteras. A miracle anyone saw the wreckage and ventured to pick us up. Thank heaven the company pays for survivors."

I walk away.

Alone I stand on the deck, thinking about things and God, and all the verses my father made me memorize.

Why is he dead? Why didn't he know how to stop it?

Part of me feels angry. The other part doesn't dare accuse God. The dull heartache never eases.

He's gone. She's gone. I'm alone and too young to know what to do. And no one notices me.

The crew goes about their duties, hoisting the rigging, swinging the sails to catch the wind.

I know how they handle it. I move out of the way at the right time. The mate nods in appreciation.

I watch two boys slice at the chopping block, where the fish are hauled in. The nets are drying across the bow.

A bell rings its signal for dinner.

From the galley, I smell ham and go in with the others to eat, *wondering how long before the Commander will send for me.* He hasn't shown his face today.

With breakfast in my belly, I wander down the hall to the cannons and take a look around. Cannonballs are stacked in wooden crates against both musty sides of the ship.

Two soldiers come to their posts.

"What are you doing here?" one asks.

I say, "Only looking. Curious about how they work."

"So, we should shoot one off to show you?" he asks.

I nod eagerly. The men laugh, amused at me.

"Be on with you, boy," the soldier sharply quips.

Back in the kitchen, the Swede peels potatoes and offers me some leftover ham. I request to borrow a knife.

Their cook looks at the Swede, who nods approval.

"Make sure you give it back today," their cook says.

I take the ham and find an empty spot where I can practice throwing. The soldiers talk about how they plan to spend their pay.

With the ham in sight, I stand behind a barrel.

I hear a squeak. Now I see it slink toward the meat. I sling the butcher knife and snag the rat.

It shrieks, blood splattered on the floor.

The soldiers run to the area and see what I've done.

"Hmph. Nice move," the first one says.

"A game we played, to practice attack skills," I comment.

They grin at each other.

"We could fire the cannon to practice," the other offers.

I raise my brows.

"Go get the powder-boys," the first orders me.

The other leaves to alert the Commander.

When I tell them, *those boys are more excited than I am.*

We meet the first soldier carrying a bucket of water. On the wall behind, a board with hooks keeps the cannon tools.

The soldiers roll up their sleeves.

"Man the cannon!" the other one shouts.

The boys scramble to the magazine and delicately bring back the powder horns, one at a time.

Both men pour the powder into muslin, making wads.

"Bring a handful of live tinder sticks," the first says.

The Swede sees me lighting tenders and grins.

When I return, the soldier says, "We clean the debris from the cylinder with the sponge after battles, so we're ready if we're attacked. Keeping the hole clean protects us from damaging the ship while we're firing blow after blow. You boys see me ramming this explosive down the neck while it's cool. But the next time, the iron will be blazing hot. There might be cinders in its belly. I wet the sponge and put any out. We make sure nothing goes amiss. In the meantime, you watch my moves and not burn ye' self."

He explains about the position of the hole and how it affects the range, close or far away.

"Most of all, we don't want to ruin their ship. Too costly. The trick is frightening them to give it over to us," he grins.

A pewter mug on the hook holds the tinders in it.

"Now watch this," the other one says.

A cannonball is thrust down the neck of the gun, and right behind it, another wad of gunpowder is rammed. The first soldier unhooks the wooden doors in front of the gun port window. Together they heave the cannon's muzzle out, and the other soldier opens the priming hole on its top.

"Get over on the far side and cover your ears," he says.

We watch him pour a tiny stream of gunpowder down the hole and lower a strand of rope until it stops. He lights it, and both men quickly step forward, shoulders heaving the cannon up against the bulwark, as the line burns down.

A moment passes. The cannonball bursts with the boom of

thunder and smoke, while the ship absorbs the impact, jerking us against the bulwark.

The soldiers have let go of the heavy cannon in time to not get burned. The barrel rolls a length backward and I am amazed at their quick reflexes. They wet the sponge stick in the bucket and clean the hole. The cannon hole sizzles. The end is glowing orange.

I weigh the danger of carrying gunpowder horns. I know what it is to be near death.

Cannonballs with such immense power would whirl the balls into other boats with men onboard. It might cause the ship to sink.

The cannon is not exciting to me anymore.

It reminds me of the metal against metal coming up our steps bringing terror.

I leave and return the knife to the Swede.

Chapter 7

"What country's ship rescued us?" I ask, in the kitchen.

"English," the Swede says.

He wipes his hands on a cloth and puts his arm around my shoulder, leading me back to the storage room.

"Let me tell you something. It may put your mind to ease about your father," he says, "The day your mother died, he was restless. He kept asking the commander to stop the boat at Flushing, to let him go by his house. He felt something was wrong. It was a lot to ask. Our ships never make personal stops. He went around, asking the crew to vote. He was starting an incident and could be punished."

I am almost in tears, and he pokes me on the chest.

"We had already passed it. One hour, Two. Your father was not reasonable. He said to us, 'What if God is trying to tell me something, hmm?'"

"So, the Commander turned the ship back?" I ask.

He nods.

"It was almost dark by the time we let him off. Try to understand. He had to forgive us. For her dying," the Swede says, "For you seeing it."

A wave of anger rushes hot to my face.

"Aw, now, don't do that," he says, "They are lost at sea. Why would I tell you now? Because your father had the rare secret of hearing from the Holy Spirit. And God is your Father now. These secrets we learned from the saints of the old country. Your mother too. God always equips His people."

I look away. *I just want to be alone* and rise to leave.

He whispers, "There's something else."

I won't look at him, and he waits.

I turn back and ask, "What?"

"It was that way when *The Zeehaen* went down," he says.

Now I take a deep breath.

"You mean he felt something was going to happen, but no one would listen?" I ask a bit harshly.

I look hard at him. He lowers his head. This time he won't answer.

That means I'm right. No one would listen.

All afternoon I sit alone in my thoughts about being at sea, being at war with other countries. My father found how to access the wisdom and help of God Almighty, and though he had fought with remarkable success, no one believed him.

Why wasn't my father put in authority to make the right choices when he had such holy gifts?

I'm frustrated. The atmosphere is choked with readiness for danger, preparations for killing. Father knew what it felt like to be the winner. He tried to tell them. He tried to tell his Commander. I could see why he told the stories at supper. It was God's victory he bragged about. Why didn't they believe God showed my father this?

I weigh the coldness of it, dissatisfied.

When the crew gathers for dinner, *The Arms of Amsterdam* Commander slips by me and whispers, "I found it. Come when you finish."

I eat quickly and hurry to his quarters to find him kneeling at the bench, one arm over his head.

He doesn't hear me come in and I gently close the door.

He pours out his heart, telling God he fears hell and asks forgiveness. He expresses his need to be with his wife and children while they are young and still remember him.

I hope now that he's found it, we will sail the seas together and always have success. I think *he will adopt me and take me into his family. I will honor him and work for him on this ship, and he will know to do this, because God's heart of love will tell him, if he's right with God.*

I cough, and he regains his composure, getting up for me.

"I cannot keep you, Gerrit. It's best you make your way in the New World," he says, crossing the room.

Immediately I stiffen to prevent myself from crying.

He finds his place in the Bible and motions for me to come see. I lean over to look, brokenhearted and quiet.

Running his finger under the print, he reads aloud, "...to one is given by the Spirit the word of wisdom; to another the word of knowledge by the same Spirit; to another faith by the same Spirit; to another the gifts of healing by the same Spirit; to another the working of miracles; to another prophecy; to another discerning of spirits; to another divers kinds of tongues; to another interpretation of tongues; But all these worketh that one and selfsame Spirit, dividing to every man severally as he will."[33]

My lip stops quivering.

We look at each other with wonder.

"Do you believe this is the secret of how Hyen Piet captured the Spanish fleet?" he asks me.

I measure the seriousness of the question, processing all my father said about Dutch victories, and how he rescued me before the soldiers burned me in my house.

With a compelling look, I say, "What do you think, sir?"

He nods and turns to the Bible again to search.

I wonder if his faith in God has love or not. Will he turn away from my need for him? Will he expect God to give him gifts when he is stingy toward me? I think not.

As I meander off to my bunk, *the depth of possibilities to change circumstances beckons. The Spirit of God could come on me. I could be like my father, only educated.*

Do I dare pray for the gifts of the Spirit, or a baptism of fire? I'm afraid to trample on sacred ground. I wrestle with the silent invitation and fall asleep.

I dream I'm leaning against a fluted column of marble, supporting a gigantic building, watching people in a meadow play with children. The sky is azure with fleecy clouds, and butterflies flit among wildflowers in the grass. Sheep graze by the brook. The children turn to a figure coming over the hill, and in my dream, I see up close, the face of my father, only younger with no beard. Across the field, he spies a hand waving at him, someone he knows and happy to meet. He runs, smiling. It's my mother, beautiful and joyous! They stretch their arms to one another embracing.

And I wake up. I'm back on the sea.

The sun is shining brightly through the window, and gulls fly close to the ship. We approach land.

I dress quickly *to speak to the Commander, to tell him my dream and ask what it means.*

He's busy with other matters and says I must wait.

As we near Manhattan Island, the forest of ship masts greet me.

No wonder the Dutch West India Company makes such fortunes.

Slave ships are lined up unloading men, women, even children of all skin colors. I lean over the starboard and take it all in. Piles of fur pelts, barrels, and crates brought by wagons are ready to ship out, and their pallets tugged by horses and ropes.

"We trade with many nations these days. Merchants of eighteen languages thrive here," the first mate says, "You can find work."

My friend, the Commander takes me aside and gives me wampum, enough for a month, he says. I look at the exquisite blue and white clam beads. He pulls the string on the leather bag and pats my shoulder, to break all ties.

"In honor of your brave father," he says quietly and hands me a satchel, "Things you may need, a letter of introduction, verification of your name, and this."

In his palm is a thin silver dagger. I reach for it. Instead, he places it in the bag, pushes me into the dingy and says, "Sew a sleeve for it under the arm. Care for a man's soul, but not at the expense of your own.

Chapter 8

"A FATHER OF THE FATHERLESS, AND A JUDGE OF THE
WIDOWS, IS GOD IN HIS HOLY HABITATION."

PSALM 68:5

Carrying my duffel across the Brewer's Bridge, *I adjust myself inwardly* and watch dozens of log rafts carrying merchants who tally the cargo, coming or going, to ships.

Noise fills the air with different languages.

I feel lost. I don't have any choice. I need a home before dark. Fear rises in my throat, but I decide to block it off.

Behind the fort are vast green forests, tall and fresh looking. My eyes gaze down the lane where several cottages are backed by the woods, leaves serenely giving way to breezes of the ocean.

The birds singing cause me to remember heaven. I almost hear my father say, "What do you think, Gerrit?"

Then I smell fish frying in a pan from the tavern where we had eaten before and hurry there.

Inside, it's dark and crowded. I bring out wampum for my meal and a mug, observing the fellows.

Fine tradesmen next to me, dine with clear glass goblets and delft plates, dressed in black coats and brass buckled shoes, wearing long wigs and lace collars. I strain to hear their conversation, careful to look the other way, savoring the vegetables before me.

They discuss the need for military protection from the Indians who kill farmers not far from Fort Nassau. I overhear the price of beaver has gone up. The Holstein cheeses are coming along well. A young merchant relates the Portuguese spice trade entirely belongs to the Dutch.

"A monopoly," he boasts, to which they lift a glass.

Among these merchants of broad experience and vast resources, where shall I find a position? I'm only a boy.

They call for their footmen to bring the carved elegant carriages, and I watch through the window, as their beautiful horses trot into the countryside.

Slowly I stroll down the rough byway past the flour mill, vegetable gardens, and chicken coops.

Here is Fort Amsterdam with its earth sod sloping sides and massive wooden gates. Today they're open. I view the inside walls are brick, protecting the soldier's barracks and the wooden Director's house. Some important looking men walk into headquarters.[34]

Passing five stone houses of a shopping district, I see the bakery and pass the midwife's house, her sign by the door. On Pearl Street sits a simple wooden church with the minister's house and stable behind. All the lanes where I'm stepping are filthy from the manure of roving chickens and loose grunting pigs.

Isack van Ostade (artist)
Dutch, 1621 - 1649
"Workmen before an Inn", 1645
oil on panel

The Lee and Juliet Folger Fund
Courtesy National Gallery of Art, Washington

So different than our city, Amsterdam.

Away from the shore there are principal streets with much noise from taverns and carpenters hammering their trade. The new building they construct has long beams. Sweating in the humidity, I glance at them, lodged high in the rafters, bracing the brackets of iron to swing at the nails holding it.

Finally I am at the edge of town and welcome the shade of a spreading oak to rest on a gnarled root at its base.

I open my satchel and spy the dagger. Making sure I'm not watched, I run my finger along the blade.

Across the field a maid leads two cows where a man plows some withered plants under the dirt. The cow moos expecting feed. I grin and think, *the maid expects milk.*

Inside I see the satchel has small men's clothes for arduous work, two shirts, one britches, three pair of stockings.

I take account of my circumstances. I am tall and no longer thin. In fact, I've built a muscular back.

Should I ask for farm work? Will I like tavern keeping? Can I load ships? Not if I don't have to.

Maybe I will trap beaver. I have to think what I can do.

Any grown man would go to the man in charge and get information. I have a letter of introduction. To summon my courage, I remember the talks with my father. I think of how he was among the crew. That's how I need to be.

Standing tall, I decide I will go back inside the fort.

As I near it, the guards at the gate go about their business.

Bravely I proceed to pass the cross-hatched guardhouse, then the soldier's barracks. *I don't know if I'm allowed to walk here*, but I go toward the Director's brick house.

Apprehensively I look around, clutching the bag.

By the hedge I hesitate, *making a speech in my head.*

Suddenly a thin man is beside me, and I jump with a start.

He steps back, removing a black plumed hat.

"Do you speak Dutch?" he asks.

"Ya," I say, unsure of myself, noticing his silver rapier with baldric, a majestic sword sheathed to his tall side.

"I see you carry a satchel and wonder if you are new here?" his voice trails off.

I nod and stand straight, almost his height.

"My name is Gerrit," I reply.

He looks me in the eye and bursts into a grin, his teeth white and even, his right brow raised.

"I'm Lodewyck Wildebrand. I've had a miserable trip on *The Den Eyckenboom*.[35] I'm surprised there is no pier or loading dock. My boots are still wet. Can you ride a horse, Gerrit?" Wildebrand asks.

"No sir," I say, "I have ship experience."

Behind us on the porch now stands Director Boydin.

In contrast, the Director is stout and ruddy faced with greying whiskers about his nose.

Wildebrand turns his head looking about, *unaware that the Director is sizing him up.*

Boydin grits his teeth and even I understand he resents the youth and authority Wildebrand represents.

I speak up, "Sir, I'm seeking work."

Boydin quips, "We always need laborers. Talk with Adam Voor Reyns, the overseer for Bos Huybrecht."

Wildebrand lifts his hat as a courtesy to the Director and tucks it under his arm, plume, and all. He has long wavy brown hair.

Wildebrand tells me, "Adam is in the tavern. Hurry. You will know him by his red tam with quail feathers."

Boykin shoos me away like a fly.

Inside the tavern, I buy myself cherry cider. Looking around there is no one wearing a red tam.

I ask if the server knows Adam. Could he point the man out for me?

Adam hears and locks his gaze on me. I walk to his table.

There lies the much worn red woolen tam, its leather edges peeling and indeed there are scruffy quail feathers.

It has seen better days. This is a working man.

Frans van Mieris (painter)
"A Soldier Smoking a Pipe"
c. 1657/1658 - oil on panel

The Lee and Juliet Folger Fund
Courtesy National Gallery of Art, Washington

"Director Boydin thinks you will hire me," I manage.

Adam has hairy arms and red curly hair. He's freckled and weathered around his brown eyes.

He leans back, amused at me, "Well. I have authority to obtain a young man your size. You will serve at the plantation house in any manner required. In exchange, the master will supply your provisions and sleeping quarters, plus a yearly good behavior bonus. You'll be schooled, of course. Follow me."

He pays his tab, and I follow behind him to a carriage waiting with an African driver.

We stop at the fort, where Adam walks me right in. He's a respected man on common ground with the Director. He holds my shoulder.

"Gerrit will belong to Evert," Adam says, holding the attention of Director Boydin.

Respectfully the Director introduces them.

"Adam Voor Reyns, meet the sheriff of Berkenkotter, Lodewyck Wildebrand. Adam oversees the ships and cargo for the Huybrechts, Evert, and his father, Bos," Director Boydin says, "He's hired this young man."

I stand by silently as I should.

Adam attempts a conversation about people requesting to meet with the Director, *which Boykin dismisses as trivial.*

I shelve the information, thinking I have come to serve a master like Joseph in the Bible. I intend to please God, be a manager and embrace the experience.

The African waits stoically.

We begin the journey away from New Amsterdam.

Too frightened to speak, I jostle along in the carriage with Adam while we follow the trail along the Hudson River. I'm amazed at the Palisades walls that have been raised. The forest begins to envelop us, serene and haunting. The trip is not long.

Adam talks of his apprentice days, *and I find him likable and intelligent.*

He does not treat me as a boy. I will not disappoint him.

It is high noon when we arrive. He shows me the fields our patroon owns, the houses and barns.

Another African meets us at the carriage in front of the house. *My Dutch heritage seems to be in my favor.*

Stepping out of the carriage, my mouth drops open to view the elegance brought to this wooded location. Before me rises a broad yellow bricked mansion with four chimneys of red brick, one at each corner. The tall windows face every direction under the baked tile roofing. The massive front entry door is majestic, painted black and foreboding.

I exit the carriage slowly, looking up three stories. Every side is flanked with shrubbery and flowers. Each walkway is as neat as Amsterdam itself. The fencing about the yard is painted and even.

It's a showplace.

At the rear doorway, I see the exquisite plaster cast designs up close and follow Adam, lowering my head.

"Sit here," he says, pointing to a forlorn stiff chair.

Adam removes his tam and holding it, he spits on the other hand and smooths his hair.

His jaw tightens as he looks up.

"Evert," he whispers, glancing quickly toward his left.

The hallway echoes with the sound of metal taps attached to his wooden soles, as he clicks toward us.

When I first see him, Evert wears a scowl under his pointed nose. He's pale and has thinning dark hair stark against his ruffled white collar.

They disappear within the house discussing me.

Across the room is a long mirror where I look at me for the first time in my life. My hair is unruly tousled, my face red and my nose too large. My cheeks are fat, and I look sullen. If I had met myself on the street, I wouldn't like me. I appear too sad, too bashful.

I fidget until I'm called.

When they come back in the foyer Evert is impatient. He dismisses Adam with the flick of his hand and points to me.

"Come along now. What are you called?" he inquires deliberately walking ahead of me.

Before I can answer he chides, "Don't dawdle. It's beneath you."

In the office, I sit on a tall chair of black carving, *very uncomfortable.*

"Gerrit Brinkendorf," I say *cautiously and dare not look about.*

With his clean fingernails, I watch Evert ruffle papers and draw a quill from the drawer of a wide mahogany desk. The ink well is ornate, gold, and glass. I watch him dip the quill and tap it to measure.

I notice my own chapped hands, rough and dirty. I bow my head in shame, pulling them out of sight.

"You are the son of Arnoldus Brinkendorf, who sailed with Commander Piet Heyn. Well, my sympathy for the loss of your father. I shall take you to task and make it worth our effort. What is your year of birth?" he asks.

"1629, sire, after Hyen took the treasure fleet," I say.

"Well, I expect you have inherited a sort of rudimentary talent. I make a decent offer in the name of charity. I propose to send you to Collegiate School and buy you books and clothing to be presentable as a student may require. In turn, you shall work for my father at his bidding for six years and not run away. You will work all hours except what is mandatory for your membership in the Dutch Reformed Protestant Church. At the end of your six years, you will be eighteen, have an education and experience with Indians and furs. This outpost is part of the raw end of the mercantile trade, which our people are proud to be the best. Make your mark here."

He is through talking, handing me the quill.

I mark "G" as Mum taught me.

He takes me back to the rear entrance.

"Show this young man where he can sleep," he says to the African servant and points for me to leave by the door.

I follow the African out to the houses by the fields.

The African shows me a bunk and tells me in broken Dutch to leave my bag. It's time for supper.

We eat on one side of the barn, *some things I have not tasted before. He notices I look curiously at the food.*

"Tomatoes," he says, "Turkey, okra, squash. Good."

All the slaves jabber to each other in their language. I eat and listen. This is the new crew I work with.

I will learn their language and be their friend.

Tonight, I sleep on land.

That may take some getting used to.

I am an indentured servant.

Does this mean I'm a slave?

I don't know and I don't have a choice. I'm among others who don't have a choice either.

In my excitement of having found a job, I forget to ask God for the baptism of fire.

I forget about pursuing spiritual gifts while I try to make a good life for myself.

Chapter 9

"THE LORD WAS WITH JOSEPH,...AND HIS MASTER
SAW...THAT THE LORD MADE ALL HE DID PROSPER...
AND HE MADE JOSEPH OVERSEER OVER HIS HOUSE
AND ALL THAT HE HAD, HE PUT INTO HIS HAND."
GENESIS 39:2-4

On the Huybrechts plantation,[36] cleared land is separated by stone walls, stacked by the strongest men.

Boogard is the crop overseer. We grow tobacco mainly, but also some indigo, wheat, and barley.

In the fields, several "half-free" African slaves work among us, required to make a fixed payment yearly to the company for their freedom.

They are better off than the rest of us. Soon they'll be on their own, getting ahead.

Indenture is not half-free. *We are working prisoners.*

Monday mornings, I report to the cook for weeding the garden at the big house and cut ripe vegetables. If it's dry, I water them and that can be backbreaking.

I wish for rain, but I don't pray for it.

I don't even think about praying.

We haul the wheat in sheaves to the mill and haul back the flour, stacking the muslin bags in the pantry.

We dry the indigo into blue dye bricks to be sold to merchants of Amsterdam. Tobacco is the most profitable commodity, the rage of the marketplace. The lead overseer practices ways to refine it, hoping to drive the price up.

I hear him talk about it to Evert.

I enter school in the third grade, the same month the company opens trade with friendly nations in the passage of the Articles and Conditions, charging them ten percent import duty, requiring them to use Dutch West India ships.

We get busier. The merchants get richer.

Foreign trade causes our town to swell with Germans, Swedes, English, and Finns, not to mention slaves, and indentured servants on every boat.

My education *is enjoyable, including speaking English.*

On the way home from school, I overhear an English housewife nagging her husband as he corrals the pig to sell and I understand what she says.

"If Wildebrand can be trusted, you'd already have a voice with the Director. What are you afraid of? Tell me what?" she nags from the back stoop.

I keep my eyes off them, nonchalantly meandering along.

He grabs the fencepost and ties the rope around the pig's neck, wallowing in the dirt.

"Don't we have any rights here?" she complains, hands on her hips.

He frowns and pulls himself to stand up.

"Shut up. You want the whole town to hear?" he hisses.

He crosses the yard to open the gate as I turn the corner.

I see Wildebrand with his black plumed hat under his arm, coming out of the tavern. He walks with two men.

I keep my head down as they talk.

"It's us that's taking the risk. He's in the fort," one says.

I walk home briskly, *wondering what is going on.*

Not far from the river, I meet the Huybrecht carriage on the road. The driver is attempting to manage the horses, spooked by a sizeable, coiled snake in the way.

Evert is jostled about furiously in the seat.

I draw my dagger out and hit the rattler square in the head, diffusing the incident. The horses calm and the driver tips his hat, while I retrieve my knife and hide it.

Evert opens the door and asks the driver about it.

"Boy fix," he says in broken Dutch, trying to explain.

With a haughty stare, Evert nods to me.

I return the nod and kick the snake in the ditch.

In the Autumn, I pass to fifth grade. Evert orders Boogard to take me to town for a reward of a new shirt with buttons, woolen knee britches, white stockings, and brass buckled shoes. Also, I am fitted for a woolen coat and given a smart hat. With my yearly bonus, I buy a raccoon tail for my hat and a leather tie to pull my hair back. I have a little beard.

I develop myself a system of efficiency while at work in the field and bringing kitchen supplies. I tell myself managing time gives me the advantage. I count my steps competing with the last day's speed. I stack it right the first time. I finish each row faster than the men around me. It makes for a feeling of adventure and builds a little self-esteem when the days are so mundane.

I am not the best-dressed boy that comes to school the following November, nor am I the worst. Some of them stand out. I take great care to keep my best things looking new for church.

From Manhattan Island, little rascals come to be taught, and none of them pirates' sons. I know because I ask. It makes me feel important, and I'm proud of my father. Whether it helps me to weave my stories, I can't tell. The young men grow quickly bored, and the wee sons act frightened. I settle in and listen and get excited about learning for another year.

Our schoolmaster, Danel Zegerzoon, is supplied as part of the company's investments to our province.

I learn that shipbuilding and our Protestant religion has benefitted the Dutch Republic to become the world's wealthiest nation.

When the lesson tarries on the Spanish treasure fleet

captured off Cuba, I marvel in every detail, knowing the memory my father told the sailors, the night he died.

Danel tells the intention of the company from the beginning was to carry on economic warfare against Catholic Spain and Portugal by striking at their colonies with their raw resources of gold and silver.

It's late when school lets out. Some mothers have come for the small boys.

That makes me miss Mum.

Lost in thought, I wander along, head down, when a surly remark takes my attention right away.

"Never a pirate like the mighty Pien," comes a menacing slur.

A group of thugs slink carelessly at the rear of the pub laughing at me.

I know them. Troublemakers.

At school, they sit in the back of the class. Almost men, they entertain one another by interrupting our teacher.

I walk farther from my usual course.

Ignore them, I think. *No friends of mine. Evert expects I won't dawdle. He'll be waiting for me.*

The five follow me. Men at the pier see what's happening.

I pretend I don't notice, purposely not quickening my pace.

Their taunts continue, taking turns.

"Dutch boy with lies in his pockets. Look at the calloused hands and common manners. It's pirate's brags of gold and treasure," the fattest one says.

"If his father was who he said he was, why is he grubbing in the dirt with the slaves? I don't believe a word of it, do you?" another asks.

They mock, poking each other.

I feel the hot tears in my eyes, which I force back.

Then the tallest one bumps into me knocking me down.

The others kick me, many at once, then back off.

I clench a hand of mud and climb up.

They surround me like a pack of wolves, watching my hand, grinning with devilish glee.

I single out the tall one, the one that ruined my clothes and hurl the dirt in his face, pulling the dagger from my sleeve.

The ruffians step back when they see the knife.

Now the tables are turned!

I twist it in front of me, making it glisten in the sun.

Panting, I cower for a plunge and the tall one's courage is met with a challenge. The air is tense.

In the eyes of his comrades, I am no longer easy prey.

Noise from loading on the dock means no one will hear what will happen now.

All eyes are on him, the pressure mounting.

The odds have suddenly accelerated.

I look at his rib cage, and a coldness must be on my face, for they look frightened, and one runs away.

The tall one says, "You'll be caught."

"So what?" I return gruffly.

He swallows.

"Throw it down and fight like a man," he says.

"A man would be a fool to throw down when he's the winner," I retort coolly.

His friends look at him anxiously.

"We only wanted a friendly tousle," he steps back to the wall, nowhere to run.

My jaw is clenched. I raise the dagger, *aware their eyes are wide* and pitch it at my target.

His sleeve is caught to the boards. He jerks. His shirt rips.

Before he can grab it, I run over and pull it out.

It's in my hand again, shining as I turn on the others.

Now I'm between them, *like a caged dog daring a rumble.*

If they doubted my ability or accuracy before, there is no doubt now.

A shadow falls on the dirt to my left.

Chapter 10

"HE THAT IS SLOW TO ANGER IS BETTER THAN THE
MIGHTY; AND HE THAT RULETH HIS SPIRIT THAN HE
THAT TAKETH A CITY."

PROVERBS 16:32

Someone in the alley causes the rest of them to scramble in all directions, over stumps, into the woods.

I look back.

It's our schoolmaster, Danel. We are alone.

He walks over eyeing the dagger.

"Maybe I should have a talk with Evert. Can you explain this altercation?" he asks.

I put my weapon away in the sleeve.

"You know them better than I do," I say, *not looking at him, in case he plans to take their side.*

"Yes. Well, that being considered, I think it would be useful to us both if I escort you home and vouch for the time lost to your master," he suggests.

I face him.

Does he mean it?

He's smiling. *For that I'm grateful.*

I enjoy the long ride to the plantation beside Danel on his wagon seat. I tell him how I got the dagger, how we practiced killing rats, and what I learned from my father.

He likes me, I can tell.

The African butler greets us in the front garden of the mansion, and I introduce Danel as our teacher.

Danel asks him if he'd like to come to class.

I like that in Danel, friendly and kind.

The butler walks us to the front door.

I've never been through the front before.

In the foyer, we wait.

My dirty hand embarrasses me. My nice new clothes are dusty. Certainly, my hair is in disarray. I spit and smooth it down.

Danel pats my knee.

"Calm down," he says, "I'm here to restore your honor."

"Evert will receive you in the library," the butler says.

Danel prods me up, guiding me by the elbow.

The aroma of baking ham through the house stirs the juices in my mouth.

Evert seems apprehensive, sitting alone. Danel greets him with a handshake and makes a jovial remark, leading me in.

"I hear the turkey are so fat near these woods that a small boy might knock one over with a rock and carry it home for his mother to dress for dinner," the schoolmaster chuckles.

Evert nods cordially.

"Please, have a seat," Evert invites, and Danel puts me on a leather ottoman by the fire while he sits on the divan.

"I want to call your attention to a valuable asset you have in your company, sir, a developing investment that may be worth its weight in gold," he begins.

Evert raises his brows, "Do say."

"May I speak freely?" Danel asks, walking to the bookcase.

Evert nods, *appraising my position, noticing the mud, aware I am uncomfortable with his expression of criticism.*

Danel says, "Labor is labor. We have a stark need for all we can get. Uneducated labor is not as important as one that has been groomed to manage."

Evert listens, *somewhat obliging.*

"In my classroom, I have various personalities suited to a wide range of work duties. I usually can tell by their attitude and study ethics how a boy will fare in his future. I see intelligence. I watch the stamina. I endure their clumsiness and strive to help them master themselves," Danel says.

"Mr. Zegerzoon, your service does not go unappreciated," Evert says.

"Thank you, sir. Now to the matter for which I have come. You possess a property so unique and worthy that I wish to extend my tutorial services for the betterment of the Huybrecht firm," my teacher offers.

Evert shifts his weight, leans forward, and clasps his hands, *looking me over.*

I dare not move.

Danel pushes the proposal.

"He exhibits a sort of courage not found in many grown men. We know his father was a remarkable man," he says.

Evert balks, but Danel confidently looks back at me.

"Given the circumstances, any man may have had his story," Evert says, "You or I."

Danel stands straight, arms crossed.

"I think not," Danel says, "I caught Gerrit this afternoon with a dagger in his hand, and five larger boys afraid of him."

Evert's eyes dart toward me with a frown.

I blink.

"I have no doubt that the gang confronted and threatened him. I didn't stop the fight. I wasn't there in time. Gerrit handled them alone, with no bloodshed. He could have damaged them, I'm sure," he says, "You see, sir, on the docks, those older boys cause a lot of fights. They think it's amusing to hurl insults at new sailors and old women. They throw rocks at the little boys. Daily they are a disruption at our school. No one has taken them to task until now. I myself was at a loss how to handle the matter," he pauses for effect, "Gerrit put them down alone."

Evert walks across the room and fills his pipe. He offers tobacco to Danel, who declines and goes to the window.

"You can thank your lucky stars Gerrit is your property," he says, *making me want to cry in gratitude.*

Of all things, being labeled "property" upsets me.

My father would be ashamed to know I was property, his proud son.

Danel says, "I believe you have on your hands a brave soul that has learned to control himself. These are characteristics a man builds in his son by example."

I swallow, beaming with esteem. Yes, my father did that.

Evert appraises me differently, and I feel it, though I continue looking forward.

"He killed a rattlesnake, somehow, by my carriage," Evert responds and softens as he remembers.

I feel some confidence, some hope in my heart.

Between us three a new bond is being formed.

"Sir, why not allow me to come evenings this winter and polish your diamond in the rough?" Danel requests.

I hold my breath.

"At what cost?" Evert asks, returning to his desk.

"Let's say, dinner and feed for my horse. If we sense the efforts are useless, we cease. Neither of us is worse off. If he surpasses my expectations, you may reward me as you deem fit," Danel says, "I'll need to use your library, of course. We'll need ink, vellum, quills, lading books, maps."

I think of Joseph standing before Pharaoh.

Evert gets up, walks to the fireplace, knocks the pipe into the fire, and lays it on the mantel empty.

"I'll have that dagger," Evert says, opening his palm.

Danel steps between us.

"Don't," Danel says, "He'll lose face."

Evert considers.

Will he let me keep my self-respect? It crosses that proper line between master and servant.

Evert cannot pass up the offer. What Danel says carries weight. Evert's lips are tight. He raises his chin.

"All right. Get your supper, my 'valuable asset'. Clean up for bed," Evert says and walks Danel to the dining room.

Chapter 11

"THE HEART OF THE PRUDENT GETTETH KNOWLEDGE;
AND THE EAR OF THE WISE SEEKETH KNOWLEDGE."
PROVERBS 18:15

Throughout the winter, I trudge to school in the freezing cold, bundled up and by myself. I learn what the other students learn, all of us in one room together.

After school, I ride with Danel on the wagon seat, and he discusses subjects I need to know. He and I study in the library until dinner at six.

Then I eat with the butler and cook. I bring in firewood for the four fireplaces and at seven, Danel moves to the dining room where I do mathematical sums and write essays.

By March, we've covered history, science, and geography.

As the ice melts and the blinding sun shines off the snow, Danel tells me he thinks he's taught me all he knows.

"I'm proud of you. See if you can prove yourself and earn me a reward from Evert," Danel quips and wears a grin.

In the library, he closes the pocket doors for privacy this time and tells me to write. He rambles through a summary of all I've learned and tells me to add what I think.

Then he coaches me in a speech.

"Show confidence. Stand up to being 'property'. Make Evert recognize your intelligence and fortitude," he coaxes.

I think and sip some tea.

"Use your head, Gerrit. This is the test," he says.

I rise to practice my speech haltingly, gaining composure, reading my notes.

"Try it again. Don't lean on your notes. Let it come from your mind, what you know you've learned," Danel points to his temple, "In your own words, it's more effective."

I do it again, *more assured than before.*

"Read over your writing. Get it settled in your head. I'm going to let you rest your voice while I talk with the butler. I want to tutor him next," he says.

After dinner, Evert waits in the library for me to return from bringing the logs in. Danel stands by the bookcase. The butler sits across from Evert, who lounges in the comfortable chair.

Danel beckons me to stand by the windows. He introduces my speech and nods for me to go ahead.

I pull myself erect and look straight at Evert, soundly relating my education, in subjects separately, and then joining their importance to his company business. I finish by offering myself as a lading counter, protector of his interests and a ready substitute for any position that might come under duress.

The butler's eyes rivet on me. He finds pleasure in my success, and the wonder in his countenance reveals hope that he can accomplish the same education.

Evert congratulates me with a clap on the shoulder and tells me to take the rest of the night off while he converses business with the schoolmaster.

Danel looks pleased.

As I leave through the rear entrance, the butler gushes the news to the cook.

I'm glad for them and head out in the cold to go to bed in the barn.

In the morning, I'm told school for me is over. Evert is waiting in the carriage and the butler hands me a biscuit with ham. Danel has advised him I should be employed for a time to Wildebrand, bringing in the furs from the wilderness. It will involve me doing business with Indians.

"The English are moving into our area rapidly," Evert says, "Their country's in a religious civil war. Not finding acceptance with the Pilgrims, these Protestants come to our doorstep seeking liberty to practice the dictates of their conscience. Director Boydin makes them swear an oath of allegiance and gives them land. To make matters worse, the fur is getting harder to get. So, our trading post is developing into a settlement. It's no longer prosperous for the Dutch West India Company and the town people complain about its management. They want laws."

I try to understand it all and wish I had a drink of water.

"Before I leave you in the backwoods with Wildebrand, I want you to understand why," Evert says, "I trust you to be my eyes and ears for what goes on behind my back."

"I'm going to work for Wildebrand?" I ask.

He nods. *I'm solemn.*

We are riding along a lonely stretch of road. The driver knows little Dutch. Still, Evert almost whispers what he expects me to do with Wildebrand.

"After you arrange the shipment today. Show me you can count. I want you to study Wildebrand, Boydin, any others that jeopardize our success. I don't ask you to lie. You will keep a low profile. Don't show how smart you are. Don't watch with an eagle eye. Appear to be unfocused. Be slowly careful, correct in your figures. Make it seem like you're, well, no one to worry about. In fact, hold off letting others know you speak languages and understand law," he says, "I want them to think you've dropped out of school because you're dim-witted. I'll spread this rumor at the tavern, saying how disappointed I am, how I had high hopes for you."

This is a smack in the face from the encouraging buildup Danel always gave me. It's not what I expected in reward for my service to Evert.

I worked hard. Now, I feel cheated.

I cover up my shame by facing the countryside. How cruel this is, ruining my reputation for his profit.

He schemes to lie about me. It hurts. He smiles.

I don't. I know now, I'll be a spy.

"You will walk into an explosive political crisis with every man you see. You will go innocently into places to overhear information," he says.

I remember the English wife, what she said to her husband about Wildebrand. If Danel couldn't confront the bully gang, he has already done all he can do for me.

I'm on my own.

We're coming into town. The driver slows for walkers and carts. Our voices may be heard.

Evert raises his brows to question if I understand.

I tighten my lips and nod.

"You will be my messenger service, going back and forth at my bidding. Always your defense will be that you are taking care of the company business. That will be your reply to any questions," he whispers, "Gerrit, never lie to me."

His eyes blaze with cruelty meant to warn me thoroughly.

We pull up as the wagons are being unloaded, and the fur stacks are on the beach.

"Your test is to load the furs in order, separate the trade goods from the fur smell and bring back the tally to me. Let's see if it's accurate according to the lading I have in my hand. I'll be in the tavern. You have the authority. See what you can do," he says and steps out smiling to the men.

He leaves me alone to command the operation.

I look older than my age, an advantage at this point.

The woodsmen scowl as I approach with the tally board. I acknowledge them nodding and say nothing, pointing to the work, making them untie the rope. I count it quickly.

The expensive beavers are first. Moving through the pile by placing them on an empty pallet, I peel off the pelts in tens and lay them to raise a new stack.

"Two hundred, forty-six," I announce, "Tie them tight."

The number verifies. The skinner signs. The fur wagons turn and leave. The timber wagons rumble in.

The otter are next. *I am careful to lower my eyes as if I'm not noticing anything about me. Some men idly whisper on the ship as they observe my way of doing things.*

I say, "Eight hundred and fifty-one. Rope them. Set them on the beach."

Next are the mink, a small stack of forty-eight. Thirty-six lynx skins and thirty-four water rat skins.

I dismiss the skinners.

The timber wagons are full of oak, and *I know already it needs to go in the middle.* I watch the logger guide the wagon driver as he backs the horses down to the water. Maneuvering the logs onto a heavy raft at low tide is the trick. They steady the horses as they unload for my count.

It makes for a smoother transition if I can manage to get the tally while they move it.

The raft gets across, and I climb up to oversee the logs to the cargo hold, away from the ship pumps. *As I walk the ship's deck, out of the corner of my eye, I see a skinner pull two lynx skins from the bundle. He stuffs them under the horse's blanket and returns to guard.*

I haven't seen Adam since the first day he hired me and took me back to Evert. He comes from the tavern now and talks with the skinner while I ride the raft back to load the fur stacks.

It's painfully slow.

"Hello, Gerrit," Adam says, "It will be nice working with you. I haven't had decent help in ages."

He slaps me on the back, as if I'm his son.

I smile, remembering I must seem like an easy one to fool.

The skinner attempts a joke.

I order the fur stacks on the raft. With the furs crossing over, *I have a period of reflection to analyze why Evert asks me to be his eyes and ears. I will tell him about the skinner stealing. Does Adam know the skinner steals?*

Do I want to be a spy? It's risky.

Someone must help protect the Huybrecht Company.

I do seem unlikely. I take on a new perspective.

Besides the fur, Huybrecht Company ships desirable trade

goods out of New Amsterdam, transporting cacao beans, vanilla, cassava, coffee, and molasses coming from the West Indies that we buy for resale. We ship locally grown wheat, rye, oats, caraway seed, and flax. These are known as profit-making grains. Each supplier signs off with his wagon of goods. Evert has paid for their delivery.

By the time the raft takes me ashore, these goods are waiting to be counted for shipment. I place them in dry areas of the fluyt. Storms can cause water damage.

In all, it takes six hours for me to count and arrange the cargo ready for transport.

Evert has come out to meet me.

Back in the carriage, the dark prevents us from going over the figures. I'm tired, but the test is not over.

At the mansion, he takes me to the library, and we sit down at the table. I hand him my tally book and he draws out his.

I watch him go down the columns.

"Did you see anything you think I should know?" he asks.

"I saw the last skinner, the one that talked to Adam, take two lynx pelts and pad them under his horse blanket," I say.

He sits back and looks serious.

Then he goes down the lists to see if they coincide.

I watch.

"The otter count is off too," he says, "My counter in the woods had eight hundred, fifty-four."

He finds no fault with the timber numbers but rubs his forehead looking over the grain account. Five sacks of wheat less than my numbers."

I lay my head on my arms, weary and worried. He walks to the kitchen and comes back with two apples and hands one to me. I'm soberly quiet.

I guess he feels he needs to confide in me, and I'm not sure I want him to.

"Gerrit, you see we live in a colony with no government in place," he says, "If I complain to the Director, he more than likely will overreact. It's his position in the community to make money for the Dutch West India Company. Boydin is not handling things very well. As a trading post, there are other ports more promising. Brazil, for instance, Ceylon, Jakarta. We are falling behind here. He feels threatened to guard company interests. They pay his salary."

He takes a deep breath and sighs. He gets up and looks at the ceiling. Turning back, he opens his hands to me.

"I don't want to put you in jeopardy. A lot of people don't like the Director's policies. He won't listen. We think Wildebrand is attempting a takeover," he says.

I jolt up straight. He walks across the floor.

"He will not suspect you. You have an innocent way about you. I want you to be his friend, visiting the people's cottages. Find out what they plan to do. Tell me what is going on so I can make the best choices," he says, "My father has everything invested here. You can see how important it is."

I finish the apple and ask for some water.

He comes back with a glass and waits, looking at me.

I say, "I have heard some talk. It's true people are unhappy with Boydin. But they don't trust Wildebrand either. You think I can do this, but I don't know."

Evert grows impatient, "If you know there is trouble brewing, what is it that bothers you?"

"I think it may not be in me to pretend. It goes against all my father taught me," I respond.

"You will obey me, and this is what I need you to do. Do it well and I will reward you. Fail and expect the full punishment I can exact. I can have you excommunicated from the settlement, removed from the protection of the Dutch West India Company, and driven out to the Indians."

He means for that to terrorize me and blows out the light.

He walks me to the back entrance, where I head out in the night, *none the less frightened.*

Chapter 12

"HAPPY IS THAT MAN THAT FEARETH THE LORD ALWAY: BUT HE THAT HARDENETH HIS HEART SHALL FALL INTO MISCHIEF."

PROVERBS 28:14

The following day is Lord's Day. At church service, I hear stories of brave men who stood for the glory of God. Men like Moses, Joshua, and Paul.[37] We Dutch fought for the Reformation and opened our cities to persecuted people.

I love the faith of my country.

Coming from the church, I spot the Swede by the tree.

"How are you?" I ask, "Do you live here now?"

He smiles shyly and squints at me.

"No, Gerrit. Probably I will always be at sea. It's my life. I look for you today with a matter on my heart," he says.

I don't know what to expect.

Is he dying? Has he done something wrong?

"Come to the tavern and we eat," he requests.

We move briskly in the blowing wind, and he holds the door for me, *which reminds me of my father.*

Seated with a mug of mulled cider, *I dread the conversation and guard my feelings.*

"Your father was my friend. We shared dangers where some men died. He protected me more than once."

I stuff my mouth with sausage and cabbage. He leaves off eating his food, *more excited to visit with me.*

"If you seek the spiritual gifts your father had, I want you to know, he was a simple man. Not perfect," he says.

I don't like how he is putting this.

"What does it matter?" I ask.

"Because if you think you must be perfect, you won't have faith to hear from God," he says, "That's been in my mind, I searched to find you and tell you. Now, I said it."

I eye him curiously, the fork poised in my hand.

"Why should I seek something so mysterious that didn't keep my mother and father alive?"

I stab my sausage with a frown.

"Oh," he whispers and his countenance falls.

He pulls his hands together under the table and hangs his head.

It does not matter to him that the food gets cold. It doesn't matter that others see his withdrawal.

I finish and lay my fork on the plate.

He's withdrawn.

I gulp the rest of the cider and wait.

He raises his tearful eyes and tightened lip.

"Would break your father's heart, you hardened so," he says.

I can't look at him. War is in my soul, and it spills over precisely as my father said it would.

I'm lonely and afraid. What do I work for? Survival.

I want to blame something.

"It is kind of you to find me and say my father was your friend. Only, don't talk to me of useless tragedy," I bark.

He nods sadly, and *I am sorry already for having lashed at him with my words. I should give him respect, words that could comfort him on lonely nights at sea.*

Our eyes meet.

I think *he should understand how busy I am.*

"Evert is at the doorway, looking for me," I say and leave.

Evert is agitated. He hurries me out to the carriage.

"Get in. We have a lot to cover, and time is of the essence," he says, "I didn't find you in the churchyard after service."

"I didn't expect you needed me," I say, "It's Lord's day."

"I know," he says, "I'll make it up to you. My wife says Marcus de Yewen's ships are arriving before ours and fetching higher prices. I want you to think of some way, come up with a plan to remedy that. It embarrasses me at home. I want it to have your immediate attention."

I struggle to comprehend how I should answer.

He goes on, "Tomorrow, when I deliver you to Wildebrand on his grounds, he mustn't know any of this. I will continue business as usual. You use that God-given ability you have like Joseph or Daniel.[38] We need to have our shipments brought in before his. That's your assignment."

He thinks I have the gifts my father and Piet Hyen had. He thinks I bring him an inside link to God. How can I do that and be deceitful? There's no way. Besides, he expects holy knowledge to come from me. I don't have it and I'm not even trying to. It's not something you buy and sell.

In the fog of early morning Evert takes me in the carriage out to the Berkenkotter plantation where I will be left.

Wildebrand is the hired sheriff of the wealthy Berkenkotter estate which manages most of the fur trade with the Indians and brings in hides for the Huybrecht firm.[39]

As the carriage rumbles along, Evert reads a pamphlet from Leiden and contents himself skimming the figures on three ledgers.

I'm apprehensive about going into the wilderness. My eyes scan the woods and rocky places. Deer watch us.

We travel along the Hudson River continually north.

The large geese squawk flying in formation overhead. The sun is rising in the sky.

"I didn't tell my father I leased you out. He'll be back any day," he says, "Tell the driver to stop at the next creek."

When we jostle away again, he lowers his voice and whispers,

"The director plans to charge the Indians taxes for what we do for them."[40]

He leans back, perturbed, shaking his head.

Through the afternoon we manage with only a slab of ham for the three of us and a half round of bread.

I'm supposed to spy on the Indian situation and Wildebrand's part in it. He doesn't have to spell it out.

As we approach the stone monuments and wooden gates of Berkenkotter Plantation, we find the bushes near the road are cleared. Six black iron lanterns are held in the stone, three on each side. The watchman lights them before we reach the turn in. It's almost dark. He rocks a wolf between the trees and asks us to get out please.

To this request, Evert is offended.

The watchman shows the driver how a large ditch has been cut across the entrance and an iron pipe crosses it. There is no place for horse footing.

Evert steps out cautiously.

"Keeps our cattle in," the watchman explains humbly.

Evert looks at me and rolls his eyes whispering, "Keeps others out too."

I focus to learn everything I can.

The watchman takes the horse's reins and walks aside where he lifts four rails of fencing, sliding them out.

The carriage is maneuvered through the meadow and turned back onto the drive while we follow, and Evert gingerly avoids muddying his boots.

No one will ever be hastily coming through that entrance.

A bull paws the dirt in a distant field. Cows moo.

Mounting the carriage again, we proceed slowly past cotton fields snowy white and workers with bags over their shoulders picking the bolls, pricking their fingers.

I know how that is.

In the air the smell of salted pork drifts to my nose and we pass many open sided barns where long rows of tobacco leaves hang to dry. The ham smell is dense, though the barns are shut tight.

Near the farmer's house, a rooster warns we're coming.

Wildebrand rides to the carriage and looks in.

Good day to ye, Evert," he salutes, moving ahead.

We pass workshops. There are smiths and glaziers and brick makers. Here are bakers, wheelwrights, cobblers, and coopers. I sit in view of the community of workers.

"Must get out. Please, I take you," a foreign servant says.

He has slanted eyes, yellow skin, and straight black hair, braided behind him.

The carriage stops while the driver walks the horse out to brush him down.

We follow the foreign man to a canoe where he paddles us toward an island.

Across the water is Wildebrand's thatch-roofed house.

He has lit the fire and comes bearing a lantern to greet us.

"I hope you've had a peaceful journey friend," he says, with a quick grin, "I'm the lawman. If ye had any trouble, it would be my responsibility."

Evert smiles but does not reply, tiptoeing over the bank.

I fetch his duffle watching the canoe glide away.

We sit at a table drinking rum while Wildebrand talks of Galileo and his inventions. *I want to hear him,* but soon my eyes cannot stay awake. I fall asleep, head on my arms.

Evert wakes me and I hear hounds baying. The moon is bright and golden. The fire has burned low.

"Climb to the hay loft, Gerrit. I'm saying goodbye until spring," he says, "Should it be important, make your way to the house. I left you a horse in the stall."

At daylight, I lay still in this strange place *thinking of Mum because the thatch reminds me of our house.*

I sit up.

"There's never enough money for the company back home is there, Dutch?" Wildebrand teases.

I eye him for calling me "Dutch" and climb down.

"Nothing wrong with being called Dutch," he says, "Don't ye like it? I like it."

"I guess so," I say.

He pokes me.

"Today you must learn to ride a horse," he says, and his eyes are wide, "First we eat. Wash up."

We walk across the drive and up to the owner's house.

I'm introduced to the Patroon's nephew, and we sit at a cloth covered table with china plates and mutton brains. There are pumpkin muffins and coffee with cream and sugar. I reach over for a slice of ham. Wildebrand slaps my wrist and looking away, he holds the plate close to me while conversing with the nephew.

I realize it must be unmannerly to reach. Thereafter, I move more thoughtfully at the table.

Wildebrand excuses us and assures the host we enjoyed the meal. I bow.

Outside, he details our plans to embark into the backwoods scouting our territory advantages and keeping peace with our neighbors, the Indians.

Then he helps me mount while a servant holds the horse. *I'm shocked how tall being in the saddle is.*

The horse snorts uneasily and steps backward.

Chickens squawk to get out of the way.

"He knows you are not accustomed to riding. The way you sit hurts his back. Lean into him. Wrap your legs loosely about the stirrups, Dutch."

I try. The horse steps about.

I make him nervous I can tell.

With leather pouches filled and rolled blankets, we head off. Wildebrand leads with me bumping along.

I soon feel blistered in the thighs and my rear is sore.
We stop to rest. Wildebrand helps me down. I groan.

He smiles, careful not to laugh.

I let him talk the most, so he doesn't know all about me.

He bubbles with the science and philosophy knowledge he's gained at the University in Leiden. He wants to tell me about how the rainbow is formed and the swirling planets around the sun. He talks about natural laws. He is awed by the mathematical genius of Galileo, the ideas of Descartes.

"Without these theories Dutch, we would not have attempted to sail around the world. Why, we would still be in our superstition, thinking it was flat and we'd fall off the edge," he laughs, "Men like these were persecuted for their lofty ideas and intellectual ability. Don't you know that using the windmill created our land from the sea?"[41]

"Yes, my father told me that. I've been to Amsterdam and gone down the canals," I reply.

"When?" he asks, drawing back.

I shrug and say, "When I was ten, after we went to Leiden."

"Now I remember. You have ship experience. Did you know that our craftsmen created the fastest sailing vessel to bolster our shipping economy? The fluyt is a Dutch idea."

"I know," I grin behind his back.

"Hmm. Well, as we go, I'll teach you Indian languages. We have a long ride ahead," he says, "Mostly uphill."

After a while I say, "The vast forest astounds me."

Wildebrand says. "We are in the Catskill Mountains. April and May are the finest months to explore. The trees are in bloom, full of sweet smells. Following next are the strawberries, whole fields covered naturally. And you will probably see a pitch black bear. I've seen a herd of deer with a buck out front. He must have had fourteen points. And I've seen a strong eagle swoop down like a flash and scoop up a living fish from the waters. There are mulberries, raspberries, watermelons, artichokes, and leeks growing wild.[42] I fell in love with the land the first time I explored it and decided I would be an American."

I've not heard such a term before. Hmm, American.

Chapter 13

"HE THAT IS GREEDY OF GAIN TROUBLETH HIS OWN
HOUSE, BUT HE THAT HATETH GIFTS SHALL LIVE."
PROVERBS 15:27

"The sheriff's job requires I collect late payments from the tenants, bring back runaways, things like that," Wildebrand divulges, "Some are so poor, they can't pay. What good is it that I harass them? If they work steady, I leave them alone, and keep things running smoothly. I decided we needed a brickyard and made improvements to the sawmill and the gristmill. I didn't consult the Patroon. His nephew is the commercial officer. He complains about me. I see what's needed to make our business thrive and ignore his petty complaints."

I venture to ask, "Sir, have you had occasion to use your sword or is it merely a show of force that you wear it?"

He brags, "This is a raw continent. Naturally, it glistens before the Indians and vagrants as a reminder. I don't flaunt it. Nor will I use it to urge men to take an oath of allegiance to the Patroon, although he presses me for that. I have opposing views about a man's freedom, understand?"

"Yes sir," I nod.

"You may call me Lodewyck. Only in attitude will you remember I'm over you," he says.

We have to pay attention to handling the horses on the rough trail. We stop at a waterfall for a drink.

I pick some berries and offer him half.

"You'll find Indian culture is interesting. They don't want to fight with us. For our part, keeping peace is an important business asset. You'll agree when you watch how I do it. I'm truthful. I respect their way of life. Mohawks live by their agriculture, while the Mohicans mostly rove to hunt. I like to learn their techniques in fishing and planting. I watch their rituals and customs. I'm welcome on their territory and in their shelters. You'll see," he says.

When we get there, *the Indian boy's eyes are on me, deciding if they like me or not.*

Wildebrand greets a few women and asks about what they're cooking. They smile and show him the roots and meat they prepare together. The medicine man walks by us.

"This is the medicine man, Gerrit," Wildebrand says, "A man of high standing in this community. I've seen wounds he tended that healed rather quickly. He teaches me cures."

I nod and bow my head.

The medicine man looks curiously to Wildebrand.

"Don't do that," Wildebrand warns, "He thinks you don't wish to face him. Look him in the eye."

Immediately I look solemnly in his face. *That works.*

We walk our horses into the grass and tie them to a tree, unloading the saddles and our bedrolls. The smell of fresh cooked food lingers in the camp, while the men begin coming in from hunting. They pass us silently until one of the chief men comes over to talk.

Wildebrand is articulate with the language.

I admire that.

Soon we sit on the ground eating from pottery bowls.

To celebrate, they do ritual dances for us after the meal. One of the dancers bows with open hands to show I am welcome as their guest. I nod smiling.

They show no emotion.

We are on their territory for now.

As the winds blow the rest of autumn's color to the ground

we continue to visit Indian villages to learn their ways and Wildebrand teaches me their language.

In the winter, *I don't bob my hair, knowing it is cover for me that God Almighty provides for all creatures.* Tobacco fields rest as the snow flurries blow, but I don't.

I learn to trap in the backwoods, and the more we hunt the interior, the more I see Indians behind rocky places. The trapper, Auguste, scouts ahead of us early each day, marking the streams, pointing where we should set traps.

We have a wagon and a wide hauling sleigh with horses harnessed to both. Eight of us set fifteen hundred traps on the banks near fallen trees. My muscles ache from sheer exhaustion in the cold clear air.

Mondays and Tuesdays, we set traps, working in a circuit. The animals have had two days to die. Then it's time to spring the traps, skin the animals, and rinse the blood off, in the streams the beaver live by. That is what we do Wednesday, Thursday, Friday, and Saturdays.

The days are grey. We rest and eat leftovers from breakfast we carry in our knapsacks. We drink water from the cold streams. No one talks. We are too weary. The trapper scout mounts the wagon seat signaling it's time to go back to work. We ride in the back, jostling over the hill to an area where we left traps earlier. When we get there, he hands us all a butcher knife. Time to harvest the pelts.

"Soft gold" they call it at the fort. We take the dead animals from the traps and cut the fur, stacking it in piles.

"How many?" I ask the scout, in frosty breaths as the sun breaks through a little in the distance.

"Around a thousand, two hundred, this time," he says.

We quickly get our loads turned around and all of us jump on where we can, on top of the furs. The wolves roam near, drawn by the scent of blood. Two guards stand with muskets on each side of us. As our sleigh hauls away, they gobble what's left in the piles of snow. They rip and tear, growling at each other, fighting viciously over it.

It's bloody work. All of us have it on ourselves. Our leather fur-lined coats and hats are serviceable, not for style. We smell of sweat and *could care less if anyone notices.*

Come spring, we tow the furs down the Hudson to the big ships at New Amsterdam. Evert has spurred us to be there as soon as the ice melts. We crunch through slivers on the water surface.

A young African sees us passing by and runs toward the Huybrecht house.

As we tie up in town, Evert's carriage drives in, sloshing through the brown patches of snow.

From his carriage window he motions for me.

"Where's the account? Bring it to me," he demands.

Wildebrand doesn't like it. He keeps the lading.

Walking across the road, Wildebrand enters the door of The Wooden Horse without so much as a word.

Evert darts a look at me. I'm speechless, still as a mouse.

Evert is a proud man. In a huff, he gets out of the carriage and follows Wildebrand.

The carriage driver searches my face. I roll my eyes.

Alone I must stand in the cold to oversee the transition from rafts to boats, until it is all done.

Later, Wildebrand and Evert reappear, jolly and apparently resolved in difference.

It's not that Wildebrand did anything wrong. It's his way to enforce the understanding that Evert cannot lord it over him. Wildebrand resents feeling owned and I'm the same.

I stay in town at a boarding house, warm and friendly.

Wildebrand insists on it. Evert compromised.

Wildebrand himself pays for my bath and change of clothes.

We have sliced pork, eggs with cheese, and fresh oats before church. Wildebrand and I sit with the men of the shopping district, all of them I recognize from my duty as delivery boy in the care of the Huybrechts.

In church, my mind is not on spiritual matters. I'm embroiled in the gravity of my position and its mission. I deliberate on how I will hold my head while fine tuning my ears to listen and it occurs to me that my father may have had at one time, similar circumstances of conflict.

That stays in my thoughts while the sermon commences.

The minister beckons us to partake of communion at the altar. Wildebrand and the district friends rise. I remain seated. They pass to my right, single file.

The room is hushed. An ivory cross hangs high below the loft, sunlight flickering on it.

I remember looking down from the loft, watching my mother pray by her bed.

I close my eyes.

"Lord," I pray in my heart, "I haven't been your servant like I told my father I would. I belong to others. I don't know if they're good or not. Please, guide me to do what's right in Your sight and not bring a curse on myself."

When we go out the church door, I notice the men separate, giving each other knowing looks.

I look away.

Wildebrand walks over to the fort, and I tag along.

Quickly catching up to Boydin he says, "Director, might I have a word with you? Have you eaten? We could go to Sailing Days tavern. It's off the busy road, quieter."

Director Boydin agrees. I tag along behind as they expect.

With steaming chicken and seasoned rice before us, the conversation turns to currency.

"The standard of good polished seawan we are using now is a sign of the progress that has been made since you issued the directive," Wildebrand says, "And it was good that you presented the warning you gave in the letter to New Sweden. Congratulations on a job well done."

"Thank you," Boydin says, "My next order of business is to tackle the Indian question."

Wildebrand acts surprised and wrinkles his forehead.

I pretend to be occupied cutting my meat carefully.

Boydin leans toward him and says, "How to apply justice

to that matter of Swits getting killed.[43] The Indians will learn their place. We'll have us an understanding, we will. I'll anger them to create an incident and show them our military power. Secretly, of course."

"Of course," Wildebrand says, "Then you've already considered the balance of power that could develop in distancing us from the furs they bring in? And then, there's the safety of the folk around us, their families, the sailors."

Boydin crosses his arms.

"With the authority and men to back you up, you can do anything," Boydin says with relish.

"I suppose," Wildebrand reasons.

Boydin eyes him. He looks about the room.

"Sir, do you think to mock me?" Boydin questions.

"Never Director," Wildebrand says, "It makes us nervous, that's all. We don't live inside a barricade."

"You've been talking behind my back. Is this treason?" Boydin growls lowly and pushes back his chair.

He stands, looks about and dons his coat to leave.

I dare not look up. A serious disagreement has taken place, and I'm in the middle.

Wildebrand rubs the rim of his glass with his finger, head bowed.

I pull off pieces of the roll and stuff it slowly in my mouth, looking at nothing particular.

Boydin goes out.

Shortly, a few men crowd the tables around us and wait for Wildebrand. He tightens his lips and shakes his head, *a sign they understand.*

We leave for the livery stable. No smithing is allowed on Lord's Day, still the livery is full of wagons and behind them a crowd of men meet.

I climb on the stable post to watch.

"He's determined to pick a fight with the Indians. I told him to remember your safety. I tried to reason how that would hurt our business," Wildebrand laments.

"What can we do? When will he start it?" one asks.

Wildebrand shakes his head.

"If we could get word to the company, I feel sure they will take measures to put a halt to it," Wildebrand says.

Now I see Evert's carriage by the church.

"I left my sketchbook in the Huybrechts's carriage. I need it to draw maps of our circuit. May I get it?" I pretend.

"Hurry then. Catch up with me. You don't need to be riding in the dark," Wildebrand answers.

Evert walks from the minister's house as I ride up. They discuss the different faiths moving into our village. He closes his talk and hurries my way.

I dismount and tie the mare quickly.

Evert slaps my shoulder, acting glad to see me.

"What is it?" he asks.

I open the carriage door, aware the driver is close by.

"Get in," Evert says.

"Boydin plans to punish the Indians. We don't know when. The men in town listen to Wildebrand," I whisper.

The driver climbs on the seat.

"I need to take my sketchbook back with me. It's my excuse to speak with you," I say.

He pulls it from the rack, and I race to catch Wildebrand.

Back at Berkenkotter, the trappers bring news every week. They say the chiefs laugh at the Director's demand for taxes. Meanwhile anxiety is growing. Wildebrand comes to church every Lord's day and meets with the town people after service. Everyone feels the Director has plans.

There's a rumor that Indians stole pigs from a Dutch farm. Everyone is talking about it.

On the way home, Wildebrand talks to me in confidence, "My friends tell me it wasn't Indians. It was a set up. Then Boydin sent a posse to the nearby village and killed several

Indians. The town people have a council of twelve[44] hopefully to prevent further bloodshed and impeding war."

All spring the Berkenkotter plantation thrives. More workers move in, bringing abundant prosperity, while I scout the woods on Mondays and spend the rest of the summer learning trades from the craftsmen.

Monthly, Wildebrand goes to Sail Away tavern and sends me off to run errands. I take sealed messages where he specifies. Then I eat alone at The Wooden Horse.

Now I'm part of the undertow of political unrest. A spy.

One Sunday in October, the ground outside the fort is covered with tents and Indians living there.

The tavern keeper tells us they came under our protection while the Mohawks are on the warpath.

I eat flapjacks with molasses *and pretend I don't care.*

Then Evert comes through the door. He walks right over to us and Wildebrand stands to shake his hand.

"We need to talk," Evert blurts.

I hurry to finish off my buttermilk.

Wildebrand pays, following Evert out. Evert motions for me to come with them and we get in his carriage.

"Drive toward the shore," Evert says to the driver.

"Why the urgency?" Wildebrand asks.

"I've obtained information that Boydin plans to raid the Indians late tonight," Evert says.

"We can't be sure," Wildebrand says, "I'll try to talk with him again. Who told you this?"

Evert is terse, "I have a soldier informant."

Wildebrand's jaw drops. He covers his mouth.

"I don't know if any of us will be safe," Evert says.

Chapter 14

"Bread of deceit is sweet to a man; but afterwards his mouth shall be filled with gravel."

PROVERBS 20:17

IN THE YEAR OF OUR LORD 1643

On Monday before we get back, a rider overtakes us and breathlessly says, "He killed all the Indians in the square!"

Dismounting, he describes it, "They were hollering about midnight. I got up and saw fire and the soldiers attacking them. I helped some squaws escape to the woods."

He's winded. The three of us stare in silence.

"Water your horse. We'll go back with you," Wildebrand orders and we make haste.

In the men's meeting, Wildebrand presents the dangers.

"The gravest possible threat we have, is if they unite and this could force them to it. I urge you to be ready to get into the fort at the slightest hint of attack. I must go back as sheriff and protect my Patroon's interest. Meanwhile we'll send our joint complaint to the Dutch West India Company," Wildebrand says, shaking his head.

We ride home looking over our shoulders, *me wishing the way was not so long.*

No sleep, no food.

Into the fall, arrows fly, and muskets kill the white faces that live on plantations and farms in the area. Attacks come without warning in the dead of night. Years of hard labor building houses, barns and planting crops are reduced to ashes. The cattle are hacked.[45]

One night loud noises come from the pork barn, and we hear shots being fired. I hurry downstairs and meet Wildebrand by the door, shuddering in the wind. He lights a lantern and in our night shirts and boots we step out to see what's wrong. He has the sword in his hand. Lanterns glow from across the water. A woman screams. Another shot, then another. Boom! Men are talking gruffly. What is it?

Wildebrand shouts, "What's the matter?"

"Bear, sir, trying to get the cured ham. We kilt him. He's down. Ripped the door off. I'll fix it now," one says.

As snow flurries fly, we hear the news that New Amsterdam's people huddle inside the fort walls, during freezing temperatures. The situation is desperate.

Below the Catskills we are packed in ice, the river currents frozen solid. The trappers continue working dangerously close to the Indians, hoping the Indians sleep days because they raid after dark. Regularly the scouts bring us news in exchange for a meal. We stay close to the farm, busying ourselves with community needs.

I help the wheelwright and the cooper.

And all this time I watch Wildebrand studying at night, preparing documents, and reaching for his law books.

When he talks, he refers to our colony as the New American World.

I wonder if he wants to be the director, having favor with all the people and a love for the land. I admire his education and viewpoint.

The months pass by slowly while I grow tall and New Amsterdam grows with families, if not profits.

Evert sends us a letter and Wildebrand tells me why.

"News of the torture of Isaac Jogues by the Iroquois, after he escaped to Ft. Orange enforces my decision to send you back to Evert," Wildebrand says, "Let me teach you to fire the hand cannons. I have a set of two I will give you, for your faithful service at my side."

"I don't expect so generous a gift," I say and step back.

"How long will you call me sir? We're business associates. You're almost grown and trained. It's a loss to me that you go. Never let it be said I didn't appreciate you," he states.

"And I, you," I reply.

He brings out a wooden case, velvet lined wherein lay two polished wood pistols, finely etched, and the cleaning tools.

In my memory I can hear the cannon exploding from the gunpowder.

He lifts one and puts it in my hand.

I blink at him, grateful.

We spend the afternoon practice shooting, laughing about nothing, enjoying being men in a world that challenges us.

For supper he brings out wine and roasts a hog on the spit, rolling it over while we listen to the whippoorwills.

When the yellow eyes of some varmints come close, we scurry inside with our meat and eat all we can hold.

He falls asleep at the table, and I climb to the loft as usual, *thinking how this will be my last night here.*

Next dawn, two French trappers accompany me to the Huybrecht land. By the fence I salute them and saunter in to meet Evert, who is waiting to see me safe. I pass smiling, leaving the reins with a field hand by the barn. Evert hands me a cup of water.

"Well, assuming my valuable asset has improved himself, I will be happy to ask many questions long overdue," he queries, "Significant I suspect."

"Do sit on the ottoman and not dirty our divan," he says.

I enter the library and put my backside to the fire for a moment, rubbing my hands and adjusting my eyes.

He is anxious and talks first.

"Because of the Indian massacre at Ft. Orange, I had to bring you out. My investment you know," he says.

I wince at his cutting sarcasm of me as his property.

This time he notices and shakes his head.

"Ah Gerrit, ever the sensitive one. I thought you would have hardened some being in the backwoods," he remarks.

To this I'm ready to comment.

"I'm stronger. I mastered several trade skills, and I can speak four Indian languages. Besides, I know now what makes Berkenkotter successful, whereas New Amsterdam is failing," I say confidently.

He balks.

"Sounds to me like you have changed who you're party to. Do you think you'll be his right hand, when Wildebrand tries to stage a takeover?" he accuses.

This change of respect brings me to a frown as I speak.

"He may convince the company that he can manage it better than Boydin. He probably can. I won't be in on it. There are grown men that want to do that," I recoil.

Evert says, "Well, good. Managing ships and crews need a focused man with courage. Certainly, you've excelled in developing that characteristic living among the fur trappers and going in and out of Indian territory."

He crosses the room and turns his nose up.

"Oh my, you do smell like a horse," he says, "Go wash and have your dinner. I can't abide that horrid stench. Come early in the morning. My father will arrive this month. I need everything loaded and shipped out before he comes."

I eat my cold corn pudding and bacon with a mug of warm beer, I find in the kitchen.

The fireflies flit about above the garden I once tended.

My bunk is taken. I move my blanket and duffel to the ground by the barn door and leave it cracked, gazing up at the stars.

Within my heart, I wish I had a home and a family.

I haven't prayed in a long time, and I miss feeling loved.

Chapter 15

"...AND SOLOMON, SEEING THE YOUNG MAN THAT HE
WAS INDUSTRIOUS, HE MADE HIM RULER OVER ALL
THE CHARGE OF THE HOUSE..."

1 KINGS 11:28

Still weary from the long ride, I toss and turn all night. I roll over and groan, uneasy on the ground.

I had a goose feather mattress in the loft and a quilt. My blanket is not long enough.

By daybreak, I rise and wash my upper body and hair, though it chills me. The others wake and soon the barn bustles with activity.

I'm confused why I can't calm down, asking within myself, "Why?"

The carriage driver eyes me curiously.

"Sick?" he asks.

"No," I say, stuffing the pistols in my belt.

I wear the leather hat with its raccoon tail and my red sash.

Evert chatters all the way to town, *as I remember my manners and wish I had more coffee.*

He tells me the skinners are afraid to go back into the woods and he has only a small number of pelts.

"Keep your eyes open this time," Evert says, "Look the part of a brawny opponent. I want them to fear you. If needs be, draw a line they don't dare cross over. See?"

He lets me out at the beach with the tally board.

"They know you're in charge. You don't need me. I'm going to the counting house. I'll be back before noon to check things over, Gerrit," he says.

It has been a long time since anyone called me that. I almost forgot it was my name.

The tobacco is arranged so that I can ship it first. Three rafts pull away the first hour.

The farmers wait with their wagons. They have pulled up in front of the loggers. I step across the seaweed and tell them to turn around. Loggers first. They will have to wait.

We unload the timber on the raft, and I oversee it to the hull, while I check the grain and molasses barrels.

I need to load the pelts and put them far from the rations.

The raft moves slowly out to sea. As I approve the beaver count and get it situated, we hear a commotion on shore.

I hurry to board the ship and climb to get a better view.

The first thing I see amiss is the farm wagons are gone.

Alone on the beach sit the grain barrels. I send the raft to get them.

I hear shouting from the woods and see smoke rising, a lot of black smoke. Soldiers shoot muskets.

"Indians!" a woman screams.

The sailors look at each other. We are nearly finished putting the load in place.

I call for the dingy to be lowered and two men go with me.

People run away from the cottages, some into the fort, some toward us on the seashore.

The Huybrecht carriage comes rattling over the ridge with the horses lathered.

"Take us out! Immediately!" Evert shouts.

We row in haste. As I reach the shore, he sees me brandishing a pistol. His carriage driver urges him to step in the water, climb in the boat. I stand guard as they clumsily board, bringing a small trunk. The carriage is left unattended on the sand.

Downwind, the raft poles awkwardly jerking the float while

they lose two barrels and fearfully watch Evert's reaction. But he pays no mind.

Oh, the scene that lies before us!

Indians and our countrymen fighting in the street, and few Dutch can hold their own. Screams fill the air. People are being chased with hatchets. Soldiers fire in volleys.[46]

Before they can reload any guns, the soldiers are scalped.

Small boats come toward me loaded with families, shop-keepers and merchants, the smith, and the minister.

I get Evert on the ship, and he orders the Commander to launch. Leaning over the side, Evert motions for everyone to get onboard with us as we hoist sails and pull anchor.

"Don't fire the cannon! Watch our neighbors," he shouts.

The towering vessel sways slowly adrift, as we see the soldiers overwhelmed by the number of attackers and wrestling around the fallen, far outside the walls of safety.

The boat clears a safe distance before attackers reach the water's edge.

The people crowd among us, in their work clothes, in their fear, united as a group.

I take a deep breath, and Evert turns to me.

"Prepare the inventory of food supplies and number of persons on board," he quietly says.

The crew are busy removing the ship to sea, while the question lingers. *Where will we go?*

Shortly, I go to the Commander's quarters to report.

"Do we have wounded passengers? Did they finish securing the beaver pelts?" Evert asks, his mind on the expensive cargo.

"No serious wounds. We loaded the beaver," I say, "And the tobacco, but not the indigo. We have food enough."

I lay the count before him.

He sighs and turns away, tapping a graphite on the desk.

"Gerrit, I remember when I first signed you on, there were rumors that your father had a holy gift of foreknowledge about danger. Is that true?" he asks.

He searches my face. I look down, uneasy.

"Do you have it?" he asks in a demand.

I take a deep breath, thinking again how I couldn't sleep last night. Was it being on the ground that kept me tossing and turning? Or something else?

I say, "I believe it's possible to have God's guidance. I haven't pursued it because when my father knew of danger he had no authority to act on it."

I wear a stubborn frown.

"But you believe that's how Piet Hyen took the treasure ships, don't you?" he asks, staring long at me.

It is a question echoing deep in my soul.

Since I have been treated as an equal with Wildebrand, I've grown more independent.

I ask him outright, "You are the one in charge. It's your business. Did God show you danger was near?"

That makes him look away. *He knows he hasn't given God reverence. He is shocked by my boldness.*

I stand as tall as he is now, no longer the boy, no longer afraid.

All the same, we both desire something to hold onto in this crisis.

Who can reach out and touch the hand of God?

Maybe my soul was troubled last night. But I don't tell him and walk away.

I think I've said enough and if God wants me to have that gift, I want the authority to use it.

Having been forced to flee their homes, the people need some hope.

I remember how I felt when our village was attacked, and people lay in the street.

I tell the cook to bake a double round of biscuits and I walk on deck with a basket, keeping them warm in muslin. We offer them to the children.

I'm doing my best.

By sunset the ship arrives at Mayhew Plantation on Martha's Vineyard Island. They're English.[47]

Will they help us?

We draw up to the landing. Evert orders men to row the dinghy to the shore taking me along.

He says, "A business associate of ours. Pay attention."

The landowner, Thomas Mayhew the Younger, listens while Evert explains our plight.

I stand aside.

Thomas opens his arms wide, "We offer all we have."

I watch his servants find a place to rest for every passenger and help prepare the food available. His old father smiles watching the order taking place. None of us knows how long we might be their unannounced guests.

In the backroom, Evert offers payment. I sit unnoticed as they go over accounts and point to the fields outside.

Then the two of them go to a harnessed wagon and Thomas drives them away.

I fall asleep on the floor of the library, without disturbance, *enjoying the cool it offers.*

When I awake, the tide has come in and the moon rising.

"Gerrit," Evert says, shaking me, "Meet my friend, Thomas Mayhew, the Younger."

Thomas offers his hand politely.

I wipe my sweaty palm on the seat of my britches, stand and shake his hand stoutly.

He is directly open-faced.

"Thomas has been showing me his crops and telling me of the Aborigines, uh the Indians, he pastors," Evert catches my eye just in time to keep me silent.

"Extraordinary Sir," I say.

"Would you like to go and help me?" Thomas asks.

I look to Evert, who nods with closed eyes.

"It would be my pleasure Sir," I say, *pretending it doesn't scare me,* glancing out at the twilight.

94

At dawn, Thomas stands over me, giving me a little nudge. I rise quietly, not to bother the others who are bedded down on all the floors of the house. We silently creep out in our stockings, carrying our boots and put them on, sitting on the steps of the wide veranda, while the sea dashes heartily against the *Morgenster*.

A rooster crows from behind the barn and Thomas and I walk up the sand dunes, into the sea brush.

I put my hand on the silver dagger beneath my belt, prepared as I can be, to meet my death by wild Indians.

It's not quite morning. A few stars are fading as we trudge west, silently. Only our breathing and the early call of birds is heard in the salty breezes that whip at us.

My keen eyes scan the woods in apprehension.

Then Thomas stops and looks intently at me.

"Are you afraid, Gerrit?" he asks.

"Indians will torture even a good missionary," I reply.

It embarrasses him as though he has been unkind.

"My Indians are peaceful," he says, "Believe me."

From that point on, as we hike the trail, he opens his heart and shares how he became their pastor and how he loves them. He quotes the Bible, of which I am all too familiar.

I'm eager to know what he's discovered in the good book.

He has a pleasant personality, daring and yet meek.

My idea of a "gentleman" means keeping a set of etiquette rules. He projects a code of honor above that.

As he shares about his life, a humbleness is revealed that he cares genuinely for others, never considering himself and makes me think of Jesus.

We reach the Aborigines by hot midday where he introduces me as his friend.

That means a lot to me.

They greet him warmly as a family might do, entirely at ease and he converses with them in their tongue.

Thomas teaches them a hymn and they sing as I look curiously about how they live and try to eat the eel.

They bow their heads for prayer. Then opening the Bible, Thomas teaches them the holy principles of Christianity. He's patient and answers their questions, stopping to retell it in Dutch, for my benefit.

As the afternoon wears on, he explains what Jesus means by His parables and why He died.

"Your sins separate you from the one true God that made the heavens and the earth. He is the God that created you and me. He made animals, trees and seas and fish in the water. Some sins are noticeably mean, like stealing from your neighbor and striking your wife," he preaches.

An old squaw covers her eyes in shame as Thomas paces around the circle of us.

"There's sin in your thoughts when you're proud of yourself and can't speak nice to your own family. Heaven won't be a place of hurting others," he says peering at the woman's husband. "When God measures a man or a woman, He counts the words and the actions."

Now he sits on a rock.

"What do you plan to accomplish with your life? Jesus taught there are more important things than mere survival. What if God has a plan for your life, Gerrit, and you never found it?" he says, centering in on my face and smiling with compassion.

I hang my head feeling the need for personal religion.

He continues along happily, making certain I fit in, and I smile sincerely at all of them.

"I ask you all to let Jesus come into your heart and be the master of your life. He will forgive your sins if you abandon them. He will cleanse your dirty heart with His own blood," he says softly.

Finally, with the most earnest look at us, Thomas says, "How could anyone walk away from the heavenly invitation of God? In truth, I extend on His behalf, the opportunity of a lifetime. The question is, Will you be one of Jesus' disciples? Will you love Him for richer or poorer, in sickness and in health, with all your heart, all your mind and all your soul? He sent me to ask you personally if you will give your life to Him?"

I look away, lost deep in thought. Give your life to Jesus?

The old Indian, whose wife had covered her eyes, puts his arm around her and both of them have tears.

Thomas likes that and he turns his attention to me.

"Gerrit, might it be God's providence that you're here to make a life commitment today?" he asks me.

I cannot answer. No one has ever inquired about me like this. It is the most personal thing to talk about. I have not been aware of my soul, or my heart.

I loved my mother and my father from my heart.

Only, my life has been absorbed in learning and working for the past six years.

At once, my conscience pains me.

He realizes he has caught me unprepared and smiles at the others, leaving me to think.

How could I have been a member of the Dutch Reformed Church and not realize my need to ask forgiveness of the Savior and commit my life to Him to be my Master?

I feel ashamed I've not even thought to give Christ my heart, much less my life, my future. This is all I have.

But what if I don't accept a holy invitation? How dare I risk offending the Lord of all Creation? Does anyone easily tell God "no"?

Suddenly, I understand those historic wars of my country.

It matters little to kings if men have religion if it doesn't reach their hearts. Selfish men rule the masses as long as they can be controlled by fear and persecution. It is the courage of "being right with God" that wicked men hate about true disciples, the age-old battle of darkness and light, satan plotting against God. That's what it really is. How plain is that?

Now, God is calling me into the light. What should I do?

Will I give God my future, all my choices?

I know I don't want to be part of the dark side.

I am at a crossroads. Jesus is waiting. According to the Bible, there are only two choices. Heaven or Hell?

Only a fool would choose hell.

Whatever it costs me, I want to go with God.

Silently, with my eyes open, I pray with all my heart and ask Jesus to forgive my sins of pride and thinking only of taking care of me. I tell Him I want to live the life He has planned for me, and I will try to please Him in everything, even if it means dying for the gospel.

It doesn't take long, a prayer of two minutes – opening the doors of heaven for me and closing out the despair and loneliness I've learned to live with.

I know at this moment, because I have given my whole heart to Jesus, He is giving everything in the Bible to me.

I have an immediate faith in the love and power of God.

Amazing.

I watch Thomas lead six converts in prayer and afterwards, he says something precious, "When you want to stop sinning and completely give your heart to the Lord, a miracle happens. His Holy Spirit comes to live in you, and you become like a new baby, fresh and clean inside."

I nod. *Yes, I understand.*

All these years I thought the Holy Spirit coming on a man was the greatest thing anyone could have.

Do I have it now? I wonder.

Is this what my mother and father found?

I do feel tender, yet strong. It seems I've become mature all at once. I'm aware God is with me. I'm excited to find out what is His plan for me.

All this I hold back in my quietness and wait while Thomas is finished making his kind farewell.

We leave both of us with much on our mind.

Then after we have walked through the woods and are back to the sandy shore, I tell him of my prayer.

"I surrendered my heart and future to Jesus Christ today," I confess, "I made Him my Master."

He simply grins and blinks.

He says, "I know."

Chapter 16

Walking in the afternoon breeze, Thomas urges me to read the Bible morning and night, with my heart open for counsel from the Lord.

He says, "Reading the Bible changed us all."

I'm intrigued, "How?"

He says, "Back in England my grandfather was a yeoman, farming the manor of a lord, always poor. My Papa got apprenticed to a shopkeeper in London. That made the family proud. There was trouble if a man didn't keep quiet about what was wrong with the Church of England and King Charles I as God's chosen ruler. My father heard of arrests and cruel punishments to any objections. These measures affected everyone, even prominent citizens. What was in the Bible they didn't want us to know? Countries were at war because of it."

He stops in the shade and picks a few blackberries.

"Because I was the oldest, I lived with Papa at the shop. Mother and the children stayed on the farm. The day he bought a Bible, he latched the shop door and drew the curtain across the front displays before lighting the lamp and gingerly heaved the giant volume onto our table. I can hear him now: 'Dinner in a while eh, my son?' He had saved for years to buy it."

Thomas says, "We kneeled before it. Usually my father was vibrant in personality, self-assured in public. Now, loosening the buckles of the scriptures, he was so humble, the mood of whispers. That's how he showed me the manners required before Almighty God."

With a shrug of his shoulders Thomas says, "I could read for myself. Side-by-side, we read among the wares and staples of life. 'In the beginning God created the heaven and the earth; and the earth was without form and void, and darkness was upon the face of the deep and the Spirit of God moved upon the face of the waters. And God said, Let there be light: and there was light. And the light he called Day, and the darkness he called Night.' We read where each day God would speak and say, 'Let there be heavens and there was sun, moon, and stars. He spoke into existence land and seas and, plants and animals, fish and birds and seeds and weather and when the world was done, man was handmade, in the image of God. And Eve was made from Adam's rib, to be his appropriate help in life. Then God rested on the Sabbath."[48]

We climb a hill.

I'm thinking of how big the earth is and how many kinds of people and places there are.

"Papa put the Bible away on a crimson velvet cloth and lay his hand on its cover, as if it would impart to him a special grace, a power longed for. We ate and I went to bed with those thoughts in my head. I couldn't understand the vastness of it all. I questioned how could God make the earth in seven days?" he says, "Gerrit, The Bible said He spoke it into being! That was hard to believe."

He stops and rests at the top, and I see awe on his face.

"In the darkness of midnight, I was awakened by a bright light in my room, the wind swirling mightily."

"You had a window open?" I ask.

"No, the wind was in my room. The very Presence of God had come. I hit the floor on my face and dared not move," he says, "His presence was a revelation, stripping me of all argument. I was immediately aware of His power and the weight of His holiness. Never again have I doubted what He can do."

I see Thomas has the assurance with God, my mother had. My father too. The secret I long to know is the connection God's Spirit makes with someone personally. It's what Jesus died for. Because I dedicated my life to Him, I understand immediately. It's obvious in all the Bible heroes, in all the Dutch heroes. God Himself makes a man the best he can be. It's Christ living in me I've been searching for. Finally I have found the treasure.

Thomas talks on about troubles that try to hinder us, *but I think what an astonishing life God had for Thomas pastoring Indians in his area.*

It's humble, yes, but I see the power of God working on his behalf. I can't explain the impact he has on me, like the brother I never had.

It's dusk as we enter the yard, and he closes the gate.

"I'm to be married this week," he confesses, "My father arranged it, a Puritan girl from Plymouth. I'm not sure how to act. Am I ready for a wife?"

We both blush, bowing our heads.

His father, Thomas, the Elder, comes on the veranda, with Evert Huybrecht, each holding a glass of brandy and peering earnestly at us. Behind them are a well-dressed man and woman.

Thomas, the Elder introduces Nehemiah Lloyd and his sister, Fairchild and then says, "They only arrived an hour ago. We will allow them time to freshen up."

Fairchild curtsies and a servant shows them up the staircase while Thomas's father grasps his arm and takes him inside for private conversation.

I raise my eyes to Evert in anticipation.

"You clean up too. You're invited to dinner," he says and pushes me toward the *Morgenster.*

I hop on a rowboat and make my way out, planning to wear my best and glad to be included.

Over a dinner of clams, pork roast, yams, corn cakes, beets and field peas, the conversation centers on the recent turn of events with the Indian attacks.

Nehemiah tells us, "When I was a boy, we fought those miserable Indians in the Pequot War and did a thorough job of it.[49] God gave us this land and we have mastered it."

This does not set well with Thomas, and he looks at once at Fairchild who has lowered her eyes.

Our host, Thomas the Elder, attempts to make peace at the table, "I bought this island with every hope of living away from the casualties of religious war."

Nehemiah agrees and says, "Our Puritan fathers did too."

Thomas, the Elder continues, his hands folded, "I sent my son ahead with thirty families to start a community and develop the land to provide for us. He had always been an asset beside me in the shop, wonderful with my customers, untiring in labor."

Nehemiah and Fairchild beam at Thomas, the Younger.

Thomas the Elder hesitates, holding the attention of all.

"Five years went by before I could sell my business in London and join him. What I found when I landed, was a thriving Christian mission in the wilderness, my son the pastor of dozens of consecrated believers living in harmony," he says, leaning on his hand looking directly at Fairchild.

She gives him the sweetest smile and nods, eyes shining.

Nehemiah asks, "How did he find so many souls to come?"

"They were already here," Thomas, the Elder, replies.

Nehemiah is baffled, frowning.

He blinks, searching Evert's face and mine.

We know what he's talking about and smile.

"You mean Indians?" Nehemiah asks.

No one moves. Nehemiah covers his eyes.

102

"Forgive me. I have made a grave mistake. My sister and I will reconsider," he says, rising to leave the table.

Fairchild gently puts her hand on her brother's hand and interrupts him, "I consider this marriage has been a holy arrangement. My heart is with Thomas, the Younger and his calling to the Indians."

Thomas, the Younger, speaks up, "There is no danger with our Indians. We have a sweet communion, and they respect us. They have accepted Christ."

We can see Nehemiah no doubt trusts her judgment.

He sits humbly back in the seat, the image of repentance.

Thomas, the Elder, orders more tea to be served.

Evert uses the opening to bring up a pressing problem.

"Back to the shipping. I've been forced to bring my goods without a Dutch guard to get my boat across the Atlantic past Spanish and Portuguese pirates. Do any of you have any suggestions? I can't think of an off route that hasn't been touched. There's only a small crew, and the cargo is valuable," he confides.

"We have sixty muskets and four cannon," I interject, "Five barrels of gunpowder, less a farthing and plenty of musket balls and nails."

"What good will nails do?" Evert asks.

"When you load the cannonball, you add nails to scatter over enemy heads and rip sails on the deck," I say.

He sits back astonished.

"When did you learn about firing a cannon?" he asks.

I'm aware that now everyone at the table stares at me.

"Aboard *The Arms of Amsterdam*, before I was left on Manhattan Island, in 1641," I say, "I can show the men. I can teach them how to use the muskets too. Remember Wildebrand and I hunted deer?"

Thomas, the Elder, gives a promising look of approval to Evert, while Evert raises his brows.

The maid asks who will like plum pudding and takes plates

and glasses away. The small talk involves the wedding guests and minister coming in tomorrow.

Thomas, the Younger, is excited to have a moment in the parlor with Fairchild and asks if I will sit in view, because it's proper.

I oblige, watching Thomas the Elder take Evert alone into the library.

I assume they're settling accounts but, no. It's about me.

Within the hour, Fairchild is ready to retire and as her fiancé watches her climb the stairs, his father opens the pocket doors, and walks toward me.

Evert is smoking a pipe and the smoke wafts behind him.

Thomas, the Younger, turns to join us, waving the smoke out of his face.

"I've reconsidered your future, Gerrit," Evert says in a jolly mood, "At the recommendation of Thomas, the Elder. Step into the library. We've prepared a contract," he says.

Among shelves of books and by lantern light I learn the contents of their decision.

My master offers a stewardship binding me as property to the Huybrecht family for a term of seven years. In the first paragraph are notations and figures amounting to my debt to them for "my keep" the past six years. This is the basis for their claim to me as their property.

The rest of the document *describes further education and duties which include risk of war and obligations to all lengths of servitude, which my imagination reels in the reading of, yet it is not my choice to refuse, as I see it.* Therefore, I comply without so much as a word, lift the quill and tap the ink, to write in my best penmanship, "Gerrit Brinkendorf."

Inside my heart, I'm again "put in my place" because I have no choices, only obligations. Did Joseph feel this way when he stood before Pharoah? He was being promoted but maybe he wanted to go back to his father. He had no money. He had been cast away from the family. His father was alive and did not come to look for him. Questions I imagine he had that do not plague me.

As I lay on the floor, I can hear the sea pulling the sand in a hug and letting it go again. Letting it go again. And again.

Tonight I comfort myself that I have made peace with God, and I have a new friend. My own dreams are put off.

Next morning, Evert leads as we cross the seagrass to the beach. He motions to an older gentleman on the ship.

Promptly with a stern face, the old man rows toward us.

On the beach, Evert addresses him, "Commander Oloff, meet your protégé, Gerrit Brinkendorf of New Amsterdam, a steward of my employ for six years and duly appointed as Second Counter of the *Morgenster*, Quartermaster next."

Commander Oloff eyes me up and down.

"Aye get a grip boy. Ye shan't be a "watergeuzen" like the rest of the lads on board," Oloff says, "Ye take a man's wage, ye show a man's fortitude."

Evert says, "He's in your hands Oloff. Make him worldly-wise and add to my guilders, for he is the one to replace you, and upon his success will decide my generosity to your retirement in New Netherland, for Elsje and yourself, a few cattle, sheep, and a salaried position as overseer of the tithe barn."

Oloff bows saying, "Thank you, sire. My pleasure. Make us both proud. Keep him God-fearing, I will."

Oloff nods and nods.

"That will do," Evert says, dismissing the Commander.

Turning to me, Evert draws from his coat a fat letter, sealed with red wax and a black velvet pouch. *I manage to gather my wits to take it. I am quite taken in wonder.*

He says, "The pelts must be delivered before winter. The next ship to New Amsterdam will take these people back. A letter to the Dutch West India Company and guilders for your needs. See that you be fitted at the tailor, for a fine set of clothing to present yourself at the counting-house in Amsterdam, and most likely, The Dutch Republic. I expect correspondence from Amsterdam upon your departure back with a precise account of expenditure. Send it by another ship, should yours go down. If you take a prize vessel, (he raises his brows), careful there is no confusion about the inventory. I hire mercenaries for prosperity and safety of the cargo, of course. My eye is on you."

He concludes by slapping my shoulder.

I'm happy about this turn of events but hide it.

I say, "I promise having been given this opportunity, I will seek God's help with my whole heart."

I mean spiritual gifts, but he does not mention it.

He clears his throat and squints, then walks on. I follow.

He eyes the ship.

Evert says, "You're traveling without the customary military guard. I have to take the risk. It's a monetary decision, plain and simple. I hope it fares well with father."

With a swish of his coattails he hurries to stand beside Thomas, the Elder, while new food supplies are loaded.

I step out to climb the gangplank as we lift anchor and I walk the deck, hearing Evert give orders to the men on shore as we sail away.

I'm headed back to Holland!

Chapter 17

"For promotion cometh neither from the east,
nor from the west, nor from the south. But
God is the judge: He putteth down one and
setteth up another."

PSALM 75:6-7

Back on the *Morgenster*, I pass a lad of maybe twelve years, who salutes. He struggles hoisting the sail, his hands chapped, and shirt sleeves tattered.

"Good day," I say.

He trips and an old mate shouts at him. The sail flounders and the rugged seaman comes hurrying, clapping the boy on the head and grabs the rigging with a firm right hand.

I meant no harm, still I caused it, to my regret.

I look about. Not seeing Commander Oloff, I proceed below to find him and receive my orders.

The cook eyes me as he chops cabbages on a barrel top.

I squint back, *remembering Commander Oloff's words, "that I'm not like the rest of the lads. I must show fortitude." I am hired to show fortitude. Yes. My hand clasps the gold under the jacket, and I consider the man's wage. I'm a man now with some respect and it came so suddenly.*

The hull is musty and dark. A single lantern sways.

It's a long time since I've been at sea. Fond memories of my father trickle through my mind. I can almost see him, telling me to wash my hands. Ha! What would he think of me being quartermaster?

"Aye," the Swede would quip.

I grin to myself.

Now, to find the commander. Oloff, Captain Oloff.

I almost ask the cook, then think better of it, entering the blackness. My eyes adjust momentarily, to see the rows of hanging hammocks and crates of cannonballs among kegs of gunpowder. Behind them against the wall lean sixty muskets. A skull is carved on the stair with the words, "Keep It Dry."

It's "stuffed to the gills", Father would have said.

I organized it well, but it reeks with the smell of animal hide, mildew, and tar. I maneuver past the thousand-pound hogsheads tightly packed with tobacco and tall roped stacks of beaver pelts, to a door at the end, where I hear voices and knock.

"Open!" Commander Oloff bellows.

As Oloff sees me, he concludes his business.

"Gerrit, meet Jakob Damen. Jan Damen, his father, has the house on the South Side," Commander Oloff says.

It's the bully that picked a fight after school.

He won't look me in the face.

I extend my hand as expected. Our calloused hands clasp with *an immediate knowing both of us are hard workers.*

I say, "I know his father's house. I passed it many times on my way to school. Beautiful roses, tulips, violets, lilies, and marigolds. Your father must be proud."

"It's my father's practice," he says, "He plans to sell the bulbs, seed, and cuttings, so he painstakingly guards them to thrive. Were you there when Danel Zegerzoon was schoolmaster?"

He's pretending he doesn't remember me.

I go along with the charade and say, "I was."

The Commander stands, "Be on with you now, Jakob. Business comes first."

He lifts a box of tobacco powder to his nose and pinches a sniff, inhaling. Commander Oloff comes from behind the desk. His thick greying eyebrows lay low over his eyes and his raspy breathing prevails as he waits for my fullest attention, face to face.

He says, "We use maps, customs, and percentages, to trade with understanding of other cultures. And if an opportunity is inviting, or necessary, we make war."

He crosses the room to a map of Europe. *I remember we studied it in my school days.*

Oloff speaks deliberately slow, "There is a pressing situation in our time waging for the soul of all of us and, that is why, we Dutch are in a long war."

"On the one hand our landgraviate invests in shipping and trading, praying to God we succeed. On the other hand, he joins with members of the Dutch West India Company to protect the Dutch Republic and our good Dutch Reformed faith. To this end our people have paid with our lives and gold," he says, steadying himself as the ship tosses.[50]

"God Almighty has blessed us to become wealthy and united. Why do you think that is Gerrit?" he asks.

I draw in my chin, "For the sacrifices at Haarlem and Alkmaar, Leiden, and Antwerp. For the starvation, cruelties, and trickery of our enemies."

"Go on. You are correct," he whispers low.

"Death of thousands," I answer.

His brow furrows.

"I was born in Antwerp," he says, pinching another whiff of tobacco, back at his desk, beckoning for me to sit.

"My father and his father handed down the stories of our suffering to maintain the liberty of conscience, which is enviable to all true Christians. Wretched souls in many countries are yet to have such liberty. We turn down no one escaping the persecutions we have long endured. In Holland there will be Jews from Portugal and Huguenots from France, Mennonites, Anabaptists, and Separatists.[51] We don't follow their teaching, but we will not hinder their right to serve God as their conscience dictates," he says.

I am quiet, absorbing his words and studying him.

"This is why we are on this ship and what it means to our country," he says, "Greater still, what it means to our heavenly Father and His Son, Jesus Christ. To be the best Quartermaster, you will need the help of heaven and for that, heaven needs your heart and soul. Have you made a dedication of your life to Christ, to live for Him and to die for Him if necessary?" he asks me straight out.

I'm shy. He's patient.

We can hear the crew sighting dolphins.

"Sir, I am a member of the Dutch Reformed Church and by heart I know the Commandments and the Lord's Prayer, as well as many psalms and hymns. I never eat without offering a prayer of thanks. But only today have I made that commitment, when I heard the invitation made by the Rev. Mayhew to the Indians," I answer.

He scowls, weighing my response.

Maybe he doesn't believe me.

"All right then. Walk this ship. Learn its secrets and study its capacity. Watch the men and their ways. When you are satisfied with that, avail yourself of the wonders of the sea and the expanse of the skies, in all weather, night and day. And while you are learning from your observations, ask yourself one question, 'What is worth dying for?' When you can answer that, come back and I will teach you all I know," he says and rises for my dismissal.

"What are my work duties, sir?" I inquire.

"You've been promoted son. You are a leader now and no longer serve in common tasks, although you will find the work as Quartermaster more strenuous in ways you've not known," he says, "Evert trusts you."

He turns his back, looking at the horizon with his spyglass.

I spend the day observing and become familiar with the men before evening.

After supper I find my quarters and put things away. Then

I weigh the situation, get down on my knees, and have a silent prayer with Christ.

I ask God if Quartermaster is His will for me and how shall I be man enough?

I feel something right about it and sleep well that night, with a peace in my heart, knowing I want to please God.

Come morning I eagerly pull two men and a boy off the nets and take them below beside the cannons,

"We're going to shoot the cannon," I say.

"But I don't know how," the first one recoils.

"I do," I say confidently, "When I've shown you everything, you'll be proud of yourself and nothing about it is hard to learn. You'll be the one we all cheer for, when we take ships from Spanish pirates. You'll be a hero."

The two standing by are excited now and ask what to do.

I show them the steps I learned and send the boy up to announce we will practice firing the cannon.

A few curious men follow him back down to watch. The boy brings the bucket of water for the swab.

The gunpowder goes in, the string is lit.

I tell them, "Quickly! Help me heave it close to the wall! And it will be hot. Be ready to jump back!" I shout.

Boom! It explodes!

The heavy barrel lurches back as we jump clear.

Then we hear hoorahs and grin at each other.

Confidence is on their faces. Confidence in me and themselves that we can protect ourselves.

I swab the red-hot hole and show the others how we make the wads. Then I line the men up to take a turn in firing it.

"I'm only going to train the ones who came on their own accord," I announce, remembering Gideon sending back the fearful.[52]

I want a band of mighty warriors like those with David.[53] *He was young too. I can do this.*

We shoot all four, proving the gunners and the equipment. I explain what I learned about the range and the timing. By dinner I have trained twelve men to man our four cannon.

"After breakfast in the morning, I'll teach every man how to use a musket. We're the soldaats now, eh?" I say.

Every morning for a week, I make them load and learn to fire the muskets. They rotate duties, and we sail on.

The remainder of the month I inspect the workings of every aspect of the ship. I ask questions about the winds and the sails in the early part of the day, checking to see what they can do, how the rigging is arranged, how sound the rope is.

I find the crew curious about me. They speak nothing, only suspicious and wary looking. I visit with each man and memorize names and stations, leaving the cook and his helper last. I poke my nose into corners and cupboards and open barrels and look into crates and scan the inventory.

I educate myself on emergency procedures for capturing another ship or defending ours.

I ask questions about running out of food, water, or lemon juice. I ask about wounds and fevers. How do we deal with the pox? A torn sail? A rotted rope? Do we have canvas, hemp, tar?

What if the ship begins to take on water in a storm? Who mans the pumps? Show me. We have practice drills.

I teach how we do rat killing after supper.

At night I ask, 'What if we get off course?'

Answers come cautiously. I continue my assignment.

There is quite a gale this afternoon and I stay on deck to observe. The pumps sloosh feverishly, our men taking turns bailing. Four weeks out, we move at a crawl, the sails down, suffering the typhoon all day.

No one must know, but I hate it when a storm comes.

My usual faith struggles with fear of it, weighing the faith of my father, his loss at the bottom of the ocean.

"Lord," I pray, "You understood the disciples were also afraid on the Sea of Galilee. You came to them walking on the water.[54] *Here in my time, come to me and change my fear to courage. I'm ashamed before You and my crew that I am afraid. Fill my heart with a trust beyond my ability. I need You. I need help."*

Daily I read the Geneva Bible in the Commander's quarters, not yet ready to speak to Oloff as he requested.

Now, in the fifth week, I approach to give my answer.

The door is open and when I catch his eye, he rolls up the map he's been looking at.

"Come in, Gerrit," he says, "Sit. I'm anxious to hear what you've been thinking."

I sit with my arm on the rail.

"Sir, many die of circumstances not their choice," I say, "As did my mother and father. Your question probes my sense of values, the worth of this grand ship and the souls on board. I can't say I'd be willing to die for the cargo, yet the sum is all three, isn't it? To lose the ship is to lose the crew and its cargo. A weighty responsibility, I comprehend."

He nods, leaning back, twiddling a fire starter.

I search his face and continue.

"I haven't fought in war. Still, we must be prepared for that, and we left New Amsterdam under flaming arrows. What a man may do in danger is to react, naturally," I say, "May I stand?"

"By all means, go ahead," Oloff replies.

I pace, saying, "Now, to thoughtfully think what I would die for, my answer is clear. Knowing I would face God after I die, then I want to do what would please Him; what matters to His kingdom. I don't want to die having my crew despise me or suffer because of my pride or incompetence. Nor do I want to die leaving Evert or the company having aught against me. I have searched my heart, and this is my conclusion, sir," I say, satisfied with myself, "I'm willing to die for what would please God as best I understand it."

Chapter 18

"APPLY THINE HEART UNTO INSTRUCTION, AND
THINE EARS TO THE WORDS OF KNOWLEDGE."

PROVERBS 23:12

Oloff places both hands flat on the desk. He draws his breath and rises.

"You need some advice from experience and knowledge," he says, "As an old man to a young man, hear this above all, you should be willing to die for the national unity of our faith that holds together all the Dutch people and the economy that keeps their faith free," he says, watching my response, "Upon pure motives hangs the unity of the crew. If you're not listening to God, you're a burden to them."

He spreads his hands out as he talks.

I recognize the same patriotism of my father, for God and country, for the good of all. He speaks wisdom, probably hard-earned. I take it to heart, and he sees that. Like a son, I listen.

"When your conscience is clean, it makes you the best you can be," he tells me, turning to go out the door, "I'm going to call muster. You make a speech."

"What? I don't..." I stammer, hurrying behind him.

"All hands on deck! Commander calls muster! All hands on deck!" Jakob shouts ringing the bell.

The men and boys scramble and line up according to seniority. I have not seen their order before.

Oloff ambles along inspecting them one by one while I watch, hands behind my back.

"Aye Meindert, eighteen years aboard this October, I recall. And Frederik, the faithful, who served on ships to Hollandia Nova," he says with a graveled voice and gives a slight salute, "Here's Skylar, our ready munitions captain and Cornelis, Overseer lineman. This is Simon, been on the *Morgenster* since he was twelve, hmm. Let me see your palms, boy. Yes, rugged calluses."

He brushes him slightly on the chest.

"And Gabriel, one fine seaman ye are!" he turns and says to me, "Able-bodied crew, them all, not afraid of storms or pirates. Well, you know Quartermaster Gerrit Brinkendorf by now. I ask 'im to have a word with ye."

He nods to me.

I stand erect, before fifty-one men and two boys.

"I've been observing your operations from poop deck to forecastle, the managing of the masts, the ratlines, the galley and the magazine," I shout as I walk across the main deck, wind whipping the sails, sun at my back.

They eye one another nervously.

The breeze subsides and I can lower my voice.

"You have good reason to be proud. It is important work we do. We make it possible for our faith to be free for the people of our nation. We protect that for which our fathers and grandfathers died. Men, be strong in the Lord and the power of his might.[55] And should we face death together, let us not live with regrets. I expect we will do our best day by day, ready to meet God with a clear conscience. That's all," I say, loud enough.

The men mull around the deck. That's when I hear Jakob grumble, right below the forecastle deck.

"Big words for a land lover with no experience, given a silver spoon position," he says in a mutter.

I jump above him immediately on the quarter-deck, high enough for all to see.

"I went to sea at nine without a peep of grumbling from

my mouth. I know the ache of tired arms and the burn of the sun on my back, not from the fields where I worked plucking tobacco worms off the expensive crop, but from hoisting sails, harnessing the wind. I know the ropes. I know navigation. I know the cannon fire and the grit of the enemy we may encounter."

My nostrils flare. My voice lowers, "I have seen their heartless deeds up close. I am the son of Lieutenant Brigadier Hiram Brinkendorf that served under Piet Hyen in 1627 and captured the thirty-eight Spanish treasure ships for our Republic. I am pure, Dutch, blood, and the salt air is in my veins."

Now I stick my chest out demanding respect, "I will manage the *Morgenster* above the water as I managed to go down with a ship and wash ashore alive! I'm Quartermaster by the hand of God, and if a man says a word against it, he may well find himself like Jonah in a whale's belly!"[56]

Jakob lowers his head, walking to his post. The others slink away, until Oloff and I stand alone.

Once back in the great cabin, Oloff eyes me.
"You show courage," he says, pouring me a jigger.
He puts his fingers to his lips and forgets the glass.
Instead he squints at me silently.
I down the rum in one swallow and nod at him.
"This is my life," I say, "It's no tale for drinking brags."
He leans back and considers me.
I rise and leave to be alone in my room.

After lunch, Oloff takes a nap and I survey the run of the ship, check in with the navigator, and look to see how many fish we've caught.

Walking toward the rear a rope catches my footing and I'm jerked face forward smack into the fishnets, hooks clawing my hands and clothes.

Surprised, I lift my head just enough to see Jakob laughing, which he stifles quickly.

Too late. I've seen him.

Other men rush to help me. The hooks are tangled in the netting and my clothes. My hands bleed and my eyes dart about, not sure who I can trust.

I inspect everything around the area where I fell.

Yes, it was rigged.

Accustomed to hiding my feelings, I make light of it as they get me untangled. My heart is burning with revenge.

"Raise me a bucket of saltwater," I say, as they clear the deck of rope and nets.

Taking the bucket below, *I make no effort to deal with it now, not trusting my temper.*

I plunge my cut palms into the saltwater, grimacing.

How would my father deal with this? I don't know.

Should I tell Oloff? He might not believe me.

He's had Jakob four years. I'm new.

I should forgive him,[57] *pray about it, but I don't want to.*

If I let it go, he'll do something else. It's his way. I should have realized that when I saw him again.

But how could I've known he would set a trap like that?

Probably has a group of men he pushes around, that do what he wants.

I consider setting a trap for him, something like the one he did for me. No, that won't work.

How can I gain respect and stop his bullying?

I don't know. I just don't know.

I skip supper, locking my door, determined to devise a plan, and I wrestle with it until I fall asleep.

In the morning I have a fresh perspective. *I remember my life belongs to God and I tell Him I'm sorry for my pride and anger. On my knees, I ask Him to give me grace.*

As I come into the galley for breakfast, a hush stills the room.

Jakob sits at the head of the table. I fill my plate and come to sit by him.

"Scoot over," I say to the man at his right.

Jakob lowers his head and says for all to hear, "How are your hands?"

A guffaw is muffled at the far end of the room.

I say, "We all know you rigged it."

He looks away defiantly.

"As you superior officer I have no conflict with you or your work. There's no reason for this contention," I say, "But there is a problem you and I have not dealt with."

He shows a smug face. I fork my ham and take a bite, chewing slowly. The men wonder what Jakob will do.

They're watching to hear what I say.

I use my fork to point at him.

"We need you. We need your experience and knowledge. You know we're short-handed," I reason, "It will take all of us to protect each other. A divided crew is like a leaky hull. Now, what am I going to do about the hole in the hull? That aggravating leaky hole that threatens to take the ship down with all of us in it?"

He looks sideways. The men are quiet.

Enjoying my food, I keep a serious face and sip my coffee. I butter my biscuit and add some jam.

"In the backwoods we set traps to take the skin off the animals and sell the fur. It's profitable for us, but cruel to the beaver. His leg is clamped. He can't get a drink from the brook or eat or get away. He slowly dies from starvation," I tell them.

"It's just an animal," Jakob shrugs.

Now I confront him, "What will you gain to set a trap for me? Is this the same game you played when we were in school, and you and the boys meant to ruin my clothes and kick the life out of me in the mud?"

With a frown he rises to go.

"Don't go," I challenge, "Stay and finish this like a man."

All the men stare silently. Jakob reluctantly stays.

He is fuming and breathing deep.

"A real man doesn't set traps to wound his fellow worker. A

real man comes right out with it to seek peace," I say, "What is your quarrel with me? Let it be known in front of all our friends."

Jakob sneers, "I don't want to compete with you."

"No, of course not, that's obvious. You want to hurt me because you're jealous and mean-spirited and don't even like yourself. No one trusts a man like that," I say.

"What are you trying to prove?" he blurts.

I continue with calm authority, "That you're not the best man for your job when you're thinking about foolish competition. When you waste time being a childish troublemaker you let the rest of us down. Not just me. Which one did you pick on before I came? Which one before that? You act like this with everyone, don't you?"

Now I have him cornered. All eyes are on him. No one disputes what I say.

I fold my napkin and lean back, "Did you bully Oloff too? Your father? The Bible says a fool does these things."[58]

"Why don't we go out and fight now?" he says gruffly.

"Yes, why not now?" I counter.

He looks me straight in the face.

I keep a confident smile, "You know I will whip you to a pulp. The only way you can beat me is to be underhanded."

I push my plate away and stand up, towering over him.

"Jakob, I forgive you this once, as a matter of Christian principle. I'll show you respect and appreciate you as part of our crew, as long as you don't start trouble," I warn, leaning close to his face, "Because, if you do, mark my words, I'll tie you up until we reach the next port and put you off the ship without mercy, no matter where it is."

Gradually the crew wanders away and Jakob remains seething.

I go on about my duties in my normal manner.

At midday, Oloff finds me cutting fish bait.

"Come talk," he says and points to his quarters.

I wash my hands in the kitchen and go sit with him.

"I heard what happened," he says.

I nod and respond, "It's something I had to do for myself. He was a bully at my school."

Oloff raises his brows and turns his head.

"I thank you for handling it well. We grow sick of his rebellion. No one is safe. All the new men eventually hate him," he tells me.

The conversation is over, and I go back to work, *thinking of the proverbs that describe our lives.*

Tonight, I stand guard on the sterncastle deck under a golden moon amidst a thousand stars, listening to the constant slap of the sea against the vessel. Several dolphins play in the water around us and our flags flap in the breeze.

In my world of thoughts, I consider recent events.

Where did it come from, my sudden burst of courage?

What has changed in me?

What in my soul came bursting forth today?

I think about it long and hard.

Finally, I come to rest with this. I do believe God is with me, has appointed me, will enable me. I believe it is in my blood, my Dutch blood. I do believe in my country, its faith, and prosperity. I cannot be more, or less than I am.

This is me.

Chapter 19

"THE HANDS OF ZERUBBABEL HAVE LAID THE
FOUNDATION OF THIS HOUSE; HIS HANDS ALSO
SHALL FINISH IT; AND THOU SHALT KNOW THAT THE
LORD OF HOSTS HATH SENT ME UNTO YOU. FOR WHO
HATH DESPISED THE DAY OF SMALL THINGS?"
ZECHARIAH 4:9-10A

Oloff steers clear of me four days. I bear it in silence, studying the Bible. I read all the Proverbs.

On deck, I imagine what I will do if confronted by a pirate ship. In my mind, I envision the men making preparations hurriedly, watching the enemy through the telescope, giving orders when the cannons are in range. I can see the broadside and hear the gunfire at my ears, men falling wounded, being moved out of the way, and shouts for powder among the smoke and blast of cannonballs. Then we are close enough to board and capture them. I give a courageous command and lead with knives all of us, taking the victory. We lower the men into the longboats and set them to sea with some water and food, sailing away in both ships.

My eyes scan the horizon. The wind is in my face until the sun goes down. The water is choppy. The crew restless.

I recall the Psalm, "By terrible things in righteousness wilt thou answer us, O God of our salvation, who art the confidence of all the ends of the earth, and them that are afar off upon the sea."[59]

We are those that travel the wide oceans. Oloff says we

have ships with sugarcane coming from Brazil. He has been to Tuticorin, India and to Dejima, Japan. He says the Dutch East India Company plans to establish a trading post at the southern tip of Africa.

Will they send me to the east? I'm Evert's property.

Maybe it's God's plan. I have no choice.

I wonder if Jesus will give me the spiritual gifts. How will I know what to do with them?

Will I be given more authority if I am faithful?

Silently, at night, *I sense crisis may be brewing.*

I turn and enter the Orlop deck below *to consider what I would do if we contracted smallpox, a possibility when taking on a foreign vessel. How would I manage it? A few ideas come to mind, nothing satisfying.*

I pray in the corner alone, "Lord, I will be in authority on the Morgenster. Humbly, I ask for the gifts of knowledge, wisdom, and discernment to take care of us and be Christ-like in my actions, that I will not be guilty before You, Who know all my thoughts."

It comes to mind that I should be keeping the fourth watch of the night. I notify the boy to rouse me at three in the morning and that he shall continue to wake me at that time throughout the rest of the voyage.

In my quarters, I light the candle and read Matthew, chapter fourteen, how Jesus came to the disciples in the storm during the fourth watch of the night,[60] walking on the water.

In my heart, I think, "If I want the power of the Holy Spirit, I need to follow the example of Jesus."

To me that means "love one another." I have been given disciples, in a way. I'm responsible and have the authority to protect them and teach them.

How can I teach? By the way I live. A heavy duty to be sure. To be like Jesus and be capable with holy gifts of the Spirit captivates me in awe.

Who am I? A castaway found on the shore, raised an indentured servant.

And a firebrand of faith in what my father found, the essence of hosting the presence of God.

I wake even before the boy comes for me. Turbulent waters mean a strong gale is brewing. The ship is pitching.

"Go to bed, son. It will be all right," I say as I takeover.

The spray whips my face when I step on the upper deck..

I relieve the man in the crow's nest, and pace in prayer.

It comes to me that I should rebuke the wind and the waves, speak to it, like my Savior did.[61]

That thought arrests me. Me?

Why not me? Am I His disciple now? Is He with me?

Do I believe? Yes. How much? A mustard seed size?[62]

I smile squinting at the pouring rain.

I raise my hand and say, "Storm dissipate, in the Name of Jesus. Cease and do no damage to property or people."

A gush of wind knocks me against the back wall. I stand with a defiant face, *like my father did to the ragman.*

A warm breeze blows over me. The rain subsides and becomes gentle. The clouds part a little and stretch apart for the moonlight to peek through. The storm is gone.

I'm soaked. Smiling to myself, I shudder with a chill.

I'm the only one that knows what just happened!

God is with me and hears me. I bow my head humbly, overwhelmed, strengthened in my faith, worshipping.

Tuesday morning Oloff casually asks if he might have a word with me, below. Silently I follow him and when the door is closed, he offers me a cup of tea with lemon.

"Gerrit, I didn't know about your father, the hero that he was, or you washed ashore," he says, "We are fortunate to have you on the Morning Star."

I say nothing.

He puts his cup down and unrolls a map of the Holy Roman Empire, placing his finger on Spain.

"Our cruel enemy," he says and taps the paper, "Protestant Waldenses and Abligenes were driven from France and the

Alps seeking refuge among us from the Church of Rome. They brought the Romaunt Version of the Bible which was translated into Low Dutch rhymes. Spanish ruler Charles V had direct control over us and vowing to stomp out all Protestant heresy he pledged to sacrifice armies, treasures, kingdoms, and souls in the attempt. Nearly one hundred thousand in the Lowlands died. For thirty-three years the war continued, until it looked as if our land would become desolate and our harbors empty. The newfound religion spread in spite of it."[63]

He frowns and refills his cup.

"On a cold day in February 1568, the fathers of the Spanish Inquisition decided all the people of the Netherlands were guilty of high treason to be immediately executed," he says.

"Death to the whole nation?"

I'm appalled.

He says, "Yes. Our people were pushed back to the sea, so we made more land with the invention of the windmill. Our enemies found gold with the Mayans and bought mercenaries to kill us. So, we designed faster ships and took the gold. Riches have power. We printed Bibles. They burned such men at the stake. What did these men find they were willing to die for? And why were our enemies so desperate to stop it?"[64]

I say, "It was holy insight from God to protect His will."

"Yes, well, the independence of people touches everything they are Gerrit. It involves spiritual standards, hard to gain and easy to lose," he says.

Jakob knocks and opens the door. He glances at me and turns aside to ask Oloff, a matter of ship rations.

"That's a question you will ask Quartermaster Brinkendorf," Oloff answers as a reprimand.

Jakob recoils, and his eyes narrow.

I rise and salute. He returns it quickly.

"I trust your judgment and experience," I say, "Do as you see best and give me the account in an hour."

He takes it well and leaves with a bow.

"Thank ye sir. Good day to ye," he says.

Pointing behind him, Oloff says, "He'll be in good spirits all day. He couldn't be sure if you made yourself look good yesterday or if you meant it."

I raise my brows and look sideways.

At the sound of the conch shell he rouses and slaps my shoulder, "Time for dinner!"

Six stay on deck to watch, and the rest crowd around the long tables. We bow to thank God before we eat.

I'm chewing a mouthful of sausage when the navigator comes tumbling roughshod down the stairs.

"Spanish Galleon on the horizon, sir!" he says.

All eyes look to me and forty seven leave to scurry up.

As we bump into each other I remind them, "The important thing is work together. We don't have the soldiers."

I take the spyglass and focus where the navigator points, but as the heavy ship comes into view, *a thought crosses my mind. I could fly the flag of distress.*

I hand the glass back to him and glance at Oloff.

The deck is lined with muskets ready, all looking my way.

"Get down," I say to them, motioning with my hand.

I dart below to the ship stores.

As I pass, men are poised, waiting to shoot the cannon.

I find the flag and hurry back into the sunlight pitching it to toward those closest to me.

"Put it up, quick! Set the muskets on the floor and step down. Be ready if I signal. They have rowers that can pull fast. Hurry. They can see us too," I say.

I take off my hat and sit on the floor with the men.

In my mind I think, what would I do if I were the enemy?

Oloff sweats, mopping his brow, leaning back.

I calculate with the size of their ship, they most likely have one hundred trained militia armed with long swords and the boat itself boasting sixteen cannon.

They could blow us out of the water. Or they could take everything and kill some of us, enslave the rest. My heart is in my throat.

Closer. Closer.

I don't want to surrender without trying. I know every man feels what I'm feeling, as they wait for my word.

And then, the boat turns. A strong wind fills their sails and pulls them north. We blink at each other, afraid to move.

They fell for the trick!

I motion with my hand, whispering, "Stay down."

We wait remaining quiet, until we are sure they cannot sneak back on us. The boat drifts listlessly with no effort.

I say, "Every other man, go below and eat. You, you, you and so on. The rest of us will stay and watch. Be quick about it, so others have a turn. We'll lay low until dark."

When the plates are stacked again and taken away, there is one pewter mug of rum for each of us.

Jakob sits across from me.

He does love to make the men laugh if he can. Mostly he makes up stories of some amusing mishap or mischief.

Today I tell the joke when I say, "Imagine the crew on the Spanish Galleon talking about how glad they are they didn't get the pox."

We grin at each other because we had pulled it off.

Chuckles ruffle down the row.

I say, "Farmers have no idea what we suffer in the weather, in the lonely stretches across the sea. They know nothing of swinging in your sleep or harnessing a wind, heh? They go to bed with their wife in their arms and their children close by, maybe a dog. We, on the other hand, face the morning sun for another blistering adventure against pirates and storms. Or even boredom."

As I get ready for bed, I think *the sea life is a lonely, wild adventure and by Providence, it is mine.*

Tomorrow we shall reach Leiden, but tonight it is raining.

Chapter 20

"BUT WITHOUT FAITH IT IS IMPOSSIBLE TO PLEASE
HIM: FOR HE THAT COMETH TO GOD MUST BELIEVE
THAT HE IS, AND THAT HE IS A REWARDER OF THOSE
WHO DILIGENTLY SEEK HIM."

HEBREWS 11:6

I stand on the deck praying at my fourth watch altar, *while
a tune my mother sang floats in my mind. Words of adoration
for Jesus are on my heart and I sing.*

"You are my heart's great song, my joy, my peace, awesome
God of heaven and earth. You are holy and righteous and excellent in mercy, Abba, Father,"[65] I sing.

Worship fills me with delight. I want to praise more.

"Nothing is impossible for You, Jesus. Nothing is too hard
for You.[66] Sweep over all of us with a holy hush of pure clean
reverence and fill our minds with the truth," I say, humming
along, and raising my hands.

From the first day I began meeting with God this way, *I
live confidently with an understanding beyond myself that I
can accomplish His priorities and manage the responsibility
expected of me.*

He helps me in every way.

*Suddenly a feeling of danger checks me. I stop. What is it? I
am still, sensitive to being obedient.*

I think, check the fire in the kitchen.

The rain is pounding heavier, no lightning. As I walk toward the sterncastle steps, I notice the ship beginning to toss and I take hold of the rail for balance.

I reach the galley, and all is in order. The cook snores sleeping deeply, the embers of the fire burn orange in the dark. *I feel confused* and lay my hand on the table, waiting.

The ship lurches, a wallop of a wave sends it up and sideways. The embers of the fire roll over the grate and out on the floor catching a greasy place on the wood and at once, a stream of fire runs across the floor. I gasp and run for a bucket of water. I throw the bucket of water on the flames. To my surprise the breeze from thrown water spreads it quickly across the greasy trail. The flames are now leaping up the wall.

I think, *the wall that gunpowder is stored behind.*

Oh God help us!

The kitchen rags are blazing. The boat is pitching. No time to wake the men. Act fast!

I see it spreading toward the lard barrel. With godspeed I grab quilts and pile them on the fire. I slosh the keg of kitchen water on the wall and stomp my feet on the quilts until it goes out. I am panting when the cook begins coughing from smoke. He jumps up and stares.

"Gerrit, what?" he asks.

Winded, I can't answer.

Through the smoke he surveys the aftermath, scorched quilts on the floor and blackened wood up the wall.

He bends over the firebox with the lantern and sees the ashes piled over the edge.

We look at each other and I take a deep breath.

I say, "Get some rest. Clean up in the morning. And make sure you keep the grease scrubbed off the floor, hmm? I want the lard barrel rolled away from the kitchen. You may have to take a few more steps, I know. Tomorrow we relocate the gunpowder."

I climb up to the Navigation Room, *weighing the consequences had I not stopped to obey the urging of the Lord. How easily I could have thought it was only a distraction.*

I marvel at the accuracy of the Holy Spirit in guiding me, how unaware I am of His hand of mercy.

"Thank you for Your protection, Jesus," I say.

I ponder this is how the Lord trained David the shepherd boy. God saw in David the heart of a king, a boy who protected his sheep with his life,[67] *trusting God.*

In that, I am like my father and that warms my memory of him and makes me smile.

Since aboard, I have joined the men in their duties and shared the scriptures I read the night before. Now they ask questions about faith and holiness. They tell me their problems and dreams in private, and a general goodness prevails among us, to be helpful to one another.

I'm content with my calling, peaceful as it is thus far.

It has been three months.

I feel I am one of them.

We put in close at Zeeland,[68] but only for fresh water and food, peeling our eyes for any sight of Spanish opposition and weary of being on board.

The crew draws straws to choose who may go ashore with Jakob and I don't win.

"This is where our journey gets a vacation," he shouts above the shrill wind, as the snow tosses flurries in the air.

Soon it will be night. I wave him on and take shelter.

The men bring back three large hams and apples a plenty. We eat buttered carrots, potatoes, cabbage, and cinnamon buns. There is cheese and wine, salt, and pepper. Everyone is ecstatic and all the lanterns lit when the conversation turns to Leiden and Oloff blinks at us.

"We are almost home," he says with a rasp.

The room grows quiet. He continues chewing the ham and looks at us.

"This is the last time I will see her, my last journey, you see," he says with a tear in his voice and reaches for another slice of bread as his head goes down.

"I know what war is," I say, tightening my lips, reaching my glass for more wine as the bottle is passed. "As a boy I witnessed slaughter, in my town, of every breathing soul, except me."

Jakob is frozen and Oloff pushes his chair back.

The effect is astounding to the others. Only the creaking of the hull is heard, while I disclose the fear I had, when the armored men lit the barns and houses where I once played.

I tell them how the ragman stole the dignity from the corpses and as I share my mother's prayer, my voice cracks a little. It's been ten years.

It feels like another world, so far away.

"She asked God in heaven to take care of me. My father came to get me. He was part of the crew with no authority to turn the ship. He felt the Holy Spirit needed him to go home. He told the commander. He begged the men. They had a shipment to deliver. It was out of the way. He paced and fretted and begged some more until," I stop.

I see the cook standing in the door listening intently.

"When a man listens to God to obey him, God talks to that man. He was warning my father. How I wish his commander had brought help for my village in time. Maybe my mother could have escaped. I don't know. Maybe they would have forfeited the ship. I don't know."

I nod, then look up with a determined resolution.

"My father came that night. He came after the attack and rescued me in answer to my mother's prayer. I am seeking to have that gift of discernment for us," I say, "Furthermore I pledge my allegiance to Holland, and to her flag flying on our mast and the protection for which it stands for religious liberty. I stand with her offering open arms to Protestants and Jews suffering from persecution. Realize men, for me, it's personal."

Oloff places a hand on my shoulder.

Around the room, looks are shared that have meaning and then Oloff takes the reins of the conversation.

"This is what an old man knows, mates," Oloff says, "When God looks down on each of us, He must see a good heart, else we fail to make it through. Measure carefully by the knots of the history you live in, that you hold well your position for Jesus Christ. Who's to know if you will indeed be the final knot on the string?"

He eases back, propping his boots on a nearby stool.

Meanwhile men scoot their chairs closer, and more wine is brought out. The cook has cut the cheeses and put them on trays on the tables, along with a few candies, some dried pear slices, and the rest of the buns.

Oloff points his finger in the air.

"Throughout this war, can't you see the Almighty favored us? A small band of us, walled in by the ocean, battling a combination of kingdoms, nationalities and armies that opposed us?" he asks.

"Know this my good men," he says, "When we unload tomorrow, look around at the people and the country. Be proud of the ships of the Dutch West India Company, our benefactor. And be respectful of Quartermaster Gerrit Brinkendorf. He has the most important quality of a leader, an anointing to make you unite. This is more valuable than the experience you have as seamen. You're powerful when you have one mind, and one accord."

I like to think my father and mother in heaven heard our conversation tonight. Surely if they look over the rim of the portals of glory, this would have been worth listening to.

The Bible says, "We are encompassed by so great a cloud of witnesses.[69]*"*

At three in the morning, by lantern light I read the Bible on the Sterncastle deck, as the *Morgenster* glides smoothly making headway.

The night is calm, a steady autumn wind obliging to us.

My place begins at Psalm 73. When I reach Psalm 75:6, I am struck with a point of wisdom that seems directly for me. It reads, "For promotion cometh neither from the east, nor from the west, nor from the south. But God is the judge: he putteth down one and setteth up another.[70]"

I remember what Oloff said last night, that "I was anointed to bring the men into unity with one mind."

What a compliment. My father's crew had it.

I know that it's so valuable.

In the morning we come into Amsterdam. As far as eye can see along the shores are various sailing vessels and low boats, for the canals.

Eventually we find a docking pier to tie up.

Jakob is left to route the baggage, while I finish the lading list for The Dutch West India Company.

Later in the streets, Oloff leads me to the tailor who measures me and says it will be ready late tomorrow. Behind him are rows of seamstresses.

As we pass the shipbuilding, I study the construction, awed with the sleek framing, *ideas bursting in my head.*

I think of the unending timber forests along the Hudson, bursting with the raw material for more ships.

Now we must find lodging for the winter.

Oloff has a family in town. They know of an attic room near the university I should rent.

"Can you skate?" his brother-in-law asks me.

I nod and he writes an address with his recommendation.

At my room the next day, I receive an appointment in a sealed with wax invitation, delivered by a well-dressed courier. I sign for it, smiling with apprehension.

Father would be proud.

In my new clothes we are received by a boardroom of twelve richly clad and collared Dutch investors. The lading is read and approved unanimously, and I'm asked to stand. The men eye me.

"It has come to our attention that your late father had not redeemed his severance pay of our employment, which is twenty acres in New Netherland. Also his reward for twenty years' service and the accumulating interest, which is our custom to pass along. The settlement is made to your account this day. Sign your acceptance that it is paid in full on his behalf," the somber one reads.

I step forward and scribble.

They are finished.

That's it, quick and to the point.

Chapter 21

"OPEN REBUKE IS BETTER THAN SECRET LOVE.
FAITHFUL ARE THE WOUNDS OF A FRIEND..."

PROVERBS 27:5-6A

In the street, Oloff suggests we have coffee.

"It would be wise for you to attend university classes while we're laid over. The opportunity may never present itself again in your lifetime," he says, removing his gloves as we hurry in and see the bakery sweets. The smell that greets us is intoxicating and the pastries warm. We sit for a long while, watching people go about their daily tasks, enjoying the coffee and iced cinnamon buns.

A bundled man enters and there is something familiar about him. He asks for Jamaican coffee and lemon cake. I watch him remove his scarf and gloves.

"Excuse me Commander. I think I see an old friend," I say, rising with my cup to cross the room.

I'm not sure if it's the Swede.

I follow him as he sits. He turns to face me. It is him!

He's overcome, biting his lip, and shaking his head.

I smile and sit down with him at the table.

"Gerrit Brinkendorf, my moon and stars! Look at you. Clad in silk and pearl buttons. And so tall," he says.

"I'm so happy to see you," I say.

He throws up his hands.

He says, "How have you been getting along? Tell me."

"I'm hired, an indentured servant. Graduated from school. I'm in training, a quartermaster for the Huybrecht firm, with the West India Company," I say.

He blinks hard and smiles.

"But of course," he offers.

He coughs deeply and his face gets red. He wipes his mouth with a dingy kerchief and sips a little coffee.

"What are you doing these days?" I ask.

"I log in the backwoods," he says, "The overseer scouts ahead of us early each day, tagging hardwoods chosen for wear of the sea and long enough, from thirty to fifty feet. Once we chop through the bark, the core is tightly wound. We work hard. My old bones ache in the cold. When we finally fell the timbers, and avoid being hit, we pull the sleigh up. I lop off the small branches and throw them in a wagon to sell. We chain the biggest trees and run them on the snow. We stack them and they go out by sleigh pulled with a team of eight horses."

"Eight horses?" I ask, amazed.

"Massive animals. Takes all their might too," he says.

I ask, "How many trees does it take to build a warship?"

"Three thousand, seven hundred, Gerrit, if they are sound, with no damages," he explains.

My eyes widen.

Then I lean toward him.

I say, "It's an answer to my prayer that we found each other today. I apologize for my rough words when last we met. I'm much removed from that way of thinking these days. I see things, well, from a man's point of view."

He raises his brows.

"Uh huh," he returns.

"I have surrendered my life to Christ," I whisper smiling.

He quietly ponders that, eyeing me.

"Your father used to talk about that. Told me I needed to surrender my heart. Said it was necessary," he confides.

Tears well up in my eyes. He pats my sleeve.

I notice Oloff has left.

"Know why sailors say, 'my moon and stars', boy?" he asks.

I look him in the face.

"Because the Almighty guides us. Brought you here for us to cheer each other up, hmm?" he says.

I nod and wipe my eyes.

I don't care who sees me. This is my heart's moment. I'm so glad to see him.

We finish our coffee and sweets together discussing the weather and sharing about our lives.

Walking out in the street we cover our heads in the wind.

The Swede grabs me and holds me with a tight grip.

Then he is gone.

I watch him for a minute and walk back to the courtyard and through the front foyer to climb the stairs to my little room.

Inside I light a fire.

I am accepted at the Athenaeum Ilustre by a letter from the Dutch West India Company and lose all sense of time, continually absorbed in discoveries.

My father wanted me to read, to go to the university and here I am by the grace of God.

My teachers appreciate my concentration. I take English writing and learn to speak French. Eagerly I approach map-making, astronomy, and navigation. Each day we begin with current events and debates. Each evening we finish with history and discussion.

I think the presentations give us an understanding of our times by learning from past mistakes and successes.

All of us are required to know the basics of skilled trades, the universal science of the elements and the etiquette of gentlemen.

Additional courses are offered in mathematics of building architecture and ship construction, cultures of Japan, Africa and India, and profitable agriculture.

When the air grows frosty and the inlets freeze hard, the

entire city gets about skating on the ice. I haven't worn skates since I lived with my mother. Yet it comes back to me, and I feel the skid of my feet swiftly take me across the expanse.

Snow covers the rooftops and alleyways. It is the first time I've seen the old windmills iced over and still. Smoke whiffs from the tall stone cut structures of the inner city. I frequent the bakery evenings as I skate home.

One afternoon under a hazy sky I chance upon a little textile shop where *I stare forlornly at a red plaid shawl.*

Not the same pattern, still it woos me to purchase it. I want to put it around my shoulders as my father did on that night long ago.

I almost hear Mum say, "Do you want some chicken?"

Lost in time I pass my entrance and end up by the lake.

"Get a hold of yourself, Gerrit," I say in my heart.

When I go to my room, I keep the shawl over my shoulders to remind me, they loved me.

I smile remembering the first time I tasted a cinnamon roll, the day the men cheered and called me "Tiger", and how my father bragged of his adventures.

Tonight I take a holiday with my memories, thinking of what my parents left me.

All the other nights I study close by the fire in the room, gaining an education, nibbling cheese and crackers.

I buy a traveling trunk and more clothes, *feeling I've quite "come into my own"* now that I own a fur coat of good standing and high leather boots.

At first, I dress the old way, but in time elite style appeals to me, and I give in. I let my hair grow long and frequent the tailor. The silver dagger shaves my whiskers off.

All the young men attend the winter solstice ball, and I go along, *unsure of myself.* They dance politely with beautiful young women as I watch from afar, hugging the wall covered in tapestry and content to sip the refreshment.

The instruments enchant my ears with cheerful melodies.

As I walk to the house, I hear the deep crack of ice giving up its hold on the canals, reminding me we will depart in a week. The ship will load another haul and carry paying passengers and apprentices from the Lowlands to New Amsterdam.

I wonder what kind of people will want to leave the sophistication here for the crude life in America. Maybe they don't know what it's like, but I do.

Chapter 22

"LET NOT MERCY AND TRUTH FORSAKE THEE: BIND
THEM ABOUT THY NECK; WRITE THEM UPON THE
TABLE OF THINE HEART: SO SHALT THOU FIND FAVOR
AND GOOD UNDERSTANDING IN THE SIGHT OF GOD
AND MAN."

PROVERBS 3: 3-4

Report to Master Evert Huybrecht of New Amsterdam
    The Lading Account~
    Two hundred muskets
    Twenty kegs of powder and five barrels of musket
balls
    Eighty seven crates of stacked yellow brick
    Four crates of shipbuilder tools
    Two crates of stonemason tools
    One hundred and sixty pounds of high-grade wool
    Two hundred fifty bags of seed as specified,
    One hundred seventy bags of coffee beans
    Twenty pounds of pepper
    Twenty pounds of cinnamon
    A crock of fine buttons
    Passengers:
    In the Eight Paid Rooms:
    Dr. Ezra de Aguilar – physician Jew
    Isaac and Naomi Spinoza - printers, Jews
    Two Dutch stonemasons - Gerhardt brothers

Four Lutheran shipbuilders with apprentice papers –
Evan Fisher, Separatist - Welsh scrivener
In the cargo hold: One hundred Dutch Republic
soldiers
Below deck: One sailmaker and his sister, one
stonecutter, one butcher, one glazier, one wheelwright, and fourteen approved and contracted indentured beggars, authorized by the Dutch West
India Company.

We expect landfall by June. There are no repairs
to be reported. All hands are healthy. I remain,
Your Trusted Steward,
Gerrit Brinkendorf, March 2, 1646.
Quartermaster, the *Morgenster*

Monday, I post the account on the *Faer Hope*, as our sails
hoist. The *Faer Hope* is still loading.

We travel without distraction through the English Channel
and out on the Atlantic by the end of the week. For that, we all
breathe easier. The wind is with us and the day balmy.

*I've gained the confidence of an older, wiser man because
of my education. Has it only been five months? The world is
changing and I with it.*

I watch the passengers with interest, especially a young
woman named Emma and her brother Charles Wiloughby. This
is probably because they make it their practice to read from a
Lutheran Bible early mornings, in the hearing of all nearby,
taking turns by page and continuing until the hourglass is
turned and we ready for breakfast.

They brought several chickens on board. Though I welcome
fresh eggs, I steer clear of their odor. Charles notices this and
winks at me.

"When the rations run low, we'll have a nice supper of these creatures," he says jovially.

I raise my brows and nod.

"Now there's a promise," I answer, equally amused.

He must be some younger than I and the sister, younger than he.

"I understand from your registration that you're a sail-maker. Where do you come from?" I question him.

He sizes me up as friendly and leans toward me.

"Originally, from Zurich. Our father and brothers were drowned in Switzerland.[71] We escaped to Wales," he says.

I hold my tongue noticing a passenger is listening.

His sister comes up the stairs, the wind blowing her hair.

She gathers it in her frail hand, tying a frayed ribbon tightly to hold it back from her face and walks toward us.

While I am distracted by her presence, another ship approaches in the fog. It bears down heavily close, flying colors of distress. I see it and push them back against the sideboard reaching for the spyglass.

Oloff hastens to the quarter deck, and I hurry to participate in our course of action. He peers long through the glass and taking a deep breath, hands it to me.

"What do you see Gerrit?" he asks.

"A Dutch ship bearing the flag of distress," I say.

"Is there a blue robed maid on the bow? A crown of shells on her head?" he asks.

I look closer and hand the glass back.

"I can't tell yet," I answer.

"Maybe it's Van de Boogart's slave ship. What would it be doing here? His route crosses from Africa to the West Indies. Mutiny. Pray," he says low.

And pray I did, motioning for all passengers to get below.

"What should we do sir?" I ask.

"We can't know until it is upon us. We are obliged to help if we can, but no one wants the pox." he responds.

The men look at each other, and word passes quickly across the decks until all sense impending trouble.

I tell them to prepare their weapons and the cannon.

Everyone moves into place.

Oloff watches how I manage.

The ship draws nearer.

"What name does it carry? Your eyes are better than mine," Oloff sweats, his eyes glued to the horizon.

"The *Salamander*. Africans on deck," I say hastily.

He looks again, but I am up the foremast ratline signaling my crew and the soldiers poised with crossbows and muskets, daggers strapped to their sides.

Oloff nods.

In the lower deck, the cannons are positioned.

Smoothly, alongside the *Morgenster*, rolls the great ship *Salamander* and in fact, she is taken over by a revolt of Africans.

The one in charge shouts orders as our firing commences.

"Don't break her," I yell, "Shoot high. One volley."

Four cannons roar, the balls flying above the boat.

It frightens the revolters and they scatter to hide around the water casks.

"For God and our Republic!" I shout, grabbing a rope and swinging to the deck across from us. The others copy my move and more of our soldiers come in boats and by planks as the ship is tugged within our grasp.

The first one in, I face the one closest to me and slash his arm causing him to drop his knife. Our attack is on.

With orders to not destroy the persons if possible, the fight spreads across the deck, wrestling and tumbling.

Jakob knocks a man overboard, yet another grabs him round the neck. They struggle, falling over a wounded man in the row. I draw the dagger from my sleeve and fling it to stop the arm of Jakob's assailant. It strikes the man's shoulder forcing him to drop the cleaver. Jakob jerks back and shoots a look at me. He hits the slave in the jaw and retrieves my knife. He holds it up to show me, as I am attacked from behind.

In the turmoil I manage to heave my attacker away from me and draw my sword at his belly.

Two of my crew grab him from behind and tie him up.

A sudden pain stabs my side. I flinch. *Have I been cut?*

Panting, I survey the situation. We have taken control. The last men fighting are moving toward the mast.

I shout back to the *Morgenster*, "Cease fire!"

I pull up my shirt to see my wound, a cut the length of my finger. *Not deep.* The noise ends.

Within the hour, thirty two stout slaves are tied, sitting in a line. Seven are dead, one severely hurt.

Commander Oloff stands afar, hands on hips.

Glaring eyes stare from where the Africans sit as I count.

"Find out where the ship's crew is," I order.

No one moves.

I'm perplexed.

"I don't mean no disrespect sir," an oarsman says, "Most of us have seen what disease can do. We're not willing."

Then facing the flag of distress, he nods at it.

Cowering, most of them climb back on the *Morgenster*, back to their duties in the bright sunlight.

Three soldiers guard the slaves, but not too close.

I know a little Swailhili from the plantation and attempt a question, "Where are the white men?"

The Africans' eyes dart in fear, expecting execution or torture. I walk down the planks, my boots heavily plodding, and my brute strength apparent.

Then one points down. Whatever the situation holds, the answer lies below.

Across the way, Commander Oloff looks ominous. He's not giving permission or orders.

The decision is mine.

Flies buzz on the wounded man and his groans are growing faint. It will be merciful if he doesn't suffer long.

The guard catches my eye. I jerk my head in that direction, meaning, "Take care of it."

The slaves visibly dread their future.

I pause and look at them, not knowing if they have killed my countrymen.

Then I hear voices below.

I think what Oloff said when Evert promoted me, "He expects you to show fortitude."

I decide to dive into the blackness.

My eyes adjust as I make out the crew lying in hammocks and on the floor, pitifully weak and reeking of sweat and excretement. Their eyes are closed.

I check their breathing, shake their arms, hurry from one to another. They are quite emaciated, a wonder any are alive. I roll up my sleeves and carry them some water from the galley quickly.

I shout to the guards, "Bring more water."

No one answers. I carry up stinking blankets and give an angry look as I throw the filthy things overboard. I order Jakob to notify Oloff, while I attend the sick.

Jakob returns and stands in the doorway.

"Oloff warns, don't go near them," he says, drawing back.

"Stay there then," I say, "I will do it."

As I bathe away days of sickness perspired on his skin, the Commander tells me what happened. They had met up with *The Rotterdam* on its way to India and requested a barrel of oranges as theirs had become moldy. I wring the cloth and wet it fresh, going to the next man.

Behind me, he describes the events.

"The next day I came down with fever, red spots, and chills. My first mate and several of the crew fell sick too. The quartermaster was overtaken when he tried to feed the slaves alone. They killed him and took his knife," he explains, "But they steered clear of us, afraid of sickness."

"A godsend," I say, checking others on the hard floor.

"I've been counting the days, knowing we were off course," he says from across the room.

I go back up and shout to the guards, "Bring more water."

The guards shrink back, looking at Commander Oloff.

At that moment, the Christian in me loses all patience.

I bellow, "My mother nursed the plague. This isn't it. They have measles and are pitifully dehydrated. They may all die if you cowards don't help me."

Filling the bucket, I turn to face them, "And not only will you lose respect in my eyes," I say winded and bite my lip.

Then shaking my head and angry, I threaten, "I will cease to pray for you!"

Commander Oloff's face falls and the men come from all sides to help me.

I remember Mum doing what I was doing, taking care of the sick. She had faith that God would protect us from it. Her courage lives in me, a faith to not be afraid.

From where I stood, it seemed Jesus Himself was urging me to pursue conviction on the Commander.

I pull up a stool and put my back between him and the others. Leaning close, I have a private talk.

"Sir, the Almighty has spared your lives in a most unusual way," I hold his attention and he nods, "Had we not come along. Well."

The moment passes as he has sobering thoughts.

"May I speak my heart?" I say.

"Please do. I am grateful for your kindness," he says.

"You have been given another chance at life. Please leave off this rotten slaving business. It is a curse to you and our nation, I believe," and I bow my head meekly.

I pull the stool away and leave him to think.

I think about it while I search for cleaning supplies.

Then I climb to the deck and issue orders.

"Scrub down everything. Make this ship worthy of the Dutch name," I shout, "Make it arrive home with honor."

We scour the *Salamander's* deck and hull with all the lye

soap and vinegar they have, then fasten the slaves back in the hold. I portion out their food and give them water.

Two whites have died. The crew removes these to the sea. The slaves are not infected, though they look thin.

I do not know how to communicate with them.

Still, common decency is a virtue.

In a few hours, I have five of the sick people in the sunshine. The fever has subsided, but their eyes are weak. Four have not awakened and I fear they may die too. All together fifty-one onboard have the disease.

Oloff joins me on the *Salamander*. He has had measles and is of a mind to leave them behind. But as their commander rallies enough to sit up and keep his supper down, I ask Oloff if we might support them one more day so they can get on by themselves to Leiden.

"Might put us in a bind, son," Oloff objects.

"Yes, it could," I reason, "But we feared smallpox and it was only measles. I think we'll see the majority up and about tomorrow, able to run the ship. Their morale is low. If we give them say, six of our soldiers, they'll feel like masters of the ship again. And it builds Christian character in our crew."

He squints and looks back at our men, weary and quiet.

"I suppose everyone needs compassion sometime," he obliges, "If we give them six soldiers, our food supplies won't be low. They'll dock in a few days."

I add, "Considering the investment of the *Salamander,* the cargo, and the recovery of the sailors that man it, I think the company would approve if we secure their wellbeing."

He nods pursing his lips.

I sigh, resting my soul in the Lord. Now I can get some sleep. I did what I would want done for me.[72]

If saving the Salamander is the highlight of this week, it cannot compare to the finale that welcomes me when I carry my weary bones back to the mother ship.

As I board the *Morgenster*, Emma's eyes meet mine.

"Bless the Lord you're safe and sound," she says with tears, "I have prayed for you night and day. The rumors said small-pox. We heard the fighting with the African slaves. We saw the dead going into the sea. I was so afraid for you," she gushes and immediately is embarrassed as the crew stand gawking.

Oh how she melts my heart!

I am smitten and it's obvious.

She sees the men staring, covers her mouth and pulls her skirt around vanishing into the hull.

The sailors return quickly to their duties leaving me standing alone, covering a smile with my hand.

Chapter 23

"WHO CAN FIND A VIRTUOUS WOMAN? FOR HER
PRICE IS FAR ABOVE RUBIES."

PROVERBS 31:10

*Below in my cabin, I weigh the balances of the day. Not
only had I spared the Salamander and its crew for The Dutch
West India Company, but I also discovered someone cares for
me. Hmm.*

Exhausted, I fall on the bunk and sleep hard in my dirty
clothes. I wake up disgusted with the smell of my body odor as
my arm covers my brow. I sit upright and peel off the clothes I
fought in the day before.

My mind races to the young woman. She's so serious.
I like that.

I scrub my neck, head, and body. The water is dark.

Out the door I call to the cook, "Bring me another tub of water!"

Then I pull the stiff brush through my hair and tie it back.
Opening the chefarobe, I choose a white shirt and lace it, as I
bound quickly topside.

In the sunlight her brother feeds the chickens. I want to get
away from the foul smell. Too late.

He joins me. I take his elbow and route him to the galley.

"Do you have relatives ahead? Have you left family behind?"
I ask him.

Charles peers cautiously around, "Only Emma's fiancé. He
was the minister. We heard he hid in a cave."

I'm arrested by the word fiancé and stand still.

Because of what he was telling me about their faith, my abrupt halt causes Charles to fear me.

I immediately notice this and look him square in the face.

"Don't be afraid of me. We Dutch protect your right to obey God from your conscience." I say and walk slower.

He breathes a sigh of relief.

We reach the galley steps and I squint in the sun.

"You're telling me, Emma, is spoken for?" I ask.

Charles nods, heading down and leaving me behind.

I take a deep breath, *readjusting my excitement about her* and follow. The galley is cooler and smells of baking.

Emma's voice flits along the lapboards and *enters my ears as a melody.* She is reading from Psalms, "Trust in the Lord with all thine heart and lean not to thine own understanding."[73]

There she stands at the head of the table. My eyes meet hers and she pauses.

Does she feel something like I do?

She wears black ribbons in her auburn hair and a smocked dress of green print.

I can't help staring.

Charles bends over the pans on the sideboard. He takes a plate and I come quickly behind him before he notices anything between us.

Emma continues the passage.

I watch her from the corner of my eye.

I'm not hungry.

Out of habit, I spoon eggs and gravy, forking a slab of ham and sit down. Charles shovels gravy and eggs on the biscuits, talking incessantly, finding me a ready audience.

"I arranged the engagement in case I was martyred. She's a good girl," he says.

Emma quits reading and comes over to sit by him.

She's guarded.

I pick at my food, watching the other people in the galley

rake their plates at the barrel and leave. The cook pitches the cat out and it whines.

Charles whispers, "Mr. Brinkendorf assures me no harm will come to us because of our beliefs."

"You must call me Gerrit," I say, "Both of you."

Emma offers her hand, eyes down appropriately.

"A pleasure to meet you, Gerrit," she says softly.

I kiss it, without looking in her face.

Her presence touches me, but I remain calm, and turn saying, "Charles, have you made connections in New Amsterdam?"

"They can't build ships without sailmakers," he says with satisfied esteem, "Emma will help me. We plan to apprentice men and women. I understand there is a great deal of shipping going on there. Have you seen it?"

Emma turns to face me during the conversation.

I'm aware she scans my broad shoulders and admires my rugged jaw. I feel her eyes studying me as I laugh at the question.

"Hah! I was stacking beaver pelts when I was thirteen. All through the winter. We drug them by sleigh to the shore. By the time I was fifteen, I helped load ships, count furs, and keep lading accounts. This past winter I've been at the University in Amsterdam on scholarship from the Dutch West India Company," I say bragging, "They've just begun building ships in the New World. Wait til you see."

Her eyes are light green. Even in the shadows I can see her skin is delicate and ivory smooth.

She leans over her plate. A tendril of a curl hangs from her brow, another loose curl at her nape.

Charles talks on and I am polite, *but my mind is not on anything he says.*

Instead I marvel how much I feel like part of their family, and it seems like they are taking me home.

I'm drawn to them. My soul warms in their company.

I make myself not look at her, but I think of holding her close, of the sweet feminine qualities I miss, living alone.

I admire her sanctification.

Her innocence is refreshing.

I want to be near her and listen to her and know what she thinks. It's her purity I find most attractive.

A genuine soul is hard to find. This is what I think about while I'm in her company.

Her hands are gentle compared to mine, almost fragile. She moves them gracefully, naturally as she talks.

I believe she and I could talk of spiritual questions, and it would hold her interest. Yes. I wonder if she knows about words of knowledge and the Holy Spirit coming on a man.

I must find an opportunity to see how spiritual she is.

Now my days seem like a dream.

All I can do is think of her.

Jakob wanders over to me before bedtime about a week after the incident with the *Salamander*.

"I owe you," he says, "That dagger whizzed right by me. Been meaning to have a talk with you ever since," he says.

"You would have done the same for me," I say.

He shifts his body and looks uncomfortable.

"Now that's where you're wrong old boy," he reveals.

I grin, but he doesn't.

He says, "You know, what you need to realize is the fight we had securing the *Salamander* was a piece of cake. A few bewildered Africans chasing a dream to get away. They didn't know how to maneuver the ship, shoot the cannon, or wield a sword. It stands to reason we could overtake them quickly. If we hadn't done it, someone else would."

"True," I say, "You don't think a Spanish crew would have taken it as a prize? The Dutch East India Company would have lost it, if we didn't help them."

He frowns.

"What if it had happened to us?" I say.

He makes a face at me.

"I don't think we got what it takes to fight a Spanish ship if we meet one. Do you?" he asks.

"You mean because we gave up six soldiers?" I ask.

"Yeah. Risky decision. Who made it, you?" he asks.

I step back.

"Look Jakob, you live with your fears and your criticisms. Leave me out of it. God will help us," I retort.

"Yeah, I know, run a ship with Dutch secrets from God like your father did. I don't believe in all that, and I never will," he scowls.

I watch him walk away with an arrogant canter.

It gives me no pleasure to think ill of him. I've prayed for him so many times. Why is he so blasted rebellious?

Because he's jealous? That's sad.

Chapter 29

Early every morning in fair weather, Emma is on deck, beginning with a sweet hymn and reading aloud the scriptures for most of an hour. If the weather is boisterous, she reads in the galley. After supper too.

Her devotion gives me a fondness for her. From the day she told me she was afraid for me and prayed for my safety, I thought of her in a personal way, like family, like a sister. It comforts me that I let my heart be open to her.

Their religion is gentle like Thomas, like Oloff. I'm drawn to those with true religion. I wonder why it's found in only a few.

The weeks go by pleasantly. Charles, Emma, and I eat together often sharing about our past, and our hopes for the future. The chickens taste good near the end of the journey.

I make myself get acquainted with each of the passengers, having conversation when we eat or when they walk the deck.

They have dreams of a better life, of liberties and opportunities. I do my best to prepare them to give up the things they took for granted.

I pray for them at night when I take the fourth watch.

Tonight, my heart is heavy for Jakob and his need for faith.

It's raining. The ship has been tossing a great deal. Before it got cloudy, I determined we were right on course. The watchmen share a beaver coat and hat to protect us. It hangs in the navigation room when it's not in use.

The quiet time always soothes me. I like to speak the Psalms I know aloud, praising the Lord.

"The heavens declare the glory of God, the firmament showeth His handiwork, Day unto day uttereth speech and night unto night uttereth knowledge. There is no speech nor language where their voice is not heard,"[74] *I say, pausing to think how large the world is, how deep the ocean, how vast the sky. I consider every tiny baby and the wide variety of animals and plants.*

"You've made a magnificent world, God," I pray.

I pray for Evert and Wildebrand and Oloff. I mediate on the Sermon on the Mount, how Jesus taught, "Seek ye first the kingdom of God and His righteousness and all these things will be added unto you."[75]

I turn to lookout on all sides. There's a dark figure moving along the rail, bending over in the rain.

I wipe my face and look again. Someone's sick, heaving. Should the boat tip, they may lose their bearings. I hurry to assist, down the wet steps, across the slippery deck.

It's a woman. She's vomiting yellow gall. *Oh my.* As I get close, the ship tethers. She almost goes overboard. I grab her arm tightly. She's soaking wet, shivering. I plop her down on the deck.

"Wait here," I say, struggling against the shifting floor.

I face the wind spray and reach the hatch door to open it.

I call, "Don't try to stand. Crawl to me. Can you do that?"

Now my clothes cling to me. She makes her way over the careening deck until I reach for her hand and pull her by the shoulders into the hull. Water pours over us and the steps.

It's Emma. *Oh, bless her heart. My little darling.*

She's choking. I get her below and run for a blanket. She is barefoot and her hands are icy. I rub them between mine and we look at each other in surprise.

She wipes her face with her arm. I hand her a cup of water. She's shivering.

From my room, I get one of my shirts and woolen socks.

When I return, her clothes lay in a pile and she is bound tight in the blanket, her lips blue, her eyes trusting.

I put the clothes by the cannon and excuse myself to get dry myself. I hear her raspy cough.

By the time I return, the ship is calm, and she is braiding her long blonde hair, unaware I watch. She braids it on both sides. Raising her head, she draws hairpins from her mouth and secures them in circles over her ears.

I look at her wearing my long shirt and we smile.

I offer for us to sit in the galley.

"What about your watch?" she asks.

"I have sent another man," I reply.

I think I must betray my affection toward her, because she casts a thoughtful eye on my person.

"Is that normal protocol?" she asks, walking forward to the galley.

I don't want to answer that, and I don't.

"I'll see if we have something to settle your stomach," I say instead and disappear into the kitchen.

She sits across the room near the windows, waiting.

I find some ginger and make us both tea, carrying soda crackers and cane syrup.

Her face is cheerful for one who had been sick.

"I enjoy your company," she says, taking my breath away.

Oh heart, do be still.

I set the tray down. She takes the cup.

"I consider it part of my position to be hospitable to our passengers," I say, "I can sit with you until you feel better and can get some sleep. Eat something."

She nibbles a cracker. I stir some syrup in my tea.

155

"I notice you turn in early and take the fourth watch," she says, "Why do you do that?"

Suddenly I'm shy. I get up and move about.

"It's my prayer hour. I chose it," I answer.

"How long has it been a habit?' she asks between bites.

I'm caught off guard.

She searches my face and sees that.

Does she have discernment?

I blink.

Could she be checking my spiritual commitment?

My hesitation embarrasses her.

"I'm sorry. I assume too much. I was beside myself. I'm too young to hold an acceptable conversation," she says, rising to leave.

I hold her arm and lower my head to look in her eyes.

"Emma, nothing you say could be less than honorable and nothing I feel toward you is unholy. Your age has nothing to do with it," I say, letting her go, "Go dress. The deck should be drying. Let's talk some more, hmm? We can discuss our faith, our dreams."

I watch her scoot away wrapped in the blanket and put the cups and syrup up. The crackers I take back up with me.

It is still dark. The clouds are edging back to reveal stars.

She quietly joins me, with the folded blanket, and shirt in her arms.

I arrange the blanket over the fish hatch and help her up to sit there. Her shoes have little heels.

I am amazed how small she is and probably full grown.

Her ivory hand brushes stray hair from her face.

She says "Tell me about your faith, your dreams. That's what you said we would discuss."

I look away and say, "My faith, now that's the center of my heart. I want to please God according to my conscience, a Dutch custom and I read the Bible to know how. To me, that's the way God meant it. He planned how Jesus would make the sacrifice

156

to redeem us from sin.[76] He plans how I should serve Him with this body and brain in the world I've been born to. It's the world my father showed me."

"Is he a Dutch seaman too?" she asks.

I tell her all about how I went to sea with him, how he drowned, how I went to work for Evert on contract.

She says her father drowned too, at the hands of church leaders. She and Charles heard it, hiding in the bushes, not far from them. She describes her agony, her fear and I at once break into tears, talking about my mother.

Her red rimmed eyes care for my sorrow while I understand her grief.

We are bonding with the things that we both hold dear.

Presently the purple hues of dawn creep on the horizon.

We talk on about Charles' dreams and his apprenticeship before their trouble. I find out she's been tutored, a great asset for a woman. Her father had been rather wealthy, investing in Virginia tobacco.

Finally, she asks, "What do you dream for your future?"

I want to say to marry someone sweet like you.

"I don't have any really," I say.

She gives me a look meaning, "That's not fair, you're holding back."

She opens up anyway, "I want a large house where I can have room to help people, poor people, people of like faith. I want to have meetings and sing hymns. I'd like to have flower gardens and vegetable gardens and a carriage. And plenty of fireplaces in my large house to keep us all warm," she says, giggling, "Plenty of food and quilts and meat on the table."

It makes me grin.

Her outlook on life is a good one, hearty and robust with kindness. She has faith in herself.

The sun is rising, coral and purple.

Charles finds us and comes by my side.

"How long until we reach our destination?" he asks.

"Sometime today," I say, "It's no Amsterdam. Charles, I

want to ask you a personal question. Did you sense the Holy Spirit warning you before your group was arrested?"

Charles looks to Emma.

Her hand shields her eyes.

"No, Emma did. She woke me up during the night, urgent, begging me to help her flee. I was sleepy. I couldn't calm her down, so I thought I'd indulge her, and in the daylight, she'd be ready to go back home," he said, "No sooner had we climbed the hill behind our house, the lanterns came from the woods. We heard them arrest our neighbors, then they took our family."

"Don't say anymore Charles, please," Emma asks.

She walks away from us, out of hearing.

"All of them?" I ask.

"Yes. A warning to others, not to join us and not to say baptism was under the water," he says frowning.

The two of them walk to breakfast and I head down for a nap. Their story is one of persecution unfairly rendered.

I am moved by their sorrow. I love them both already.

I lay thinking about what happened to them a while.

Soundly I sleep until midday and hear birds and voices. There is activity everywhere. We're there.

As we sight land and New Amsterdam comes to view, *I see the disappointment on all their faces.* The fort is downtrodden and most of the woods are now just stumps. Rows of thatch roofed cottages and muddy thoroughfares with filth and animals straying make no welcome like the beautiful cities of Europe. It's only a crude settlement around the fort protecting the trading business.

Charles turns his gaze on the panorama view of ships anchored on the shore. The colony is desperate for all kinds of labor, forging a place to live in the wilderness.

We dispatch the lading, and I am finalizing the account when I see her and her brother crossing the deck with their belongings.

I'm sorry to see them leave my life. I decide I will visit them after they're settled. That would be polite. With her engagement, there is little more I can do and not be considered rude.

I go back to the task at hand.

Now I see them on their knees praying, before they lift their bags and load our small boat.

I won't get to say goodbye.

I wonder how I can see her again?

The woman is spoken for, I keep telling myself.

But my heart won't listen.

I could speak to Evert and recommend their character, I suppose. I could go by next week and visit. I could make an offer to invest in his sail-making business.

That would provide opportunities to see her often. It probably will be beneficial to all of us. Yes, I'll be their proprietor.

There is little else I can do and still be proper.

I can almost feel her near me, even though she's not.

Now I see Jakob helping them in the boat. He says something that arouses worry on her face.

What? I discern it's important.

Maybe I should go with them now. Yes.

Why wait 'til next week?

They need housing tonight and directions for tomorrow.

Hurriedly I call the oarsmen back. He looks baffled.

To that, I give him a stern look.

Jakob moves aside and I climb into their boat, noticing Emma covers a smile lowering her head.

Chapter 25

"...BOAZ COMMANDED HIS YOUNG MEN, SAYING,
LET HER GLEAN EVEN AMONG THE SHEAVES, AND
REPROACH HER NOT: AND LET FALL ALSO SOME OF
THE HANDFULS OF PURPOSE FOR HER, AND LEAVE
THEM, THAT SHE MAY GLEAN THEM,..."

RUTH 2:15-16

"Charles, allow me to assist you in finding room and board. I know most everyone. Come with me," I offer.

I carry Emma's satchel and walk them down the lane to The Wooden Horse.

A chicken scurries across our path clucking and splatters Emma's dress. She steps back in dismay.

Charles laughs, but I don't.

"Do you have another dress?" I ask with concern.

"Only my best," she says, "I should have parted with it and packed work blouses."

"Never mind," I offer, "All the neighbors cross the animal paths too. You won't be the only one."

We sit together dining on breaded veal with green beans and rice with raisins and cinnamon.

"I like cinnamon," Emma says, savoring the meal.

"It's one of my favorite things. Always reminds me of my father," I tell her smiling.

"Is he a seaman?" Charles asks.

"He was. Died in a shipwreck," I answer.

He and Emma become quiet.

I say, "I wonder if you'd like to open your own shop near the water, if you have the funds?"

"I don't of course, only enough for us," he replies.

"It would prove to be a wise investment for any benefactor to set you up in business and receive a share of your holdings," I say, "Don't you think?"

He's eager to talk about it.

"Do you have the connections? Someone here maybe?" he wants to know.

"I suggest you show me what it would take and where to put it. Make a list of supplies and furnishings to make it profitable. I'll be laid over for three to five days. During that time, I'll visit some people I know," I say, "Pray about it. Give me something solid to present."

"Thank you Gerrit, thank you so much," he says.

I settle them in with a widow who has two rooms and a view, a separate outhouse and well to the rear. It's the best I can find.

I make haste in a small boat out to Martha's Vineyard Island and I'm glad to see Fairchild's brother is docked there.

Well, they built a dock. Small, but welcoming.

"Thomas, the Younger, is gone," his father says at the door, "Please, come in. You remember Nehemiah, from Massachusetts? He trades with us often, an excuse to visit his sister and the baby I suspect."

We all laugh a little.

"Of course, I remember you, Nehemiah. How have you been?" I respond, reaching to shake his hand.

"No ship this trip Gerrit?" Thomas, the Elder asks me.

In the library, having tea and crumpets, I disclose my reason for coming.

"I present an investment opportunity to you of a small dependable trade," I announce.

I describe the number of ships frequenting our port from the Americas and the West Indies and the sure profit in backing the sailmaker company. I vouch for Charles and Emma, the conduct I observed at sea and that I, myself, intend to further to them five thousand guilders.

"I'll match your investment," Thomas the Elder says.

"I too," says Nehemiah, "If Mayhew trusts you, I do."

"Good," I respond, "I'm going to Evert and my friend Wildebrand. Both are good businessmen. With twenty-five thousand, that will secure all he needs until the business rakes in the rewards of his work and profits for us."

"Won't you stay and have dinner with us? Roast pork," Thomas the Elder asks, "You can talk with my son and rest yourself."

"No, I must get back. I've been on the night water half my life. It's nothing to me," I say, and they walk me out to the dock, waving as my oarsman pulls us away.

The next morning, I spy Jakob standing outside the house where I roomed Emma and Charles. His back is to me and as I near him, I realize he is talking with her by the roses.

"It's the reason most of us don't try to marry. There's always that chance that we will go down. It takes a lot of courage to be a sailor. If a storm doesn't get us, a ship full of Portuguese pirates will," he says and sees me coming.

"Good morning Emma," I say, tipping my hat, "Don't listen to this scoundrel. He is the storyteller every night at supper. Jakob, have the loggers brought the wagons to shore? We should load them first. Why don't you check?"

Across the way I spot Wildebrand coming in with the trappers. Their wagons are heavily stacked. Behind them are barrels of rum.

"I have to go now Emma. Tell Charles I will meet with him this afternoon," I say in a hurry.

"Hello Dutch," Wildebrand quips, spying me, "How's the weather in Leiden? Did you bring me a batch of jonquils?"

I laugh out loud.

"With all the flowers of the field and wood, you miss the daffodils?" I throw back at him.

"Of course. It wouldn't be the Netherlands without them. What is happening in your world today my friend?" he says watching the traffic coming from the bowery.

"I have an opportunity for you to invest in a sure thing," I say with my brows high and a look of confidence.

He and I use the first wagon that's emptied to drive back to the Huybrecht house and approach Evert with the proposition. He's at the barn, in a good mood, watching the tobacco weights press the broad leaves for stacking.

Wildebrand punches me, knowing we came at the best time. He climbs down complimenting Evert on the crop.

As soon as I present the offer, Evert is quick to take us into the house and offers brandy, a drink of his choice. I decline.

Evert says, "Let me find the location. I have a hand in these things. Can you bring the proprietor's list today? I'll draw up the contracts and send the next ship out to Mayhew before Nehemiah leaves. I think it will be loaded by now. Meet you at The Wooden Horse."

When Wildebrand and Charles sit down with me, none of us thinks Evert would take advantage of the agreement. We put the funds and the contract into his hands. Charles is happy with the building and Evert is happy with his figures.

I don't get to see Emma again that layover. I did what I could to help them and keep in their good graces.

Spring runs into summer and summer is our busiest trading time. I take loads out and passengers in, constantly.

I visit once with Charles and Emma when they have been in New Amsterdam seven months. He talks almost the whole visit, interested that I'd be glad for his success.

I say there's five equal partners, that's how it's set up.

"No," he counters, "The Huybrechts are the main share-holders. The ownership consists of eight shares, which are:

Mayhew, Lloyd, Brinkendorf, Wildebrand, me, and three parts Huybrechts. They manage the business."

I'm stunned. Friends trusted me on this.

He wants to show me the cabin he's raising in the forest on Manhattan Island.

I'm not interested today.

He takes me to the back of the building where they have set up house. Emma is busy about the kitchen and never has time to eat with us, though she serves us potato soup and hot bread with molasses.

He describes the process of soaking the hemp that comes from the field and how he uses it for both the sails and the ropes. He describes the long ropewalk needed for making the rope and says he has to spread it with tar. He opens his blackened hands.

"How can I get a wife when my hands look like this?" he laughs, "All day Emma sews sails. It's rough on her."

I attempt to see her face, even once. It does not happen and *discourages me from staying longer.*

I decline to go to the shipyard with him and make excuses about my time of departure and business obligations.

Word of our recovery of the *Salamander* has made me a hero in Amsterdam and when the news reaches New Amsterdam, Evert Huybrecht gives me a fine parchment commendation with a gold seal, saying I am rewarded for my bravery in time of distress in the amount of fifty thousand guilders, safely placed in the account set up in my name with the Dutch West India Company.

I show no one. Why should I?

But I sign a draft to the church for the tithe I owe.

It was God who gave us safety and prospered me. I would not forget to thank Him, my true benefactor.

At The Wooden Horse, Evert makes his point about his dislike for my friendship with Wildebrand.

"Lately I hear you eat at the Sail Away tavern. You won't do that anymore," he says, "I forbid it."

I try to defend myself when his hand shoots between us.

"Not a word. You're not going to be involved. Our company reputation," he states, "Non-negotiable."

Walking along Front Street, I see the newly painted sign, "Strong Sails in the Sun" over their establishment. It's closed on Lord's Day.

At the widow's house I call for them, but she says it is their practice on Sunday to meet with those of their kind.

She sneers when she says it, *in a tone I don't like* and watches me walk away.

No one has seen Wildebrand. They say he's gone to Amsterdam. It makes them nervous when I ask.

Chapter 26

"MY TIMES ARE IN THY HAND: DELIVER ME FROM
THE HAND OF MINE ENEMIES,..."

PSALM 31:15

At the beachfront, Evert waits for me in his carriage.

"Get in. A private conversation, Gerrit," he says.

I climb in and there sits Jakob.

"I'm told you're more than friendly with the Anabaptists. Not in a business way. Personally. Is that true? Don't lie to me," he accuses.

I look nervous. *He gives me no chance to talk.*

"All right. You may go, Jakob," Evert says, placing coins in his hand.

"Nothing at fault with your work Gerrit. From this moment, you will meet our shipments at Mayhew's plantation and transport them with my sealed orders. Your shipments will be received there, and you won't come to New Amsterdam, until I send for you. Is that understood?' he asks.

I frown and nod my head.

"Should there be any failure on your part to be honest, join a revolt against Stuyvesant or interfere with the shipping empire I'm building, I will see you in irons or worse." he says.

He keeps his hand on the door handle and stares me down so quietly ugly. Again he has succeeded in putting me beneath him.

Only when he sees I'm resigned, does he open the door with a stony look.

I ride the dinghy out to the *Morgenster*, sad that I will only see it ofttimes. I've grown attached to it as my home.

The trip to Martha's Vineyard Island is dreary. The fog lays over us most of the way adding to my dismal feelings.

Jakob avoids me. He should, the weasel.

Disappointed in him and Evert, *I feel haunted by the indenture that binds me and being separated from Emma and Charles. I hoped for happiness in their company, even invested much of my savings in them.*

Going to the Mayhew house is like home for me.

Over dinner, Thomas the Elder says, "You seem out of sorts, Gerrit. You're among friends. Can we be of help?"

I tell them, "I didn't get to see the man we invested in. From out of nowhere, my master scolded me about them and forbids me to come to New Amsterdam. I'm to use your port as a base to swap ships until further notice."

Nehemiah says, "Things grow increasingly unstable."

Thomas the Elder, elbows on the table, hands folded under his face, says, "The fact is the Dutch West India Company is considered a failure. Men with revenue are in a quandary. The pressure mounts as to how to make the raw materials bring the income to cover their overhead."[77]

He sits back and takes a deep breath.

He says, "Not only are there large monies on the table, but authorities that would perhaps imagine empires. And given the climate of New Amsterdam, there's opposition to religions that have broken off to themselves. Your Director-General, with an administration to protect trade is enforcing his opinion on the populace. He thinks one religion brings unity. They say Quakers have come in."[78]

The room is quiet.

I think about that for a minute while we eat.

"Why, when they're protected in the Lowlands?" I ask.

Nehemiah turns to me saying, "Son, all of us try to keep

war from destroying our efforts. Huybrecht most likely knows you are a valuable asset others might make a pawn."

His words strike me like lightning. Who wants to use me as a pawn? Evert? Or Wildebrand? My mind goes back to the day Jakob picked the fight. Has he always been jealous of something I have? I don't understand.

What is he trying to do, behind my back with Evert?

Does he want Emma? I called him a scoundrel in front of her. If I can't get into New Amsterdam, he can't either. And if he goes behind my back off ship, what about at sea?

The men discuss problems in England. I hear only part.

"England is in a civil war. To have a Catholic queen was absurd. King Charles sports himself above God," Nehemiah says, "The ministers here have written The Cambridge Platform, uniting as a body politic to enforce their position.[79] Meanwhile Cromwell's army is taking over, and the king is locked in prison."[80]

"I didn't know. I'm sorry to hear it, really I am," I say.

"The Stuart family of Scotland has been on the throne for years. I fear the worst for them should Oliver Cromwell take over,"[81] he says and sets his glass down frowning, "I won't send my ship to England. I'll trade at Jamestown. My profits will be lower, but it's better than losing my ship."

I ask, "Do you believe God shows people things to come?"

Thomas the Elder breaks the ice, saying, "We hope so."

"I mean to warn us? Guide us?" I ask.

The silence that follows causes me to excuse myself.

I don't see Jakob when I come back to the ship in the morning. I'm told he kept the fourth watch, although I was on the veranda at the house and didn't see him.

We sail away under a good strong headwind, the stores full of food for us, the best we've ever had.

By and by the cook asks my opinion.

"Most of these vegetables will only last this week. Do I have permission to use them as I think best?" he asks.

"Whatever you think," I say, "As much as you want."

A week goes by and still no Jakob. He is dodging me.

The cook complains of rats getting in the flour. That won't do. We must keep it clean for our survival.

I call for a dagger match next three nights.

After dinner that night, the cheese is by the back wall, and we wait. Suddenly Jakob appears, slinking behind the fellows that work close to him and I sense danger.

The crew crouch in the shadows, daggers in hand.

Out run the rats, scurrying in a herd. We do have a lot.

The tinging noise and thud of the flying knives fills the air along with the squeal of rodents wounded.

One dagger, out of nowhere, flies by my chest.

Quickly I look back at the source. Jakob has fled, two men with him.

No one saw it but me.

The game is over. I quickly remove the blade.

Unknowingly, the crew dispatches to their duty posts and hammocks as determined.

The cook sweeps the varmits in a pile to fling overboard. He passes me standing alone, with the bucket in his hand.

"Now when did that get there?" the cook says to me.

"What?" I ask.

"That cut in the wood," he says frowning, "Weren't there before. I pass this door every day. Weren't there before I say. Somebody trying to get you Captain?"

"No," I say, "I assure you. Nothing will happen to me. You probably didn't notice it before."

He's a jolly man, fared from Ireland last year.

"I'm sure of it. The cut is fresh. See, the wood is light. Hasn't had time to weather. You need angels watching you, ye do," he says, "Like me. I felt the Spirit of God say, 'Git up. Git outta' this place, Jerome. You don' a want to be here when the killing comes. So, I caught me a rowboat and we crossed over. When you came to port, I liked the sound of ye boat's name. I asked the others, 'What's it mean, *Morgenster?*' They say, Morning Star. I said, 'That's the one for me. Yessir, Captain."

He carries out the rats and rinses the bucket.

I wait curious.

As he enters the galley again, no one is around.

"Come on back and have the last peach sir," he says, "and I'll give ye a bit of advice."

I walk behind him cautiously, *wondering if it's a trap.*

"Here, it's shriveled, but sweet," he says, handing me the peach and taking the mop out to the floor.

"I'll rinse it later. Don't want to keep you waiting. Ye might make your footsteps heard on the stair just in case they think you're down here with me," he says, "Go on."

I step deliberately loud down the aisle and climb most of steps, softly retreating back into the kitchen.

"That's better," he says, and closes the galley window, leaving only a slat that he perches himself to look through.

"They plan to stiff you," he says, "Anyway they can. It's a game to them, see? They bet on who can get you first. The tall one, he wants to take your place. Tells the others, you're dim-witted. Says he's got favor with the company and the House of Hambrick."

"Huybrecht," I correct him, "How many of them?"

"Five," he says searching my face with a frown.

I consider the information and search his face.

"You better go now, before they suspect me," he says.

Chapter 27

"FOR MINE ENEMIES SPEAK AGAINST ME; AND
THEY THAT LAY WAIT FOR MY SOUL TAKE COUNSEL
TOGETHER,"

PSALM 71:10

In the twilight, I watch the sharks skim about the boat.

Two more rat killings fill the cook's bucket, but I don't go. I take my dinner alone in the navigation room.

We're in a lull. The wind has died down.

I need to sleep *but I don't know if I trust the soldiers.*

Every time I go to prayer at three, Jakob assembles a fishing group and prevents me from being alone.

I can't complain. The storeroom is full of salted catch. We've had no storms since we left.

The cook acts always busy.

I don't want him at risk.

Then while eating a biscuit, I bite into a sliver of metal. I pull it out, blood on my hand *and thank God I didn't swallow it.* I fork through the rest of the biscuit and see several chards of metal. My eyes dart over the rail.

Who brought me my breakfast? I wasn't paying attention.

That man could be innocent.

Someone put it in before it was baked. Of course, I suspect the cook. But why would he tell me, then turn?

Quietly alone, I pray, "Lord, protect me."

In my heart, I hear, "I am protecting you. The knife missed you and you caught the slivers. No weapon formed against you shall prosper."[82]

Suddenly I grow bold. My thoughts shift from fear to worship. He who sees everything knows me and I am His. I'm His property. His will can triumph over Jakob, Evert, anything.

I feel the Spirit of God come upon me like a rushing holy courage. Angels fight with me. I'm really in no danger.

I laugh within myself, so relieved.

"Thank you, Jesus," I say in a whisper.

Stepping out in the midday sun, I fairly skip down the steps to the main deck.

"Enough fishing in the night. We have more than I can possibly sell now," I command, "Every man gets a good night's rest. We may need your strength if we meet up with an opposing vessel. Hear? No fishing tonight."

Things go back to normal. Jakob does what he has to.

He won't look at me, but I don't ignore him.

My Irish cook is singing in the kitchen one morning.

"Do you ever have someone help you make breakfast?" I ask, "Someone who mixes the biscuits?"

"Yeah, Beauregard," he says smiling, "On rainy days."

I say, "We haven't had any rainy days."

"I told him that, but he insisted. He said he got up early to help me," he says, "That's him, with Jakob."

I don't turn around.

"What are we having tonight?" I ask.

Whatever he replied, *I didn't listen, only pretending to.*

My ears are tuned to the conversation echoing in the galley.

"Should be easy to get rid of him," Jakob says low.

I turn and walk out. They're looking hard at the cook. To them, he's in the way. They want to get at me.

I fast my supper tonight and turn in early.

I'm not afraid anymore for myself, yet my soul is anxious. I toss and fret.

Later I fall into a deep sleep.

I wake abruptly to find someone on the floor by my feet.

No moonlight. It's pitch-black in my room.

I don't hear snoring. I don't hear breathing. I reach out and touch an arm, a head.

Footsteps run away from the door. *Two men,* I think.

Fumbling, I step over this person and find my way to the top, grabbing the deck lantern and seeing no man.

I return and hold the light over the floor. My Irish cook lies dead with a knife in his back. I jerk back in shock.

Then I hold my lantern out the door to see up and down the hall. Nothing. I get my pistol, load it, and sit on the bed.

Was he trying to help me?

Was he hoping I'd protect him?

I don't know how many are in on this.

Telling me cost him his life.

There are voices in the galley.

Quickly I get dressed, keeping the pistol close and ready.

I decide to face them. What else can I do?

"Lord, I believe and declare Your angels surround me.[83] *Like Elisha, I have angel armies here with me. I'm your servant."*

I step into the kitchen and there are five men with knives drawn. I face them holding the pistol.

"What's this?" I say, standing firm.

Jakob grins.

In a snarly voice he says, "The rats come out at night."

One of them snickers behind him.

"We thought we'd have a killing and feed the sharks," he says, "Do you think you'd like to have a go with us?"

"Why waste my gunpowder on rodents?" I say.

He steps forward.

I stare at him.

"We don't like it that ye tell us we can't fish late. We were doing so well. If it makes more profit, we could impress the Patroon. Or do ye want all the glory for yourself?" he questions.

My face hardens. I feel my muscles tighten.

"We have enough fish. We may have too many sailors," I hiss and walk across to view them all carefully.

"Ohh, mighty pirate's son," Jakob mocks, "No one will find your body. Do you have a visitor in your room, eh?"

I see a man targeting me. He lifts a dagger. I shoot him in the belly. He groans and bowls over.

The pistol aside, the others decide to charge me.

I draw my knife from the sleeve and face them.

"Which one wants to be fish bait?" I ask and hear footsteps hurrying down.

Two soldiers with muskets come behind me.

"What goes on here Commander? Mutiny?" the first asks.

"Indeed. Make your mark men. If they lay down, we'll be merciful. If not, fire away. They murdered our cook," I say.

It's apparent Jakob wants to attack. The others hang back. I throw it at his feet. His nostrils flare. *Hatred is in his eyes.*

He hesitates and the soldiers aim at him.

His hand drops the knife and the others lay down too.

I retrieve my dagger as the soldiers tie their hands, leading them to the supply room where they're separated between the cannon and their feet shackled and chained.

The noise wakes everyone and sets the crew on edge.

We wrap the cook in a sail, and I speak a prayer for his burial at sea, knowing the rats will gouge him if we tarry.

How many knew about it, I don't know.

More than ever I feel alone, except for Jesus. He who had enemies for no reason knows my heart. I can't pray like I did. My spirit hurts from the sad events.

I wrestle with how I should manage the outcome.

After breakfast, I sit in the Commander's quarters and write an explanation to the Dutch West India Company.

It's hard to put into words.

I go about the daily routine, asking if the prisoners are fed, are they well?

I know they are not comfortable and that is no fault of my own. I hardly have accommodations for prisoners.

I will send a soldier to the Dutch West India Company administration ahead of me with the letter.

In that way, I allow them time to consider before I bring the general report.

I wish for them to bring the charges before the Republic and not I. After all, a murder was committed. The ship was in danger. The man who tried to report their uprising is dead. Surely, they have the right to make the complaint.

I merely took the authority required to halt their attempt to rob the company of their rightful ownership.

The charge? Piracy on the high seas. Murder. Attempted mutiny. The two soldiers and I are witnesses.

As soon as we come to Amsterdam, I send the letter ahead. I expect the prisoners to be taken to the authorities where I can go back to business as normal. Evert will be waiting.

While we are unloading, the messenger returns, not the soldier I sent. He hands me an official wax sealed envelope.

All my appointed soldiers have gone ashore except one that guards Jakob and his gang.

The letter says I must stay for the trial. Nothing about the soldiers. They've been questioned and say they don't know what happened before they got there. They believe we had personal differences and that was the rumor onboard.

The ship belongs to the Huybrecht House and though it contracts to the Dutch West India Company, the final responsibility is theirs.

Within the hour, the ship is impounded, the prisoners carted off and I face a crew waiting to be paid with nowhere to go.

I have sufficient funds in my account and settle the payroll, saving receipts signed from each man.

I post the letter to Evert on a ship that goes out today and look at the balance of my guilders. Forty-six.

They make me wait a week before we have a docket in The Hague. A legal representative for the Huybrechts meets me by the columns, outside the entry.

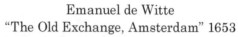

Emanuel de Witte
"The Old Exchange, Amsterdam" 1653

Wikimedia Commons / Public Domain
Museum Boijmans Van Beuningen

"You're Commander of the *Morgenster*?" he asks, "She's no longer impounded. Lucky thing I heard of it. I'm doing them a favor. You hand deliver this bill of my expenses to Evert Huybrecht. Should it not arrive, you'll not be hired again, understand?"

He expects a bow, *obviously knows I'm indentured*. I do.

"When we come before the States General, you'll hear our discourse, but make no comment in the chamber. None. Keep your place," he warns.

We are called. I follow him. He talks confidently and in legal terms. Jakob is convicted for killing the Irishman. The sentence is banishment. The others receive servitude until their fine is paid, five thousand guilders or five years, for participating in attempted mutiny.

The gavel falls and we leave.

"There's the ship. Do whatever you do," he says.

I go to the Dutch West India Company Administration building and ask for the Huybrecht cargo from eight days ago. I sit for an hour while someone checks at the warehouse.

Passengers approach me about the fare, wondering if I will refuse.

Why should I?

They show me identification. They are Jews. I meet their faces with honesty.

"You are protected in my country, and you are welcome on my boat. You travel as a group?" I respond.

"We are relatives of the same grandfather," he says.

"I will give you a special price. One is free. Only pay for seven and eight travel," I say.

They smile at each other.

"Which one is free?" the old woman asks.

I look at the group, *all of them strong, bright-eyed.*

I bow and answer, "You are my lady. For you, no cost."

The messenger returns and the clerk calls my name.

"Go there and show them your credentials. They'll pack it again if the supply is inhouse," the clerk says.

By sundown it's loaded. I haven't seen my crew all week.

Time is of the essence.

"Lord, I am so tired. Please give me a new crew," I pray.

Some men are standing around the docks as usual.

Down the street march twenty four soldiers, all ordered for our journey. When the sailors see them coming to me, they flock over asking for work. In one hour, I hire forty men. *Hopefully, I've got a better group.* I had fifty-three.

Well, this time I've got two cooks, one named Dirk.

We pull anchor and catch the wind before the evening tide. The sun is low.

I assign duties, bunks and hammocks, weapons, and schedules. Most of these men are Scots. *I ask no questions.*

We all eat heartily tonight and work at understanding each other's language. Half of them will fish through the night and sleep tomorrow.

I have six Englishmen and four Dutch. My navigator is Dutch. Good.

Before I go to bed, I go over the cargo inventory.

Some things I haven't shipped before: medicine, damask, fine writing paper, measuring equipment, saffron, sassafras and sarsaparilla.

As for me, I plan to start this crew out fresh with Bible study. I will tell them what my father learned and how we need it. I'll build a crew that can agree in prayer and all of us know the Spirit's gifts. And that will keep the peace.

Maybe I didn't reach Jakob.

I won't hide it from them. I'll tell them how jealousy poisons a man's heart. I'll talk about sensing danger and becoming valuable assets.

Maybe these men don't love Holland or its World Bank. But they came to us, and we took them in.

In the morning mist, down the English Channel a fishing boat rows hard to signal us coming from Adelburgh.

"Don't turn 'em away Captain," the men on board plead.

We can see they're peasants, scrawny and fearful of us.

"What is it you want?" I shout in English.

"Sire, not for me self, mind ye. For these young ones. Sons and nephews. Take them with you. Please?" a broad backed fisherman asks.

The crew looks to me, hopeful.

The fisherman is frightened at something behind him.

I say, "All of you then. You, too. Come on. You'll earn your keep. Jobs and enough to eat. Come on."

My men drop the rope ladder over to them and reach to help the boys climb.

"Not me. Just the boys this time, thank ye. I got to stay with my missus. She ain't well. Hurry lads," he says.

We pull the last one up and he steers the boat away.

I order the boys below to be fed and watch with the spyglass as a group of men take over the fisherman and his boat. They wrestle him and throw his body over the side.

It numbs me the rest of the day.

Chapter 28

"BUT THOU SHALT REMEMBER THE LORD THY GOD: FOR IT IS HE THAT GIVETH THEE POWER TO GET WEALTH,..."

DEUTERONOMY 8:18

After dinner I ask, "Who's been to the New World?"

No hands. I shake my head and smile.

"I have a proposition for you. Each morning, I will meet with everyone that wants to know about the Bible, about Dutch pirate secrets and about the New World. My father was a great pirate. I have read the entire Bible and I lived in New Holland for six years before I became Commander," I say, "Besides, I have been to the University at Leiden and can tell you many interesting things about science, and nature and philosophy."

Our Jewish family politely leaves.

"Can you tell us how to get rich?" a hairy Scotsman asks.

"Yes, I know many rich men. You are going where dreams can come true. And where everyone must work hard. There are those that are becoming quite wealthy. I can't say they're happy," I raise my brows and grin.

I pace and proceed to say, "Now most of you have left war behind. In all its ugly venom, killing has always been the devil's tool to sour your heart and turn you from God."

Every eye rivets on me when I talk like this.

"Dead religion murders without conscience. The Pharisees did it to the Prince of Peace. Jesus went about doing good and healed all that were oppressed by the devil. People loved Him. And Jesus died to change dead religion. He told Nicodemus, 'Ye must be born again, like a newborn baby.' He told the religious experts their hearts were like corpses in the grave.[84] There's a lot of difference in a dead body decaying in the cold ground and an innocent newborn baby. In your heart, which are you?" I say, "Each one of you were destined to be on this boat with me tonight so I could say, Jesus invites you to become His disciple. He told me to ask you that."

Heads turn and the men look at each other.

"I won't have the war you've come from spill over into useless fights between us. Last month I had to take six of my men prisoner because they let the poison of jealousy and hatred takeover their minds. They murdered an innocent man and attempted mutiny," I say.

Dirk comes out wiping a pan and listens.

"Here is the first Dutch pirate secret. God warns me of danger and angels protect me. That's how I knew what they we're trying to do. It's how the Dutch took the twelve million in gold from the Spanish fleet, along with forty ships. I invite you to surrender your life to Jesus Christ, with all your heart, all your mind, all your soul and all your strength.[85] To do that will cause you to become the best you can be," I say.

The boys look nervous.

"No one forces you to take on my religion, understand. God calls you to come of your own free will.[86] I have hired you as you are." I say, "I command you to keep the peace. I want a crew that's in one accord. But the invitation to be a disciple is a personal one. If you don't accept it, that's your choice. I won't bring it up again. It's between you and the Almighty. You may pray anytime, anywhere and answer His call to follow Him."

I look about the room. Some hold their heads down, some look away. *I think I'm finished* and leave the room.

I sleep soundly and Dirk wakes me at three as I asked. He starts the fire for breakfast, and I start the prayers for our day.

All is quiet, the ship making good headway under a strong west wind. I approach the night watchman and he stretches.

"Aye, Captain. Out to sea now," he says, "I'm a mite frightened of it, the deep may have monsters."

"What's your name sailor?" I ask.

"James Sutton," he answers.

"Old wife's tales, mate. Nothing like that. No dragons or fairies or such. Hmm?" I say, "No ghosts or goblins."

He searches my face. I smile assuredly.

I say, "Get yourself some sleep. Angels are real. They protect us and only do good. God controls the storms and hides us from our enemies."

"I been thinkin' 'bout what you said to us, about Jesus and our whole heart. I like that," he tells me.

"When you curl up in your hammock, turn yourself away from the others and have a silent talk with Him. He'll be glad to hear from you. He'll give you a new heart," I say.

As he walks the deck, the moonlight breaks through the clouds and shines around us. He looks up to the sky.

I pray for my new crew and those I knew back home. I pray for Emma and hope I'm not intruding because she's married. I ask God to help me train my men how to coordinate their duties and I thank Him again and again for delivering me from the schemes that Jakob planned.

I don't know how Evert and his father will take it. I'm young to be Commander. A lot has happened. Evert made it worse when he paid Jakob to spy on me.

I decide to cast all my care on the Lord and not worry about it, as I open the Bible with the coming dawn. I slip below to get a tinder to light my lantern, smelling buttermilk biscuits and fried bacon. I pour myself some coffee and climb back above. It's good to be on the water again, I think.

Good to be at peace in my soul.

As we finish breakfast, I stand to teach 1 Timothy and read: "Have nothing to do with irreverent folklore and silly myths.

On the other hand, discipline yourself for the purpose of godliness.[87] Godliness is of value in everything since it holds the promise for this life and for life to come."

The boys are seated close by me. I speak toward them.

"Let no one look down on you because of your youth but be an example and set a pattern for the believers in speech, in conduct, in love, in faith, and in moral purity,"[88] I say, "Jesus taught 'Love your neighbor as you love yourself.'[89] Do for other people what you would want done for you."

I say, "That means here on this voyage and everywhere you go. When I was a boy, I became an indentured servant. That opportunity will be available in the New World. The men that buy you for six or seven years can treat you harshly. For that God will punish them. They may humiliate you, overwork you, even punish you with pain. If you run away, you'll be caught, and things will get worse. But if you have self-control over pride and your temper, God can reward you in ways others don't receive."

Dirk brings the last of the cooked food and sets it in the middle of the table. A few men take that interruption as a good place to leave. The boys grab a biscuit or bacon and crowd closer. I talk about Joseph and his trials. I describe the backwoods beauty of the Catskills and trapping beaver.

The first week some stay for devotions.

I remember Emma reading from her Lutheran Bible. She'd be proud she had influenced me if she could see me now. Thomas would too. This is what he would do.

The second week, I teach them how to memorize like my father taught me. At dinner, I tell them the stories of Piet Hyen, Moses,[90] Solomon,[91] and Daniel[92]. When I talk about the battle when the sun stood still half a day,[93] they roar with laughter at how God did something extraordinary. And when I tell how Peter denied Jesus, they are still.[94]

Eventually most every man and boy seek me out to tell me what's on their mind and I counsel what the Bible says.

I must help with duties because most are inexperienced.

I'm patient in training them knowing they can become valuable assets. I talk about the trade skills and the emerging community that surrounds the trading post.

When there's time I urge them to learn languages and I share a few common phrases.

We complete the voyage a week early and I send the dinghy ahead to notify Evert I'm in, explain the attempted mutiny and the trial, and give him the bill from the lawyer.

Dining at the Mayhew house, I can't wait to ask about our investment and how do things look?

Thomas the Elder, passes the sliced turkey breast and nods, "You recommended a favorable investment. Yes, we received a pleasing dividend. The business was liquidated. Seems your friend Wildebrand went to the Dutch Republic with signed petitions as a citizen representative and has been refused permission to return to Manhattan."

Oh no. I don't know what to think. How could that happen? Wildebrand loved the New World.

Fairchild comes to the door and the old man sees her, motioning her to come to the table.

I ask, "How long since you've seen Nehemiah?"

"He was here in September. King Charles was beheaded in January, you know. The civil war goes on. Nehemiah left me with two Scottish orphans, hoping they could work for me. Cromwell is enslaving them, Scots and Irish. It was Nehemiah's last trip. He sold his ship to a man who trades in the West Indies. Sugar, I suppose. Jamaica," he says.

Upset, I stop eating.

Fairchild shows us the new baby, a boy this time. She says Thomas the Younger's congregation has grown. He has a teacher helping him.

She leaves, saying, "I only came for a cup of flour."

Thomas the Elder smiles watching her out the window.

"I eat alone so much of the time, Gerrit. It's good to have you, someone with whom I can have a decent conversation," he says,

"Nehemiah has had serious thoughts about the strict punishments in his colony. He watched them brand a man for burglary with a letter 'B' in his forehead. The same man stole again, and they clipped one of his ears off, warning him if he was caught again, they'd execute him. A neighbor's boy was rebellious and was heard to curse. They put him to death. For every piece of fruit on a tree or pumpkin in the field, punishments are written and the people in the strictest way, pride themselves righteous if they catch one breaking the law. They turn on each other, he said."

Before I leave, he takes me to the closet in the hallway. Thomas the Elder hands me a folded English flag.

Silently he is giving me the key to visit him.

In the night, the replacing Huybrecht fluyt arrives. I hear it creaking on the water, being familiar with such things.

I sit on the veranda and see them lower the sails and drop anchor. The watchman spies me and drops the plank to hurry over and give me a return letter from Evert.

I have new orders. On the next trip back, I'm told to bypass Martha's Vineyard Island. Trouble with the English.

Tomorrow I should sail this ship south one day, then straight up to Holland. Don't stop at Leiden. Make our rations last. Return loaded with Scottish refugees to become indentured servants as soon as possible. Report to him on my return, at any hour.

Back in Amsterdam, I check my account balance when I go to the Dutch West India Company Administration building. Nothing. No reimbursement for the wages I paid. No deposit for my investment in Charles' business.

Every time I come in, Evert meets me at night, and he sends him right back out, without chance to ask about Charles or Emma. Always I bring in Irish and Scottish refugees. Always I take out the raw resources so plentiful from the New World. Eight trips I make in three years.

And always I think about Emma.

Chapter 29

"LET NO MAN SEEK HIS OWN, BUT EVERY MAN
ANOTHER'S WEALTH."

1 CORINTHIANS 10:24

In the spring of 1656, I dock in New Amsterdam and pick up a letter from Thomas:

My dear friend Gerrit,

I am constrained to write, having not heard from you in three years now. My work with the Indians has progressed so heartily that I am making a trip to England in hopes that the missionary society will see to it I have some help with caring for the two hundred and eighty three Wampanoag converts now in my care. I have formed an Indian school and hold two meetings each Sabbath. Hiacoomes sends you greetings, and we both wish to know if you are well. He says please come to Great Harbor and meet with us. You will be surprised to see how many sons I have and how tall they are. The seasons have been good for our crops. Refresh our hearts and come by soon.

Yours in Christ
Thomas Mayhew, the Younger
April 1652
Mayhew Plantation, Martha's Vineyard Island

I had only read it when another is brought by carrier and given to me at the landing. It's from Charles. I instruct the crew to hoist the sails and lead out to Martha's Vineyard, while I gently peel back the wax and *prepare my heart for news from the love of my heart.* In privacy, I sit alone absorbing the few lines.

> December 1653.
> Our brother Commander Brinkendorf,
> I am posting this note hoping it finds you healthy and prosperous as you serve Christ in your given capacity. We have new opportunities and are obliged to move to Rhode Island, although the particulars are vague, so I must be.
> Please look us up. We are always and ever happy to be in your company.
>
> With warm regards,
> Charles

Why is he referring to "we"? Does he mean to include Emma, or is he speaking of his wife and children? What particulars must he be vague about? Is he in some kind of trouble? Perhaps he is ill. I should go to him. Or maybe there is a business loss that has strapped him, and he needs help. I do count him a friend and honest. Which port? He doesn't say. The letter is three years old.

My mind stays continually on Emma. Is this his way of beckoning me toward her? Surely by now, she's married and settled down. It's likely she's moved to her husband's place of trade. Maybe she's no longer with him. But what if she is? What if she's waiting for me?

I smile in spite of myself. That thought keeps tickling the edges of my mind like the ripples of the water below us. It runs deep, my feelings for delicate little Emma. She must be twenty by now.

Evert has me meet him in front of The Wooden Horse. In wet boots I walk to the carriage. Inside I view the new red leather seats. Evert has shaved off his beard and coifed his hair. He makes me talk by cover of night in the carriage going down the road. I haven't been to the Huybrecht house in five years. No one is up. We go in the rear entrance, and he makes me leave my boots inside the door.

In the library hangs a framed world map almost the size of the wall. I walk over, amazed at the view.

"Where is Jakarta?" I ask, running my finger up close, "And New Zeeland?"

He fills an ivory pipe and relaxes on the divan.

"Would you like to go farther away? It can be arranged," he says, "I have a ship loaded now for the Caribbean. Let me see, (He reads the lading), seven hundred twenty-four planks of pine, twelve hundred forty-five pounds of English hardbread, two barrels of bacon, seventy-five skipples of peas and ten Irish slaves, women to be cross bred with Negroes, each worth one hundred, thirty pieces of eight. Light skinned Negroes are more valuable sold as house servants."

"My indenture is up in a week," I respond, weary of his greed, "I haven't received the reimbursement for the payroll or the dividend from my investment in Charles' business."

"Yes, well, I have it all on record. I'll see you get it. I rather thought you'd put it to better use to become a shareholder with us, a partner in the Huybrecht firm. I would recommend you marry my sister. She's rather well-to-do and widowed, recently. She lives in Amsterdam in a fine house. I don't think she'd approve of living here, but if you're at sea, it shouldn't matter. We're moving our trade routes to the slavery business. That would mean trade routes from the West Indies to Africa and back."

I sit by the fire and think *what a schemer he is, saturated in making more money. He does not even look at my face.*

"I've drawn up a new contract. That's why I invited you here. It's for another seven years. I included the particulars of the partnership when you marry my sister. To marry her will make you then the ninth richest man in the world."

And make me a permanent slave of yours, I think.

"I have six more days. What do you require?" I ask.

He rises and comes near me, *a fraudulent pose of caring.*

"Use those days to visit your friends at Martha's Vineyard and think it over. You'll adore the posh mansion you inherit on the Herengracht Canal, two plots wide, near the Golden Bend. After seven more years, you'll be independently wealthy and retire to your pleasure, won't you?" he peers at me with raised brows.

I rise to leave, and he continues rehearsing his "deal" while seeing me outside.

"I have an English flag I use when I need it. Do you want anything from Martha's Vineyard?" I ask.

"I could certainly use a gardener," he says, and I nod.

The boat is being unloaded on the beach at dawn. As the merchants and carpenters come with their wagons, I distribute their wares and tell them I'll be back in five days with fresh vegetables. The tavern keeper wants it all. He and the general store clerk go away arguing.

We have a strong headwind and swiftly make Mayhew's plantation in two days. Thomas sees us approaching and I view him ordering the servants to prepare landing for us with a welcoming refreshment. *How like him, so kind.*

I stay by the bow, leaning forward in anticipation.

They are the only family I feel I have in the world, and I bless the day I met them.

Thomas and I sit on the cliffs overlooking the ocean and share the sweet rolls from breakfast.

"We are at war, our countries," I say, turning to him.

He shrugs, *as if it does not matter to us.*

"I need to talk to someone I respect and has my best interest at heart," I blurt, all at once.

He smiles slightly and squints at me.

"I knew that when I saw your face," he says plainly.

"It's like this. My stewardship is up. Evert is pressing me to marry his sister and come into the firm."

"Lady Flortina? His Lordship Sir Ruebensen must have died. I didn't know," he remarks.

"Lost at sea. *The Fentress*," I say, "I don't want to marry her. I've been in love with the same woman seven years and feared to ask her hand. I've been at sea. I don't know how to make a living if I give up shipping. My indenture is finished. What do you think?"

Thomas looks out across the land and smiles.

"You lose some things when you marry. I haven't always been grateful for my wife, Gerrit. Consider how stubborn your habits may be," he says wisely, his face soft, "At first marriage is exciting, warm, and tender. Then a responsibility of relationship chaps one's selfish side. You've been alone a long time ol' boy."

He gives me a knowing grin and pulls off his jacket.

"Fairchild aged some after the last child's delivery, her face wrinkling round the eyes, the veins in her hands protruding. I paid little attention to the vast workload she carried, until that long winter. It was to be the Lord's correction for me, an ungrateful husband. It was bitter cold when our fifth child was coming. We were stuck in the house while the birthing came. When it was over, the midwife left the newborn on her. She had fallen asleep nursing. The midwife, with her hands on her hips, glanced at the four little ones huddled by the fire and then at me. 'Sire, it be none of my business to say, but if'n ye can't carry on this house for at least three or four days, these children will be without their der mudder come summer," she remarked. I stared at her in disbelief. 'A body has only so much strength. Men are more careful to their harses then thar womenfolk,' she mumbled looking down, afraid of me, I suppose."

"I was in a daze as I watched her clean the bloody floor and toss the rags in the fire. The boy's eyes were wide, and they backed away. John clung to my leg, 'Papa,' his innocent face searched mine. Little Matt held his hand to his mouth. As soon as the nurse had left, John took Matt's hand and pulled him to the chair. Pushing him up on it, he climbed beside him and snuggled into the quilt lying on its arm. Andrew leaned over on his brother, and they looked at me. Jedediah blinked and frowned, kicking a cinder back toward the fire in defiance. All this while Fairchild was sleeping with the wee girl on her shoulder. I decided I must keep house, setting my mind to fix the meals, the fire and help my own. They needed me," he stares out at the sunset.

"I guess I can't have a wife and be at sea," I question.

"Men love adventure, challenges, the openness of nature. Women were created with a desire to please a man. It's torment to leave them alone. God is grieved with our selfishness. We hide it behind the necessity to provide. Even my simple Indians, going out to hunt or fish, occupying great lengths of time as they choose. They ignore the emotional emptiness they create at home," he sighs, standing to stretch his legs.

I lift my knapsack and join him walking back to his house.

"If you marry her, Gerrit, be kind to her. If you can't, leave her be," he says softly, "Marriage is God's mirror to show us our selfish nature. The Bible says we have either war or peace inside ourselves. My family has managed to stay out of the Dutch war. I see you fly our flag."

He points. I return a nod.

Again he has given me heavenly guidance.

Returning to the *Morgenster*, I find it loaded, the crew watching for me. We eat supper as the boat drifts slowly in the sunset, steering us back home.

I pray God will show me. Then I lay awake most of the night, settling things in my mind, weighing every view of my situation. By dawn, I surmise a business plan to present to Evert.

Hastily I dress and walk the deck.

Assured all is in order, I give James the run of the ship, telling him "I may be in my quarters until dark. Please bring my meals to me. Secretly, I'm devising a plan for us. How would you like to command a ship and report to me?"

He nods eagerly. And with that, I hurry below.

I set out the graphite pencils and parchment.

Already the figures and details bounce in my head. I plan to build faster frigates and market the towns within three hundred miles. We would buy their goods, trade off our perishables and stock, shipping staples back to our cargo vessels for the homeland. We could start with three in the first year and build to six or ten with the profits.

Would Evert invest in my enterprise? He owes me eight thousand, seven hundred guilders, besides my severance. Could he secure backing from the West India Company? I will supply trade to new settlements that need the business opportunity, such as New Sweden, Rhode Island, Martha's Vineyard, a circuit close to home.

First, I draw up the cost account. I list the goods I feel will do well and my design of shipbuilding requirements. Next, I list the colonies and destinations that seem to me worthy of this venture.

I can personally build a good relationship with the officials, merchants, and farmers in each town. I will guarantee fair prices and steady delivery.

I'm excited.

I make maps with routes and a timetable, including weather considerations and harvests. The next account is of the seasonal products we could supply and a list of goods we would buy from them or trade. I can resell citrus, spices, wool, and medicine.

When James comes with my supper, I have papers scattered across the desk and on the table. He looks at them and the object of my proposal, with his eyes wide.

"Gerrit, this will make us rich. It's good!" he rallies a fist in the air excited.

I smile, stuffing potatoes in my mouth and stacking the papers in a pile. I'm hungry and happy. The boat tilts.

Instantly he grabs the sliding papers, losing their order.

We look at each other and break out in laughter, saying no

more and enjoying our meal. The pickles are still crisp, a wonder. The bread is dark, but warm. I drink a whole pitcher of lemon water, having been thirsty and busy.

Finally, he belches, and we smile at that too.

He searches my face.

"Tell me, will the ships be easier to maneuver? Can we get them into small harbors and up rivers?" he asks.

"That's the key. I learned it at the university. I've had it in my mind for years, but it didn't seem to fit anywhere. You know my stewardship is about to end?" I say.

He asks, "What's changed? I thought you and I would work together until you're too old to do this anymore."

I poke him in the arm.

"We make a good team. I won't do it without you. I trust your diplomacy with clients and management of your crew. You'll keep our ships safe, leaning on the gifts of the Spirit I showed you. We won't be on the high seas. I'll give you a percentage," I offer.

Tears are in his eyes, which he fights back.

The opportunity wouldn't be his if it weren't for me.

"I could buy land," he says swallowing casually.

"I could get married," I say, expecting his surprise.

"You don't say-y-y-y," he teases.

"Well, I have someone in mind," I grin.

A call comes from the starboard. He takes the dishes and hurries away. The halibut are running, and every man is needed to haul them in and salt them down.

I'm alone again with my dreams and my paper, to which I put to good use, scratching out my ship building plans. The measurements keep changing as I calculate the ideas in my head. As soon as I think I've made it swift and streamlined, the angles are not right. I have to start over.

By night, I've exhausted myself in the attempt and it has been a long, good day. I fall on the bunk, entirely clothed, *with visions of the business still in my head.*

Chapter 30

"THE LOT IS CAST INTO THE LAP; BUT THE WHOLE
DISPOSING THEREOF IS OF THE LORD."

PROVERBS 16:33

I awake to bright sunlight. I missed breakfast. The bell for land is ringing and we're coming into New Amsterdam. I look at my wrinkled shirt and open the door.

The cook's helper speaks to me.

"I saved you two buns, sir," he offers.

"Very good," I say amused, *simply because life is promising, and I am well enough to enjoy it.*

There's hope for more happiness than I've ever dreamed. I want to get to her, speak to her.

Then I remember that the ship plans are not materialized, and I cloud.

The cook studies my face.

"Something the matter sir?" he asks respectfully.

"Nothing prayer can't fix," I motion for him to join me.

"Me sir?" he wavers.

I set him at ease putting my arm around his shoulder.

"Why not? Your soul and your prayers weigh as much in heaven as mine. Come now," I coax.

He pulls off the apron and dips his hands in water, drying them at once and hurries behind me.

"I need someone to agree with me[95] and if you're my friend and love God, then you're the partner to help me in this matter," I encourage him.

He humbly bows on his knees at my bunk, and I get on the other side, kneeling to pray.

"I'll pray and whenever you feel it's good, you say 'Yes, Lord, I agree'. Are you ready?" I teach him.

He nods with his head still bowed. *I like that in him and realize I've taken him for granted.*

"Father God, you have brought us thus far and blessed us and kept us safe. I thank you," I pray.

"Yes Lord, I agree," he prays.

I say, "I stand in awe of You, so perfect in all Your ways, loving and kind. I am grateful for the Blood of Jesus that washes my sins away and the Holy Spirit that lives inside me to guide me into righteousness. I thank You for the Holy Bible and for our Dutch Reformed faith and for the hope You put in my heart," I pray, believing myself standing before God.

"Yes Lord. I agree," he whispers.

"There are three matters I wish to bring before You and ask Your hand to be upon me in the business I request, Lord. First, may I find favor with Huybrecht in obtaining funds and permission for my business plan. And second, may I find Emma pleased to be my wife if she is free to marry. And last, may James and this cook be given to me for the Coastline Trading Company for the mutual profits and happiness of us all," I request with assurance, "I will give you the tithe and the glory and live to serve You always."

The cook weeps in his hands.

"Yes Lord. I agree. I agree to go with Commander Brinkendorf whatever he is asking for and be his cook and be faithful to him and You, God," he manages, "Only please save me from my sins, so I don't disappoint His Excellency and make a fool of myself."

He rises quickly and looks fearfully at me, about to hurry out. I gain my footing and stare him in the eye.

"Will things in the kitchen be all right unattended?" I ask.

He's unsure of himself, feeling tense in my presence.

"Sit in the chair. Remind me. What's your name?" I say, setting my captain's chair across from him.

He's trembling.

I'm ashamed. How had I started out so thoughtful and per-sonal with my men, and hardened in a selfish, busy way not to know him better? He works near me. He serves me every day. I've never heard him complain.

"Dirk Stevensen, sir. My father took one look at me when I was born and said, 'His head looks like a dirk', so he named me that," he explains, twisting his shirt hem.

I'm careful not to smile, assuming it has been a source of embarrassment to him, whenever he gave it.

"You make it a fine name, mate. I ask forgiveness that I've not given you my time and friendship before now. Tell me about yourself," I lean back and open up to him.

He nervously looks out the windows, knowing the men are tying up now and will be unloading.

"I didn't get the scraps out in time, sir," he apologizes.

"Never mind. I'll see it's taken care of. Tell me about your-self," I continue.

He's impressed and I mean for him to be.

"Well, I never been in trouble with the law. Always honest," he starts and looks up at me, "I come from Ireland and learned Dutch from the street. I ran away from home you see. There wasn't enough food, and they wouldn't speak of it, but I knew I was getting old enough, so I left. I write my mother and send my wages when we're in port."

"I understand. Do you like being a cook?" I inquire.

"No. I do my job as best I can, for everybody who has to eat it. I try not to waste anything, and make it taste good. I keep the galley clean," he says proudly, no longer uneasy.

I smile and he warms to that.

Shifting in the chair, he tosses his head and looks me in the eye, "I have dreams," he whispers, "I want to be captain myself someday. Maybe it take years. I don't care. I will do my best, be available and like you showed me, pray."

I soften and realize I have been one-sided.

I offer, "Would you like me to pray with you and agree? About your dreams?"

He looks back at where we knelt and without a word, gets up and kneels in the same place.

"I start," he looks to me.

I get up and kneel across from him, nodding.

"Father God, I am happy to call You Father and I need you to be my Father. Please forgive me all my sins and with Your help, I don't want to do them anymore. I believe Jesus Christ died for me to be saved from hell. I am happy to not be afraid of hell. I would also like to ask for three things, please sir. I ask that I can learn to read and own a Bible. I ask that I can be a captain and have a ship. And if it's not too much, I would like a wife and family that I can love and go home to when I am at shore. That's all. Thank you very, very much, God," he says with joy and faces me.

"I agree, Lord," I pray.

"As soon as we get unloaded and your duties are done, come see me on the sterncastle," I instruct him, "I'll buy our dinner at The Wooden Horse tavern and make you a stewardship offer, hmm?"

"You be my friend?" he asks, watching my face.

"Yes," is my swift reply, "and probably bring some answers to your prayers."

He leaves in a hurry, *and I feel better about heaven smiling on me than I have in a long time. Faith comes from obeying God, being kind and reaching to lonely souls. I believe the ship measurements will fall into place without any effort now. How do I know? I know God is pleased, that's why.*

After Dirk and James and I put away a fine dinner of leg of lamb, turnip greens, creamed carrots, egg bread and butter, we enjoy a generous portion of cinnamon apple strudel. We drink sweet tea from first to last and groan because our bellies are stretched to the limit, excitedly talking, and keeping it low, not wanting anyone to steal my idea.

That night we make a partnership. James's stewardship to me for seven years includes two acres of my land, ten per cent of profits and the ship he commands will become his, at the end of the tenure.

For Dirk, seven years stewardship include a wardrobe for church and school, time to go to Collegiate School equal to two months a year, a Geneva Bible, one acre of land and the apprenticeship under James as quartermaster. With this covenant, I have more insurance of success to submit my business before Evert, and I go to the lodge light-hearted, eager to draw my ship plans.

It does flow out of me as I expected, a perfect drawing that correctly measures this time.

Expected to report the next morning, I want to be my best.

There is a humbling that accompanies me from praying with Dirk, that I will not soon forget. I kneel as I did when I was younger and needier of God than I have been of late.

I ask Him to forgive my pride.

The moon shines brightly through the window and streams on the floor beside me.

Such peace fills my heart and I fall asleep with Emma's face in my mind.

Chapter 31

"THE KEEPER OF THE PRISON LOOKED NOT TO ANY
THING THAT WAS UNDER HIS HAND; BECAUSE THE
LORD WAS WITH HIM, AND THAT WHICH HE DID, THE
LORD MADE IT TO PROSPER."

GENESIS 39:23

The Huybrecht carriage arrives for me in the morning, and I wear my tailored silk embroidered jacket and new buckled shoes. The driver remembers me as a youth and says nothing to acknowledge that, only raises his brows in recognition. I nod, as he holds the carriage door.

We pass Oloff at the tithe barn. I wave. He sees me and grabs his cane, hobbling along, in a hurry to greet me.

I order the driver, "Pull off the road, only a moment."

Oloff shakes my hand continually as he talks.

"Aye, so good to see you Gerrit! A sight for sore eyes, my son," he says.

My, how he's aged in seven years.

I pat his shoulder.

"I invite you to my wedding, dear friend," I oblige.

He rears back his head and grins wide, raising the cane.

"And who might the fortunate bride be?" he quips, with a jolly manner I still find likeable.

"The very same Emma Wiloughby that read the scriptures on our first return voyage, when we regained the *Salamander*," I say lighthearted.

He scowls, stomping the cane "She be that Anabaptist girl. I don't know about that Gerrit. I think they run them out of town. They were holding their meetings. Heresy. The Director didn't want trouble."

I interrupt him, "Run them out of New Amsterdam?"

His eyes calculate right away I won't listen to gossip.

"Probably Rhode Island. What else could they do?"

He is sad to tell me this.

I run forward to the carriage, shouting, "I'll come and have supper, next time I'm in."

He waves and shakes his head, *an old man, set in his ways, precious to me and intolerant of her.*

I smile as we jostle along.

I have business to do and need my mind to be clear.

At the door, a new butler meets me and announces that Evert is not available. He tells me my appointment for the account is with his father, Bos.

It is unexpected.

I wait, standing in the grand hall, surrounded by oriental porcelain and marvelous oil paintings of ships at sea and relatives dressed in finery with their wigs and jewels. One outstanding painting, the largest of them all, is of the Dutch West India Company Merchants, at a time when they were younger, with their black frocks and wide collars and high hats. They look soberly from the oil, and I shudder. The thick Turkish rugs I recognize from the Amsterdam marketplace as well as the lengthy silk draperies with delicate tassels.

If ever a waiting area could make one feel put in their place, it is here, I think, *peering at the Delft tiles on the floor.*

I shift my bag of plans and maps on my other shoulder and hear a small yipping dog from behind the door.

The butler opens.

"He will see you now," the butler waves for me to enter.

The ceilings are tremendously high with wide wooden beams

and carved trim. The colorful rug is so thick, I drag my boot not expecting the pull.

With a raised brow and no expression, Bos Huybrecht offers a nod.

I open my bag and draw out the accounting, laying it on the desk.

"A good profit this run, sir. No losses, all men, and goods intact," I state and wait for his response.

"Hmm, yes. Have a seat," Bos curtly addresses me.

I sit still. He takes his time, running his finger down each page slowly.

He obviously is accustomed to bookkeeping and managing the considerations.

When he seems finished, he makes a faint sound to himself and turns to look out the window with his back to me and *leaves me wondering what to do.*

He remains in that silent position for some ten minutes, *making me more uncomfortable with my business proposition.*

In my worry, I tell myself to wait patiently for the Lord. I have committed my plans to Him and now it is my part to trust in faith.

I relax. Whatever the outcome, I give my plans to God.

Finally, Bos Huybrecht turns back to me.

"Your stewardship is expired. Evert made the contract without my approval. He was generous to a fault. I want you to know it has been a matter of contention between us these thirteen years," he says, leaving me shattered.

I blink, *not knowing how to answer, in a quandary really.*

"What's that you have there? A claim you wish to make, a legal complaint in writing?" he accuses.

"A business plan I thought would be an asset," I say, stammering in a loss of confidence.

"You thought. You thought of something we wouldn't have thought of?" he says condescendingly rude.

"I would not offend you in my wildest dreams, Sir. Ever

since I have been a steward to the Huybrecht firm, I have given my best talents and hard work and brains with never a lack of persistence. It is my choice to be grateful for every benefit shown to me by your house and I have repaid that debt honorably and cheerfully. This is no kind conversation to an innocent party of your ill will to your son," I say, and quietly bowing, I whisper, "As always I am your servant."

He taps a graphite on the pages I prepared.

"I expected you to be done with us," he says.

"Nothing of the kind," I say.

"Your profits are good. They have been," he admits.

It's my turn to make him wait. I hold my peace.

"Do you intend to propose a business plan to me as you might would have brought to my son?" he asks, rising and walking to the bookshelf.

He faces me, *challenging*.

"I am prepared to present it as God wills. I have put the matter in His hands. I trust He will deliver a good decision, whomever I do business with, sir," I say, composed.

"Then show it to me," he says, "and be quick about it. I have another appointment."

I lay it out and talk quickly, *sorrowing for the loss of time it's not permitted and hoping for his favor.*

But he doesn't give it and I wait in vain as he shoves all the papers into my bag again.

"I need more time to look it over. Leave it here," he says.

Our eyes lock.

I cannot hide my distrust. Immediately I believe he schemes to take my ideas, my plans, my maps and use them to his advantage, leaving me completely out of it.

He could. He has the power to do that. He doesn't have to give it to me. It is his money, his ships, his men on them.

He walks to the door and dismisses me, sending me out empty-handed.

I am no longer steward and no longer Commander and no

longer full of excitement. A thorough job he has done of putting me in my place, back out in the vast waiting hall.

The butler sees me out and secures the door. The carriage is nowhere to be seen. *I am on my own again, like the boy who first set foot in the New World.*

I walk down the drive in my fine new shoes, getting them dusty and sweating in my silk frock, *all the time feeling the eyes of Bos Huybrecht on my back from the mansion window.*

Chapter 32

"UNTIL THE TIME THAT HIS WORD CAME: THE WORD
OF THE LORD TRIED HIM."

PSALM 105:19

*I won't break the news to James and Dirk. I can't face them
until I have some faith myself. I worry I've made them lose their
jobs, at least put them in ill favor because of me.*

I walk to the sailmaker shop and ask about Charles. The
shopkeeper gives me a onceover and answers brashly, "Doesn't
work here. Possibly removed to Providence."

All the men in the shop stare at me, until the shopkeeper
sternly looks at them and they commence sewing.

My heart is still on Emma.

I pack up and secure passage in a small sailboat the next
day for Rhode Island.

We arrive and tie up alongside four slave ships unloading.
But I am in a hurry and light out to find the shipyards, knowing
the sailmakers will be there.

I do find Charles in a good way and friendly. Yes, they moved
to Providence two years ago and Emma is well.

Charles is married and his wife wanted Emma to have her
own house. Hers is beside theirs and small. Would I like to have
supper with them tonight and come to meeting?

I couldn't have planned it better myself. Thank you, God.

I'm careful not to mention the disappointment I feel about my business plans. The sting eats away at my faith, and I am not ready to let it go.

All afternoon as I walk and look over the village, *I ponder the circumstances of my life.*

I told God what I wanted. I made a life commitment to Him. What if He knows something I don't? What if there is a storm with my name on it? Or a battle at sea?

What if the ship I want to build isn't seaworthy, and men die because of my haughtiness?

Furthermore, how shall I make a living for us?

Yet I'm here, with nothing but my heart to offer, some money in the account in Holland and my good intentions. Will she marry me?

I stop at the bakery and buy two loaves of white bread and a ball of butter.

It is almost lantern lighting time. Charles will be closing the shop and I step swiftly to meet him.

His cottage is thatched roofed and common.

Immediately my heart is in my throat to be in a home like my Mum's.

I meet his sweet wife and two little boys, tumbling about on the floor with their father. I sit by the fire and turn my memory back to childhood and the love of my mother. A dog barks and I try to calm it to no avail. The wife thanks me kindly for the bread and takes it away to slice it. She places the butter on a bone china dish and returns smiling.

And Emma comes in.

Her face is flushed, *and by her expression she delights to see me.* Behind her are two small children, a girl with curls about three, and a frail boy of maybe six.

She must have married. I close my mind to the personal hopes I brought on my journey.

My heart is not in the conversation, though I try, and Charles asks me twice if something is wrong. *I'm too sad to open up to him and my spirit too low to hide it.*

As soon as supper is finished, I leave without a slice of pie and although Emma says, "Please stay for meeting", *I can't bring myself to be disappointed anymore.*

I quickly find lodging and fall asleep, *not willing to pray or think about anything.*

Before dawn, I head back to New Amsterdam. *The only place to start is to go to my land, and see what I can make of it, so I do.* It lies behind the Huybrecht plantation, where I set traps in my youth.

I withdraw funds from the New Amsterdam account, as much as allowed, knowing I need the Huybrecht signature to withdraw my savings from the West India Company, *and decide I will make do while the paperwork is being processed, a good four months at best.*

Evert has cheated me more than once. I fume, remembering.

I buy an axe, a hatchet, pots and food, some rope and four blankets. Camping will serve my needs until harsh weather. I wear my worst clothes and string the rope from two trees. With the blankets hanging from the rope, I have some shelter from the sun, the wind, and the rain. I sleep on the ground, making a campfire of stones.

Soon I clear an area of trees and stack them to build myself a better shelter. The blankets make a roof, until I can add one. Then I dig up flat rocks and fill in the floor, stacking a fireplace on one end. I cut and notch the logs, stacking them with a hand-made pulley for walls. After three weeks, I beam out the roof and thatch it, satisfied with my new home.

When all the food is gone, I count the money left and go out to buy fish traps and a musket with powder. I need coffee, salt, flour, oil, beans, and cabbage. *If I get a couple of deer, I might get by until spring.* It will take that long to receive funds from my account in Holland.

I find out I am no good at hunting. Never got the hang of it. Waste four days. Use all my powder.

Oloff comes hobbling through the fallen leaves to find me and we sit on the rocks.

"You never did come back to see me," he scolds.

"I know," I say, "I meant to."

"You find the girl?" he asks, pressing me.

I take a deep breath saying, "I found her. She has children."

"Hmm," he says dropping his jaw, "You feel let down and come back here to lick your wounds?"

He has me pinned. I sulk.

"You went to see Huybrecht, and he disappointed you. So, you come out of that big house all beat down and out of work," he looks away at nothing.

I don't want to hear it. That's the way with old folk. They muddle all in your private affairs.

He raises his head in the way I remember so well.

"How's your relationship with God?" he asks.

It stings and it wouldn't if I had a good answer. But I don't. I'm out of faith because I'm out of luck. And I don't care about my friends or church or anything. I'm running away from God, not trying to get back.

"You're barking up the wrong tree," he says.

"Yeah, well if I had a hound dog, I could tree myself a coon at least, a rabbit or quail. That's a good idea," I say.

"Well, Job's friends blamed God foolishly,"[96] he spurts.

I won't look at him. I'm no boy anymore.

"What are you all riled up about?" he asks, "I came to bring some news and set you straight."

I'm getting angry.

I stand up to walk away.

His voice follows me.

"A month after you sailed away, news came that her fiancé had drowned. That girl had no suitors. Always at work with her brother. As for the orphans, Emma adopted them," he says, "Cost her five hundred guilders. People say they went to Rhode Island, the sewer of New England.[97] All riff raffs."

I'm stunned.

He groans as he leans on his knee to stand up again.

"You need to see Bos Huybrecht. He's been looking for you at the docks," Oloff says.

I say, "I won't do another seven years loading, being humiliated. While I have strength and determination, I'm going to make a home for myself on this land and be an apprentice doing something else, Commander."

He pokes that stout finger on my chest and challenges me.

"No, you won't. You got the sea in your blood Dutch boy, and you are too good at it. Now admit it. I was always so proud of you! But the trouble with you is not that woman or Huybrecht. Your trouble is with your faith in God. You quit believing?" he says in my face, "I don't see you at church."

His words shoot clear to my heart.

Tears fill my eyes.

He pats my shoulder gently.

"Listen here, when you quit believing in God, you quit believing in yourself and others. You can't see the good in other people. You just see your own needs and survival becomes your god," he places his hand on my arm, "Now then, talk to God. Talk to Huybrecht. And go tell that girl you'll raise those children with her."

Silent tears course down my cheeks.

I swallow my pride and look at him.

"You are a precious friend, Oloff," I hug him.

He nods and hobbles away.

Without changing clothes or bathing, I walk over to the plantation, up to the mansion door and ask for Bos.

Chapter 33

"...WHEN THE ENEMY SHALL COME IN LIKE A FLOOD,
THE SPIRIT OF THE LORD SHALL LIFT UP A STANDARD
AGAINST HIM."

ISAIAH 59:19B

Evert comes to the door and gives me a cold stare.

"Take a walk with me. You owe me that much," he says.

He is ahead of me, briskly stirring a dust cloud down the lane toward the tobacco fields.

"You ungrateful urchin," he hisses, "After the education, the careful tutoring and inside experience I've invested in you, is there no decency that strikes you as necessary when we've given you every benefit the last thirteen years?"

He glares at me menacingly.

I meet his look with solid composure.

The fieldhands stare. He turns on them and they swiftly assume work.

Calmly I say, "I'm no longer bound to you. Don't you think a man can have dreams of his own?"

He sighs, his lips tight, his jaw protruded.

"Gerrit, Gerrit," he says, shaking his head.

I lean on the fence and face the house, just in time to see Bos looking out the window at us. I turn back around.

The slaves and indentured servants work on steadily.

"All those years I thought, what will I do when I'm free?" I plead, "Are you so caught up in making money you don't care about people's feelings anymore?"

He frowns cold faced.

"I bought two big ships. Slave ships. Already I've made contracts in New Zealand, Africa, and Brazil to export sugar. I was counting on you, my valuable Commander, my indomitable seafaring agent. But no. You want to hug the shore and take a wife. Oloff told me," he says.

"And how can that be so wrong?" I ask.

He rolls his eyes, aware he's making a scene and other ears are listening. He clips down the road toward town *keeping me a pace behind as he rattles on. It's so like him.*

He says "You're throwing away a golden opportunity. I thought you were smarter than that. I thought you had brains, but no. You're like these misfits who come here for their conscience sake. Well, I didn't. I'm here to make money."

I stop walking, *uncontrolled by his tirade.*

"Did your father send you out to try to convince me to keep shipping overseas?" I ask.

He looks at me *with defiance.*

"No, I'm the one that found you. I'm the one that saw greatness in you. It's me you should have asked, not him," he complains.

"I came with every intention of bringing it to you. The butler said you were unavailable. Your father required me to report to him. He told me he never approved of the deals you made with me," I say, "He sent me out penniless."

Now Evert says, "Oh, I doubt it was all so bad as that. You knew we needed you. You planned to take it over my head. You knew I'd never stand for it and passed me up."

I quietly look at him shaking my head, and it dawns on him what an innocent victim I am of their family strife.

He glances back up at the house.

I feel sure he sees his father listening.

He swallows, seething. *He's drawn a line in the sand with me and is stunned. This time it's to his own hurt.*

And he won't apologize. He's too proud.

"Gerrit Brinkendorf, I will be the richest man you ever met.

I'll pass you on Wall Street and you'll remember what you gave up. You'll regret you turned your back on my offers and grind your teeth, wishing you had let the girl go," he fairly hisses.

I want to say something nice, but he has soured the air with his curses.

Instead, I blink and walk away.

Behind me he says, "My father will go ahead with your plans. He let me appeal to you first. You were my protégé."

I turn to thank him, but he abruptly puts his back to me, a thing I remember as a family habit, so rude.

This is his goodbye to me.

I go to the front door. The butler stands with it open.

Bos doesn't keep me waiting, *nor does he seem to care about my humble clothing.* Instead he stands politely when I enter and opening my bag, he discusses the terms of our agreement. He tells me he has carefully absorbed the details and decided it is a solid investment.

He has prepared a request to the Dutch West India Company for backing before I arrived. He reads it to me, "To build three ships by your design and after you've proved them one year, to be awarded sufficient monies to build seven more and outfit them with crews under your direct command. They are to be designated cargo fluyts, merchant ships for coastal loading only. You will receive fifty per cent of all profit, ten per cent out of that for James and our agreement will be for ten years steward-ship, since the investment in your company will be large. After ten years, the ships will belong to you and the rights to the busi-ness, insomuch as you can protect it from foreign competition."

From the window, I see Evert outside, looking up at the house.

"I will recommend this contract in view of your humble and cheerful service to us and for the West India Company the last twelve years," Bos says, seating himself, "I did attempt to locate you and comply with your wishes. Please, have a seat."

"Sir, it pains me that I have been a source of trouble between you and your son," I offer, still standing.

His face *at once is harsh. I meet it sincerely.*

With a deep breath, he folds his hands and leans forward.

He says, "It is pointless to try to manipulate other men. Evert enjoys the game of making money. He uses everything to his advantage. Somehow that sours with age."

He too sees Evert. Both of us stare quietly out the window.

He turns back and says, "This document will go out Thursday. Upon its approval, I expect the ships to be launched in a short time and you can begin trading as soon as the boats are ready. Now, for your share of the liquidation of the Strong Sails Enterprise, I included it with this document as your down payment of shares in the new company which I named the Coastal Trading Company. I thought that was the way you would apply it, when you sought the investment with us," he says.

The parchment is long, consisting of two pages. I read it over, sitting down, while he watches Evert mount a horse.

While I'm signing, he softens and ventures a kind word.

"It was callous of me not to mention your share of the investment to Wiloughby when you were here last," he says, "You also haven't collected your severance from the duty on the *Morgenster*. This is yours."

He opens a drawer, then pushes a bag of coins across the desk to me and turns the contract back facing it to himself. He powders it and nods.

"You have seven hundred thousand guilders in your account. I hope you will make another shipment for us and return in November, Commander. If you accept that assignment as agent, you may take twelve per cent. What do you say?" he asks.

"You are generous. I will make it worth your while," I reply, "There was the matter of a payroll I've not been reimbursed since the impound of the *Morgenster* four years ago."

He says, "I'm appalled. Forgive me. I trusted, well. I will issue it with the interest of those years forwarded today."

He closes his eyes and nods, then walks by my side into the grand hallway and to the door. The butler stands by.

"Have the carriage take Commander wherever he would like to go today," he orders.

We wait for the carriage, and he steps out with me.

"You've been clearing your land behind us," he says.

In the sunlight, *he seems frail, not commanding at all.*

"I am your neighbor, sir," I say.

"Dispense with calling me sir, Gerrit," he says plainly, "I should not have offended you and I beg your pardon. A better man would have had more sense. You are clearly a good businessman, surely my equal. The Coastal Trading Company is assigned only to me. I look forward to our joint enterprise and have no fear of its success. May the good Lord watch over you and give you every happiness."

Chapter 34

"Whoso findeth a wife findeth a good thing,
and obtaineth favour of the Lord."

Proverbs 18:22

I have the business. *It happened so suddenly.*

Now, will I get the wife? It means nothing to me if she won't have me. Or if she's taken.

I waste no time in telling James and Dirk the good news and hire passage to Providence.

On the way there, *I rehearse what to say.* Then I think *that's of little use because Charles stands between us.*

I enter the sail maker barn and he sees me at once, *not with a friendly face.* I walk around to where he has the broadcloth stretched across the wide loom.

"You obviously have some business on your mind Gerrit, but I grow impatient that you don't come out with it. You left hastily without reason when last we met, and I have come to think of you as an enemy, spying out our freedom. You reject joining the brethren for meeting, a bit convenient to a persecutor of our faith. To you, I suppose I'm just another Anabaptist," he accuses fearfully.

I'm so startled I can't speak.

He stops work and puts his hands on his hips.

I burst out laughing *at the accusation and myself.*

"Oh Charles! How inconsiderate of me and awful for you.

Please, hear me out. I'm by no means an enemy of your faith. I have the deepest heartfelt respect for you and Emma. My clumsy emotions got in the way of good manners. Do forgive me. I will gladly go to meeting tonight. I come as a brother, not an enemy," I say and hang my head.

He blinks and shakes his head.

He lays a hand on my shoulder saying, "I spoke in haste, trapped by fear of my own. Let us speak of it no more. I'm cheerful to have you join us around the Word of God, and supper at our humble house."

"You can't imagine how I've longed to be at your table again. May I bring a baker's dozen and fresh butter?" I ask.

"We haven't had such a treat since last you came," he agrees, "But I must deliver these sails today. It's the last of the fittings before they depart tomorrow."

"I've nothing better to do. Let me help," I offer, and he does, putting a large, curved needle in my hand and the twine to tighten and knot, as we make the fastenings secure for the sail. We wax the seams evenly and move to the next bolt. My hands are stained black now.

Eventually I ask him questions *because I can't wait.*

"Will Emma eat with us tonight?" I venture.

"Yes," he responds, concentrating on the sail.

A few minutes go by. I'm so anxious.

"Do women attend meeting?" I probe a little more.

He stops and reviews me.

I pretend not to notice.

"Myra keeps the children. Emma does our laundry in exchange to be free to go to meetings during the week. All of us attend on Lord's Day."

His tone is flat.

More time passes.

"Why aren't you at sea, Gerrit? Are you looking for work?" he questions.

I quickly answer, eager and excited.

"I've been granted a shipping contract of my own. I'm creating a new trade company in America," I say.

"America, hmm. That's good," he says, "And you come looking for? Sails? Shipbuilders? A wife?"

He had me. We both stop and look at each other.

A half hour passes working, while no more is said.

I'm nervous. He knows it.

It reminds me of how my Father knotted thoughts in his head and I need to read what Charles isn't saying.

Finally, he levels with me, "It would break her heart if she had to give up her religion, or the children. Both are the center of all she loves and lives for."

He studies my reaction.

I know enough that I should show I have put plenty of thought into this.

We keep tying, tightening.

He cuts me some slack.

"Why don't you come to meeting? Let us pray for God's guidance in the matter," he suggests.

"Without Emma's foreknowledge?" I hesitate.

"Let me explain it to her. I'm her guardian and have her best interest at heart," he compromises.

"Of course," I answer lamely, wishing I could speak for myself and that things might be more personal.

"Stay here a week, maybe," he asks, "To find God's will."

Supper is excellent and I eat two plates of fresh garden pickings and a leg of chicken.

Emma's eyes dance at me which preoccupies me in a way most welcome.

The children watch me, and she reprimands them not to stare. The boy especially is curious, staring at my tall boots and sword.

Charles eats four rolls *and I'm happy he enjoys them.*

The three of us walk a short piece to Ivan Sattler's cottage and there find twelve brothers and three sisters for the meeting.

I've never been to a home meeting.

The younger men sit on the floor and the women are in rocking chairs. I take the chair by the hearth and remove my plumed hat and coat, unhinge the sword, and lay it on the stones.

Ivan cannot disguise his disapproval at seeing it.

When everyone is in the room and the door shut, they bow their heads and Ivan prays first, "Heavenly Father, we come together in the Name of Jesus Christ. You said, "Where two or three are gathered in my Name, I am in the midst of them.[98] We revere Your presence and the Holy Spirit that teaches us all things."

We bow silent while the candles flicker and burn low.

I reflect on my pride about the shipping line and the presumption in which I have come, feeling unsure of myself.

Charles opens the Geneva Bible, to the book of First John reading, "Beloved, let us love one another: for love cometh of God, and everyone that loveth is born of God, and knoweth God. He that loveth not, knoweth not God, for God is love. If we love one another, God dwelleth in us, and his love is perfect in us[99]."

Charles says, "I bring tonight, Commander Brinkendorf, a good Dutch Reformed Protestant that we made friends with, when we crossed from Holland seven years ago. Gerrit showed us much kindness and loves the Good Book."

At this, the men generally turn my way and nod.

He says, "His desire is to marry Emma and I have advised him that I would like us to agree in prayer for guidance."

They look me over *and I meet their looks with honesty.*

"Where is your residence?" Mrs. Sattler asks.

Charles says softly, "This morning, Gerrit came to my work. I accused him of being our enemy, through no fault of his own, except he was nervous about asking for Emma's hand on his last visit, when he saw the children."

Emma quickly interrupts, "You don't want the children?"

I respond tartly, "I do want them. I was moved to the heart

that you took it upon yourself. It made me love you more. I will love them and you together, as a family."

It brings tears to her eyes. Everyone looks back to Charles.

"You see," he whispers, "We sin in not opening our hearts to a man that has come to us. He can be baptized. It may be in his heart to join us. Still, we serve ourselves and not our Lord Jesus when we narrowly judge him because of fear. John 4:18, "...he that feareth, is not made perfect in love."

Charles maintains a firm countenance.

Ivan prays, "Forgive us Heavenly Father for allowing fear to rule us, rather than wisdom and truth. Show us Your will about a marriage. We ask the commander's forgiveness."

A hymn rises from the back, and we sing it together. The melody is simple, *the words of a Psalm I recognize, and it sticks in my mind all the way home.*

Chapter 35

"Finally, be ye all of one mind, having
compassion one of another, love as
brethren,..."

I Peter 3:8

We meet the next night, while Emma is told to stay home.
Ivan opens in prayer.

Next he says, "Our decision is to let you decide if we are
what you want to be associated with. We won't favor Emma
giving up her faith, nor do we believe in forced religion."

I'm put on the spot right away.

Edmund reads from the Geneva Bible lying open, "Chapter
three of Matthew, "And in those days, John the Baptist came
and preached in the wilderness of Judea, And said, Repent: for
the kingdom of heaven is at hand. For this is he of whom it is
spoken by the Prophet Isaiah, saying, 'The voice of him that cri-
eth in the wilderness, Prepare ye the way of the Lord: make his
paths straight.' Indeed, I baptize you with water to amendment
of life, but he that cometh after me is mightier than I, whose
shoes I am not worthy to bear, he will baptize you with the Holy
Ghost, and with fire. Which hath his fan in his hand, and will
make clean his floor, and gather his wheat into his garner, but
will burn up the chaff with unquenchable fire."

He halts there and stares at me.

Proceeding he reads, "Then came Jesus from Galilee to
Jordan unto John to be baptized of him. But John earnestly put

him back, saying, I have need to be baptized of thee, and comest thou to me? Then Jesus answering, said to him, Let it be now: for thus it becometh us to fulfill all righteousness. So he suffered him. And Jesus when he was baptized came straightway out of the water. And lo, the heavens were opened unto him, and John saw the Spirit of God descending like a dove, and [lighting] upon him. And lo, a voice came from heaven, saying, 'This is my beloved Son, in whom I am well pleased.'"[100]

From that point he defines their position, "I notice that John the Baptizer separated himself from the Pharisees who persecuted him and later killed him and our Lord, their religion being hateful, and their concern was not for men's souls. In them, I only see political power, wealth, and prestige as their motive.[101] John recognized Christ. He preached repentance of sin, as fruits worthy of baptism. Jesus said we should do it to fulfill all righteousness. I believe the obedience of water baptism in the Name of Christ opens our hearts for the light of the Holy Spirit."

As the night goes on, I agree with everything they say, except for the vow of non-violence.

I decide to stay on for the week, bringing in food to add to supper and helping Charles at his work.

At the Sabbath meeting I express my pleasure in their company and say I hope I meet their expectations.

"I want to be baptized. Tomorrow is good," I say, "I want to live among you in one accord. But I have one objection."

I take a deep breath.

"I've been a steward where I'm required to take up arms to protect. I have been born of stock that took up arms to weather eighty years of persecution for the Protestant faith and many of you were protected by the open arms of the Netherlands. We live in peace because we don't let them take from us that which God intends."

I open my hands.

"It seems to me, if we had not taken up arms, none of us would be here now. There would be no freedom anywhere. You all know full well the powers that be in Europe were determined to put us in the ground. Even as we sit here, you have been run out of other colonies for pure and holy standards. I cannot think how sorrowful it would be, if we drew back now, after all the fathers have done to bring us this far.[102] Should we let that light be swallowed up in darkness? Do nothing?" I ask.

I get up, pacing.

"Hear my heart. I have carried a silver dagger since I was eleven years old. Never have I used it for personal advantage, though I have been across the oceans many times, in danger and in circumstances justifying it. I answer to God always for everything I do, every soul under my watch, every guilder my company has me give account for. In this way I am honest with God and man. What is faith in God if it does not supply the courage to live ready to face Him? I bear arms only to protect and may I never have to quit my company because they ask of me to do damage unless it is a necessity. I do not run slaves for them. I think it's wrong. Men should be free," I expound.

Squinting eyes are on me. I nod.

"I promise before God, I will not do anything to hinder my wife's faith or hurt any of you. I will support and provide and be a comrade as long as I have strength. Do not ask me to lay down arms, to not fight for what I believe in and find necessary. As a Dutch seaman, do not ask me this," I plead, at the brink of tears.

A heavy silence hangs in the room. I find a place to stand near the door and bow my head.

Without a word, Bernard crosses the room to embrace me.

"I will not condemn you Gerrit. I believe your heart is in the right place and there is much merit in what you say. I consider you my brother and would be glad to baptize you in the morning," he says loudly, looking around the room.

With that, he steps out the door and leaves.

I hold my head low, not expecting the best.

Felix comes by and shakes my hand. He too, goes quietly.

Howell and Vincent get up together, nod at me and go out, unhitching the horses and climbing into the wagon alongside one another.

Edmund has a stern lip.

He leans on one knee and frowns, "I must pray about your position here friend. There is merit in your argument and merit in our beliefs. I do not count you an enemy. No."

He turns to Charles.

"You have the most to gain or lose," he whispers.

Charles shakes his head with raised brows.

I sigh.

"We best be putting forth the results of our consideration to the sister who will live with her own decision," Ivan says, "Gerrit will be baptized, and we can't withhold that from him. On the important foundations, we agree."

Ivan and his wife stand watching us as we walk down the road in the dark. He closes the door silently and she carries the candle with them, away from the window.

The night is clear and inviting with fireflies darting above the meadow grasses. Crickets chirp from the woods and in the distance a hound bays at the moon.

"I don't know what to say, Gerrit," Charles speaks softly.

I nod, looking down the road.

"It will be up to her," I remind him, "And that is what I want. Understand, I can't change to please them. I live my life to please God. I'm not a hypocrite. That you know."

"I'll be disappointed if it doesn't work out. I've grown fond of you, and I respect you," he says at his door.

"Then we'll trust God for the outcome," I say, and walk to the boarding house alone.

Chapter 36

"THEN SAID SHE, SIT STILL, MY DAUGHTER, UNTIL
THOU KNOW HOW THE MATTER WILL FALL: FOR THE
MAN WILL NOT BE IN REST, UNTIL HE HAVE FINISHED
THE THING THIS DAY."

RUTH 3:18

As I undress for bed, *I wonder if Emma is anxious for them to make a decision.* I saw her waiting by the door as Charles went in. *I'm sure she was asking how it went.*

Though he is certainly tired and needs to work tomorrow, his heart must weigh how to speak to her about me. He will carry the most influence on her view of me as a man.

I lay back looking at the low ceiling.

I've come too far to put down my sword now. It's a service to my faith and so much a part of me and my heritage.

If they say I must comply, if she says I must, I can't.

"Lord, keep me back from presumptuous sins. Let them not have dominion over me.[103] Show Your wisdom in the choices we all make in this matter," I pray.

I have peace the marriage will be stopped if it's not His will.

Silently, I drink in God's presence and drift off to sleep.

I dream of orphan boys, their dirty faces aching for love and acceptance, the teaching I could do at night and the strength they gain by day. Then I see younger boys and girls laughing around me, singing, and asking questions, tugging on my sleeve.

When I awake, *I understand The Lord is showing me my future, only I don't know if Emma will be with me. I thank Jesus for the children I can be kind to, and I tell God I will love that.*

Come daybreak I scrub my face and dress myself, smiling. As I pull on my old boots, a knock sounds on the door.

Charles says, "She sends me to tell you she has made up her mind and expects the men to honor it. We'll baptize you this morning, before we go to work. I brought you a boiled egg."

Is that good? I wonder what she has decided.

I peel the egg and step out into the sun with him. Around the street faces view me, men and women going about their daily tasks.

Children frolic in the grass and then they see something, something past the buildings, I cannot see yet.

Women stop. Men stare as something comes parading in front of them.

"It's Emma," I say hushed to Charles and stuff the egg down to meet her.

She carries a bucket to the well, but she looks so grand, in an elegant full skirted green velvet gown with an embroidered bodice trimmed in lace. Her hair is braided in rolls, and she walks like a queen, stately and poised.

Her eyes rivet on me.

Be still my heart! Hurry to the lady, my feet!

"I'm so pleased to see you, Emma, that you've come out to meet me. How perfectly beautiful you are in the fine velvet," I manage, as her bucket moves to my left hand and my right goes to hold hers.

She smiles quietly.

It fairly takes my breath away.

I'm swept up in love with her. Does it show on my face?

I dip the pail, clasping her hand still.

Is she going to be my friend for the rest of my life?

Everyone is looking at us and she lowers her gaze.

Charles stands at the corner, as Emma and I walk back.

All too soon we are at his house. I open the door and follow her in, setting the water on the table.

"I must go to be baptized now. They're waiting," I say, "Will you marry me, Emma?"

I'm trembling.

The house is quiet. Her eyes meet mine.

"I came out in hopes to find... I couldn't wait... yes!" she says, embarrassed, "Was that unseemly?"

"Not at all. I'm honored," I speak plainly.

At this, Myra comes drying her hands.

"Charles told me, if you're ready, the minister will perform the wedding soon as you come up from the water," Myra says, turning the gridiron away from the fire.

Myra removes her apron and changes to buckled shoes, wrapping Lucie in a blanket, and calling Marcus inside.

All this I watch, *knowing we are becoming a family. It is happening so suddenly.*

I think I'm going to cry with joy.

I take Lucie up in my arms, and Marcus by the hand, while we walk down toward the Bay, Emma by my side.

I suppose the news of my baptism and her acceptance of marriage has rippled through the neighborhood.

As we walk, people leave their duties and in their work clothes, follow us down the road. Near the dock, Emma whispers that Roger Williams is there to observe the ceremony.

And there is Bernard at the water's edge. Around him stand the elders all, no one missing.

I'm so relieved. This is good. I want their blessing.

When we stop, I give Lucie to Myra. I remove my coat, folding it and handing it to Marcus. He's proud to be trusted.

In her face I see the question, "Where will we live?"

Before I walk away, I relieve her understandable fears.

"We will live here, with your people, the Mennonites you love," I say, touching her cheek gently.

She wants to kiss me and say, "Thank you."

I know. I feel it.

I leave my boots and stockings on the bank and walk toward Bernard. When I turn, *for the first time she realizes how tall I am. Taller among the other men. She has always paid attention to my face at the table and my manners around her family.*

I look at her on the shore watching me.

She's thinking, "Who is this man that has wanted me from afar? And how will he make a living when he comes here?"

She watches me solemnly profess repentance and my commitment to Christ and then, I'm going under, all wet.

As I come up dripping, I walk toward her.

Governor Williams offers for the ceremony to be in the courthouse. I agree. Everyone moves inside.

It touches her heart, me standing in my wet clothes beside her, humbly ready to make my vow.

Tears are in her eyes and a broad smile on her face, that expression so innocent.

My heart melts in the vows we make, looking at each other.

Charles says he gives her to be married. The room resounds with "Amens", and I turn to smile at them.

The ceremony ended, everyone leaves going back into the sunlight. They return to their daily tasks.

We have two days of our own in her cottage, while Myra thoughtfully takes care of the children.

I must buy Myra something in gratitude.

The children warm to me quickly, needing a father and I enjoy their playfulness.

When we go to the square, we're approached with more respect because we're married.

I'm learning the high regard marriage has in society.

The first day I go out while she freshens herself in privacy, saying "I won't be long."

I consult with Charles and purchase land within walking distance of the family and hire carpenters for a large house to be built, paying a deposit, leaving the oversight to her.

When I return, I sit her down across from me and tell her.

"It faces a nice river, dear heart," I say, looking for approval, "They are choosing the timber and are instructed to carefully build it to your liking. Spare not the cost, within reason. I have some funds in Amsterdam that by letter will be paid out. This year the company invests in me. But next year, with my profits, I intend to invest in myself. And, may I say, there is much wind in this man's soul with your tender love behind it."

I'm excited, my words tumbling along like a waterfall.

I say, "My business is called The Coastal Trading Company because I will service along the coast. I'll begin here at Narragansett Bay, then Newport, New Haven, Brooklyn, Ft. Christopher."

"In New Sweden?" she asks.

"Yes, then Hartford, Saybrook, Martha's Vineyard Island, all the small ports. My cargo will be the fresh crops each has to sell, like pears, peaches, grapes, melons, plums, nectarines, cherries, raspberries," I say, and see her smile.

I tell her the produce, "Cabbage, carrots, beets, spinach, dill, parsnips, maize, onions too. I can haul piglets, chicks, calves, and goslings. Wherever crops are plentiful, I will buy them. Wherever there is drought or blight, I can sell."

"Gerrit, This will be such a good service. How did you ever think of it?" she says.

I whisper, "I have never quit thinking about you. You captured my heart the first time we met and the more I watched you, got to know you, I admired you so. When my indenture was up, I was wrestling with my love for you and my love for the shipping trade. God gave me the answer. I only have one more run overseas darling. When I return, I'll bring flower bulbs from New Amsterdam and seed too. My new company runs once a month and I'll be home with you for a week in between, March through December. All winter I'll be home with you, my family."

She giggles.

I continue, "You can stock our pantry and Marcus can care for the animals you wish to keep on our land. You should have them build you a barn and a chicken house."

"Charles has chickens, He'll give me baby chicks. Marcus knows how to keep them alive. What do you want the barn for?" she asks.

"Horses, a carriage, a wagon. You can have sheep or cows. Anything you want sweetheart," I say and sit back to watch her reaction.

It's priceless for me. She feels promoted in life. The plenty of my estate takes her weariness away.

She stands up straight and looks around the shanty, where she has lived in one room.

I can almost read her mind rising above the "don't haves".

"Buy for you and the children anything you need, with my blessing," I say, and lay in her hand the bag of gold guilders.

She does not open to look at it, knowing what I would carry. She honors me already. I feel her profound respect.

That's how she sees me, awed at my success.

I need that too. I've worked hard. It's good to be the hero.

The next day I watch her braiding her hair.

"I'll bring back beautiful and useful things for our new home Emma," I say, walking across the room, "Do you like lace? What colors do you prefer? You were a vision in loveliness on our wedding day," I say, remembering to appreciate her with kindness, the advice of my friend, Thomas.

As the day wears on, I explain how I had designed a boat without cannon, designated only for cargo and using block and tackle to operate it.

I say, "It will have taller sails and a shallow draft for getting into ports and harbors other ships can't. It'll be faster and so my shipping will be cheaper."

I remind her "I always thought of you. I couldn't come. I didn't know what happened to you until I got the letter."

She says, "I always thought of you too. I didn't want another suitor. I had already found the best man."

My whole inside smiles. She admires me. Wonderful.

Chapter 37

"Defend the poor and fatherless: do justice to the afflicted and needy."

Psalm 82:3

In the year of our Lord, 1655

Emma builds a three-story stone house, with ample pantry shelves and firewood storage in the basement. She has a large room for meetings, rooms for guests, and plenty of light with windows on every side. She oversees whitewash on the walls, inside and out and makes eight good mattresses, stuffed with husks. The six fireplaces open on all floors, for adequate heat. She has them cut windows in the loft and reinforce the roof with a gabled layer. She fences the side yard and edges the walk and river with large stones. In between, she digs a wide flowerbed for tulips and daffodils, thinking it will remind me of the old country.

She tries to please me. I love that.

Workers are painting, and she's dragging a mattress through the door, when I come across the meadow to our path hauling a wagon of goods and waving gallantly at her.

On the buckboard I have two boys, sullen and apprehensive. I jump from the seat and run to Emma, lifting her up and kissing her face here and there. She has to giggle.

"What's this?" she asks, eyeing the boys and the load.

Quickly I stand in front of her and explain.

"I couldn't turn them away. They would have been put in the street," I say, wondering how she will take to them.

She hurries past me to make them feel welcome.

Oh, good.

I say, "This is Lance and Faron. Their Lutheran parents sent them to the Netherlands from Palatinate, the Rhineland."[104]

I whisper, "Please ask nothing more now."

She leans toward the youngest who is, maybe five.

"Are you Faron?" she guesses.

He nods.

"They've been learning English on our trip," I insert.

She wrinkles her nose and lifts him up in her arms. The older boy shifts, looking down.

"You must be Lance," she says a little gruffly, "Tell me, are you as strong as your name?"

His eyes meet mine expecting rejection.

She squeezes his arm muscle.

"My!" she exclaims, "You will be a good help with the new calves. We have two you know."

He perks up, hops off the buckboard and dons his jacket.

She points, "In the side yard there, you'll find Marcus feeding them. Go and tell him you've come here to live with me and Papa Gerrit."

She put Faron down and they both run to see the calf.

I'm speechless with tears and happily want to show her my presents. She begs me to unload at the back of the house.

I brought three fine dresses for her and accessories, (too many to mention), a silver locket for Myra, coats and boots for the children, tools, pots and crocks, a case of fine china, two cartons of silver serving utensils and a chandelier. I chose elegant carved furnishings, four chairs, a chefarobe and dainty curtains and oil paintings, (two). Books and maps and vellum and India ink. Spices of cinnamon, nutmeg, pepper and saffron. Fire grates and fire shields, (four). The last barrel is full of flower bulbs.

She is ecstatic, laughing.

How I love to see her happy.

As we walk outside, she shows me the place for the bulbs.

We watch Lance petting the calf and Marcus showing Faron the piglets.

"Will you be sorry to have four orphans?" I ask.

She beckons for me to come near her.

"Tiger, look at me," she orders, "Nothing could have made us closer than doing God's work together. Believe me. You made the best choice. I've heard many poor families in London have children taken from them[105] to be put on ships as laborers in the colonies. As long as we have enough, we're compelled to be family to them and share what God has given us."

In five days, I must be off again, this time promising it will be only to Manhattan and oversee the shipbuilding.

She draws the children around her, teaching chores, reading the books together and bringing them up with the Word of God in their minds.

I love that too.

All in all, I prove to be worthy of Bos' trust and the first year the Huybrecht firm builds three ships by my boat plans, awarding me the management. I hire on two quartermasters and make them Commanders. Then I train Bernard and Felix to do our buying and selling on those ships. I trust them. The trade agreements I write myself, making new friends with the Swedes and the English.

Dirk is in school in New Amsterdam until Spring.

We keep a low profile, humbly carrying small goods and staying close to shore away from recent pirate activity. They are scouting for gold, but I don't want to tangle with them to prove we don't have any.

Six days a week we come to port somewhere, ready to buy, ready to sell. All the men are home to rest on the Lord's Day.

By Christmas Emma is carrying my child and our basement is full of barrels and crates of food. I bring her a mink muff from Ft. Christopher, that she finds comforting and puts it to use especially during meeting.

In our new house, we hold meetings and share our bounty, our hearts full and our town peaceful.

There is news of war Vincent hears on the docks. Arrests are made on the converts of George Fox for the fast-growing group called the Religious Society of Friends.[106] When George Fox suggests the judge should tremble and quake at the Word of the Lord, the judge dubs him a Quaker. The papers make sport and the name sticks.

"Quakers are jailed in England by the hundreds and dying there," he says, "In northern Italy, the Duke of Savoy put force on the Waldenses to attend Mass or remove to the high Alps in twenty days. Through icy waters, climbing frozen peaks they at last reached the homes of other Waldenses who took them in. By Easter, the Duke sent troops into the mountains and demanded the people quarter them in their homes, which turned out to be a trick to gain entrance. Seventeen hundred persons pitifully destroyed in unmentionable ways," Vincent tells us at meeting.

He becomes silent, then says, "Things so brutal I cannot speak it."

His face is seriously sad.

We leave in shock, having forgotten persecution far away.

In a meeting the following week, Bernard tells us he has been talking with the Religious Society of Friends who settled near Providence.

Felix asks if they are heretics. The air is tense.

"That's not for me to judge. I find them devout and peaceable, though there are stark differences. In their zeal to separate from all the rituals of the Anglican Church, they have forsaken Holy Communion and baptism," he answers.

Edmund raises his brows and looks to Howell.

At once I speak up, "Jesus said, 'By their fruits you'll know them.'"

Vincent agrees with an input from the back, "If that is the measure, heretics are what we fled from."

We grunt at the absurdity of our persecutors having love and decide what we know of the Quakers, won't cause us to harm them.

"Which gives us reason to question the hanging of Quakers in Plymouth,"[107] I make my statement, unafraid, "This news I heard straight from my friend Nehemiah himself."

Everyone looks wide-eyed one to another.

"Yes, yes," around the room they agree with me.

"We who have made friends with Indians, shall find a way to be neighbors and not Pharisees," Bernard offers, "I live closest to their community. Tomorrow I will take some sugar and tea. I'll ask if they need anything, for we are brethren."

I agree, "We'll go too. Maybe Emma can talk with the women. Sometimes they open up more than the men."

There are many poor among the Quakers, who indeed need food and quilts. They lost cows and oxen.

Four orphans come home with us. Three are older girls that can cook and clean, sew, and help as Emma nears time for the baby to be born.

The boy is very studious, and I allow him to read and tinker, encouraging his scientific curiosity. He will only be a boy once.

Our son is born in the heat of summer, in the middle of the night, by firelight. Emma lays by the fireside and nurses the tiniest person, ninth of the young in our house.

I can't help beaming, considering a grand name and when I ask, she says, "It's up to you."

I take our baby in my arms. A tiny fist winds itself around my finger.

"I want to name him 'Gerritsen' after me. He is Gerrit's son. My son," I whisper proudly to her.

She falls asleep exhausted and content, watching me by the window tell the baby of the sea and ships and things.

The Quaker girls marry and move to new settlements, at Barrington, Pawtucket and Westerly.

News from Europe comes. Today Bos has a runner fetch me from the boat and invites me in the library. He proceeds immediately asking if I would like to make a mercy run to the West Indies in the *Morganster*.

That night back home, I call Emma outside and say, "There's been a heavy massacre of Waldenses in the Piedmont on Easter.[108] The Dutch and Swiss have smuggled one hundred and sixty-seven Waldenses underground escaping to Holland. Oliver Cromwell paid a great sum on their behalf and rescued them. The city councilors have hired three ships to transport them to The Christina River. Bos Gillis Huybrecht wants me to bring one of them back from Pembroke, Wales."

"There's no one else can do it?" she asks.

I blink.

She already knows my heart is making the journey.

"I'll leave at sunset, to keep the cargo running on schedule. I shan't be back for Christmas," I say, eyes waiting approval, "I did offer my services."

"But it's almost winter," she objects.

I look down.

So, she gives me a kiss, saying no more.

She understands I'm a man trying to please God and her.

The storms come heavy. I'm out on choppy waters, hurrying the course, icy conditions inside the hull.

Keeps our food well, but frigid on the bones.

The men's hands and lips crack and bleed in the wind.

It's March when I get home. I have taken cold and go to bed four days. Emma makes me laugh, telling me how Gerritsen learned to say his first word.

Balancing himself by the firebrick his hand touched the hot stone. "Burn," he wailed to his mother.

She tells me how she hurried to cover his fingers in salve and wrap them, which did little good, for a toddler thinks only to put his fingers in his mouth. Later as he slept, she inspected and found them blistered, red with pus.

He sits on her lap, watching her tell me the story. Then he shows me the finger, completely healed.

"Burn," he says, sending us into laughter.

By the time I'm up, he has named me, "Da".

Yes, a boy after my own heart.

Chapter 38

"Unto me, who am less than the least of
all saints, is this grace given, that I should
preach among the Gentiles the unsearchable
riches of Christ;"

EPHESIANS 3:8

IN THE YEAR OF OUR LORD, 1657

When I pull stopover at the Mayhew plantation, Thomas the Elder strolls out on the lawn to greet me.

"We've had a good deal of rain lately. Our vegetable crops are plentiful. Could I interest you to take some of it off our hands? Perishables, you know. Won't keep. Tomatoes, squash, cucumbers, strawberries, and such," he says, "As well as eggs and butter."

I shake my head and grin.

I say, "Is this meant to twist my arm?"

We chuckle and cross the bridge to the fields. I see the baskets being filled by workers, bent picking the produce.

"Whatever you have, I'll buy it all," I say.

Fairchild calls the boys from her doorway, and I watch them quickly obey their mother.

I say, "My son is learning to walk."

The old man nods.

"I recall the day I taught my Thomas to walk. I had closed the shop early. It was dreary cold and rainy, a brisk wind whipping about and no customers. His mother and I lived in the back, and she had made us a hearty beef soup.

While the bowls cooled and her flat cakes were on the spider, I would stand the child across the room a little and with my legs spread wide, bid him come to me. 'Com'n, my boy, come to your Papa,'" he recalls.

His eyes twinkle merrily savoring the memory.

"He loved me to rough-house with him. He haltingly stepped out and reached his arms toward mine. And fell. I laughed and stood him up again," he says, turning to go to the house.

He says, "Now, he does that at his mission, teaching them how to get back up again.. It's incredible the transformation in those Indian's lives. It's grown to be more than he can oversee. They're sending him to London to gain support and helpers. Got his minister's credentials too, Gerrit. You really should go out and see for yourself."

He pokes me on the chest, "Will do your soul good and give us time to bring in the harvest. He'll leave this week."

I say, "You've convinced me. I'll have my men rearrange the cargo to make room. They can fish while I'm gone."

Early the following dawn, Thomas the Younger wakes me and I hurry along to keep pace with him.

He's a fountain of joy, talking serious and contagious.

How I missed him, this sincere man of God.

I sense the presence of Jesus as Rev. Thomas Mayhew stands opening the service at the "Place on the Wayside", with prayer, and preaching to the fifteen hundred Indians standing in a semicircle around him.

They follow him as he comes down toward Lexingtown. Taking his text from first Psalms, he expounds on the third verse, saying, "He shall be like a tree planted by the rivers of waters, that bringeth forth fruit in his season; his leaf also show not wither; and whatsoever he doeth, it shall prosper."

With compassionate eyes he stresses the love of God in contrast to the superstitions they used to believe.

"I'm going to purchase books and bring back teachers for

our school and ministers to help me in this work. Thank you to the sachem of Sanchakantackett for the "powwow" you gave me at Farm Neck and the excellent dinner of split eels. I leave you in the care of Stephen Breckworth, and he will guide you to understand God's Word," he says at the end, "Remember the Lord is your Shepherd, watching over you tenderly, knowing all of your needs."[109]

He then prays and they sing a hymn. Hiacoomes was his first convert. He comes forward and shakes his hand, placing a large stone at his feet.

"I put this down here in your name and whenever I pass, I shall place a stone in your memory until you return," Hiacoomes speaks loudly for the honor he feels toward Thomas Mayhew and backs away.

Thomas responds, "Hiacoomes, not in my name, nor in my memory, but in the name and memory of the Great Master of whom I taught you, Christ."

All the Aborigines chiefs in turn, place a stone where Thomas stood and throw a blanket over their faces and bow in their grief, following by tribes, and leave Indian file, tracking back over the plain to their homes.[110]

Walking back, Thomas is quiet, his Bible held up close to his chest. I respectfully leave him to his thoughts.

The baskets and crates are being loaded as the house comes into view. My men give a signal. They are ready.

I run ahead and inspect the cargo as well as the fish they brought in. A very good day's catch.

"I think you should fish a little more in the wee hours. I'll be back onboard to keep my watch at three. Tell every man you can spare to eat now and go to bed. I'll rouse them before sunup," I order, jumping back on the pier.

At dinner I meet Stephen Breckworth. Our conversation centers around the Indian student's accomplishments.

I return to the ship to catch a few hours of rest, thinking how different the vision was that Thomas the Younger had for the Indians, than the directors of New Amsterdam.

What God could have done with a Christian heart of love?

I'm glad we live in Rhode Island. Other colonies say we are "riffraff". Roger Williams says it was founded on love.

The next morning, I watch Thomas leave, taking Fairchild's brother and the first Indian graduate of Harvard College, a preacher among the Aborigines. As their ship sails away, the Indians stand on the beach with bowed heads and Indian runners follow as far as they can.

It causes me to weigh what my life could be and how I need to let God use me like that.

Because the rains are abundant and the winds contrary, it's three days before I arrive back at Mayhew plantation.

"Governor, I hear you've been given a formal consideration from King Charles," I say, meeting him at the door, the rain slicing my face as he quickly lets me in.

"With so much mud, we scarce can send the workers out. Do give me your cloak, my good man," he welcomes me.

It's late and we sit by the fire drinking tea.

"Fairchild and the children have already eaten and went to bed. I made her come to the big house because of this dreadful weather. Won't you have some chicken with rice? It will only take a moment to set some by the fire," he asks.

Suddenly the roaring sound of a hurricane blasts our ears.

As the shrill night wind of the Atlantic Ocean blows aggressively against the house, the Governor opens the windows back and latches the wooden shutters, one after another, while I help him. Then upstairs, going down the hallway, he passes the children's beds and I'm below, bolting the doors, front, and rear.

The gale intensifies. The house creaks in the storm. We hear trees cracking and the sea pounding the rocks violently.

I peek out at my small ship, careening in the water.

Back in his study, Governor Mayhew dons his spectacles.

"Come here Gerrit," he says, "I have a projected inventory of the upcoming harvests. You know we cleared eight more fields last fall. I want to build a flour mill, but up til now, all my budget has been used for the Indian school."

I seat myself by the doorway.

He's attempting to concentrate despite the howling storm.

Fairchild in her bed bonnet tiptoes down the stairs with a lamp stick.

She says, "M'lord, might I have a word with ye, if I'm not disturbing your concentration?"

Her father-in-law is attentive, yet silent.

He puts his finger on the page and peers over his glasses, responding, "Is this a serious matter?"

She nods and waits permission, never looking up.

He bookmarks the page, closing the volume.

I say, "Should I leave?"

He shakes his head, "You're like family."

She's solemn, entirely respectful.

The Governor removes his spectacles and faces her saying, "I'm ready to hear you, my child."

"Thank you kindly, sire," Fairchild says, "I will establish two things before I state my business."

He clears his throat, "Business. Humph."

Fairchild says, "I've never given my mind to dwell on foolish fears or entertain vain imagination. Always, I'm practical, logical and serve God in all my thoughts."

Over the howling wind he nearly shouts.

"Yes Fairchild. True no doubt," her father-in-law replies.

Fairchild ventures to look at him momentarily.

Rain begins to smack the windows sideways.

"My gentle husband and I have been one heart and soul since our first day of marriage," she confides.

The old man melts, with crinkles around his eyes. Obviously, he appreciates her place in his family.

Fairchild chooses her words, "I honor him from my heart. We've never gone to sleep with anger toward each other."

Governor leans forward compassionately, "I believe you."

"I have been lying awake a long time trying to decide if I should tell you," she says, studying the ceiling.

The Governor's face freezes.

She takes a deep breath.

"I think Tommy is giving me a message in a dream I just had. In the dream, the ship was heaving. The mast broke and fell crashing down. Water surged over the side and the ship tilted. The sailors were struggling. The storm raged and suddenly there was a light around Tommy. He looked at me and smiled," she says pacing.

I immediately turn to see Thomas the Elder's reaction.

He interrupts her, "A good sign. He'll be safe."

Fairchild continues, "He reached for me and took my hand. We were no longer at sea, but in a beautiful meadow, full of sunshine and bird songs. I could smell the sweet fragrance of fruit and flowers. People were singing and calling him to come along. They were going to celebrate with the King. He let go my hand and joined them."

Outside, the rain stops. Governor Thomas opens the window and unlatches the shutter, turning it back. The moonlight shines clearly over the ocean.

He looks back at Fairchild.

She crosses the room to the base of the stairs.

"I think he's gone," she says resolute.

The Governor has burned the lantern low and is still bent over the books when I go outside to pray at three.

Fairchild's dream disturbed us both.

The sky is overcast in the morning. Tree limbs are scattered over the ground and I see two ripped sails. Field hands remove the debris, working happily.

I stand on the veranda watching my men pull the canvas down to repair it, drinking coffee, awaiting the Governor.

Inside, Fairchild has dressed the children and they wait while she bakes biscuits and turns bacon.

The smell is enough to bring the Governor out.

He salutes me and we sit down to a glorious breakfast.

In the fall we are trading near Virginia and my mind was on the storm that took my father not far from there, when I hear Thomas's ship never reached England.

It devastates me. I could not bounce back all day.

When I meet Jesus for prayer on the fourth watch there is no moon and I pace quietly, *mulling questions of why?*

And there in the dark, the Comforter reminds me they are blissfully worshipping before the sapphire throne of God.

In my mind I see the serene joy of Thomas's face and recall the dream Fairchild counted personal.

God meant for me to be there that night, to know He had taken young Thomas in His arms.

No, he is not dragging the ocean floor as some who have no hope.

He is waiting for her and his converts, his children and his old father. Thomas is resting in Paradise and I will see him again someday.[111]

Chapter 39

IN THE YEAR OF OUR LORD, 1681

Gerritsen is raised among other children from the start.

I love him more, of course.

When he's nine, I insist he's old enough to travel with me.

Having been a young orphan myself, I always hire and train boys I see on the shore. If they survived the turmoil they came from, *I know to be sensitive and help them make their way.*

Many are already hardened. I have felt that way too.

I tell them to look at the horizon until they get used to the waves tossing the ship. I show them how to stay out of the burly men's way, yet be helpful. I take them on a tour, explaining how the ship works, what is dangerous and what is expensive.

I gain a reputation for it. People bring me orphans from Holland and the New World. Sometimes they drop them at Martha's Vineyard, sometimes Boston. They are half breeds mostly, wiry-haired vagrants, rough and tumble survivors.

Often, I'm the only soul that knows their language.

I do what I can to get them to a job and safety.

Gerritsen tends to latch onto the English boys. Maybe because of his mother, he feels he's was one of them.

They carry a disdain for the Dutch from the prejudice they've heard. At dinner they sit away from the other boys.

I notice it affecting Gerritsen toward me when he's about twelve.

Ever since New Amsterdam fell to the British in '64, it has been a source of shame and regret.[112]

I know firsthand how mismanaged the outpost had become. The complaints of the people were justified. The attack on the Indians was senseless and brought a bad reputation for us who had no part in it.

Looking back, I can see why Evert had need for me to spy. And Wildebrand wanted to govern for certain. He had a love for the land and a heart for the people. But I think the greed of the company spoke louder than sentiment and the longer I live, the more I see my people have become enslaved by their own wealth.

So the English control the land along the Hudson, Manhatten Island and all of New Netherland. The Dutch are pushed aside, no longer revelant.

Our old ways have been beaten down.

I thought it would wear off when those boys moved on, but it didn't. It seemed that every English orphan I take on, is drawn to Gerritsen and he to them.

Every week we pull in at Boston. Nehemiah has become like a grandfather to my son and his grandchildren are Gerritsen's friends. He watches over the bow as we near the dock and runs down to meet them.

"Do you believe 'All things work together for good?[113]'" Nehemiah asks, "I need to talk. My heart is heavy."

We let Gerritsen and Noah walk ahead, looking in shop windows with money in their hand for a treat at the bakery.

We tell them we're going back to the boat galley and they can fish while we talk.

Alone, I bring out two mugs and some cider for us.

Nehemiah says, "My oldest son, Noble, is my right hand. He is good and kind, quiet and always dependable. He has ten children, seven boys and three young sisters. Their house is near mine in the field. Recently, at communion he looked long and hard at me with a yearning I didn't understand."

I sit by the window where I can watch the boys fish.

"All through the Bible study I couldn't keep my mind on church. I wonder, "What's bothering my son?" he tells me.

"How old is he?" I ask.

"Forty-two," he says, "As soon as it's over and we're walking away from our wives, I caught up with his clip and tugged on his sleeve.

"What's come between us?" I ask.

He looks over his shoulder fearfully, "'Father, if ye count my heart precious, I need to speak to you privately, not in the street,' he whispers so serious."

Nehemiah says, "For two miles I'm perplexed, until we are behind shut doors, in the barn among the horses. Noble says 'I've been struggling in my soul all winter, how to say this to you because it may part us forever.' I bear hug him tightly, then wait for his explanation."

I'm on the edge of my seat wondering what will come next.

Nehemiah's lips are tight. He shakes his head.

"'I no longer agree with our church and I no longer want to live here,' Noble admits and I cover my mouth. The shock is in the air. I stare at him," Nehemiah shares.

I can tell he's heartbroken and shoot up a prayer, "Lord, show me what to say, how to help."

Nehemiah's expression pleads, "Noble's heart is resolute to please God. I know him. He said, 'Father there is a pride in this colony I cannot abide. It's harsh and cruel and infects my children, cancelling everything I want them to be.'"

Nehemiah isn't finished, "He said 'The Quakers should not be hung. They shouldn't be afraid of us. It's not Christian love. Jesus told the story of the Good Samaritan.[114] Father, these people were strangers among us.' Up to that point I was ready to argue how our ways keep a pure society. Who were we to question the elders?"

I nod, *perplexed at this information.*

Then Nehemiah says, "My son said, 'I'm ashamed to be this kind of Christian.'"

Nehemiah shakes his head, "His innocent eyes bore a hole through my heart. We stood facing each other for a few minutes. I knew he was resolved. I leaned against the stall. Our eyes locked, father to son, heart to heart. Then he tells me, 'We want to sell off my inheritance and move west.'"

Nehemiah's eyes stare at the fire. On his cheeks rivlets of tears course twinkling in the firelight.

Now he whispers, "He said it so softly, wishing not to hurt me, I know. Still it came crashing down on my dreams with a thud. I put my hand on his shoulder, before I left. I did not want to break ties. I couldn't find fault with his conscience."

Nehemiah wipes his face with his sleeve and gets up, crossing to the window, overlooking the town and says, "As the week wore on, I watched him in the fields with his boys. I weighed his words while I drove the horses to market and again when the plowing gives a man time to think. The colony has a stranglehold on my faith. Faith that was once pure between me and God. My soul wrestles with Noble's convictions and it's been a long time coming."

I'm speechless, blinking, absorbed with his dilemna, truly.

He sits back down, and sadly faces me.

"I've been praying and I trust your advice. We've been business associates all these years. I have no one else to go to, that can understand and I'm getting old," Nehemiah says, "My seed is in the soil. I can be gone three weeks. I read of the land grant given to Admiral Penn's son, the preaching Quaker who has been in prison several times. His pamphlets are scattered across England and Europe. If you agree it's good to put out a Gideon fleece,[115] I'll let you take me to Pennsylvania. I can look around, see if anything speaks to my heart and no one need know where I'm gone."

I squint at him in awe.

A test of faith. A test of all a man's fortune and all of his family.

Actually, I can't take my eyes off him.

I didn't need to say I agreed about putting out a fleece. He had already made up his mind. His trip was the fleece.

I say, "Of course, I'll take you."

When the boys come back, Nehemiah's packed bag is in the passenger's cabin. He tells Noah to take the wagon home.

Gerritsen takes Nehemiah on a tour of the ship and shows him all he knows. I'm busy and the day's sun holds promise. All afternoon the grandfather occupies my son conversing about his life and Massachusetts.

At dinner, Gerritsen urges me to tell our family history about Piet Hyen and the city of Amsterdam.

Nehemiah watches the dagger match after dinner.

Later we walk the deck as I pass Long Island, and I tell Nehemiah about myself, about my father dying in the storm and being washed ashore as an orphan, while Gerritsen fishes from the other side.

"There is an estate up the Hudson," I point, "Belongs to my benefactor. I served the Huybrecht family six years in the fields and woods, and on the dock, before you met me. When the Indians attacked New Amsterdam, we fled to Martha's Vineyard. Young Thomas led me to give my life to Christ. He challenged me to not just believe, but live it and love people. I gave Jesus my heart and surrendered my life to Him that day, and to practice the Bible," I say, "It was the same day you brought Fairchild to get married."

"But you were Dutch Reformed," he ventures.

"Well, a member of the church, yes. That's not getting born again," I challenge him, square in the face.

"I'm a Puritan. I love God and live piously," he bargains.

We stand on the bow observing isolated cabins and farms.

I say, "My people fought eighty years, dying by the thousands for religious freedom. Our enemies committed cruelties in the name of Christ with no love in their hearts."

"My people too, in England," he says.

"What causes men to turn on others, even when they read the Bible and have the example of Jesus?" I whisper, looking into the dark, questions hanging in the silence.

Nehemiah excuses himself and goes below *to wrestle with pleasing men or pleasing God.*

When morning comes, he finds me in the cargo hold, counting barrels. He looks at me with a grin, *knowing we would continue our conversation of the forenight.*

"How did you end up at Rhode Island?" he asks me.

I answer, "Because of my wife. She and her brother had been chased out of England. I knew her to be a believer with the strictest devotion. I admired her faith and had been her acquantince three months at sea when they crossed over on my ship, the *Morgenster.* They were fleeing persecution. Part of her family were drowned for being Anabaptists."

I finish the count and turn back to him.

I say, "Friend, no man can find happiness from being a church member. Faith comes from following Christ. It must come from your heart. Are you looking for that peace in your soul that only God can give, not manmade religion?"

His expression is troubled.

I open my hands, asking, "Do you think you'll draw closer to God, away from the Puritans back home?"

He rubs his beard thoughtfully and says, "Quite possibly, Gerrit. It's on my mind. I'm going to seek a suitable parcel of land and buildings. If my venture proves Providential, I'll resign the Church and find faithful friends who love the Bible among the neighbors where God moves me. You know one of the things Penn wrote was, 'Force makes hypocrites, 'tis persuasion that makes converts.'"

Our eyes lock.

We who have seen religious hatred know its venom.

He lowers his eyes, "Could it be God Almighty has re-warded a man with a tender conscience by giving him land like a king? Pennsylvania is over forty-five thousand square miles.[116]"

It did not escape my attention that this was definitely the second time I was aware of a great wealth transfer.

I say, "You will know. God will make it clear, in your soul."[117]

After he walks away, I think, *that's what he needed to hear, and it will echo in his mind with the power of prophecy.*

Chapter 40

"Now the end of the commandment is charity out of a pure heart, and of a good conscience, and of faith unfeigned:"

1 Timothy 1:5

In two weeks, I meet him on the dock in Philadelphia among many ships and much loading.

"Will you be long Gerrit? I'm ready to get home," he says.

"No, I have plenty of help. Let me see the merchants. Go on up and settle in. Ivan, come carry Mr. Lloyd's things to the first passenger cabin," I order.

When I return, Dirk has chicken soup with rice in the kettle and some cole slaw ready. He fries cornmeal mush on the griddle, hot and crunchy.

We drink fresh buttermilk and then Nehemiah and I talk.

"So did you meet the famous William Penn?" I ask.

With his mouth full, he nods.

"At the land office," he says, "He came up the river and a group of people welcomed him.[118] I followed them just to observe. He was quite respectful with the Indians and gave them the same attention as the magistrates.

"He did?"

"Yes. And he took off his coat and hat in the building and turned up his sleeves. They unrolled the surveyor maps, and he came out in the mud with the rest of us. He was overseeing the clearing, surveyors waiting to be hired. Loggers. Men waiting to work, standing, watching things."

"Hmm," I responded, as the boat swayed launching out.

He says, "I thought if he's going to be Governor, I want to know what I'm getting myself into. He's mild mannered and humble, a true Christian. Then, when the opportunity was ripe, I approached him and said, 'Mister Penn, I'd like to buy land.' I looked him in the eye. He shook my hand and faced me too. Didn't act like an aristocrat, high and mighty. He says to me, 'You can obtain a warrant for survey at the Land Office in that cabin over there. I welcome you friend! If there is any way I may be of service, come to me.'"

"Treated you as an equal?" I ask surprised.

Ferris, Jean Leon Gerome, Artist.
"The Landing of William Penn"
J.L.G. Ferris. Pennsylvania, ca. 1932.

Cleveland, Ohio: The Foundation Press,
Inc., July 28. Photograph. https://www.loc.gov/item/2004669764/.
No known restrictions on publication.

"Yes, he did," he goes on, "Gerrit, it's a whole different atmosphere. You'd love it. Well I went back over by the land office. All those axe men and surveyors with their chains, wanting to be hired looked at me in anticipation. There were Germans, Swedes, French and Danes settling in their communities, building, and cutting timber. They had brought millworks and had set up shops. You know. You can see it's prosperous when you come into port here."

I roll a warm corn patty, load it with coleslaw, and stuff it in my mouth.

"I filled out an application and paid the fee," he says, "There were old men standing in the corner. One came to me and offered to be a guide for a fair price. 'What's a fair price?' I ask him. He spouts off, 'Ye kin buy me supper and remember to be kind when ye have extra in the fields, eh?' showing me a toothless grin from his leathered face. He had a horse and wagon tied out back. 'What ye be needing the land for sire?' So I follow him and explain, 'My son and I are farmers, and we have sheep. He has a large family Then he says, 'Everyone has to buy one hundred and twenty five acres.' That was something I didn't know. We drove on in silence so I could see the area and consider the situation. The woods are dense, the land slightly hilly. The soil is rich. By the Schuylkill River, the horse trotted on a worn path along its bank. What are you grinning about?"

I lean back and say, "I've been there. Long time ago. Used to trap in those hills."

He gives me the eye.

"You've done everything," he says, shaking his head.

I reply, "Just about. Had to. Not for the fun of it."

We laugh and eat the food while it's hot.

"The best plots were bought first by investors in groups," he says, "They chose land to the north and off the Delaware River. But I looked at a place I really liked. I had the ship money and funds from the investment we made years ago."

He was smiling so contentedly, I knew already.

"You bought it," I guess.

He smiles full faced to me. I laugh and readjust myself.

"And you didn't tell your wife? You old rascal," I tease.

He's excited, caught up in the joy of his decision.

"Oh Gerrit! If you could see what pretty land. I walked it and envisioned what I could do with it."

He got up and stretched, crossing the room.

"It's two hundred acres," he says, "A good stone barn with

cleared and fenced fields around it and windows below. The doors are stout, wide enough for a good-sized hay wagon."

My eyes widen, thinking *there's no house. He expects they'll live in the barn for a while with the animals.*

He solemnly looks at me.

I brace myself to keep a straight face holding his stare.

"I invested my savings and a note until I sell our estate in Massachusetts. I've got the surveyor's diagram and my warranty deed. I want to be part of the Holy Experiment.[119] I pray my wife will not resist. Can you understand what it means that an old man like me has a dream to start over?" he asks, waiting for my answer with his heart in his hand.

I fold my hands and lean forward.

I'm smitten with his faith.

"You inspire me, Nehemiah, honestly you do," I say.

When I arrive home, I tell Emma how Nehemiah found out that William Penn had made a loving impression on the Lenape Indians, paying them for their land and working out a respectable treaty.

His excitement had triggered me, and I couldn't hide it.

It was something to be admired and I say, "He told me he saw the Indians frequently moving peacefully about the scattered houses, bringing their fish and maize to market, buying tools and imports. He said, "They walked the byways without a care."

This touched me as nothing else could have. I'd been in the meetings Thomas held at his mission and rode with Wildebrand to the Indians in the Catskills.

I believe Jesus opened His arms to all men, Jew, and Gentile. I've seen many a soul cross the ocean to have a clear conscience.

When Nehemiah decided to move, he did it for his.

Chapter 91

"AND THEY TOOK STRONG CITIES, AND A FAT LAND,
AND POSSESSED HOUSES FULL OF ALL GOODS, WELLS
DIGGED, VINEYARDS, AND OLIVEYARDS, AND FRUIT
TREES IN ABUNDANCE: SO THEY DID EAT, AND
WERE FILLED, AND BECAME FAT, AND DELIGHTED
THEMSELVES IN THY GREAT GOODNESS."

NEHEMIAH 9:25

There's no telling what would become of all of us, if something happened to you," Emma corners me one night after the house is quiet, "How would I take care of us all? How could I run the company?"

She gives me the look that implies, "Do you love me?"

"Nothing is going to happen to me," I reason, *knowing she's thinking about what Nehemiah said about Pennsylvania, guessing she wants to move there. It melts my heart.*

"I'll think about changing some things," I offer.

"Like what?" she continues, her tone irritable.

"I don't know. What do you want me to do?" I respond.

"Why don't you give up the company? Put Gerritsen in business and move us away from the coast to the country. He's long been old enough. We could teach school together and farm and raise sheep and chickens," she raises her brows, her voice trailing off.

I look silently at her, *weighing the questions.*

From the cupboard she cuts a piece of cherry pie for each of us and pours mugs of chilled buttermilk.

"I'll test Gerritsen to see if he's ready," I say, "Mind you, if he can't handle it, then it's not right for him. There's a certain fortitude the crew has to see and it's not something I can teach him. It has to come from within himself."

She nods *seeing my heart is with her.*

"I'll ask around the ports and get the news. I haven't farmed since I was very young. It's demanding work. I'm no hunter, that's for sure. Though I would like to be a fulltime teacher, with a bigger place for orphans," I confess.

That sets well with her.

"You've been working for so many years Gerrit," she says taking my hand gently, "Let's do what we love most while we're still young enough to enjoy each other, and I believe God will bless it."

The smile between us is long and I hold it dear for years.

It's her caring heart that I fell in love with, and it is my desire to be with her, doing what satisfies our soul.

So I test my son as I had been tested, leaving the run of the ship to his charge, and watching the men follow his orders.

I feel I've trained him well and he has a favorable manner with clients in his discourse of business. He keeps accurate books and enjoys the life at sea.

Within a year, I sign over six ships to him and three to James. One I give to Dirk, who tender as always, hugs me, and says, "God bless you, kind master."

There is a great sum of money in our account. And Emma has found a buyer for our house.

Four of the boys are working in good apprenticeships and tell us they want to stay on in Providence. I agree they should stay, but if they want to go with us, we're their family. If they need us in the future, don't hesitate to ask for help, or come back home. I take the addresses of their lodging and say we will correspond.

Last, I go to visit the Mayhews. I leave the ship unloading at the pier and find John Mayhew in the field with his son, Ezra, overseeing the harvest of beans for our next load. His grandfather passed away in '81, he tells me, and his two brothers moved to the mainland for other businesses. Experience eyes me quietly with a maturity keen for his twelve years.

I shake the boy's hand heartily.

"I was your grandfather's friend," I explain warmly, "He was kind and so likeable. I remember your father when he was knee high to a grasshopper."

I'm smiling, but the boy is solemn.

His father takes my arm and walks me back to the house.

"May I offer you refreshment Captain Brinkendorf? Your visits here are always welcome of course," he is polite but not with the warm friendliness of his father.

I say for him not to bother. I need to be on my way.

Then bidding him well, I leave as the transaction is finished and the Bill of Lading signed.

I wonder how the Indians are doing and if the church is flourishing. They loved Thomas so and he loved them.

Alone on board, I promise the Lord I will carry on, bringing souls to Him in my corner of the world, expecting divine appointments and excited for my new opportunity.

At Providence, Emma has a girl named Holly watching on the dock. She takes off running before we drop anchor.

I see Emma bringing the loaded wagons, the dust rising behind them. Gerritsen takes our things to the ship and carries us on a dedicated passage up the Delaware to Philadelphia.

We purchase fifty acres recommended by Nehemiah. He describes the house in good condition with ten rooms and four fireplaces, thatched roof, and a year-round spring on a well-traveled road.

"Also, a log barn, with a loft," he says, "Eight stone fenced fields that had been used for livestock, a chicken coop, a cleared garden spot and five fruit trees, seven maples and one black walnut near the woods. He made mention of the wild blackberries and says there hasn't been a bear or panther seen in twenty years."

He'll be our neighbor.

Chapter 42

"BEHOLD, MY SERVANTS SHALL SING FOR JOY OF HEART,..."

ISAIAH 65:14

We are resting in the harbor at dawn when Nehemiah and Noble bring six wagons to take us to our property. Members of the crew unload everything from the boat on wagons and at the house, set things inside.

The house is quite large, and the barn is tall enough for smithing.

Gerritsen stays on another day, to get us settled and his mother hated to see him go as I did. She does not hide her tears, hugging him, and giving advice while I watch her, smiling. Then he leaves.

I choose a school room carried away with plans of instructing children.

"Tiger," Emma whispers when at last we're ready for bed, "We left our brood in Providence. We only have three."

I snuggle her, nightcap ruffles tickling my face.

"God has sent us here for souls that need kindness and learning and some food from the field, eh?" I make her giggle with a funny face, "Soon enough there will be scrambling and pulling of braids, pranks of boys and bright eyes looking to us for instruction."

She sets the warm bricks under the cover at the foot of our bed and lays aside her quilted arm pads.

"Will you go find them?" she asks, "How will you know?"

"God shows me. My heart listens to Him. I'm like a hunter, looking for clues in the eyes. They hide near families. They want to be with other children. Some hide in the work they find. Not all have a bed when the day is done," I say.

I blow out the flame and look at the moonlight over a grassy hillside, with wildflowers along the stone wall and a gate at the top of the rise.

A path is worn to that summit and a cat scampers atop it, mewing in the night.

Emma makes breakfast for us, and Holly is eager to explore the outdoors.

"I think you should go with them," I say when the dishes are put away, "You can tell me all about it when I come in tonight. Cook some beans, and I'll find a bakery and some vegetables."

"What will you do?" she asks pouting.

"Now, you can't put a bridle on me like the goat that pulls the cart," I retort, and she pokes me with a grin.

"I'll go into town and learn what goes on along the dock, find us a cook if I can and introduce myself to authorities and such. When they ask our business, I'll make it known and God will open doors,"[120] I assure her, "We need books and writing supplies for students. I have a mental list."

She unties the apron and kisses me goodbye, gathering biscuits in her pocket and sliding the kitchen knife in her boot. One call from her and the children follow her out the door, like ducklings in a row.

I tie back my hair and put on a fresh shirt and coat.

No telling who I might meet today. I want to serve God here. I'm ready, more than ever.

I decide to walk. It's a pleasant day, not yet warm. From this vantage I can get a better feel of what lies between me and town.

I take a slow step, peering into the woods and pacing myself to quietly enjoy nature. The birds are joyful and busy capturing their breakfast. Two black silky squirrels chase across the lane and scamper up the tall trees, swiftly, cautious of me. The blackberries are in bloom I notice. I will remember their location for the future. A coyote slinks near an upcoming barn, where unsuspecting chickens peck at grasshoppers and dig for worms in the dirt.

I pick up a hand-sized rock and hurl it at him striking the hind leg. He yelps and runs. I watch him as he eyes me from the field. I bend to choose another stone, holding the guard. He scurries away.

I hear voices. An angry woman is chastising someone behind the barn. As the bend of the road takes me into a clearing, I see the object of her scorn, a young girl of perhaps twelve. The woman slaps her again and again as the girl shields her head with her arms. The laundry in the girl's hand falls in the dirt, which angers the woman more and her tirade of harsh words heightens.

Then she sees me. I smile. She gathers up the laundry and huffs away from the girl, who looks my way and brushes back the tousled hair, wiping her cheeks.

I walk slowly, watching the woman return to the fire by the laundry tubs on the rocks.

I feel I should do something and approach her.

"Good day," I quip, "My name is Gerrit. My wife and I bought the house down the lane. We want to make friends with our neighbors and live here in God's peace."

She brushes her arm across her forehead sweat and turns to one side facing me.

"That's fine I suppose. I don't have time for pleasantries if ye don' mind sir," she says a little brash, "My work must be out of the way for more washing. Business you understand."

Considering that she has given me a little information regarding her pressures, I proceed to be Christ's hand of love to her.

"Would you be thinking you could take on any new customers?" I request mildly.

At that she wipes her hands and calls the girl to finish the tub full. She shakes my hand and faces me.

"There is no comparison to the respectable job I will do for ye sire. I work cheap and keep to your schedule. I'm a widow you see. It's my living," she bows to a curtsey in the old style.

"You're Swedish?" I ask, nodding.

"Ya, born here. Father's farm is mine. More than I need. Do you have a lot of laundry?"

She's anxious to be on with it. I'm not.

The girl is holding her own by this time and has hung three garments out to dry. I notice the woman's hands are chapped and her bulky shoes once belonged to a man.

"Is this your daughter?" I implore further.

The woman scowls, "No, an indentured servant. I bought her to help, but she's lazy and ill-tempered."

I restrain from laughing and ask her name.

"My apology good sir. Molly Schwann. All the families in town know me. I'm a member of the Swedes Church in Southwark," she says and straightens in pride.

I take her elbow and walk with our backs to the girl.

Whispering I bargain, "How much did you pay for the girl?"

She draws back to consider.

"I've fed her and clothed her nigh two year. She's been a lot of trouble," she says callously.

I pretend to weigh that.

"She's worth 75 shillings," she finalizes, and I nod, looking at the chickens.

"That's a fair price madam. Fair enough. As I came down our road, I rocked a coyote that was stalking your rooster strutting far from his fat hens," I announce.

Her eyes narrow and shoot into the woods.

"That varmit. He's got four good laying hens so far," she divulges, about in tears.

She's graying and heavy, her teeth going bad. What would Jesus do in my place?

I take from my bag seventy-five shillings and hand them to her, turning her countenance to joy.

"I'll take the girl off your hands. Can you cook?" I continue. She nods eagerly. I smile.

"Good. Let us be kind neighbors and best of friends together, my family and you," I say, "How about you gather the chickens into the barn for now and finish the laundry. My wife needs a cook and I'll bring the wagon to buy your chickens. You won't need them when you eat with us. We'll share the eggs together. You and the girl clean yourselves up. I'll be back with my wagon and negotiate your salary."

Her face clouds.

"We negotiate now," she stubbornly demands.

Her mood has escalated to fight.

"How much do you need?" I banter.

"I work five days, only morning and afternoon. I be there early but not late. I go home early, only five days. Not Sabbath, not Sunday. No laundry. Twenty shillings and my food," she looks at me with a firm lip, but I know she is hoping this is the answer to her prayer.

She crosses her arms.

"Hmmm. That is considerable," I say slowly, "How good is your food?"

"Very, very good. My mother teach. You will beg for more," she put her fingers to her lips and closes her eyes, then smacks.

"I look forward to tasting it Molly. Now, here is my decision: You cook good and don't burn the food. Don't waste anything. I'll give you twenty shillings every week and be happy to have you. And..."

I pause to get my point across.

Her brows raise.

"I'll give you twenty-five shillings on the weeks that you are cheerful and do not lose your temper in my house. I don't like anger in my house. I don't let my wife, or my children lose their temper," I explain, and my expression is solemn.

She grows serious and *I'm afraid she might back out.*

I can see her thoughts crashing around in her mind. She wants the money. She's afraid she can't do it.

She narrows her eyes and sets her jaw.

"If I lose my temper, I still get twenty?" she asks.

I nod, "But you must keep the bonus a secret," I warn, "If you tell anyone, I'll find another cook."

"Hmmm," she mutters, "Five shillings for five days of no temper. We will be ready when you return."

As I walk away, I see her look at the shillings and call the girl.

"Don't forget to bundle the girl's belongings!" I shout from afar, "What's her name?"

"Lorraine!" Molly shouts and Lorraine waves at me.

Emma is ecstatic when I give her the news. She hugs me smiling and tells me about the wild strawberries they found growing near the house.

Excited, I harness the horse and climb on the wagon. I load up an old cage I found in the cellar.

As I bend to kiss Emma, I warn her about Lorraine.

"The girl's been treated harshly. We don't want her to feel rejected. She's our first sheep in the new ministry. No telling the wolves she's been hurt by," I plead, "And Molly is a widow. She needs us and we need her. She's Swedish and says she's a good cook. I bought her chickens. We'll kill five and have them for dinner. The rest will give us eggs."

Her surprise, priceless.

As I drive away, I shout, "Set the table for many guests."

So, I bring back Molly and Lorraine and all the chickens, leaving the wash on the line for later gathering and take the wagon to town.

Chapter 43

"A FATHER OF THE FATHERLESS, AND A JUDGE OF THE
WIDOWS, IS GOD IN HIS HOLY HABITATION."

PSALM 68:5

I find Goforth and Trywan at the wharf, hanging around watching for any vessel that hired hands to unload.

Goforth is ten, a slight boy, freckled and imaginative. I suspect he is German by his accent.

Trywan is a Lenape half-breed, unwanted by whites and rejected by his tribe. His father has been a drunkard, his mother disappeared.

I hire them for farm work in exchange for room and board, which they are eager to get and slap each other with glee.

I give them each a biscuit from my pocket which they make disappear quickly.

As they sit in the buckboard, I drive down the streets of Philadelphia, up High Street, down Chestnut and around to Walnut. It is already quite a town with possibly two hundred wooden houses.

The boys spy a ship coming into port.

"It's the *Henrietta*!" Goforth says as he pokes Trywan, and they raise themselves up to see.

I steer the wagon toward the dock.

"What cargo do you suspect she'll be carrying?" I inquire.

"More indentured servants probably. Sick people. Convicts and poor trash," Goforth rattles away.

I'm shocked at his criticism knowing his own destitute circumstances, but I'll take that up with him later.

We stop a safe way from the landing, and watch the boat tie up and lay out the gangplank. Merchants and farmers gather around about to see the sale of those who have secured passage on loan. From the hull come hungry looking men, women, and skinny children. The sale goes on for an hour, exchanging monies, filling out contracts, the people following their buyers.

"I've never seen so many European slaves," I state quietly, "I thought they were mostly Africans trained in the West Indies."[121]

Trywan turns to me.

"Many servants, all kinds," he says, "Children too."

He points out two red-headed girls, standing fearfully alone. Probably Irish.

I jump from the wagon and quickly make my way to the front of the crowd.

They're sisters being sold as house servants. I buy them without resistance. They carry a bag that they will not let me help with and climb into the buckboard without expression.

The sadness in their hearts has wiped every trace of feeling from the cherub faces. It breaks me down.

"Goforth, where is a bakery?" I ask cheerfully and sing silly songs *like the Swede once did for me.*

In a few moments we all stuff cinnamon rolls in our mouths and drink sassafras tea.

That's when I see Christopher. He's dirty and tall, probably thirteen. He leans against the building and watches us eat.

I figure him for an orphan.

We're close enough for him to hear, and I finish my food and offer them another bun.

"Shall I tell you why you're in my wagon?" I begin.

They are attentive, cautious.

I know the older boy watching will hear me.

"I went to sea with my Father when I was nine," I say, weaving my life story, up to when I was offered to work on the farm with a contract. I talk about being grateful for the opportunities God sends and respecting the people who were merciful to me.

"God took care of me, and He wants me to take care of orphans. I have a farm and a big house and a wife. We have a cook that makes delicious food. Roasted chicken and potato dumplings," I roll my eyes for effect.

The tall one takes the bait. He walks over and looks at me.

"Would you be needing a good strong worker, almost a man, to be showing these boys how to care for cows and pigs and sheep? I could do that for you, on a contract, like that," he offers.

"That's excellent!" I act surprised, "Have a cinnamon roll. Come sit by the small girls in the back and make sure no coyotes come near our wagon in the countryside. A brave young man is what we need."

Goforth and Trywan aren't sure they like him. Seeing as they're sitting on the seat with me, it doesn't feel so threatening to have him ride in the back.

We haven't gone far before the tall one speaks up, aiming his question at me.

"What's your name?" he says, so blunt.

I stop the wagon, hop down, and go around to face him.

"My apologies are in order. I'm Captain Gerrit Brinkendorf. I sailed the *Morgenster* for the Dutch West India Company for seven years and owned a fleet of ships for twenty more, that my son now manages along the coast. I've recently moved here with my wife and three children, Holly, Brewster, and Angel Eyes."

I extend my hand to him.

He sulks a bit, then sticks his hand out to me.

"Mine's Christopher. Whatcha got to say bout it?" he spurts.

I shake his. Next I stretch my hand to the oldest red-headed girl. Her expression is painfully sober.

"What's your name?" I ask gently.

"Honesty," she says barely audible, "I'm eight. Our Mum died. And our brother. Chessire's seven."

With that, Honesty bends over the wagon and vomits, gagging and pitiful.

I offer my kerchief, but she declines, wiping her mouth on her sleeve and settling back by her sister.

All of us know she'd been hungry too long and eaten too fast. We say nothing, as if we don't notice.

As I return to the driver's seat, I introduce Goforth and Trywan by name, then lift the reins.

"Captain," Christopher speaks up, "Could you use two more boys that are good mannered and hungry?"

I turn around and he jumps startled.

He's touchy.

"You seem like a rich man with a good conscience, talking about God and all. I know two boys who are beaten and punished. If you can buy 'em, I'd pay you back somehow," he is determined.

I like that in him so much already.

All the children look at me and wonder what I will answer.

"Of course. Where do I find them?" I assure him.

And that is how we got Blake and Maudy. Cost me two hundred shillings. They load up on the wagon barefoot.

"Don't call me Maudy," he mumbles grimly, "I hate it."

"What do you want to be called?" I ask him.

"My name is Micah. My mother called me Mike," he retorts, and I raise my brows.

"None of us ever heard of Maudy," I nod at all of them.

"Hello Mike," I say, shaking his hand and it brings a smile to every face, even Honesty.

We sing my silly song as we pass Molly's house and the children look in wonder, as I introduce each one to Emma.

Molly has baked the chickens and potatoes adding onions and cabbage.

"Where did you get the vegetables?" I ask Emma.

"Noble brought them. And a crock of cream. He wants to see you when you have time," she tells me.

Lorraine stands by the fire stirring rice pudding. She glances at me shyly and turns back away.

Honesty and Chessire wander over by her and look up in her face. Lorraine has auburn hair too. Immediately there's a bond with the three and they choose to sleep together that night. I put them in the room next to ours and lay all the boys down on pallets across the hall.

Then I bring two chairs to the doorway, and Emma and I began to talk to the children, where all can see us.

I ask for them to quiet down and look at me.

I say "I have my rules and I mean to have them obeyed. You need never fear me. Only God. Because we will live in honor toward each other and in reverence of our Heavenly Father. He who sees all, will reward and punish the deeds and kindnesses we do.[122] I have lived this way many years and I will teach you how Christ can be your constant help. We will have no angry words in this house. We will work cheerfully and eat tasty food and learn to read and write."

"You may stay here under these rules until you find your way in life. When you're old enough, you may become an apprentice, and still live here. Any problems you can bring to me and talk with me. Consider me your father in whatever way is comfortable to you. Now let us hear the scripture and I will lead in prayer," I promise warmly.

Christopher more than the rest, hangs on every word.

I feel he's ready to make manly decisions, but first he'll watch for proof. He wants to believe in true Christianity so bad.

Now Emma reads 1 Corinthians 13.

How perfect, I think.

"Charity does not boast, does not behave itself unseemly. Rejoices in the truth. Bears all things, hopes all things. Charity is kind and patient. Charity never fails." she says.

Blake is up on one elbow, "What's charity?" he asks.

"Love," Emma responds, "Pure unselfish working love."

After the candles are out and they're asleep, Emma pushes me out the door and we walk in the moonlight to the barn.

"Lorraine came with nothing," she says, "She only owns what she keeps in her pockets."

"Did you see any bundles with the children I brought home?" I ask, "See here, tomorrow Christopher and I will buy things, including what Molly wants in the kitchen. Your job will be to assign chores equal to ability and stay cheerful. Molly will prepare breakfast early and supper early. In between, you will lay out midday snacks as you wish, like cheese, fruit, rolls, and tea. Anything you need we will get. The town is well supplied and there are many merchants and traders on Market Street. Boats deliver daily. I'll look for a laundress, another widow perhaps."

"Tiger," she whispers into my shoulder, "I'm so happy we're going to be together."

Chapter 44

At the crack of dawn Molly brings her apron full of eggs to the kitchen. We hear her rebuilding the fire and pouring water in the kettle.

I walk in the room sleepily and she announces, "A word with you Mr. Gerrit."

I wander closer and give her my attention politely.

"I didn't know you'd have so many mouths for me to cook for. I think I should reconsider my wages," she blasts.

Then she turns her back to me, busy stirring the dough.

"No, we won't do that," I answer quietly.

She has not planned a rebuff strategy and did not anticipate my management ability.

"This is more than normal," she argues, "I didn't expect it. I think you have taken advantage of me."

I hold her look and shake my head.

"If these all were my children you would say nothing. You expect if I am generous with them, you can push my good nature to suit your demands. I will not. Yesterday I saw you struggling and felt compassion. It was the same with each of these I brought to this house. What if each one began to make selfish demands? How soon gratefulness dies."

Her mouth drops open, her hand on her hip.

I lean near her and remind her saying, "You set your wages. I agreed. You set your schedule. I agreed. I offered a bonus each week for extra effort in what I counted special service."

Now she picks up the bowl, stirring furiously.

I raise my finger toward her and say, "I think possibly you have a choice to make now. If you decide you do not like my refusal and yet need the job, you will probably get angry and hold it in. Eventually it will boil over and create mean words and I will hear about even if they are not directed to me, they were meant for me. This has been your attitude since the death of your husband, and I don't think Lorraine could have done anything to please you."

I set my jaw and wait for her response.

She stops stirring and sets the bowl down. Her face is hard, her eyes looking down, her breath labored.

I use my authority and very quietly continue my discourse.

"At this moment you are on the verge of losing this week's bonus. You have a little money from selling Lorraine and the chickens. What when that runs out? Who will pity the soul that bitterly creates its own trouble? Surely that is not you Molly. You are too fine a Christian," I say and put my finger on the table tapping, "God is my witness, I have not taken advantage of you. That slanderous talk is forbidden in the Bible. I am the man of this house, accountable to God and not you. He tells me what to do with my money. And, if He decides you are no longer worthy of the position I've offered, we'll find another woman more satisfactory, to serve."

I cross the room and open the window curtains, away from the hallway.

Maintaining a stern look and low voice I say, "With that made clear, I'm going to wash up and help Emma with the children. If you wish to cancel our agreement, do so quietly by leaving and do not be in my house when I return. Otherwise, I expect a happy Molly and a tasty breakfast, to which I will be delighted to continue where we left off in friendship, before this unpleasant conversation took place."

I leave the room and find Christopher and Lorraine standing around the corner. None of us speak, but Lorraine's eyes shine. She nods slightly at me.

At the washstand Emma has all the little girls in a row. She brushes hair and washes faces. Lorraine comes behind me and smiles at Honesty.

Christopher stands in the door.

"Papa Gerrit is going to buy new clothes for you," Emma gushes, "And scented soap and cinnamon for cookies."

Four pairs of innocent eyes beam at me as I take the brush and smooth my hair, tying it back. I wash my face and wipe it with the towel.

"All hands are dressed and ready for the day, Captain," Christopher salutes, and I nod.

"Can you look them over and determine approximate sizes for clothing and boots? Do that for me Christopher," I ask.

Emma grins at me and gathers her little flock into a file, proceeding down the steps.

In the kitchen Molly stands by the food platters.

"Good morning Captain!" she says in a most cheery way.

"Good Morning, sweet Molly! It's going to be a wonderful day, don't you think?" I return.

"Yes sire, if you say so," she smiles and looks me straight in the face, to which I reach over and give her a side hug.

"The children appreciate your grand breakfast and the excellent meal from last night, don't we children?" I say.

Amid the general "yeses" and nods, Emma is loudest.

"Molly you're a godsend. We're so thankful you have come to help us," she says kindly.

Molly beams a true smile, and *it is a much-needed relief for her disposition,* I think. Now she will be responsive to do her best and win weekly bonuses.

I grow fond of her and *plan to buy her gifts like I would, had she been my mother.*

The little girls will hang on to her stories and love to watch her make desserts. Molly will grow to love us and when the older boys take apprentices and younger boys come in their place, Molly can offer rooms in her house for a small fee, have the company and provide help to those deserving. I see this in her future as I stand there.

"Captain, how are we going to remember all the things we need?" Christopher asks me as we ride along in the wagon, our bellies full.

"I always ask Jesus to help me. He does," I answer, "When the going gets rough, I'm still at peace. We are a team, me, and Jesus. I respect Him and He's a faithful friend."

Christopher is quiet, and *I know it is a good quiet.*

He's thinking from his heart, about life and his obligations to the Most High. I leave him alone with those thoughts.

We stop first at the tailor. Christopher wants to wait for me and pull his hat over his eyes, embarrassed by his appearance. Instead I take him by the sleeve, smiling.

He gets measured and when the tailor comes back with cloth choices, I let him choose what he wants. Next, we find a barber, who cleans up the ratty look of the boy immensely. We drive on to the cobbler and he measures Christopher for boots and buckled shoes. I stand back with satisfaction, my arms folded. His things can be picked up Friday. I pay the man and we go outside.

"Well, I owe you plenty now. You'll get it back. You won't be sorry," he says reluctantly.

"Ah now, son, it gives me great pleasure to be your friend. Don't spoil it thinking it is more than that. I do for you what I would have done for myself. You are valuable to God just as you are. If you run away it will be my heart that will miss you, not my wallet," I tell him.

At the Mercantile, we ask for stockings of every size and frocks for girls and boy-sized jackets and work pants and shirts. There are nightshirts and bonnets. I decide Emma can trim off what is too long. I take eight and am able to persuade the proprietor to let me carry shoes home for a trial fit and exchange them if it isn't right. We buy grey yarn and bolts of fabric, white cotton, and brown wool. I buy indigo blue grosgrain ribbon and matching mittens for the girls and when I see they had them for ladies, I also buy a pair for Molly. A stunning upturned hat with dainty flowers sits in the window. That I get for Emma. They place it in a fine hatbox lined with pink.

I buy buttons and thread, charcoal pencils, five schoolbooks, vellum, India ink and eight quills. I take also, the glass jar with all its contents of candy and a barrel of apples, a barrel of freshly milled flour and bags of ginger and cinnamon. Christopher and the clerk package and load us down. When I see we still have room, I look around and buy six chairs and a stack of plates, a crate of pewter mugs and a case of fragrant soap, remembering Emma had promised it to the girls. Christopher grins at that.

As we climb up, I hand the hatbox to him and he lowers his head, *(how thoughtless of me)*.

I situate myself and take it back on my lap.

"Why don't you drive us home?" I suggest.

He balks, saying, "I've never..."

"Oh, you will do an excellent job. You're cool-headed and have strong arms. I'm here to guide you should you need my advice. Go ahead," I say, with a nod of my head.

You've never seen a boy so proud and happy.

He gently slaps the reins, and we go down Market Street, pretty as anything, with our loaded wagon and the sun shining on us before all the town.

Outside the house, I offer to let him oversee the handing out of goods. That pleases him so much.

Why should I receive all the enjoyment of giving?

He plays the man and goes to the door, announcing everyone should stand in line along the wall according to size. It must have been a hurried scuffle.

Through the window I see Molly watching with interest.

I keep back the soap and hatbox to do my own giving, standing in the doorway.

Wise as an owl, Christopher brings the least likely first.

He rolls the barrel of flour into the kitchen and sets the cinnamon and ginger sacks on top.

"For Molly. Fresh flour, sugar, and spice to make cookies and desserts!" he announces.

All the children squeal except Lorraine of course. She is too mature. She steps closer to Emma.

Next Christopher rolls the barrel of apples in and pops the lid off, lifting one shiny red apple and looks my way.

"Captain says, 'Everyone can have an apple after you complete today's chores,'" he toys with their excitement.

Disgruntled faces fill the room.

Then he comes in the door with his arms loaded with folded clothing packages, as many as he could carry.

"Here are new things for everyone! Miss Emma, would you be so kind to help each child find their size?" he turns smiling and lays them on the table.

Molly sits down checking my face for permission. I nod.

Christopher brings the chairs one by one, putting them in a circle around the room. Emma unfolds the goods and calls each name for the size that looks like it might fit.

The older ones help each other try on things over their old clothes and then Emma looks back at me sadly.

I can't imagine why.

Just a look. Then it dawns on me.

"No under garments!" I say aloud, "We'll go back!"

I hand the hatbox to Emma and kiss her lightly. The soap I shove into Lorraine's arms and hurry out the door. As we drive away, the children, Molly and Emma are all outside, laughing at us and waving goodbye at the same time.

I will never forget this day. And Christopher is laughing too, only trying hard not to make me feel bad. He grins and turns his head away. When he composes himself, he asks permission to speak openly. I agree.

"I think this is one time you were having so much fun you didn't hear God remind you what you needed to get," he mocks kindly.

I have to smile. He's right.

Chapter 45

"...I WILL PUT MY LAWS INTO THEIR MIND, AND
WRITE THEM IN THEIR HEARTS: AND I WILL BE TO
THEM A GOD, AND THEY SHALL BE TO ME A PEOPLE:"
HEBREWS 8:10B

In due time, I buy a larger covered wagon and use the small one for farm work only, not for town.

We all go to church together and when we come to church, we fill two pews.

We visit with Molly at the Swedish church the first Sunday. She introduces me to her competitor, Jane Martin.

"She does laundry for her living," Molly says, looking down her nose at Jane, "I thought you might give her your business, since I no longer need it."

"Jane, if you would like to take on our business, you may come on Mondays and my wife will show you what we need. I cannot bring it to you. It's too much," I tell her.

Her eyes grow wide, and she looks astonished to Molly.

"Thank you, sir. My pleasure. I'll be there at dawn," she answers sweetly.

"Oh no, not that early. Let us have breakfast first, please," I answer chuckling.

So, Jane will come to do laundry.

Nehemiah drops by Sunday after church. We walk out to the fields, and he recommends what I should plant and what we should clear. He advises me on seed, tools, and livestock, giving me sources of information, I need. I take Christopher along to listen and learn with me.

Nehemiah offers to start me with some good sheep.

Christopher is all ears. That's what he knows about.

As Nehemiah is leaving, he invites us to church, and I say we will come next Sunday.

This puzzles Christopher and when Nehemiah is out of sight, he asks me about it.

"How can you go to different churches? What do you believe Captain?" he questions with his head down in a casual way.

I feel it's a suitable time to survey our land and present the gospel. It's time to cover it all.

The day is young. I head for the deep woods to talk.

"I attended the Dutch Reformed Church and was a faithful member all my years in New Amsterdam. I learned the doctrines that I still to this day, hold precious and true. The sovereignty of God, the authority of the Bible, the Blood atonement of Jesus Christ, the infilling of the Holy Spirit, the baptism of water, the holy communion, holy matrimony and all the commandments that guide a holy life, acceptable to God. I was patriotic for the cost my country paid to hold onto this faith and back then, the Dutch ruled the world, with the most wealth and the largest navy.

"When you were my age?" he asks intrigued.

"Yes, I was in that church from age twelve to age eighteen, six years. Many Sundays I heard the Bible and knew by memory several Psalms and hymns. But I was not born again. I didn't understand. I thought I was good. I thought I knew the right way and thought that was all I needed," I explain.

We spot three deer and stop. The doe sniffs and turns her head. The deer leap through the sylvan shade and disappear.

Whispering I point, "Trywan must teach us to hunt."

"What did you do to get born again?" he asks.

"I realized it was head knowledge for me to believe Christ

died for my sins and I was justified by the grace of His forgiveness. I had not repented of my sinful nature, my selfish ways. I thought of how to please myself and get on in the world. I wasn't mean. I wasn't a drunkard or a thief. I wanted to be rich and successful like my landgraviate, Evert Huybrecht. He had been my benefactor, like I am being yours. I met a man that pastored Indians at Martha's Vineyard Island out from Providence. I had a fear of Indians then. My people would war with them, not like William Penn. I remember keeping my hand on my dagger as we walked to their camp," I tell him reminiscing.

Christopher hangs on my every word.

No telling how long it had been since a man had given him this much time and respect.

I find a fallen tree and we sit down there.

"To be born again is a miracle in your soul. It requires you to give up all rights to yourself. You not only ask Jesus to forgive your sins, but you also promise God to live for Christ with all your heart and all your mind and all your soul and all your strength. And that constitutes loving your neighbor as yourself."

I add, "It's a lifetime servanthood. When a person comes to God with this prayer, all heaven rejoices, and the Holy Spirit fills your heart with goodness, patience, faith, and love. Your mind becomes alert to promptings from God. Your conversation and thoughts change. Your life becomes blessed with healing, opportunities, and protection of angels. The Bible is a map showing every pitfall and danger that can cause regret or victory. It's a counseling advisor for every situation. It's holy. All of it."[123]

His eyes widen.

"Well, I have to think about it," he drops his lower lip.

We get up and walk toward the light of the meadow.

"Captain, I probably will make that decision someday. If I do, you'll be the first to know," he says, frowning.

We step in tall grass, scattered with cornflowers of blue. Christopher picks a few.

"Emma loves flowers," I spout, unthinking.

"These are not for her," he says gently.

And when we get to the house, the first face we see is little Chessire. Christopher squats down and puts them in her hand. She breaks into a shy smile, before she runs away to show her sister.

I like that boy. Yes, I do.

Nehemiah attends the Mennonite Church. Emma is much at home there and *though she would not pressure me, I can tell she wants us to stay on.* I watch Nehemiah and Noble as they serve as deacons and contribute to the service order. He in turn watches my brood and the respect they show in church.

Nehemiah sees how we live and one day he corners me, after the sheep are in the pen.

"How do you keep peace with so many, Gerrit? I've raised children. They can be like goats," he quips good-naturedly.

"Well, we're good to them and don't allow any anger on the place. No harsh words.[124] We care for one another. We stress serving and pleasing God. We tell them God has feelings and it hurts His feelings when we hurt each other," I say, shrugging my shoulders.

"As simple as that. Gerrit. Amazing," he shakes his head, "I can see you drawing them behind you. You are the man for this. My compliments."

"You amaze me too, old friend," I say, "You followed the Holy Spirit to move here first. Without you, I wouldn't have retired and come to Pennsylvania."

We share a warm look, and he leaves.

The bond of Christian love between us is strong. I decide to become a member at his church. The change I've seen in him is more convincing than any other factor I would weigh for this decision.

Chapter 96

"AND THE SERVANT OF THE LORD MUST NOT STRIVE;
BUT BE GENTLE UNTO ALL MEN, APT TO TEACH,
PATIENT,"

2 TIMOTHY 2:24

Every summer we look for a letter from Gerritsen when he should dock at Boston and post one to us. It's been six years since we've seen him, a sailor's life being what it is.

Often his mother stands looking down the road after she's divided the tulips or brought in a basket of gooseberries. She says nothing about it, *but I know the forlorn look is for our son, her heart longing for him.*

Gradually the children steal our hearts away, as they grow up and move to their places in life. At church service we nod at them and see their little ones spread out around them.

That is a reward for us.

As we sit, *Emma and I share "that look" with each other, the one that only comes when two hearts are joined as one, from a life well spent, two souls knit in satisfying service.*

In the last letter Gerritsen told me The Coastal Trade Company was having trouble staying ahead financially and he was thinking of making a change.

This morning sitting in church, *my mind is on him and what may be happening to him. I cannot concentrate and that is so unlike me. I pray silently for him, looking straight ahead and hearing nothing of the sermon.*

My jaw is tight. Emma notices. Squeezing my hand, *her eyes question, "What's the matter?"*

I shake my head and pull away my hand. Then *careful not to be misunderstood,* I smile at her and close my eyes.

She must understand, some things are not for sharing. Worries especially. They're best taken to God and left there.

As the horses travel our dusty road home, we pass fourteen fields of knee-high crops and six pastures of sheep and cattle. Soon, the harvest will be our best ever and were it not for young Luke Mayhew, I could not bring it in alone.

Luke came to me at school one morning with Noble's son, Elijah, and getting me alone by the henhouse, he bargained for an education.

"My name's Luke Mayhew, sir," he began, offering a scrubby eight-year-old's handshake, "My great uncle says you're a friend of the family and a good man to be trusted, a man with a heart for God," he searches my face and I'm flattered.

Class begins to stir loudly without me.

He hurries to the point, "I need an education. My mother has none and I could teach her to read too, if ye so a mind to trade it out with my service on the place as you need me. I'm getting taller and I don't complain. Ain't afraid of most anything. I make friends with cows and Indians. Don't mind cleaning out the hen house or the barn."

I stop him and take him by the shoulder.

"What does your father say about this?" I probe.

"Aw, he's for it, but he said I got to be a man and ask you myself and keep my part of the trade like a man. He said, if I don't apply myself, you could just run me off and he'll understand. He says it's between us. He's got my two brothers to help him on the farm. Will you do it? Will you take me with no money?" he questions, his ragged pants exposing his shins and his hair wiry and matted.

"Yes," I say nodding, and immediately he is a sunburst of smiles, heaving a sigh of relief.

Before he can waste any time, I take charge saying, "Rule number one, go see the principal, Mrs. Emma, and she will show you where to wash up and drive you to town for supplies. Tell her I have made a contract with you as a man and you'll be needing school clothes and a slate, paper, the usual books and graphites. Tell her I expressly mean for you to go to the barber and have dinner with her at the Lodge. Oh, and say that on the way home, stop at the bakery and purchase three dozen cinnamon rolls," I order him.

His eyes are wide and *his mouth watering already.*

"Rule number two, you'll find our classes interesting and cheerful. I'm an understanding man and therefore we have little need for harshness or disciplines. Still, don't test my patience for I'm serious about every student getting the most out of the sacrifice of my time and sharing my education. I expect you to be the best student and the best boy in my room," I say to make it clear.

He's sober and attentive.

"Last, remember, I choose to love you as a good Christian should. Don't lie to me and do try to be on time. Never fear that I won't be respectful of your size when you work for me on the farm, and most of the time, I'll be nearby. Tell your father I look forward to meeting him. I'll make a list of your work duties for this week, and when we see how you do, I'll chart a schedule for the year. Is that satisfactory with you Luke Mayhew?" I ask.

"Yes sir!" and his eyes look at the other children, who by now are outside on the steps, wondering why I'm late.

He waves at them with anticipation, and I see Emma behind them. I motion for her to come, and I leave Luke in her care.

Eighteen years I teach school making sure every soul in my care has a good understanding of personal salvation, as Jesus wants me to do. Many sorrowful little faces confessed their sins on their knees, as I gave an invitation to plant their lives in the field of our precious Lord.

I closed the classrooms this year.

Molly died leaving her house to Lorraine who cared for her as a nurse in her final days.

Lorraine's husband is the principal in charge of the city school with five teachers.

My job is done.

Today I oversleep and awake hungry. I step out on the porch when Emma catches my eye as she wanders up the hill and seems distraught. She wipes her face with an apron and stands looking toward the city.

I know she's hoping to see a Coastal Trading Company ship with Gerritson on it.

Slowly I climb to join her, but not to interrupt her privacy. She doesn't hear me.

I suppose her whole heart is involved in her prayers for our son. I respect that. And it pains me to see her sad.

She jolts when I touch her shoulder.

"Tiger, what if he's drowned?" she inquires wringing her hands, "It's been so long. I can hardly stand it."

I take her in my arms, and we stand together with the wind blowing gently in the sultry heat. It's cooler up here than in the house.

I can't think of anything useful to say. We have been over it a dozen times.

My jaw clenches.

After dinner that evening I walk in the setting sun.

I'm troubled and not able to watch her grieve.

Down the road I briskly saunter and when I meet a wagon coming my way, I forsake the wide path and duck under the cover of the woods, continuing at a fast pace.

My mind is determined to get some answer. Unconsciously a prayer forms in my spirit that blurts out the anguish.

"God, You have been my Father since long ago. I have never

been so helpless as at this moment. My heart is breaking," I pray aloud.

The birds became quiet while I make tracks in a fury.

"I can't fight this gnawing fear. You know where he is. Please tell us. For Emma, I beg You," I manage to say, collapsing in the grass.

There is a crackling of leaves behind me, and I turn at once.

"Captain, you all right?" Luke asks.

I shake my head. He chews his lip and looks away.

With hands in his pockets he offers, "Why don't you pay my passage and send me to the Dutch West India Company office in New York to find out what they have on record about the *Coastal Trading Company*? I could be back in a week."

I'm grateful. Yes, I nod. *We can do that.*

"But don't tell Emma. Let us find out first," I suggest.

Luke goes to the New York office, and I begin to fast.

I repent of my unbelief. I ask God to forgive my son for not honoring me and his mother. Then I regret thinking that. What if he's dead? Then I chastise myself for my lack of faith again.

I give up the fast on the third day, conflicted in my spirit.

Luke's back in four days. The report is not good. The *Coastal Trading Company* has been sold to Commander Leuder seventeen years ago. No person by the name of Gerritson Brinkendorf is on their files. Luke asks about him at the dock. No one knows him.

It's a mystery. I have nothing with which to console Emma. I am at wit's end myself. Has he died? How could a businessman sell his business and disappear? I ponder it for days with no relief.

Emma senses my melancholy. She asks if I feel well, do I have chest pains?

I can't tell her "I'm fine."

In the silence of our evening meal, *our bonded love bears it together. No words can comfort our sense of loss.*

Finally, I break down in a flood of tears that pulls me out of the house before she can see it. I hitch up the horse and drive the wagon furiously away from everything.

I don't care if others see me. I don't care if I break a wagon wheel. I'm suffocating with heartache.

I drive hard two miles before I let up and loosen the reins for a steady gait.

My breathing is labored. I pour my raw emotions out to God, crying in all my strength and now I am so tired. My hands go limp in the reins. The front of my shirt is wet. I wipe my nose with my sleeve and stop under a tree.

"Lord, forgive my unbelief. Whatever has happened, I believe You have watched over my son, and I will not accuse You. I trust You," I whimper.

I sit in His presence and open my soul. I want to go home and be good company for my little wife if I can.

Morning by morning I walk over my hill to view the ocean in the distance believing Gerritson will come home.

Chapter 47

"My tears have been my meat day and night,
while they continually say unto me, Where
is thy God?"

Psalm 42:3

Emma can't seem to bring herself to reach for unseen horizons.

She pines and shakes her head when I speak about his return. She will have none of it.

At service Nehemiah brings the sermon. He chooses the parable of the prodigal son in Luke 15. I watch Emma's frown and close my eyes. He preaches that our duty as parents is to keep watching with a warm heart, to keep a candle in the window and hope alive in our hearts. If we quit praying, if we become bitter, it hardens us.

All the way home she is silent.

And as we pass the hill overlooking the Delaware, she deliberately stares in front of the wagon.

Can a soul die from a broken heart?

I shudder in the sunshine.

Early one misty summer sunrise, I step out and *from nowhere I relive the day my mother killed the chicken.*

My mouth goes dry, and I climb the knoll *with foreboding.*

I sense trouble. I cannot pray it away. The gift of discernment is upon me. So, I wait.

Listening to the birds chirp, watching the squirrels scamper about, *I wonder what will happen.*

All seems right, but *I am tense.*

The warm rays of sunshine clear the sky and droplets of dew hang on the leaves of our fruit trees.

Emma comes out with a basket and blows me a kiss with a wave of her hand. I nod smiling.

I watch her raise her skirt, navigating the rocky places, approaching the peaches, and inspecting them, still green.

Moving along the rows, she sets the basket down and plucks the ripe pears bending to fill her basket. I'm thinking *there'll be pear preserves in our pantry when she's through.*

I feel a twinge of something out of order and then, she collapses! I run to her, pears scattered down the grassy hill.

"Ah. Gerrit. What?" she says sighing.

Her eyes search her body to understand, unsure why she has fallen. I sit on the grass and lift her shoulders on my lap.

Then she is gone, eyes open, no longer with me.

I'm stunned. She can't be gone! No!

I look to heaven.

"Oh God. God, help me," I whimper alone.

How long I'm there, I cannot tell.

Luke comes through the trees, sunlight on his shoulders and finds us on the damp ground.

He takes off his hat and kneels by our side.

I'm like a child that has lost his way.

"Captain, I'll take care of our dear mother, sir," he says and gathers her up in his arms. He carries her in the house while I follow, and he lays her gently on the long table, crossing her tiny hands over her heart and closing her eyes.

I look at him for what to do next. I cannot function, weak as a kitten.

His eyes hold so much sympathy, *I gather strength from him.* Putting his arm around me, he helps me to the bedroom.

Luke says, "Now you dress for company. We'll be holding a

wake and everyone who loves her will want to say goodbye. That will be so nice, don't you think Captain?"

He turns me toward my washbowl, "Wash your hands and face and get ready. Put on your Sunday best."

I slowly and deliberately make myself go through the motions, *to do this for Emma* and return to the main room.

He has covered her body with the fine damask tablecloth, tucking it under her sides, and put purple irises from her garden, in two vases at her head and feet. By the mantel he lights the candles, and in the kitchen, he has closed the window shutters. All of the chairs are moved along the outside walls, awaiting guests.

I walk over and gaze at her *resting so peacefully*, the cloth turned back at her chest, *as if she were asleep* and I stare.

Luke has smoothed her hair back neatly with a comb.

Thoughtfully he put the Lutheran Bible under her hands.

I glance at him, tidying the house, *quietly being the son, I needed*. Then I cry.

He comes, putting his arm around me and waiting for me to let go of my grief.

"You go ahead and cry now sir. It's better you do it now, while there's no one to interrupt your private feelings," he offers kindly.

I am so grateful for him and what he means to me at this moment.

I hug him with all my might, and he stands humbly when I pull away.

I bend to kiss her one last time, on the forehead, a gentle peck. But she is cold and turning green already.

I back away, realizing again, *she is gone*, her small boots sitting lonely by the door.

Emma's grave is out by the flower garden, her favorite place, and these days I'm restless.

Nothing feels right. The house is too quiet.

I hitch the wagon and load most of our food to take to Luke's family. *It's an excuse to see him, I know.*

His wife is charming, the children rambunctious.

They all look like her and act like him.

I carry a crate of pickles and jelly inside and set them down by the flour barrel. She holds the ham I gave her.

"Where is he?" I ask.

She points down the road and says, "Went to help bring a calf at Jorgensen's."

I climb back up and turn the wagon toward town, in a hurry, not willing to make small talk.

Something about the bushes by the river takes me back to the night my father ran with me.

I slap the reins and bustle along faster, flinging sprays of mud behind. My emotions are raw.

I don't want to pray.

I think, *it is not good for man to be alone. God said it.*

I snap the whip lightly and we plummet the ground daringly, my good mares pounding away at my command.

My teeth are clenched. My spirit roaring.

Where is my son?

Suddenly I'm at the Delaware River's edge and I whoa.

Shaking and broken, I shout into the distance, "Gerritson, come home! Gerritson, come back!"

The tears spill unchecked, and I sniffle on my sleeve.

I look at my old body sitting here, searching for answers.

The voice of my father plays in my memory, "He leads me beside still waters. He restoreth my soul."[125]

"*Restore my soul, God. I need my son,*" I say in my heart, while I get down from the buckboard and unhitch the team.

I lead my horses to a shallow place and pet their noses.

Across the way, a farmer plows effortlessly, his field well-tended.

He's probably concerned about me.

He waves. I return it.

Luke on horseback comes racing across the field. I hang my head and become teary. Bless his heart.

"Captain," he says, dismounting, "What are you thinking?"

I laugh ashamedly.

He must have surmised I was suicidal, what with giving the food away and all.

I hug him and shake my head.

"Nothing, son," I say biting my lip and forcing a grin.

"You and God going to get through this," he offers.

"Yes. Yes we are," I respond.

He motions toward the city, "Did you have business down this way you came for?"

I tighten my lips and shake my head "no".

"I'll ride back with you," he says, without invitation, *taking care of me unasked for, responsible for the care of my soul.*

Luke trots the horses slowly, letting them recover and hands me a slice of deer jerky.

I haven't eaten. *It tastes good.*

We ride in silence, him patiently sitting with me.

I need that.

Along the road home, I admit I shouted in the distance for Gerritson to come home. He listens respectfully.

His faith in me astounds me. I was that way about my parents. It is strong in me to this day.

Near the gate the stone walls are covered in lavender blooming vinca Emma planted our first year. It has amassed the fence rails and thrives in the shade.

"I always wanted to build a gable over that entry. Me and Emma talked about. Never was a good time," I tell him.

"We can still do that. I'll make time," he says.

We pass the corn and the wheat, ripe and golden.

"I don't want to harvest this year. Bring some laborers and haul it to market. You can have it," I say, "No sense it rotting on the ground."

"All right," he returns.

I watch him care for my horses and follow him as he unties his. He salutes me like he did as a youngster and says, "Something good is going to happen Captain."

Well, I hope so. I nod.

Chapter 48

"...WEEPING MAY ENDURE FOR A NIGHT, BUT JOY
COMETH IN THE MORNING."

PSALM 30:5

The Holy Spirit wakes me in the morning with a hymn in
my head bouncing joyfully like a babbling brook in the shade.
I spring from my bed anticipating something good is going to
happen.

Luke had lovingly put seeds of encouragement in the fertile
soul of my bosom bursting with life again.

I cut a potato into bite-sized pieces and fry them golden over
the fire, while peeling a green apple.

Anything tastes good when you're hungry..

I smooth my hair back and sharpen the knife blade to scrape
the whiskers from my face with suds of castile soap. The smell
of lilacs reminds me of Emma and the girls she cowered over.

I smile, no longer sad.

The floor needs sweeping. I get out the broom and dustpan,
drawing dust from the corners and scooping them into the fire.

When I turn back the shutters, I see cobwebs by the windows and swat them down, wiping the mantel and tidying up
the whole room.

Maybe I should start teaching again.

Probably not. The people send their children to better
schools in town, that have English teachers with current ideas
and information.

I sit in the plumped chair and read my scriptures, thinking I want to be useful. I want to be with people.

I need to be involved, give something to benefit the world around me.

"Lord, what do I do with my life now?" I pray inwardly.

Someone is outside. I hear a man's voice.

Before I can rise, Gerritsen comes through the door! Gerritson! Gerritson!

My jaws ache with the held back joy I want to express.

I utter sighs and break into smiles of relief. I shiver.

He comes to my knee, bowing, hugging me awkwardly, repentant, so young, and strong.

My eyes take him in, my mouth open wide, tears flowing. I look at him in wonder.

I remember Nehemiah's sermon. God knew my son was alive. He tried to comfort me.

This is happening. I'm overcome and he begins to talk.

"Father, I tried to be everything you wanted. I managed the company business and took diligent care of the ships. James and I both ran into much more competition than you had in the early days. Whenever I tried to tell you, you would say 'Go to smaller ports,' because you did not really understand why we weren't making the previous profits. I was frustrated and getting older, I wanted to have a wife and children. I needed to be a success and time was passing me by," he said, pleading in his eyes.

He's nervous, afraid, watching my face.

"When I discussed this with James, he was skeptical. 'Your father is my best friend in all the world, he frowned at me, 'What will you do with what he's given you?'"

I could only look at Gerritson, *so long gone, so close to me now,* pouring out his explanation.

I'm still grasping he's alive.

He says, "I told him, 'I have nothing else I can do. If I can't make a living at shipping, I'll be a beggar."

Gerritsen backs away, unhinging his sword and removing his coat. He lays them over the bench and looks around for his mother.

I don't get a chance to tell him. He pushes forth the speech he's been wrestling to bring me.

"'What do you propose?' James asks and I say, 'Go in with me. Sell our ships and buy slave ships. Get a contract with the Dutch West India Company for a few years and then retire on it. We can settle down near my father in Pennsylvania,' I bargained, "But he said no.'"

By now the disappointment is seen on my face and Gerritsen swallows watching me.

I loathe slaving. He knows that.

"'He must not find out. It will break his heart,'" James said. I argued, "Why? Don't you think it's a good business decision? The Dutch West India Company has decided it's the best investment."

I'm trying to hear his confession. I shut my eyes and take a deep breath, sitting up straight in the chair.

It's a heartbreaking story.

Gerritsen plows ahead, *getting it off his chest.*

"James's answer was, 'Let me think about it. Overnight. Come tomorrow,' and he showed me the door."

I realize James knew where Gerritsen was and didn't tell me. It crashes against my heart like a ship breaking on the rocks. It swallows up the fondness I felt for him as I recall the years Emma and I grieved. I suppress allowing hatred, solely due to the Bible understanding of its poison.

The selfish excuse of a man, I think.

Gerritsen requires my concentration as he shares his heart.

"Father, please forgive me. Please. Forgive James. He would not go in partners with me. He gave me two ships on credit, and I sold the five forthright. In three months, I received in Amsterdam, a contract for slaving and had purchased a large galleon, one of the largest. I hired an experienced skipper and crew, who had run the route several times. With a great advance of money, the Dutch East India Company sent me out," he says and pulls a chair across from me to talk.

I look at the man my son has become. Quite impressive. I'm proud of him, yet sorry for what he has done to be this.

He sees my mind calculating his maturity. He sees I have aged. He softens and appeals to my business side.

He says, "Arriving on the Gold Coast in good time, I was able to purchase one hundred, thirty-seven males, twelve females and three children. In Jamaica I doubled my money and bought seventy-two trained field hands and thirty-one house servants. Of these, sixteen were Indians from Spanish colonies.[126] In one journey I had made more money than I had in three years along the New England coast working our business. I quickly paid James back the loan and was eager to run another load before winter."

I take all this in. It's becoming clearer. I raised him to think as a businessman. I knew the logic behind the Dutch West India Company decisions.

Gerritsen is my boy, caught up in a changing world. I prepare myself to hear all he has been through.

He says, "Often my name 'Brinkendorf' was treated coolly and having made such a success with my new plans I reasoned that I had my father's business savvy, but I did not want the Dutch name. I lay awake pondering about it, most of the night I spent in Boston, after the auction. With plenty of money in my pockets, I found a lawyer and applied for a legal name change, for business reasons."

My smile fades.

Here comes the thing I don't want to know.
Gerritsen is determined I hear him out.
"I kept Gerritsen, but I spell it the English way, 'Garretson'. My first name is Michael," he says, "Michael Garretson. My friends still call me Gerritsen, but my business associates think I'm English. Well, mother was."

His pale green eyes hold my heart as Emma's had.

My son, my "Gerritsen", changed his name. Changed his proud Dutch name. Oh, what a shame. My one and only son.

I blink back the tears listening to him pensively.

He senses my pain and rises, walking toward the window.

I don't want him to leave. I'm not happy but not angry.

I love him. This is hard.

His expression changes as he further builds the story of his past, saying, "I began to call upon a lovely Boston miss that caught my fancy and she did carry a certain charm about her that warmed me nights at sea. Her father liked me, solely for the prosperity I offered. I found him contentious in that Puritan haughty way and would politely change his conversation to my business holdings. This granted me an open door to court his sixteen year old daughter and at length I asked for her hand, obliging a wedding of grand style, such as she wished, costing me a year's wages. I begged my family could not attend and lied, saying they resided in Holland at present."

No wonder he didn't come home. How would he tell us?

I'm almost glad Emma doesn't have to hear it.

My son says, "We were married in their Puritan church, my membership being required, and I did attend regularly when I was in port. It bored me, though I did not disapprove, for I have been raised on the Bible and its honor."

I frown and ask, "Does she make you happy?"

He blushes smiling. His face lights. *I can tell.*

"Yes. She does do that. I would cross the world for her. She loves to spend my money, live in a fine house in Boston and display our china and silver for her parties. The French seamstress makes her elegant gowns and matching slippers. Three fine wigs were fitted for her in Paris. I adore her. She is delightful and intelligent. She bought furnishings of style and comfort for our home, a copper washing basin, and a sufficient amount of powder for her wigs as might last a lifetime. Always there is a tally of accounts for my signature to release payment when I dock in Boston," he says.

I take it in with mixed emotions, nodding.

My prodigal is home now and sits near me.

He says, "I became weary of the busyness and lonely for simpler days when I was not obliged to wear my wig and be socially graceful which came with the territory. She calls me "Michael" in a beautiful sing song voice, drawing me into her kiss. I cannot bear to see her unhappy and I bought her every desire mentioned. Still, no children were born to us."

His face is drawn.

I sense the disappointment and pity him.

He leans back stretching.

"So, she threw herself into the chattering of sewing parties and various charities and kept up appearances. It would have been the crudest of sentiments for anyone to mention it, notwithstanding the gossip did go on. You know, no children," he says, looking down to his hands, "I heard it first from a shipmate, that I was accused of being unable to perform. He fought for my honor at a local tavern coming to ship with a broken nose. The next rumor was more wicked. They watched to see if she would favor a younger gentlemen. Thank God, she did not. Father, I'm eighteen years her senior."

His eyes search for understanding and I nod kindly.

We smile.

His face clouds and he looks away.

Facing out the window he says, "More each year I noticed I had become callous to everyone, while dealing in human suffering and its harsh reality. The colonies reasoned they would die without essential labor to work the land, so we did it. You pointed this out to me. You loved me so. I could not hurt you. You brought passengers willing to toil and sweat. You were more familiar with the Europeans who chose hardship to escape war and persecution. Though they died, they were slaves of labor by choice. Being sold as an animal, which was something sinister, I remember you said."

Now he was bent in shame, saying, "I made excuses when she wanted to meet you in Amsterdam and more excuses when she asked if she could write. She couldn't speak Dutch. I used that. I was shipping out to the Gold Coast, to the West Indies and Brazil, I reminded her. I was becoming richer and more empty in my soul with the seasons and the brisk business of a profitable trade."

I'm glad he shows some wisdom and has learned this much.

He takes a deep breath and confesses, "In the back of my mind, I wonder if the Dutch West India Company is not losing heaven's blessing, as it bargains across the table with the souls of men. How can slaves believe in our God? It's true they are heathen. Many American Indians held similar beliefs. The African chiefs that warred against one another, sold us the captives. Once on our ships, they were captive for life."

Now he holds anxiety on his face, searching my eyes.

I blink and I think, *"Oh no, there's more?"*

Chapter 49

"If thou count me ... a partner, receive him as
myself,"

Philemon 1:17

He says, "I did the unthinkable. I had an illegitimate son
born in Jamaica."

I fold my hands and bend over, *to silently absorb it.*

Quietly he crosses the room to the window looking out.

When I regain my composure and raise my head, his tear
stained cheeks *search for my acceptance or rejection.*

"How sad that must have been for you Gerritsen," I offer.

A whimper escapes his cool demeanor. He nods to me, lips
tight.

He keeps looking at something outside, but he rushes to my
knee and pours out his soul.

"Oh, if I had only listened to you," he manages, and his face
exposes his wounded spirit.

I pat his head, *like he's a boy, like my father would do.*

"Now then, why don't you tell me about it?" I whisper.

He sniffs as I watch him recount it all. I am seeing how he
has been become the man I prayed he'd be, right in front of my
eyes, here in my house. He paces, looking out the window, looking back at me, looking around for his mother.

"It began as an act of protection. We had taken in a new
group of slaves from Ouidah, with a sultry princess that haugh-
tily stared at the sailors in defiance. She was a beauty of fierce

countenance and defied the chains or being shoved against the others. The men singled her out to humble her and took to making her the object of rude comments and scowling looks. Although she did not know the language, she understood enough. Mostly they could not keep their eyes off of her and she resented their lust," he says.

I nod and *sense he has left something outside he's checking on.*

Too polite to interrupt, I patiently hear years of his life.

With hands open wide, he says, "I knew it would come to some sort of violence and warned them. They only looked at one another as if to say, "When he's not looking..."

He swallows and admits, "I was not a praying man, nor merciful, yet it did chaff me. I had to do something. By nightfall, I loosed her and put her in my quarters, providing her with a shirt of covering and some old pants of mine. She eyed me suspiciously, especially the silver dagger you gave me in my belt. I saw this and when I raised my hand, she recoiled. I didn't know how to speak to her. I shook my head, pulling away. The effect was accomplished. She pointed to her mouth and the cup by my desk. I poured her some lemon water, which she gulped heartily. She nodded humbly. She looked at my bunk and I walked over, latched her chain to the rail, and handed her the blanket. She lay down. I walked out the door and back on deck. The crew assumed I had taken her for myself and that ended the disturbance."

At the window he makes gestures to someone, and I raise my brows, standing up.

He moves toward the door and hurriedly says, "When the child was born, I left the boy with the Catholic bishop. He has my green eyes. Where's Mother?"

"She died. A month ago. Buried by the garden," I say.

He sighs heavily, a wail gasps from him unguarded.

"My greatest fear has been I'd come home, and you'd be gone. And she is."

He tearfully looks out the window.

I get up to hug him, but he moves between me and the door. "Sit down father," he coaxes, "Please, let me finish."

He speaks louder, "In the midst of a raging hurricane, I made a decision to break off my sins."

He knew that would get my full attention.

"What's going on? Who's outside?" I ask, cornering him.

I step toward the door. He puts a hand on my chest.

He says, "I promised God I'd quit shipping slaves if He would save us. The sea became immediately tranquil, which put the fear of God in all of us," he whispers."

I stand frozen. *What beautiful words.*

Yes, music to my ears.

My turn to sigh. I look in his face.

It brings us both to tears.

I blink to weigh that miracle.

He shakes his head.

"I could never sell slaves again. It broke me. I came to a sudden conclusion that Christ would forgive me if I would repent. I confessed my sins with pure sorrow, weary of their haunting me and thirsty for the peace to pray with a clean conscience," he says, "I sold my slaving trade to Johann Lueder. This dissolves my contracts with the chieftains in Africa and the Dutch West India Company."

"Good," I respond, *remembering the morning at church when I was so burdened to pray for him.*

I don't like that he bars my way to the door.

I step forward.

"What did you do with the slaves Gerritsen?" I ask.

He takes the doorknob in his hand and *purposely gives me a pleading look meant to draw from me all the love I've ever known for him,* and then he opens it wide.

"I brought them here to you Father," he says.

My mouth falls open.

Along the fencing and back toward the barn stand young black men looking anxiously at me as I appear on my steps.

They had been brought on several wagons, now resting in the shade, the horses nibbling grass.

It takes me a minute to adjust. I lean back on the casing. I see they are decently clothed and hold the same yearning in their eyes I've seen on many faces.

"I didn't know what else to do," Gerritsen says. "They can't go back."

"No," I say, overwhelmed, "They can't."

They silently watch my son with his old father.

"I thought you could teach them English, help them learn a trade. Start a new life," he says.

"I, I'm in awe. It's a wonderful idea," I say.

He raises a hand in worship to God in his joy, releasing the tension of the hearts watching us and the sound of "Halleluiah" comes loud from them, echoing in the valley.

I'm impressed.

I'm beaming and can't stop smiling.

The shift in my life is beginning to dawn on me. No more lonely days! Gerritsen has found Christ!

The peace is my breast swells.

Finally. Thank you, Jesus.

Two men step forward at his signal and he introduces them to me.

"Jacque, this is my father, Commander Brinkendorf. Jacque is the one who warned me during the hurricane to cry out to God, quit slaving and He would save us. He's a French chef. He needs a place to stay and knows no one. I thought he could help you," Gerritsen says.

Jacque bows low. To that I thump him on the head, lifting him back to my level and give him a hug.

The situation astounds me.

The Africans watch closely.

They don't know what to expect from me.

Next to Jacque is a middle-aged African.

Gerritsen looks at me and says, "Father, meet Sampson. He speaks English well and tells me he is a good smith."

I shake his calloused hand and look him in the eye. His grin is a frown. His eyes twinkle. He will be a loyal friend I can tell.

In Dutch I say, "Well, I have been complaining to the Lord that I needed some people to love and needed something to do."

We burst out laughing and I hear a chuckle from close by.

Who else here understands Dutch? Who laughed at that?

My eyes go to the men standing far off. They are all dressed the same.

Gerritsen steals a worried look my way but says nothing.

Jacque looks at us while Sampson crosses his arms.

There's a knowing in me that causes me to zero in on the faces.

I walk along the men, searching.

Among those sitting on the wall, one is lighter, more confident.

I step in the road and come up to him.

He holds my look with his light green eyes.

Eyes like Emma. Tall like me.

"How are you called son?" I ask.

"My name is Michaelsen Paul Brinkendorf," he says.

A chuckle erupts in my soul.

Brinkendorf. He proudly tells me "Brinkendorf."

Ha-ha! Ah yes.

I reach and hug him hard.

"Say it again," I ask, as I brush a tear.

"Michaelsen Paul Brinkendorf," he repeats and grins.

I'm beaming. *Ha-ha!*

"You are like me," I remark with a pointed finger.

His face lights up so much I can hardly contain the joy.

RECOMMENDED READING

The Light and The Glory: 1492-1793 (God's Plan for America), by Peter Marshall, Jr. and David Manual

Fair Sunshine, Character Studies of the Scottish Covenanters, by Jock Purves

The Island at the Center of the World, The Epic Story of Dutch Manhattan & the Forgotten Colony that Shaped America, by Russell Shorto

Experience Mayhew's Indian Converts, A Cultural Edition, Edited and Compiled by Laura Arnold Leibman

REFERENCES

1   Beacon of Truth – Reformation Articles – *The Siege of Haarlem*
    https://beaconoftruth.org/reformation-in-the-netherlands

2   *The Island at the Center of the World, The Epic Story of Dutch Manhattan & the Forgotten Colony that shaped America.* By Russell Shorto, Copyright 2004 published by Doubleday – p.101

3   The Island at the Center of the World, The Epic Story of Dutch Manhattan & the Forgotten Colony that shaped America. By Russell Shorto, Copyright 2004 published by Doubleday – p.25, p.94-95

4   *The Island at the Center of the World, The Epic Story of Dutch Manhattan & the Forgotten Colony that shaped America.* By Russell Shorto, Copyright 2004 published by Doubleday – p.212-213

5   Bible, King James Version, 1607, Public Domain – Psalm 8:6-8

6   The Island at the Center of the World, The Epic Story of Dutch Manhattan & the Forgotten Colony that shaped America. By Russell Shorto, Copyright 2004 published by Doubleday – p.63, p. 68

7   Bible, King James Version, 1607, Public Domain – I Kings 11:1-10

8   Bible, King James Version, 1607, Public Domain – Ezekiel 1:16

9   Bible, King James Version, 1607, Public Domain – Ezekiel 1:26-28

10 Bible, King James Version, 1607, Public Domain – Psalm 47:9

11 *Bible, King James Version*, 1607- Public Domain – Matthew 12:31

12 *The Island at the Center of the World, The Epic Story of Dutch Manhattan & the Forgotten Colony that shaped America.* By Russell Shorto, Copyright 2004 published by Doubleday – p.29

13 Bible, King James Version, 1607, Public Domain – 1. Samuel 17:37

14 Bible, King James Version, 1607, Public Domain – 1. Samuel 17:46-50

[15] *Bible, King James Version,* 1607, Public Domain – 1. Samuel 17

[16] Bible, King James Version, 1607, Public Domain – Daniel !:8, 17-20

[17] *Bible, King James Version,* 1607, Public Domain – Colossians 3:23

[18] Bible, King James Version, 1607, Public Domain – Romans 14:12

[19] Bible, King James Version, 1607, Public Domain – Psalm 119:11

[20] *Bible, King James Version,* 1607, Public Domain – Psalm 23

[21] Bible, King James Version, 1607, Public Domain – Mark 4:39

[22] *The Island at the Center of the World, The Epic Story of Dutch Manhattan & the Forgotten Colony that shaped America.* By Russell Shorto, Copyright 2004 published by Doubleday – p.61-6, p.89, p.108

[23] *Bible, King James Version,* 1607, Public Domain – Genesis 29-37

[24] *Bible, King James Version,* 1607, Public Domain – Genesis 39-41

[25] *Bible, King James Version,* 1607, Public Domain – Proverbs 4:23

[26] *Bible, King James Version,* 1607, Public Domain – Exodus 20

[27] *Bible, King James Version,* 1607, Public Domain – Matthew 5

[28] *The Island at the Center of the World, The Epic Story of Dutch Manhattan & the Forgotten Colony that shaped America.* By Russell Shorto, Copyright 2004 published by Doubleday – p. 63

[29] *The Island at the Center of the World, The Epic Story of Dutch Manhattan & the Forgotten Colony that shaped America.* By Russell Shorto, Copyright 2004 published by Doubleday – p.63

[30] Bible, King James Version, 1607, Public Domain – Matthew 17:27

[31] *Bible, King James Version,* 1607, Public Domain – 1. Corinthians 12:8

[32] *Bible, King James Version,* 1607, Public Domain – Matthew 3:11 and Luke 3:16

[33] *Bible, King James Version,* 1607, Public Domain – 1. Corinthians 12:8-10

[34] *The Island at the Center of the World, The Epic Story of Dutch Manhattan & the Forgotten Colony that shaped America.* By Russell Shorto, Copyright 2004 published by Doubleday – p.63,p.95-96

[35] *The Island at the Center of the World, The Epic Story of Dutch Manhattan & the Forgotten Colony that shaped America*. By Russell Shorto, Copyright 2004 published by Doubleday – p.93-109

[36] *The Island at the Center of the World, The Epic Story of Dutch Manhattan & the Forgotten Colony that shaped America*. By Russell Shorto, Copyright 2004 published by Doubleday – p.105

[37] *Bible, King James Version*, 1607, Public Domain – Moses, entire Book of Exodus; Joshua – Exodus chapters 17, 24, 32, 33, Numbers chapters 11, 14, 26, 27 32, 34, Deuteronomy chapters 1, 3, 31, 234 and Book of Joshua, chapters 1- 24; Paul – Book of Acts, chapters 13-28

[38] *Bible, King James Version*, 1607, Public Domain – (Both Joseph and Daniel stood before rulers and were promoted because of divine insight) Joseph – Genesis 41; Daniel 2.

[39] *The Island at the Center of the World, The Epic Story of Dutch Manhattan & the Forgotten Colony that shaped America*. By Russell Shorto, Copyright 2004 published by Doubleday – p.102-103

[40] *The Island at the Center of the World, The Epic Story of Dutch Manhattan & the Forgotten Colony that shaped America*. By Russell Shorto, Copyright 2004 published by Doubleday – p. 120-121

[41] *7 Tipping Points that Saved the World,* By Chris Stewart and Ted Stewart, Copyright 2011, The Shipley Group and Brian T. Stewart – p. 227-231

[42] *The Island at the Center of the World, The Epic Story of Dutch Manhattan & the Forgotten Colony that shaped America*. By Russell Shorto, Copyright 2004 published by Doubleday – p.130, p. 136

[43] *The Island at the Center of the World, The Epic Story of Dutch Manhattan & the Forgotten Colony that shaped America*. By Russell Shorto, Copyright 2004 published by Doubleday – p. 118-121

[44] *The Island at the Center of the World, The Epic Story of Dutch Manhattan & the Forgotten Colony that shaped America*. By Russell Shorto, Copyright 2004 published by Doubleday – p. 121-124

[45] *The Island at the Center of the World, The Epic Story of Dutch Manhattan & the Forgotten Colony that shaped America*. By Russell Shorto, Copyright 2004 published by Doubleday – p. 124-128

[46]   *The Island at the Center of the World, The Epic Story of Dutch Manhattan & the Forgotten Colony that shaped America.* By Russell Shorto, Copyright 2004 published by Doubleday – p. 123

[47]   *Experience Mayhew's Indian Converts,* By Laura Arnold Leibman, Copyright 2008, University of Massachusetts Press – Introduction p.1-6, including footnotes.

[48]   *Bible, King James Version,* 1607, Public Domain – Genesis 1:1-31

[49]   *EErdman's Handbook to Christianity in America,* Copyright 1983-William B. Eerdmans Publishing Company – p.64-66

[50]   *The Island at the Center of the World, The Epic Story of Dutch Manhattan & the Forgotten Colony that shaped America.* By Russell Shorto, Copyright 2004 published by Doubleday – p.63, p. 68

[51]   Beacon of Truth – Reformation Articles – Netherlands Reformation – *Sea Beggers, Siege of Haarlem, Siege of Leiden, Siege of Alkmaar, Siege of Antwerp.* https://beaconoftruth.org/reformation-in-the-netherlands

[52]   *Bible, King James Version,* 1607, Public Domain – Judges 7:7

[53]   Bible, King James Version, 1607, Public Domain –1.Samuel 22:2

[54]   *Bible, King James Version,* 1607, Public Domain – Matthew 14:25 and Mark6:48

[55]   *Bible, King James Version,* 1607, Public Domain - Ephesians 6:10

[56]   *Bible, King James Version,* 1607, Public Domain – Jonah 1:1-17

[57]   *Bible, King James Version,* 1607, Public Domain – Matthew 6:15

[58]   *Bible, King James Version,* 1607, Public Domain – Proverbs 20:3

[59]   *Bible, King James Version,* 1607, Public Domain – Psalm65:5

[60]   *Bible, King James Version,* 1607, Public Domain – Matt. 14:25

[61]   *Bible, King James Version,* 1607, Public Domain – Matt. 8:26

[62]   *Bible, King James Version,* 1607, Public Domain – Matt. 17:20

[63]   Beacon of Truth – Reformation Articles – *Protestants Before Protestantism* https://beaconoftruth.org/reformation

64 Beacon of Truth – Reformation Articles – Netherlands Reformation –The Reformation in the Netherlands https://beaconof-truth.org/reformation-in-the-netherlands

65 *Bible, King James Version*, 1607, Public Domain – Galatians 4:6

66 Bible, King James Version, 1607, Public Domain – Jeremiah 32:27

67 *Bible, King James Version*, 1607, Public Domain – Acts 13:22

68 Wikipedia – Zeeland is the westernmost and least populous province of the Netherlands

69 Bible, King James Version, 1607, Public Domain – Hebrews 12:1-3

70 Bible, King James Version, 1607, Public Domain – Psalm 75:6

71 *The Protestant Persecutions* from *A History of the Churches*, which is one of the 13 titles in the Advanced Bible Studies Series, By David Cloud, published by Way of Life Literature. copyright 2013

72 *Bible, King James Version,* 1607, Public Domain – Luke 6:31

73 *Bible, King James Version*, 1607, Public Domain – Proverbs 3:5

74 *Bible, King James Version*, 1607, Public Domain – Psalm 19:1

75 *Bible, King James Version*, 1607, Public Domain – Matthew 6:33

76 *Bible, King James Version*, 1607, Public Domain – Matthew 25:34

77 *The Island at the Center of the World, The Epic Story of Dutch Manhattan & the Forgotten Colony that shaped America.* By Russell Shorto, Copyright 2004 published by Doubleday – p.224

78 The Island at the Center of the World, The Epic Story of Dutch Manhattan & the Forgotten Colony that shaped America. By Russell Shorto, Copyright 2004 published by Doubleday – p.275-276

79 *Tenacious of Their Liberties: The Congregationalists in Colonial Massachusetts* – By James F. Cooper Jr., 1999, reprinted by Oxford University Press

80 *EErdman's Handbook to Christianity in America,* Copyright 1983-William B. Eerdmans Publishing Company – p.29-30

81 *Fair Sunshine* – By Jock Purves, 1985, Banner of Truth Trust

82 *Bible, King James Version,* 1607, Public Domain – Isaiah 54:17

83 *Bible, King James Version*, 1607, Public Domain – II Kings 6:17

[84] *Bible, King James Version*, 1607, Public Domain – Acts 10:38

[85] *Bible, King James Version*, 1607, Public Domain – John 3:3

[86] *Bible, King James Version*, 1607, Public Domain – Joshua 22:5

[87] *Bible, King James Version*, 1607, Public Domain – I Timothy 4:8

[88] *Bible, King James Version*, 1607, Public Domain – I Timothy 4:12

[89] *Bible, King James Version*, 1607, Public Domain – Matt. 22:36

[90] *Bible, King James Version*, 1607, Public Domain – Exodus 1-15

[91] *Bible, King James Version*, 1607, Public Domain – I Kings 1-9

[92] *Bible, King James Version*, 1607, Public Domain – Daniel 1-6

[93] *Bible, King James Version*, 1607, Public Domain – Joshua 10:13

[94] *Bible, King James Version*, 1607, Public Domain – John 18:25

[95] *Bible, King James Version*, 1607, Public Domain – Matt. 18:19

[96] *Bible, King James Version*, 1607, Public Domain – Job

[97] *United States History in Christian Perspective – Heritage of Freedom –* By Michael R. Lowman with Laurel Hicks, George T. Thompson, and the editorial department of A Beka Book Publications, copyright 1982,1983, A Beka Books Publication, a ministry of Pensacola Christian College – p.42-44 and p. 194-199

[98] Bible, King James Version, 1607, Public Domain – Matthew 18:20

[99] Bible, King James Version, 1607, Public Domain – I John 4:12

[100] Bible, King James Version, 1607, Public Domain – Romans 8:28

[101] *Bible, King James Version*, 1607, Public Domain – Matt. 3:1-2

[102] *The Island at the Center of the World, The Epic Story of Dutch Manhattan & the Forgotten Colony that shaped America.* By Russell Shorto, Copyright 2004 published by Doubleday – p.125-126

[103] *Bible, King James Version*, 1607, Public Domain – Psalm 19:13

[104] National Park Service web site www. nps.gov – Article *The Palatine Germans* – Fort Stanwix National Monument

[105] *Children Bound to Labor: The Pauper Apprentice System in Early America*, By Ruth Wallis Herndon(Editor), and John E. Murray, (Editor), Copyright March 10, 2009, Cornell University Press

[106] *Miracles and the Supernatural Throughout Church History*, By Tony Cooke, Copyright 2020, Published by Harrison House – P. 140-144

[107] *The Light and the Glory, Did God Have a Plan for America?*, By Peter J. Marshall, Jr. and David B. Manuel Jr., Copyright 1977, Published by Fleming H. Revell, a division of Baker Book House Co. – p.174-175

[108] Wikipedia, the Free Encyclopedia, *Piedmontese Easter*, Talk

[109] Experience Mayhew's Indian Converts, By Laura Arnold Leibman, Copyright 2008, University of Massachusetts Press – Introduction p.1-6, including footnotes.

[110] *Experience Mayhew's Indian Converts*, By Laura Arnold Leibman, Copyright 2008, University of Massachusetts Press – Introduction p.1-6, including footnotes.

[111] *Bible, King James Version*, 1607, Public Domain – John 14:2-3

[112] *United States History in Christian Perspective – Heritage of Freedom* – By Michael R. Lowman with Laurel Hicks, George T. Thompson, and the editorial department of A Beka Book Publications, copyright 1982,1983, A Beka Books Publication, a ministry of Pensacola Christian College – p.47-48

[113] Bible, King James Version, 1607, Public Domain – Romans 8:28

[114] *Bible, King James Version*, 1607, Public Domain– Luke 10:25-37

[115] *Bible, King James Version*, 1607, Public Domain – Judges 6:36-40

[116] https://www.britannica.com/biography/William-Penn

[117] Bible, King James Version, 1607, Public Domain – Isaiah 30:21

[118] *United States History in Christian Perspective – Heritage of Freedom* – By Michael R. Lowman with Laurel Hicks, George T. Thompson, and the editorial department of A Beka Book Publications, copyright 1982,1983, A Beka Books Publication, a ministry of Pensacola Christian College – p.49-50

The Island at the Center of the World, The Epic Story of Dutch Manhattan & the Forgotten Colony that shaped America. By Russell Shorto, Copyright 2004 published by Doubleday – p.301-302

[119] https://www.britannica.com/biography/William-Penn

[120] *Bible, King James Version*, 1607, Public Domain – Isaiah 30:21

[121] *Children Bound to Labor: The Pauper Apprentice System in Early America,* By Ruth Wallis Herndon(Editor), and John E. Murray, (Editor), Copyright March 10, 2009, Cornell University Press

United States History in Christian Perspective – Heritage of Freedom – By Michael R. Lowman with Laurel Hicks, George T. Thompson, and the editorial department of A Beka Book Publications, copyright 1982,1983, A Beka Books Publication, a ministry of Pensacola Christian College – p.29-31, P. 58

[122] *Bible, King James Version,* 1607, Public Domain – Romans 14:12

[123] *Bible, King James Version,* 1607, Public Domain – II Timothy 3:16

[124] Bible, King James Version, 1607, Public Domain – Ephesians 4:29

[125] Bible, King James Version, 1607, Public Domain – Psalm 23:2-3

[126] *The Island at the Center of the World, The Epic Story of Dutch Manhattan & the Forgotten Colony that shaped America.* By Russell Shorto, Copyright 2004 published by Doubleday – p.292-293

Printed in the USA
CPSIA information can be obtained
at www.ICGtesting.com
JSHW020957091023
49638JS00002B/5